The Devil Wears Plaid

THE DEVIL WEARS PLAID

TERESA MEDEIROS

THORNDIKE
CHIVERS

This Large Print edition is published by Thorndike Press, Waterville, Maine, USA and by AudioGO Ltd, Bath, England.
Thorndike Press, a part of Gale, Cengage Learning.

The text of this Large Print edition is unabridged.
Other aspects of the book may vary from the original edition.
Set in 16 pt. Plantin.

LIBRARY OF CONGRESS CATALOGING-IN-PUBLICATION DATA

Medeiros, Teresa, 1962–
    The devil wears plaid / by Teresa Medeiros.
      p. cm. (Thorndike Press large print basic)
    ISBN-13: 978-1-4104-3435-7 (hardcover)
    ISBN-10: 1-4104-3435-4 (hardcover)
    1. Young women—Scotland—Fiction. 2. Kidnapping—Fiction.
3. Aristocracy (Social class)—Fiction. 4. Highlands
(Scotland)—Fiction. 5. Scotland—Social life and
customs—Fiction. 6. Large type books. I. Title.
PS3563.E2386D48 2011
813'.54—dc22   2010044615

BRITISH LIBRARY CATALOGUING-IN-PUBLICATION DATA AVAILABLE

Published in 2011 in the U.S. by arrangement with Pocket Books, a division of Simon & Schuster, Inc.
Published in 2011 in the U.K. by arrangement with Simon & Schuster, Inc.

U.K. Hardcover: 978 1 445 83622 5 (Chivers Large Print)
U.K. Softcover: 978 1 445 83623 2 (Camden Large Print)

To our beautiful nieces Jennifer Medeiros and Maggie Marie Parham. Your grace, compassion for others, and love for the Lord are always an inspiration to me.

For my Michael, who makes every day of our life together a dream come true.

ACKNOWLEDGMENTS

A very special thank you to Andrea Cirillo and Peggy Gordijn, who look after me from sea to shining sea and beyond.

And to Lauren McKenna, for refusing to settle for anything less than my best.

CHAPTER ONE

"Ah, just look at the dear lass! She's all a'tremble with joy."

"And who could blame her? She's probably been dreamin' o' this day her entire life."

"Aye, 'tis every lass' dream, is it not? To wed a wealthy laird who can afford to grant her every wish?"

"She should consider herself blessed to have snared such an amazin' catch. With all those freckles, it's not as if she's any Great Beauty."

"I'd be willin' to wager she couldn't bleach them away with an entire jar o' Gowland's Lotion! And the copper shade o' her hair does make her look a wee bit common, don't you think? I heard the earl met her in London during her third and *final* Season when all hope o' findin' a husband had nearly been lost. Why, she's already one-and-twenty, they say."

"*No!* So turribly auld?"

"Aye, that's what I hear. She was on the verge o' bein' placed firmly on the shelf, she was, until our laird spotted her sittin' with the confirmed spinsters and sent one o' his men o'er to dance with her."

Even as she gazed straight ahead and valiantly fought to ignore the avid whispers of the two women gossiping on the front pew of the abbey, Emmaline Marlowe could not deny the truth in their words.

She *had* been dreaming of this day her entire life.

She'd dreamed of standing before an altar and pledging her heart and her lifelong fidelity to the man she adored. She'd never caught a clear glimpse of his face in those misty dreams but there could be no denying the passion smoldering in his eyes as he vowed to love, honor and cherish her for the rest of his days.

She lowered her gaze to the quivering bouquet of dried heather in her hand, thankful the beaming onlookers who crowded the rows of long, narrow pews flanking the center aisle of the church were attributing her trembling to the joyful anticipation any eager young bride about to speak her vows might feel. She was the only one who knew it had more to do with the chill that seemed to permeate the ancient stones of the abbey.

And her heart.

She stole a glance at the churchyard beyond the tall, narrow windows. A sky the color of unpolished pewter brooded over the vale, making the day look more like deep winter than mid-April. The skeletal branches of oak and elm had yet to sprout a single bud of green. Crooked gravestones lurched out of the stony soil, their epitaphs worn away by the relentless assault of wind and rain. Emma wondered how many of those who now slumbered beneath the ground had once been brides like her, young women full of hopes and dreams dashed too soon by choices made by others and the inescapable march of time.

The jagged crags of the mountain loomed over the churchyard like monuments to an even more primitive age. These harsh Highland climes where winter refused to yield its stubborn grip seemed a world away from the gently rolling hills of Lancashire where she and her sisters loved to romp with such careless abandon. Those hills were already green and tender with the promise of spring, beckoning home any wanderer foolish enough to forsake them.

Home, Emma thought, her heart seized by

a sharp pang of longing. A place she would no longer belong after today.

She shot a panicked glance over her shoulder to find her parents sitting in the Hepburn family pew, beaming proudly at her through eyes glazed with tears. She was a good girl. A dutiful daughter. The one they had always relied upon to set a sound example for her three younger sisters. Elberta, Edwina and Ernestine were huddled together on the pew next to their mother, dabbing at their swollen eyes with their own handkerchiefs. If Emma could have convinced herself it was happiness that prompted her family's weeping, their tears might have been easier to bear.

More simpering whispers intruded upon her thoughts as the women resumed their conversation. "Just look at him! He still cuts a strikin' figure, doesn't he?"

"Indeed! It does one's heart proud. And you can tell he already dotes upon the lass."

No longer able to deny the inevitability of her fate, Emma turned back to the altar and lifted her eyes to meet the adoring gaze of her bridegroom.

Then lowered them as she remembered she towered over his wizened form by over half a foot.

He grinned up at her, nearly dislodging

the poorly fitted set of Wedgwood china teeth from his mouth. His cheeks all but disappeared as he sucked the teeth back in with a pop that seemed to echo through the abbey with the force of a gunshot. Emma swallowed, hoping the cataracts that clouded his rheumy blue eyes would render his vision poor enough to mistake her grimace of distaste for a smile.

His withered form was draped with the full regalia befitting his station as laird of the Hepburn lands and chieftain of Clan Hepburn. A billowing red and black plaid nearly swallowed his hunched shoulders. The matching tailored kilt exposed knees as bony as a pair of ivory doorknobs. A mangy sporran hung between his legs, the ceremonial purse balding in uneven patches just like his skull.

The two gossiping old biddies were right, Emma reminded herself sternly. The man was an earl — an extremely powerful nobleman rumored to have both the respect of his peers and the ear of the king.

It was her duty to her family — and their rapidly dwindling fortunes — to accept the earl's suit. After all, it wasn't her papa's fault he had been cursed with a passel of daughters instead of being blessed with sons who could have gone out and made their own fortunes in the world. Emma's catching the Earl of Hepburn's eye just before donning the drab mantle of spinsterhood had been a stroke of extraordinary good luck for them all. Thanks to the generous settlement the earl had already bestowed upon her father, her mother and sisters would never again have to be startled from their sleep by the terrifying racket of creditors banging on the front door of their ramshackle manor house or spend their every waking moment in fear of being carted off to the workhouse.

Emma might be the prettiest Marlowe girl among her sisters, but she was not so attractive that she could afford to turn down such an illustrious suitor. During their grueling journey to this isolated corner of the Highlands, her mother had discussed every detail of her upcoming nuptials with determined good cheer. When they reached the rolling foothills and the earl's home had finally come into view, her sisters had dutifully gasped with admiration, not realizing their pretended envy was more painful to Emma than overt pity.

No one could deny the splendor of the ancient castle nestled beneath the shadow of the lofty, snow-capped crag of Ben Nevis — a castle that had welcomed the Hepburn lords and their brides for centuries. When

14

this day was done, Emma would be its mistress as well as the earl's bride.

As she blinked down at her bridegroom, she struggled to transform her grimace into a genuine smile. The old man had been the very soul of kindness to her and her family ever since spotting her across that crowded public assembly room during one of the last balls of the Season. Instead of sending an emissary on his behalf, he had traveled all the way to Lancashire himself to court her and seek her papa's blessing.

He had conducted himself like a true nobleman during his calls, never once making a disparaging remark about their shabby drawing room with its faded carpet, peeling wallpaper and mismatched furniture or casting a contemptuous eye over her own outmoded and much-darned gowns. Judging by his courtly charm and gracious demeanor, one would have thought he was taking tea at Carlton House with the Prince Regent.

He had treated Emma as if she were already a countess, not the eldest daughter of an impoverished baronet one ill-considered wager away from the poorhouse. And he had never once arrived empty-handed. A stern-faced footman always followed one step behind the earl, his burly arms laden with gifts — hand-painted fans, glass bugle beads and colorful fashion plates for Emma's sisters; French-milled lavender-scented soap and handsome bolts of muslin and dimity for her mother; bottles of the finest Scotch whisky for her papa; and leather-bound editions of William Blake's *Songs of Innocence* or Fanny Burney's latest novel for Emma herself. They might have been only trinkets to a man of the earl's means, but such luxuries had been in scarce supply around the manor house for a very long time. His generosity had brought a flush of pleasure to her mother's wan cheeks and elicited genuine shrieks of delight from Emma's sisters.

Emma owed the man her gratitude and her loyalty, if not her heart.

Besides, how long could he possibly live? she thought with a desperate twinge of guilt.

Although the earl was rumored to be nearly eighty years of age, he looked closer to one hundred and fifty. Judging by his grayish pallor and the consumptive hiccup marring each of his breaths, he might not even survive their wedding night. As a fetid blast of that breath wafted to her nostrils, Emma swayed on her feet, fearing she might not survive it either.

Almost as if she had read Emma's grim

thoughts, one of the women sitting on the front pew whispered primly, "One thing you can say about our laird — he ought to have ample experience in pleasin' a woman."

Her companion failed to smother a rather porcine snort. "Indeed he should. Especially since he's already outlived three wives and all the bairns they produced, not to mention a gaggle o' mistresses."

The image of her elderly bridegroom gumming her lips in a fumbling parody of passion sent a fresh shudder coursing down Emma's spine. She still hadn't quite recovered from having to sit through her mother's painfully earnest instructions on what would be expected of her on the wedding night. As if the act described hadn't been horrid or humiliating enough, her mother had also informed her that if she turned her face away and wriggled a bit beneath him, the earl's exertions would be over that much more quickly. If his attentions became too arduous, she was to close her eyes and think of something pleasant — like a particularly lovely sunrise or a tin of fresh sugar biscuits. Once he was finished with her, she would be free to tug down the hem of her nightdress and go to sleep.

Free, Emma's heart echoed with a throb of despair. After this day she would never be free again.

She averted her eyes from her groom's hopeful face to find the earl's great-nephew glowering at her. Ian Hepburn was the only person in the abbey who looked as unhappy as she felt. With his high Roman brow, dimpled chin and sleek dark hair gathered at the nape in a satin queue, he should have been a handsome man. But on this day the classical beauty of his features was tainted by an emotion dangerously close to hatred. He did not approve of this match, no doubt fearing her nubile young body would produce a new Hepburn heir and deprive him of his inheritance.

As the minister droned on, reading from the Book of Common Order, Emma looked over her shoulder again to see her mother turn her face into her papa's coat as if she could no longer bear to watch the proceedings. Her sisters were beginning to sniffle more loudly by the minute. Ernestine's sharp little nose was as pink as a rabbit's and judging by the violent quiver of Edwina's plump bottom lip, it was only a matter of time before she broke into full-fledged sobs.

Soon the minister's ramblings would draw to a close, leaving Emma with no choice but to pledge her devotion and her body to

18

this shriveled stranger.

She cast a wild-eyed glance behind her, wondering what they would all do if she lifted the lace-trimmed hem of her silk wedding dress and made a mad dash for the door. She'd heard numerous cautionary tales of careless travelers disappearing into the Highland wilderness, never to be seen or heard from again. At the moment, it sounded like a wonderfully tempting prospect. After all, it wasn't as if her decrepit groom could chase her down, toss her over his shoulder and haul her back to the altar.

As if to underscore that fact, the earl began to croak out his vows. Too soon, he was done and the minister was looking expectantly at her.

As was everyone else in the abbey.

As her silence dragged on, one of the women murmured, "Och, the puir lass is overcome with emotion."

"If she swoons, he'll naught be able to catch her without breakin' his back," her companion whispered.

Emma opened her mouth, then closed it again. It had gone as dry as cotton, forcing her to wet her lips with the tip of her tongue before she made another attempt at speech. The minister blinked at her from behind his steel-rimmed spectacles, the compassion in

his kind brown eyes bringing her dangerously near to tears.

Emma glanced over her shoulder again
but this time it wasn't her mother or her
sisters who captured her gaze but her papa.

There was no mistaking the pleading look
in his eyes. Eyes the exact same dusky blue
shade as hers. Eyes that had for too long
looked both haunted and hunted. She
would almost swear the tremor in his hands
had decreased since the earl had signed over
the settlement. She hadn't seen him reach
for the flask he always kept tucked in his
waistcoat pocket even once since she'd accepted the earl's proposal.

In his encouraging smile, she caught a
glimpse of another man — a younger man
with clear eyes and steady hands whose
breath smelled of peppermint instead of
spirits. He would swoop down and whisk
her up to his shoulders for a dizzying ride,
making her feel as if she was queen of all
she surveyed instead of just a grubby tod-
dler with skinned knees and a snaggle-
toothed smile.

She also saw something in her father's
eyes that she hadn't seen for a very long
time — hope.

Emma turned back to her bridegroom,
squaring her shoulders. Despite what the

onlookers might believe, she had no intention of weeping or swooning. She had always prided herself on being made of sterner stuff than that. If she must marry this earl to secure the future and fortunes of her family, then marry him she would. And she would strive to be the best wife and countess his wealth — and title — could buy.

She was opening her mouth — fully prepared to promise to love, cherish and obey him, for better or worse, in sickness and in health, till death did them part — when the double doors of iron-banded oak at the rear of the abbey came crashing open, letting in a blast of wintry air and a dozen armed men.

The abbey erupted in a chorus of startled shrieks and gasps. The men fanned out among the pews, their unshaven faces grim with determination, their pistols held at the ready to quell any sign of resistance.

Instead of fear, Emma felt a ridiculous flare of hope ignite in her heart.

As the initial outcry subsided, Ian Hepburn boldly stepped into the center aisle of the abbey, placing himself between the forbidding mouths of the intruders' weapons and his great-uncle. "What is the meaning of this?" he shouted, his clipped tones ringing from the vaulted ceiling. "Have you savages no respect for the house of the Lord?"

"And which lord would that be?" a man responded in a Scots burr so deep and rich it sent an involuntary shiver down Emma's spine. "The one who formed these mountains with His own hands or the one who believes he was born with the right to rule them?"

She gasped along with everyone else as the owner of that voice rode a towering black horse right through the doorway of the abbey. A shocked murmur went up as the wedding guests shrank back into their pews, their avid gazes reflecting equal parts fear and fascination. Oddly enough, Emma's gaze wasn't transfixed by the magnificent beast with its gleaming barreled chest and flowing ebony mane but by the man straddling the steed's imposing back.

Thick, sable wings of hair framed his sun-bronzed face, presenting a startling contrast to the frosty green of his eyes. Despite the chill of the day, he wore only a green and black woolen kilt, a pair of lace-up boots, and a sleeveless vest of beaten brown leather that exposed his broad, smooth chest to the elements. He handled the beast as if he'd been born to the saddle, his powerful shoulders and well-muscled forearms barely

22

showing a strain as he guided the horse right up the aisle, forcing Ian to stumble backward or be trampled by the animal's deadly hooves.

From beside her, Emma heard the earl hiss, *"Sinclair!"*

She turned to find her elderly groom's face suffused with color and twisted with hatred. Judging by the ripe, purple vein pulsing in his temple, he might not survive the wedding, much less the wedding night.

"Forgive me for interrupting such a tender moment," the intruder said without so much as a trace of remorse as he reined his mount to a prancing halt halfway down the aisle. "Surely you didn't think I could resist dropping by to pay my respects on such a momentous occasion. My invitation must have been lost in the post."

The earl shook one palsied fist at him. "The only invitation any Sinclair is likely to receive from me is a writ of arrest from the magistrate and a date with the hangman."

In reaction to the threat, the man simply arched one bemused eyebrow. "I had such high hopes that the next time I darkened the door of this abbey, it would be for your funeral, not another wedding. But you always have been a randy auld goat. I should have known you couldn't resist buying another bride to warm your bed."

For the first time since he'd muscled his way into the abbey, the stranger's mocking gaze flicked toward her. Even that brief glance was enough to bring a stinging flush to Emma's fair cheeks, especially since his words held the undeniable and damning ring of truth.

This time it was almost a relief when Ian Hepburn once again sought to impose himself between them. "You may mock us and pretend to be avenging your ancestors as you always do," he said, a sneer curling his upper lip, "but everyone on this mountain knows that the Sinclairs have never been anything more than common cutthroats and thieves. If you and your ruffians have come to divest my uncle's guests of their jewels and purses, then why don't you bloody well get on with it and stop wasting your breath and our time?"

With surprising strength, Emma's groom shoved his way past her, nearly sending her sprawling. "I don't need my nephew to fight my battles. I'm not afraid of an insolent whelp like you, Jamie Sinclair," he snarled, marching right past his nephew with one bony fist still upraised. "Do your worst!"

"Oh, I haven't come for you, auld mon." A lazy smile curved the intruder's lips as he drew a gleaming black pistol from the waistband of his kilt and pointed it at the snowy white bodice of Emma's gown. "I've come for your bride."

CHAPTER TWO

As Emma gazed into the stranger's glacial green eyes over the mouth of his pistol, it suddenly occurred to her that there might be worse fates than agreeing to wed a doddering old man. The thick, sooty lashes framing those eyes did nothing to veil the unspoken threat glittering in their depths.

At the sight of the pistol pointed at Emma's breast, her mother clapped a hand over her mouth to muffle a broken cry. Elberta and Edwina clutched at each other, the clusters of silk violets on their matching bonnets trembling and their blue eyes wide with shock, while Ernestine began to paw through her reticule for her smelling salts.

Her father leapt to his feet but made no move to leave the pew. It was as if he was frozen in place by some force more powerful than his devotion to his daughter. "I say, man," he barked, steadying his hands on the back of the pew in front of him, "what in the devil is the meaning of this?"

While the minister backed toward the altar, deliberately distancing himself from Emma, the earl lowered his clenched fist and slowly shuffled backward, leaving a clear path between Emma's heart and the loaded pistol. Judging by the expectant hush that had fallen over the rest of the guests, she and Sinclair might have been the only two souls in the abbey. Emma supposed some response was required of her as well — that she ought to swoon or burst into tears or plead prettily for her life.

Knowing that was exactly what the villain probably expected her to do gave her the courage to tamp down her own budding terror and stand straight and tall, to lift her chin and meet his ruthless gaze with a defiant glare of her own. She dug her fingernails into the bouquet to hide the violent quaking of her hands, crushing the lingering perfume of the heather from the crisp blooms. For an elusive second, another emotion flickered through those frosty green eyes — one that might have been amusement . . . or admiration.

It was Ian Hepburn's turn to march past his uncle, his dark eyes smoldering with contempt. He stopped a healthy distance from the man on horseback. "So now you've

27

sunk to defiling churches *and* threatening to shoot helpless, unarmed women. I suppose I should have expected no better from a bastard like you, *Sin*," he added, hissing the nickname as if it were the vilest of epithets.

Sinclair briefly shifted his gaze from Emma to Ian, his grip on the pistol unwavering. "Then you're not to be disappointed, are you, auld friend?"

"I'm not your friend!" Ian shouted.

"No," Sinclair replied softly, his voice tinged with what might have been either bitterness or regret. "I suppose you never were."

Even in retreat, the earl remained defiant. "You're living proof that it takes more than studying at St. Andrews to turn a mountain rat into a gentleman! It must gall your grandfather beyond measure to know that sending you off to university was such a waste of his precious coins. Coins no doubt stolen from my own coffers by his motley band of rabble!"

The earl's insults didn't seem to faze Sinclair. "I wouldn't exactly call it a waste. If I hadn't gone to St. Andrews, I might have never made the acquaintance of your charming nephew here." That earned him a fresh glare from Ian. "But I will make sure to give my grandfather your regards the next time I see him."

So this brigand had lived among civilized folk for a time. That would explain why the roughest edges had been polished off his burr, leaving it even more dangerously silky and musical to Emma's ears.

"Just what do you plan to do, you miserable pup?" the earl demanded. "Have you come to hasten your own inevitable journey to hell by murdering my bride in cold blood on the altar of a church?"

Emma was alarmed to note that her devoted bridegroom didn't look particularly dismayed by the prospect. With his title and riches, she supposed it would be a simple enough matter for him to procure another bride. Ernestine and Elberta were both nearly old enough to wed. Perhaps her father would be allowed to keep the earl's settlement if he offered the man a choice between the two girls so the ceremony could proceed without further interruption.

After they'd mopped up her blood, of course.

A nervous hiccup of a giggle escaped her. She had avoided swooning or begging for her life only to end up skating dangerously near to hysteria. It was just beginning to occur to her that she might actually die here at the hands of this merciless stranger — a virgin bride never knowing true passion or the adoring touch of a lover.

"Unlike some," Sinclair said with pointed politeness, "I'm not in the habit of murdering innocent women." A tender smile curved his lips, more dangerous somehow than any sneer or glower. "I said I'd come for your bride, Hepburn, not that I'd come to kill her."

Emma read his intent a heartbeat before anyone else in the abbey. It was there in the squaring of his unshaven jaw, the tension that rippled through his muscular thighs, the way his powerful fists wrapped around the beaten leather of the reins.

Yet all she could do was stand rooted to the flagstones, paralyzed by the raw determination in his narrowed gaze.

Everything seemed to happen at once. Sinclair dug his heels into the horse's flanks. The beast lurched forward, eyes rolling wildly, nostrils flaring. It came charging down the aisle of the abbey, heading straight for Emma. Her mother let out a bloodcurdling scream, then slumped into a dead faint. The minister dove behind the altar, his black robes flapping behind him like the wings of a crow. Emma flung her arms up over her face, bracing herself to be trampled beneath those flashing hooves.

At the last possible second, the horse veered to the left while Sinclair leaned right. He wrapped one powerful arm around Emma's waist and swept her into the air, tossing her belly-down across his lap as if she weighed no more than a sack of wormy potatoes and knocking the air clear out of her. She was still struggling to catch her breath when he wheeled the horse in a tight circle, forcing the beast up on its hind legs for a dizzying pirouette. As those deadly hooves pawed at the air, Emma sucked in a breath that was sure to be her last as she waited for the horse to topple over backward and crush them both.

But her captor had other ideas. He sawed at the reins with brute strength, using sheer mastery to force the creature to succumb to his will. The beast let out an earsplitting whinny. Its front hooves came crashing down, its iron shoes striking sparks off the flagstones.

Sinclair's strong voice carried, even over the shrill shrieks and frantic shouts of alarm echoing off the vaulted ceiling. But his words were meant for the earl alone. "If you want her back unharmed, Hepburn, you'll have to pay and pay dearly! For your own sins and the sins o' your fathers. I'll not return her to you until you return to me

31

what's rightfully mine."

Then he snapped the reins on the horse's back, sending the beast charging back down the aisle of the abbey. They thundered through the doorway and past the crooked gravestones of the churchyard, each of the horse's long, powerful strides carrying Emma farther away from any hope of rescue.

CHAPTER THREE

Emma could not have said how far or how long they traveled. Each bone-jarring jolt of the horse's hooves against the frozen turf scattered more of the amber-tipped pins her maid had so painstakingly secured in Emma's unruly curls as she had sat before the mirror that morning. Before long, the tumbled strands were hanging in a blinding curtain around her face.

She had only the vaguest impression of other horses surrounding them, other hooves pounding the ground in a rhythm as relentless as their own. Sinclair's men must have leapt upon their own horses outside the abbey and joined their reckless flight.

They were moving far too fast for her to put up any sort of struggle. If she tried to fling herself off the horse while it was in mid-gallop, the fall would snap every bone in her body.

Her undignified position would have been

even more precarious were it not for the large, warm, masculine hand firmly anchored at the small of her back, shockingly near to the gentle swell of her rump. Its steady pressure was all that was keeping her from flopping around on her captor's lap like one of Edwina's beloved rag dolls.

Even with that dubious protection, there was still no guarantee the horse's next leap wouldn't splinter a fragile rib or bash her skull wide open on one of the tree trunks leaping in and out of her frantic vision. As the landscape raced by with dizzying speed, blurring before her eyes, she could feel the muscles shifting in her captor's powerful thighs. He drove the horse through thickets, woodlands and across open ground as if he and the creature were one.

As the beast's hooves left the mossy turf and launched them into flight, sending them sailing across a deep ravine, Emma choked out a strangled scream and squeezed her eyes shut. When she dared to open them again, they were skirting the outermost edge of a steep bluff. She caught a dizzying glimpse of the glen below and the rolling foothills crowned by the crenellated stone towers of Hepburn Castle. Her fear deepened to an icy dread as she realized just how far they had already journeyed from both the abbey and civilization.

They rode for so long she wouldn't have been surprised had they arrived at the gates of hell itself. But when Sinclair finally hauled back on the reins, slowing the horse's gait to a bruising trot, then a swaying walk, it wasn't the sulfurous stench of brimstone that made her nose twitch but the crisp aroma of cedar.

Emma wasn't sure what she expected to happen upon their arrival at their unknown destination but it certainly wasn't to be dumped unceremoniously to her feet. As Sinclair swung one long leg over the horse's back, regaining his own footing with effortless grace, she stumbled backward and nearly fell. Her legs felt weak and rubbery, just as they had after her papa had taken the family yachting at Brighton the summer before his luck at the faro tables had taken a costly turn for the worse.

She regained her balance only to find herself standing in the middle of a spacious clearing vaulted by a moody gray sky and ringed by a lush coppice of evergreens. Their feathery branches softened the sharp edge of the wind, making it sigh instead of roar.

Here, where the very air smelled of freedom, she was more a prisoner of circum-

35

stance than ever before.

With their grueling journey at an end, she should have felt some measure of relief. But as she shook her tangled curls out of her eyes to confront the man who was now the master of her fate, she feared she was about to face a reckoning of another kind.

He stood on the opposite side of the horse, his deft hands unfastening the brass cinch holding the saddle in place. The sable wings of his untrimmed hair had swept down to cast his face in shadow, veiling his expression.

Emma stood there in an agony of suspense as he dragged off the heavy saddle with an effort betrayed only by the bulging slabs of muscle in his upper arms. He tossed the saddle on a nest of pine needles before returning to tug the bridle from the horse's sleek throat.

His men had drawn up their own horses at a respectful distance and were dismounting with equal ease. Although a few of them were bold enough to cast her sidelong glances and murmur amongst themselves, it was almost as if they were aping their leader's indifference.

Emma could feel her apprehension beginning to harden into anger. She had expected Sinclair to terrorize her, not ignore her. He was going about his mundane tasks as if he hadn't just brutally snatched her at gunpoint from both her wedding and the bosom of her family.

She stole a glance behind her, wondering if he would even notice if she whirled around and sprinted for freedom.

"I wouldn't try it if I were you," he said evenly.

Startled, Emma whipped her head back around. Sinclair was running a brush down the horse's quivering flanks, all of his attention seemingly focused on his task. It was as if he had divined her thoughts and the direction of her glance with some sense deeper than either hearing or sight.

She still felt a satisfying twinge of triumph. At least she'd proved he wasn't as oblivious to her presence as he was pretending to be.

"As your hostage, isn't that what I'm obligated to do?" She struggled to keep the quaver out of her voice. "Try to escape your villainous clutches?"

He shrugged one powerful shoulder. "Why squander your efforts, lass? You wouldn't get ten paces before I stopped you."

"How? By shooting me in the back?"

He finally did look at her then, the slight arch of one sable eyebrow warning her she had only succeeded in amusing him. "That would be a waste o' perfectly good gunpowder, wouldn't it? Especially when you're worth far more to me alive than dead."

She sniffed. "A touching sentiment, sir, but I'm afraid you've tipped your hand. If I know you have no intention of killing me, then what's to stop me from running?"

He came around the horse then, his strides as even and resolute as his voice. "Me."

Now that Emma had succeeded in gaining his full attention, she had reason to regret her brashness. Her heart began to pound wildly in her chest as she scrambled backward, knowing even as she did so that she had no hope of eluding him. He was everything her bridegroom was not — young, muscular, virile . . . dangerous.

He might not have any intention of killing her but there were other things he could do to her that many might consider even worse.

Much worse.

Her back came up against the knotty trunk of a pine, leaving her with no choice but to stand her ground before his relentless approach. The air must be even thinner up here on the bluff. The nearer he drew, the more breathless she became. By the time his shadow fell over her, blocking out the milky daylight, she was positively light-headed.

She had believed those light green eyes with their thick fringe of sable lashes to be his most striking feature but at this proximity she could no longer be sure. He might be nothing more than a common brigand but he had the high, broad cheekbones of a king. His nose was as straight as a blade with nostrils that flared slightly over a pair of full, almost sinfully sensual, lips. The faintest hint of a cleft shadowed his chin.

He planted both hands on the tree trunk above her head, leaning so close to her she could feel the heat radiating from every muscled inch of him. Both her fear and her light-headedness deepened a dangerous degree as she breathed in the warm, masculine musk of his scent.

Despite its rough edge, his voice was as soft as crushed velvet against the delicate cup of her ear. Its message was not intended for his men's ears but for her and her alone. "If you run, I'll have to put my hands on you. So unless you think you'd enjoy that — and you just might — you'll want to think twice about trying to escape."

Then the sheltering heat of his body was gone and she was once again exposed to the icy bite of the air. As an uncontrollable shiver wracked her, one that had more to do with his tender threat than with the chill hanging in the air, Sinclair went strolling back to his accursed horse as if he hadn't a care in the world.

She glanced over at the other men to discover their brief exchange had garnered an audience. A sallow fellow with a dark arrow of beard on his chin even dared to elbow his companion and chuckle aloud.

"You needn't be so smug, sir," she called after Sinclair, her stinging pride shouldering aside her fear. "I suspect your triumph will be short-lived. The earl is probably notifying the authorities and dispatching his own men to retrieve me even as we speak."

"Once we climb high enough on this mountain, he'll never find us and he knows it," Sinclair tossed back over his shoulder. "No one ever finds a Sinclair if they don't want to be found. Not even a Hepburn. But don't fret, lass," he added in a gently mocking tone. "If everything goes as planned, you'll be back in the arms o' your adoring bridegroom before his bed grows cold. Or at least any colder than it already is."

As he returned to grooming his horse, his men hooted with appreciative laughter. Emma hugged back a fresh shiver, chilled to the bone by the discovery that her captor's contempt was not for the earl alone.

Stealing brides was a time-honored Highland tradition but James Alastair Sinclair had never dreamed he'd be driven to steal another man's bride. It had long been whispered his own great-great-grandfather, MacTavish Sinclair, had swiped his fifteen-year-old bride from her irate papa while on a cattle raid when he was only seventeen. She had refused to speak to him until after their first child was born, then spent the next forty-six years of their marriage chattering incessantly to make up for it. When he expired in his sleep at the ripe old age of sixty-three, she wept inconsolably and died a few short days later — some said of a broken heart.

Jamie could only be thankful his own heart had never been in such dire peril.

As the clouds cleared and the stars began to wink to life in the night sky, his men polished off the earthenware jug of scotch whisky they'd been passing from hand to hand and settled down in their bedrolls. Jamie squatted next to the fire and ladled a steaming dollop of rabbit stew into a bowl, shooting his captive a wary look.

She sat on a rock at the very edge of the trees, shunning both the fire's seductive warmth and his company. The shadows from the overhanging branches dappled her pale face like bruises. The last of the pins had tumbled from her hair, leaving it to hang around her face in an untidy mop of copper-tinted curls. She sat with her slender arms wrapped around herself, the dirt-smudged tatters of her once-elegant gown a poor protection against the brisk mountain wind. Despite her forlorn posture, her soft mouth and sharp little chin were still set at a mutinous angle. She gazed right past him and into the crackling flames of the campfire as if she could somehow make him and his men disappear simply by ignoring their existence.

Jamie scowled. He had expected the earl's young bride to be some wilting milksop of an English miss, none too bright and easily cowed. Knowing what he did of the Hepburn, he had assumed the auld wretch would have deliberately chosen the chit most likely to die in childbirth minutes after she'd handed his squirming spawn over to the wet nurse who would raise it.

Her stubborn show of spirit despite her fear — both in the abbey and here in this clearing — had unsettled him and stirred a twinge of admiration he could ill afford. After all, the lass was naught to him but a means to an end; a brief inconvenience he could be rid of just as soon as the Hepburn conceded to the demand that would be delivered to him a few days hence.

Jamie felt as if he had already waited a lifetime for this moment and now his time was running out. But he was still determined to give the Hepburn a day or two to consider all of the grim fates that might befall his innocent bride at the hands of his sworn enemy should he fail to comply.

A bone-chilling gust of wind breached the boughs of the pines and whipped through the clearing. Although it felt like no more than a gentle breeze against Jamie's tough hide, the lass shivered, hugging herself so tightly her knuckles went white. Jamie suspected her delicate teeth were no longer clenched in impotent fury, but to keep from chattering.

Swearing softly in Gaelic, he straightened and strode over to her. He stopped right in front of her, holding out the bowl of stew. She continued to stare straight ahead, scorning both him and his humble offering.

His hand did not waver. "If you intend to starve yourself to death just to shame me, lass, it won't work. Your precious bridegroom would warn you that neither I nor any o' my kin have any shame."

He waved the bowl beneath her haughty little nose, deliberately tempting her with the succulent aroma. Her stomach betrayed her with a lusty growl. Shooting him a resentful glance, she snatched the bowl from his hand.

He watched, torn between triumph and amusement, as she used the crudely carved wooden spoon to down several greedy mouthfuls of the stuff. It was an unexpected pleasure to watch the color seep back into her cheeks as the stew warmed her belly. He had heard whispers that the Hepburn's bride was no great beauty, but her freckled cheeks and finely chiseled features possessed a winsome charm few men could deny. Against his will he found his gaze drawn to the softness of her lips as they closed around the bowl of the spoon, to the supple grace of her little pink tongue as it darted out to lick the utensil clean.

The innocent sight stirred a surprising hunger low in his own belly. Afraid he might just start growling back at her, he started to turn away.

"Just how long am I to be your prisoner, sir?" she demanded.

Sighing, he pivoted to face her. "That depends on just how much your bridegroom values you, now, doesn't it? Perhaps you'd

44

find your lot in life more bearable if you tried thinking o' yourself as my guest."

She wrinkled her nose, drawing his attention to the dash of cinnamon freckles across its bridge. "Then I'd have to say your hospitality leaves much to be desired. Most hosts — no matter how miserly — will at least provide a roof over their guest's head. As well as four walls to keep them from freezing to death."

Propping one foot on a fallen log, Jamie tipped back his head to survey the majestic indigo sweep of the night sky. "Our walls are the sheltering branches o' the pines and our roof a vaulted dome dusted with gems sprinkled by the hand o' the Almighty himself. I challenge you to find a grander sight in any London ballroom."

When silence greeted his words, he slanted her a sidelong glance only to catch her quizzically studying his profile instead of the sky. She quickly lowered her eyes, hiding them beneath the wary russet sweep of her lashes. "I was expecting little more than an unintelligible grunt. It seems the earl was wrong, sir. Your education wasn't wasted after all. At least not judging by your vocabulary."

He sketched her a mocking bow so flawless it would have done any gentleman proud. "With enough time and determination, lass, even a savage can learn to mimic his betters."

"Like Ian Hepburn? From what you said in the abbey, I gather he was one of your betters at the university?"

"There was a time when he might have considered himself my equal. But that was when he only knew me as his dear friend *Sin*. Once his uncle informed him I was nothing but a filthy, stinking Sinclair with dirt under his fingernails and blood on his hands, he wanted nothing more to do with me."

"After having known you for only a few hours myself, I can't say that I blame him."

"Och, lass!" he exclaimed, clapping a hand to his chest and giving her a reproachful look. "Ye cut me to the heart wi' that wee, sharp tongue o' yers. Hae ye no' an ounce o' pity in yer soul fer a puir ignorant Scotsmon?"

Hoping to hide the melting effect his velvet-edged burr had on her, Emma surged to her feet to face him. "My name isn't 'lass.' It's Emmaline. Or Miss Marlowe if you're civilized enough to observe the social niceties. My father is a baronet — one of the gentry."

Folding his arms over his chest, Jamie

snorted. "Genteel enough to auction his daughter off to the highest bidder?"

She lifted her chin again, refusing to quail before his scorn, and said softly, "The *only* bidder."

Her confession caught Jamie off guard. The lass might be willowy and small breasted, but there was still no denying her feminine charms. If she had been born and raised on this mountain, besotted suitors would have been lining up to cast themselves at her feet.

"And you needn't make my father out to be some sort of grasping villain from a Gothic melodrama," she added. "For all you know, I could be madly in love with the earl."

Jamie barked out a laugh. "And I could be the King of Scotland." Ignoring his better judgment, he allowed his gaze a bold foray over her. "There's only one reason a woman like you would wed a moldering auld bag o' bones like the Hepburn."

She rested her hands on her slender hips. "You just abducted me a few hours ago. How can you possibly presume to know what manner of woman I am?"

Before he even realized what he was going to do, he had stepped closer to her — close enough to stroke his roughened knuckles

47

down the irresistible softness of her cheek. He'd never been a man given to bullying women but there was something about this tart-tongued girl that made him want to put his hands on her, to coax some sort of reaction out of her, even if it was to his own detriment.

He put his mouth against her ear, deliberately lowering his voice to a husky whisper. "I know you're still young enough — and comely enough — to need a real mon in your bed."

A shiver having naught to do with fear or the brisk wind raked her tender flesh. When Jamie drew back to survey her face, she was gazing up at him, her parted lips trembling ever so slightly and her dusky blue eyes large enough to reflect the rising moon.

Before he could succumb to her unwitting invitation, Jamie turned away from her, determined to fetch her a bedroll and be done with her for the night.

Her next words froze him in his tracks.

"You're wrong about my father, sir. He's not the greedy one. I am."

Jamie slowly turned, his eyes narrowing as a prickle of wariness eased up his spine. He'd felt that unsettling sensation numerous times before, usually just seconds before he was about to be ambushed by a roving gang of Hepburn's hired guns.

His captive's posture was no longer forlorn or fearful but openly defiant. Her voice was steady, her eyes as cool as the silvery moonlight playing over her high, freckled cheekbones. "Surely even a common ruffian such as yourself must know that most women would barter not only their bodies but their souls to wed a man as wealthy and powerful as the earl. Once I'm his countess, I'll have every treasure a woman could desire — jewels, furs, land, and more gold than I could spend, or count, in a lifetime. And I can promise you I'll not lack for a *mon* in my bed," she added with a scornful toss of her head. "After I've provided him with an heir, I'm sure the earl won't begrudge me a Season in London and a strapping young lover . . . or two."

Jamie simply gazed at her for a long, thoughtful moment before saying, "My name isn't 'sir,' Miss Marlowe. It's Jamie."

With that, he turned on his heel and left her standing there, her slender frame buffeted by the wind.

CHAPTER FOUR

Jamie, Emma thought. Such an innocuous name for such a dangerous man.

As the moon crested and slowly began its descent, she huddled deeper in the nest of scratchy woolen blankets her captor had provided. They smelled of *him,* a realization that only sharpened the jagged edge of her misery.

The rich masculine musk with its earthy undertones of leather, woodsmoke and horse should have been offensive to her delicate nose. Most men of her acquaintance, including her father and every gentleman she had encountered during her three Seasons in London, smothered their natural scents beneath a choking layer of shaving soaps and floral colognes. One could hardly draw breath when walking into an assembly room crowded with dandies drenched in the most popular of that Season's sweet waters, whether it be honey or rose. Instead of being repelled by Sinclair's exotic scent, she caught herself breathing deep to draw it into her lungs, almost as if it had the power to warm her chilled blood.

She rolled over. The cold, hard ground was as unwelcoming as a slab of rock. Every time she stirred, a new stone or twig seemed to rear up to jab her tender flesh. Not that she was likely to sleep anyway while lying a few scant feet away from a pack of dangerous outlaws in the middle of the Scottish wilderness.

Not even their drunken snores could completely drown out the echo of her own mocking voice: *I'm sure the earl won't begrudge me a Season in London and a strapping young lover . . . or two.*

Emma moaned aloud and buried her head beneath the blankets, wondering what had possessed her to make such a preposterous boast. She had managed to survive her parents' forced cheer and her sisters' pretended envy over her nuptials to the earl, so why had a stranger's opinion of her proved so galling to her pride?

Somehow as she had stood there in the moonlight, being judged and found wanting beneath the cool appraisal of Jamie Sinclair's eyes, it had seemed better for him to think her a grasping shrew than some

51

sacrificial lamb marching meekly to her doom. Better to have him loathe her than to pity her. For a few precious seconds, she had felt strong and powerful and in command of her own fate.

Now she just felt ridiculous.

She might have been able to restrain her temper if he hadn't kept calling her "lass" in that infuriating manner. Thanks to that whisky-and-velvet burr of his, the word had sounded more like an endearment than the overly familiar insult it was. It had made her desperate to put some distance between them, even if it was only by insisting he acknowledge her social superiority by calling her Miss Marlowe. He would probably laugh in her face if he knew her *genteel* father was one flask of brandy and one unlucky round at the faro table away from being cast into debtor's gaol.

I know you're still young enough — and comely enough — to need a real mon in your bed.

As she struggled to pummel a fold of the blanket into some semblance of a pillow, it was his words and not her own that returned to haunt her. A fresh shiver raked her as she remembered how his knuckles had grazed her cheek with such disarming tenderness. His husky whisper had summoned up mys-

52

terious and provocative images of the things a *mon* might do to her in that bed. These images had little to do with the disagreeable duty her mother had described. Even now, they held the power to send a rush of heat sizzling through her veins, to burn the chill from her aching bones.

She squeezed her eyes shut. Was Sinclair bold enough to imply she needed a man like *him* in her bed? A man who wouldn't simply climb atop her and wiggle and grunt as her mother had told her the earl was likely to do? A man who would woo her with tender, breath-stealing kisses and skillful caresses until she was begging to surrender herself to him?

Her eyes flew open. Being bounced around on the horse's back must have scrambled her wits. It wasn't as if a barbarian like Jamie Sinclair could ever be that man. From what she'd heard of the wild Highlanders who still roamed these hills, he was more likely to bend a woman over a table, toss her skirts up over her head and take his pleasure roughly and swiftly without a care for her own.

Emma poked her head out of the blankets, hoping the icy air would cool the sudden fever raging in her cheeks. She was accustomed to hearing her sisters whisper and giggle in bed each night after their mother extinguished the lamp. It gave her an unsettling start to hear instead the low rumble of two men talking between themselves.

"She's a bonny eno' lass, I s'pose," one of them was saying. "Though a bit scrawny for my tastes."

"Judging by the girth o' that barmaid in Invergarry, any lass under fifteen stone would be a bit scrawny for your tastes, Bon." Emma stiffened as she recognized the unmistakable cadences of Sinclair's murmur. Although she had her back to the fire, she instinctively closed her eyes so no one would guess she was eavesdropping instead of sleeping.

Sinclair's observation was met with a fond sigh from the man he'd called Bon. "Aye, me Rosie was a bit o' a handful, wasn't she? Two handfuls and a mouthful, if ye must know."

"I mustn't, but I'm sure the image will haunt my dreams for nights to come," Sinclair said dryly.

"Don't try to play the monk with me, lad. I'm sure ye'd like nothin' more than to warm yerself between a certain pair o' soft, white thighs on this cold spring night."

"You heard me in the abbey," Sinclair replied, his tones clipped. "I told Hepburn

54

if he met my demands, no harm would come to her."

"Ah, but ye promised to return her unharmed, not unfooked." Emma was still puzzling over the unfamiliar term when Sinclair's companion chuckled. " 'Twould be the ultimate revenge, wouldn't it? Sending her back to the auld buzzard with a Sinclair bastard in her belly?"

Emma's blood froze in her veins as the full import of the man's words sank in. She might still be an innocent but she was no fool. If Sinclair decided to use her tender young body to slake his appetite for revenge, there would be little she could do to stop him. No one would heed her desperate struggles or her pleas for mercy. Judging by what his companion had just said, his men were more likely to gather around and cheer him on than rush to her rescue.

Emma shuddered, remembering anew the dreadful things she had said to him. Since she was the one who had boldly professed her eagerness to take a strapping young lover as soon as the earl would allow it, he might even be able to convince himself that she would welcome his advances.

She held her breath, waiting for Sinclair to deny his man's words, to rebuke his companion for suggesting something so abominable. But the taut silence remained unbroken except for the cheery crackle and snap of the fire. Though her eyes were still squeezed tightly shut, she could almost see him sitting there before the fire, his regal cheekbones shadowed by its leaping flames as he weighed the wisdom of his man's counsel.

No longer able to bear the suspense, she dared a furtive glance over her shoulder. Sinclair was sitting with his back to her, facing the fire and blocking her view of the other man. His broad shoulders and back looked even more imposing from this angle.

She had no intention of just lying there and waiting for his shadow to fall over her, blocking out the moonlight and covering her in darkness.

As she eased back a corner of the blanket, his velvet-edged warning echoed through her mind: *If you run, I'll have to put my hands on you . . .*

She rolled soundlessly out of the bedroll.

If Jamie Sinclair wanted to put his hands on her, he would have to catch her first.

Jamie glared at his cousin over the leaping flames of the campfire. Their hellish glow only emphasized the devilish sparkle of Bon's black eyes and the impish arch of his thin, dark brows.

Bon was one of the few men who could bear up under Jamie's most fierce glower. He'd had ample practice, both when they were lads running wild over the grounds of the Sinclair stronghold together and during the half dozen or so years that they'd been riding against the Hepburn and his men. The only time they'd been separated was during those long, bleak terms Jamie had spent at St. Andrews.

If Jamie hadn't known that Bon was deliberately needling him, he would have lunged across the fire and boxed his pointy ears just as he had so many times as a boy. More often than not, the two of them would end up rolling in the dirt, pummeling each other bloody until someone — usually Bon's mother, God rest her long-suffering soul, or Jamie's grandfather — dragged them apart by their collars and gave them each a sound shaking.

Their brawling had tapered off when Jamie had turned fourteen and rapidly gained eight inches in height and two stone in weight on Bon. Since then, Bon had been forced to do battle with his canny wits instead of his fists, wits that were on full display now as he returned Jamie's glower with an innocent blink of his own.

Jamie should have disputed his cousin's words outright but he couldn't deny the truth in them. There were few on this mountain who would condemn him for sampling the auld mon's bride. After everything the Hepburn had done to his family — including trying to wipe the Sinclair name from the face of the earth — it would be a fitting revenge for Jamie's seed to live on in the womb of the woman the Hepburn had chosen to bear his own son.

Jamie felt a surprising surge of lust in his loins. For the first time since he and Bon had instituted their little game of wits and wills, Jamie was the first to look away.

Ignoring Bon's triumphant grin, he picked up a stick and gave the fire a fierce poke, sending a shower of sparks shooting up into the velvety blackness of the night sky. "There's no need to play these games. I'm well aware you don't approve o' me snatchin' the Hepburn's bride."

"And why would I when the only likely outcome is for us to end up danglin' by our necks from some hangman's gibbet? Now that ye've gone and made off with an Englishwoman, what's to stop the Hepburn from callin' the full wrath o' the British army down on our heads?"

"His pride. You know he'd rather die than

ask for help from any mon, be he Scottish or English."

"Then I wish he'd go ahead and die and spare us all this trouble." Bon stabbed a finger in the general direction of the bedroll where Jamie had left their captive. "Because I can promise ye that trouble is all that lass is goin' to be."

Jamie snorted. "I doubt a prim, stiff-necked lass like that has ever done anything more *troubling* than dropping a stitch while embroidering a scripture on a sampler." He spared his cousin a sideways glance. "Besides, she couldn't possibly be more trouble than that bonny wee dairy maid in Torlundy whose husband threatened to tear off your scrawny arm and beat you to death with it when he caught you sneaking out of his bedchamber window in the middle of the night."

"Ah, my sweet Peg!" Bon sighed wistfully at the memory. "Now there was a lass worth dying for — both between the sheets and out o' them. Can ye say the same for the Hepburn's woman?"

Jamie tossed the stick away. "She's not his woman. At least not yet. And I can promise you I have no intention of dying for her. Not by the hangman's hand or by any other means."

"What makes ye think the Hepburn'll even be willing to pay to get her back? He's never had a reputation for bein' overly sentimental. There are some who say he sold his black heart to the divil along with his soul."

"Oh, he'll pay. Not because he has any particular fondness for the lass but because he won't be able to bear the thought of a Sinclair stealing something that belongs to him." Jamie felt his lips curve in a grim smile. "Especially this particular Sinclair."

"And what if Ian Hepburn isn't as proud as his uncle? What if he convinces the auld buzzard to bring in the redcoats to fight on their side?"

Jamie's gaze was drawn back to the darkness at the very heart of the fire. Even he had to admit that Ian was the unknown quantity in his carefully calculated scheme. It was difficult to pretend he hadn't been shaken by the depth of the loathing he had glimpsed in his former friend's eyes as they had faced each other in that abbey.

He gave his head a brisk shake. "If anything, Ian hates me more than his uncle does. He won't want the redcoats doing their dirty work for them. He'd rather see his own hands around my throat than a hangman's noose."

The sparkle in Bon's dark eyes was dimmed by the shadow of worry. "I don't know exactly what it is ye plan to ask of the Hepburn in return for his bride but it's goin' to have to be one hell of a prize to justify riskin' all of our necks, includin' yer own. Are ye sure it's worth it?"

"Aye." Jamie looked Bon dead in the eye. Bon had always been more brother than cousin to him and he owed him at least that much of the truth. "That much I can promise you."

Long after Bon had retired for the night, Jamie found himself standing over his captive's bedroll, hoping he would be able to keep the promise he had made to his cousin. If he was wrong about the Hepburn bringing in the redcoats to retrieve her, he may very well have sealed the doom of his entire clan.

He had long suspected that the Hepburn secretly enjoyed the little game of cat and mouse the two of them had been playing practically from the moment Jamie had been born. Jamie could almost picture the auld man at this very moment, gleefully rubbing his bony hands together as he plotted his next move. To a man like the Hepburn the mountain was naught but his own personal chessboard, and the people who eked out their living from its rocky soil pawns to be moved about at both his whim and his pleasure. There was only one way to beat the man and that was to be cannier . . . and more ruthless than he was. By kidnapping an innocent woman, Jamie had finally succeeded at both.

He scowled down at the bedroll. The girl who slept at his feet was no less a pawn to the earl. He knew that it galled Hepburn beyond measure to have outlived his three sons and all their offspring while Jamie had not only survived, but thrived. Hepburn would stop at nothing to procure a new heir for himself.

Jamie ran a hand over his tense jaw, wondering why he'd been foolish enough to assign himself guard duty when he could have easily commanded one of his men to do it. He glanced toward the other side of the fire where they had bedded down for the night. Although he'd trust most of them with his life, for some reason he was reluctant to trust them alone with Miss Marlowe. Hell, at the moment he wasn't sure he could trust himself alone with her. Especially not with Bon's taunting words still fresh in his mind.

She had the blankets drawn up so high

62

that even the coppery spill of curls at the top of her head was hidden. A frown creased his brow. She was a lady, not some sturdy Highland lass. She was probably accustomed to taking her ease in a fluffy feather bed piled high with down coverlets, not on the hard ground with only a thin layer of scratchy wool to shield her from the cold.

He squatted down next to her and drew back a fold of the blanket, seeking to assure himself that she hadn't frozen to death just to spite him.

There was no coppery spill of curls. Miss Marlowe was gone.

CHAPTER FIVE

For a disbelieving moment, Jamie could only stare stupidly at the empty spot where Emma should have been.

Not only had she managed to slip out of the camp with him sitting only a few feet away, she had been clever enough to mold the blankets into a rounded heap so that anyone giving them a casual glance would assume she was still safely tucked beneath them.

"Bluidy hell," Jamie breathed, raking a hand through his hair.

He should have known that anyone who would consort with the Hepburn wasn't to be trusted. He was a bluidy fool not to have tied her to the nearest tree when he had the chance. That would teach him to try to play the gentleman.

He straightened, his grim gaze searching the murky shadows beneath the nearest stand of cedars. He would have never dreamed such a slip of a girl would be bold enough to defy his warning and brave the night or the wilderness on her own.

He knew only too well just how unforgiving that wilderness could be. A sheltered English lass had no chance of navigating the brutal terrain of the mountain. She probably wouldn't survive more than an hour before falling into a burn where she would be lucky to drown before she could freeze to death, or stumbling over the edge of a cliff. The image of her fragile young body lying crumpled and broken at the bottom of some rocky ravine troubled him more than he cared to admit.

Jamie knew his only rational course of action was to rouse his men from their bedrolls and send them out to scour the woods for her. But some primitive instinct stayed his hand. The Hepburn had put a price on his head the minute he'd been born. He knew exactly what it felt like to be hunted through these hills; to run until you thought your aching legs would collapse beneath you and your lungs would explode; to never know if your next breath might be your last. He couldn't bear the thought of his men driving Emma before them as if she was some sort of helpless woodland creature. They could very well be the ones to spook her over the edge of that cliff.

Jamie strode to the border of the clearing and swept aside a low-hanging cedar bough. As his practiced eye scanned the underbrush for fallen needles and broken twigs, a smile slowly curved his lips. It seemed that Miss Marlow had left a trail even a blind man could follow.

Emma plunged blindly through the forest, her only thoughts those of escape. She knew she had no chance of making it back down the mountain on her own but if she could get enough of a head start on Sinclair and his gang of ruffians, perhaps she could find some hollow tree or sheltered nook where she could hide until the earl's men arrived to rescue her. She could tell by the steep slope of the land and the number of times she had stumbled over her own feet that she was at least headed in the right direction — down.

This forest was nothing like the wood that bordered her father's lands in Lancashire. She and her sisters had spent many pleasant hours there when they were children, picking wildflowers or gathering mushrooms for their mother's table while playing at being pirates or fairy princesses. The sheltering branches of elm and oak were spaced widely apart there, inviting in glowing shafts of sunlight. The mossy hollows and gentle glades seemed more like a park than a wood.

This place resembled the forest in some dark and forbidding fairy tale — a place where time had stood still for centuries and some slavering ogre might spring out at any minute to devour you.

The thickly laced branches over Emma's head allowed in only grudging flashes of moonlight. As she scrambled down a slick, mossy bank, the rasp of her own breathing echoed in her ears like the panting of some desperate wild thing.

She'd yet to stumble across anything even remotely resembling a road or a path, which was probably for the best. The last thing she wanted to do was make it easy for Sinclair and his men to track her.

Branches lashed at her as she ran, their bony fingers stinging her cheeks and tearing at the fragile silk of her gown. A sob of pain escaped her as her left foot came down squarely on a jagged stone. The thin soles of her kid slippers provided little protection for her tender feet. She might as well have been barefoot. She winced as she splashed through the icy water of a shallow creek, knowing it was only a matter of time before the slippers gave way altogether, leaving her completely exposed to the elements. What she wouldn't have given for the pair of sturdy old half-boots she'd left tucked beneath her bed at home! Her mother had refused to let her pack them, insisting that the earl would buy her all the elegant slippers she would need once they were wed.

She glanced behind her. It was impossible to tell if she was being pursued or if the sounds she could hear over the rapid throb of her heart in her ears were simply the echoes of her own clumsy thrashing through the underbrush. She wasn't about to stop long enough to find out.

She had no desire to find out just exactly how Jamie Sinclair might punish her for refusing to heed his warning. Judging from the icy composure he had demonstrated in the abbey and the authority he exerted over his own men, he wouldn't take kindly to being defied.

Doubling her pace, she dared another desperate look over her shoulder. The moon was sinking in the sky and the shadows themselves seemed to be chasing her, the billowing clouds of darkness threatening to swallow her whole, leaving no trace behind.

She jerked her gaze back to the path ahead of her only to find herself heading straight for the edge of a steep bluff. It was too late to slow her forward momentum. Too late to do anything but make a frantic grab for the slender trunk of the birch tree overhanging the rocky gorge far below.

The smooth bark slid right through her hands, offering her no purchase and no hope. A shriek escaped her lips as she slid over the edge of the bluff and into thin air.

Jamie froze in his tracks, his ears echoing with a cry so sharp and brief he might have imagined it. Or it could have simply been the night cry of some animal, either predator or prey.

He cocked his head to listen but heard only silence, unbroken except for the mournful sigh of the wind through a nearby copse of pines.

That's when he realized something was wrong. He had been tracking Emma for nearly an hour, tracking her with his ears and eyes but also with some sense deeper and more primitive than hearing or sight. No matter how far or fast he traveled, he'd known she was there . . . somewhere ahead of him, out of his reach but still within his grasp. But now that awareness of her was gone. It was as if an invisible thread had been cut, leaving him dangling over a dark precipice with no bottom in sight.

Biting off an oath, he broke into a run, heading in the direction of that helpless cry. He paid no heed to the branches that slapped at his face or sought to trap him in their thorny embrace. He'd gone charging through these same woods dozens of times before, usually with a pack of Hepburn's men hot on his heels.

This time he wasn't running away from something but toward something. Unfortunately, that something turned out to be a downward slope that came to an abrupt end when the earth tapered off into nothingness.

Jamie staggered to a halt a few feet away from that deadly drop, his heart plummeting in his chest. He knew that particular bluff only too well, knew more than one man who had plunged to his doom there due to ignorance or carelessness or a fatal combination of both.

He drifted forward, his steps robbed of their confidence now that he knew his worst fears had been realized. He closed his eyes briefly before peering over the edge of the bluff, already dreading the sight that awaited him.

Emma was going to die.

If the thin shelf of dirt and rock that had

broken her fall didn't soon crumble beneath her, sending her plummeting to a stony grave, then she was going to freeze to death. As the fruits of her exertion faded, the chill hanging in the air began to worm its way deep into her bones. She huddled against the stony wall of the bluff and hugged the tatters of her wedding gown around herself, fearing her uncontrollable shivering might further damage the fragile soil holding the shelf in place.

She cast a despairing glance upward. She was only a few feet below the top of the bluff but the distance might as well have been a hundred leagues. Even if she could manage to make it to her feet without sending the entire ledge crashing to the gorge below, the rim of the bluff would still remain just out of her reach. There wasn't even a stray rock or root protruding from the damp wall to use as a hand or foothold.

It was probably a poor testament to her strength of character that she was feeling in that moment not grief or prayerful resignation, but anger mixed with a petty dollop of satisfaction. It appeared she was to have the last laugh after all, she thought with a faint edge of hysteria. Once she was dead, she would be of no value to Sinclair, her papa or the earl. They would no longer be able to barter her back and forth as if she was some prize sheep or sow at the local market. She wondered if Sinclair would go to the trouble of burying her or if he'd just leave her body to rot on the ledge and go riding off to abduct another bride.

"Halloo down there. Is anybody home?"

Emma started violently, sending a fresh shower of dirt skittering to the gorge floor below. She slowly tipped back her head to find Jamie Sinclair grinning down at her from the rim of the bluff.

Her heart betrayed her with a wild surge of relief. To hide it, she narrowed her eyes to glare up at him. "You needn't look so smug, sir. As far as I'm concerned, you can go straight to the devil."

Her words only deepened his smile. "You're not the first lass to tell me to go to hell and you probably won't be the last."

She snorted. "Why doesn't that surprise me?"

He dropped to one knee and peered over the edge of the bluff, his sharp gaze quickly assessing the urgency of her situation. "Would you like to come up or shall I come down?"

She smiled sweetly up at him. "Oh, do feel free to come down. I'll make sure and wave as you go by."

"Now, that wouldn't do either one of us any good, would it? Especially since you'd be destined to join me shortly thereafter and then we'd have to spend eternity in each other's company."

She watched warily as he stretched out full-length on his belly and extended one arm over the side of the bluff, offering her his hand.

Remembering exactly how she had come to be stranded on the ledge in the first place, she ignored the undeniable temptation of his outstretched hand. "I heard what your man said," she reluctantly confessed. "While the two of you were sitting around the fire."

His eyes clouded briefly, then cleared as comprehension dawned. "Oh," he replied, the single word speaking volumes. "So that's why you ran. Because you thought you were about to be . . ."

"Fooked," she finished grimly.

He looked startled, then was forced to strangle back a cough. While he was struggling to catch his breath, his eyes a shade too bright, she shook her head in frustration. "I'm not familiar with the word because I don't speak Scot but I'm not completely ignorant. To prepare me for my wedding night, my mother explained to me

73

that a man has drives . . . much like an animal."

He cocked one eyebrow. "And that a woman doesn't?"

"She implied that there were women who did, but that they were unnatural creatures, given to bringing scandal and ruin upon their families. She also explained in rather excruciating detail what would be expected of me if I was to provide the earl with an heir."

The sparkle in Jamie's eyes hardened to a dangerous glitter. "And you assumed I would be expecting the same thing from you." It was not a question.

"From what your man said, you'd be more likely to demand than expect." Even though it was one of the hardest things she'd ever done in her life, she forced herself to hold his direct gaze. "Or to simply take what you wanted without begging my leave."

His rugged jaw tightened, that subtle motion only hinting at the dark things that could pass between a man and a woman when she was forced to rely upon his mercy. "As long as Hepburn gives me what I want, you've naught to fear. I won't let anyone hurt you." He paused for the space of a heartbeat. "Including me."

She gazed at his outstretched hand, still

torn. All she had to do was stand and stretch out her own arm to seize his offer of salvation.

She had no reason to trust him. He was a scoundrel and a thief. He could be lying through his teeth. Her gaze darted to the dizzying drop below. If she were a true lady, she would fling herself upon the rocks rather than risk being defiled by his hands.

Almost as if reading her mind, he said, "You're forgetting one thing, lass. Your virtue is of nearly as much value to me as your life. The Hepburn isn't going to pay me so much as one halfpenny for damaged goods."

"What makes you think he'll still want me? How can he not consider me *damaged* after you and your band of not-so-merry men have dragged me halfway to Hades without the benefit of any sort of chaperone?"

"Oh, he'll still want you," Jamie said grimly, "if only to prove a Sinclair didn't get the best of him. Knowing the Hepburn, he'll probably insist his own personal physician examine you to prove you're still worthy to be his bride."

As the full import of his words sank in, a scorching blush drove the chill from Emma's cheeks.

"Why, I wouldn't put it past the auld buzzard to invite the wedding guests into his bedchamber to witness your deflowering or to hang a bluidy sheet out the window the next morning just as the Hepburn lairds of auld used to do."

"Stop it!" Emma shouted. "Stop trying to make a kindly old man out to be a monster when you're the true villain! For all I know, you're lying about everything, including what you plan to do to me if I trust you enough to give you my hand!"

"What if I am?"

The deadly calm of his tone cut right through her agitation.

A taunting sneer curled his lips. "What if I am lying to you? Have you so little spirit that you're willing to die to preserve your precious virtue?" Even though Emma suspected he was deliberately trying to goad her into action, she was still mesmerized by the cruel cant of those sensual lips. "You set a very high price on yourself, don't you, lass? Why don't you come up here and show me whether or not you're worth it?"

Keeping her furious gaze locked on his face, Emma began to inch her way to her feet, her back still pressed to the stony wall behind her. As the subtle shift of her weight sent a fresh shower of rubble dancing its way down the side of the cliff, she squeezed her eyes shut against a rush of paralyzing vertigo.

"Damnit to bluidy hell, woman, take my hand!" Jamie's voice deepened on a beseeching note. "Please . . ."

It wasn't his roared command but that raw plea that finally swayed her.

She swung her arm upward and slapped her hand into his broad palm, choosing life, choosing him. His fingers closed around her slender wrist with the force of a vise. As the narrow ledge beneath her feet broke away from its stony mooring and went tumbling into the gorge below, Jamie hauled her up and into his waiting arms.

Chapter Six

Jamie rose and staggered backward, dragging them both away from the edge of the bluff. As the last echo of the shelf tumbling into the gorge died, reminding her anew that it could have been her fragile bones shattering on those rocks, Emma clung helplessly to him, conscious only of the warmth and solidity of his bare chest beneath her cheek. Her shivering had deepened to a violent trembling she could not seem to control.

He hesitated for a moment, but then his arms went around her, drawing her even deeper into his embrace. Through a haze of blind relief, she realized his heart was pounding nearly as wildly as hers.

"There, there, lass," he murmured, stroking a hand over her tangled hair. "It's all right. You're safe now."

Although there was some treacherous part of her that wanted to believe she was safe in the solid warmth of his arms, she knew better. Flattening her palms against his chest, she pushed herself away from him, determined to stand on her own two feet.

He watched through wary eyes as she brushed crumbs of dirt from the skirt of the tattered, filthy rag her wedding gown had become. An alarming amount of pale, freckled skin was beginning to peek through the shattered silk, a fact that did not seem to have escaped Jamie's heavy-lidded gaze.

"When I warned you about trying to escape, it never occurred to me you'd take some fool notion into your wee head to go running off in the middle of the night and tumble over a cliff."

"So what do you want from me now?" she asked, shooting him a defiant look. "Should I apologize for trying to escape or for making such a mortifying muddle of it?"

He folded his arms over his chest. "Perhaps the question should be what do you want from me, Miss Marlowe? Do you want me to prove I'm every inch the villain you believe me to be? Are you deliberately trying to goad me into lifting my hand to you? Into forcing you to my will?"

"What I want, sir, is to go home!" Emma was as shocked as he was to hear the words come spilling from her lips. She'd been

choking them back for what felt like an eternity.

Jamie stiffened. The heat faded from his eyes, leaving them as cool and opaque as paste emeralds. "I promised you I would return you to your bridegroom just as soon as I was able. I'm sure you'll make a very fine mistress for his castle. And his bed."

Shaking her head helplessly, Emma backed away from him. She sank down on a stump and rested her chin in her hand, unable to look at him for fear the tears clogging the back of her throat would finally come trickling from her eyes. "Hepburn Castle is *not* my home. My home is a ramshackle old manor house in Lancashire that's been in my mother's family for two centuries. The roof leaks like a sieve, the floorboards creak beneath every step, and there's a family of mice living behind the kitchen baseboards that creep out every night to steal the crumbs left beneath the dining room table. Most of the shutters hang crooked and don't close properly and when it snows the drafts are so cold a thin layer of ice forms on the *inside* of the windows. The flue in the drawing room fireplace sticks more often than not so you never know when you light a fire if you're going to end up getting chased out of the room by clouds of smoke."

She stole a wary glance at Jamie to find his expression even more unreadable than before. "I always know spring is coming because a cheeky robin and his mate build a nest in the holly tree growing right outside the window of my bedchamber. When the babies hatch, their chirping wakes me up each morning at dawn. The arbor at the edge of the orchard is on the verge of falling down because it's completely buried beneath a tangle of wild roses." She could not stop a wistful smile from curving her lips. "And in autumn when the apples start falling from the trees in the orchard, the whole world smells so tart and sweet you'd swear the very air could make you drunk."

"You speak o' this place as if it's heaven on earth, but what about all o' those treasures the Hepburn can give you? The jewels? The furs? The land? The gold?"

She cast him a despairing glance. "I'd trade them all for a chance to go out foraging for blackberries in the hedgerows on a fine summer morn."

"If you love this home of yours so well, then why did you agree to marry the earl?"

Emma went back to gazing into the shadows. "Before Papa sent me to London for the Season, we received a notice informing us the house was being seized by his creditors and we had three months to vacate the premises. The earl's offer was a godsend. Instead of demanding a dowry, he paid my father a generous settlement in exchange for my hand. It's too much for even Papa to gamble or drink away. My mother will be guaranteed a roof over her head for as long as she should live. And as the earl's new countess, I'll possess both the means and the influence to sponsor my sisters' London debuts. I'll be able to find them decent husbands and homes."

"While you give up your home and any hope of happiness?" Jamie shook his head, a flush of anger touching his high cheekbones. "If your father was the one who drank and gambled away his family's last shilling, why should you be the one to suffer for it?"

She rose from the rock to face him. "Because I'm the one who drove him to it."

CHAPTER SEVEN

For three long years, no one in her family had dared to utter those words. Yet here she stood confessing them to a man who was little more than a stranger to her — and a dangerous stranger at that. It was such a relief to finally say them aloud that it took Emma a moment to register Jamie's incredulous smile. It was the sort of smile one might give a gibbering escapee from Bedlam who claimed to be Richard the Lionhearted or a vanilla blancmange.

"*You?* You were the one who drove your father to the bottle and the gaming tables?" His smile escalated into a snort of disbelieving laughter. "Just what turrible transgression did you commit, you wee wicked hoyden? Did you forget to let the cat in or break your mother's favorite china saucer?"

She lifted her chin a defiant notch. "I broke a man's heart."

She half-expected him to dissolve into

fresh gales of laughter at the thought of her as some sort of temptress but as she continued, his smile slowly faded.

"When I was seventeen, I went to London to stay with my aunt Birdie and my cousin Clara for my debut. Everything went exactly as my parents had planned and I was able to secure a proposal from a perfectly nice young curate with excellent prospects for a decent living in Shropshire. After he had obtained my father's hearty blessing, all of the betrothal documents were drawn up. But less than a month before we were to be wed, I decided I had no choice but to beg off the engagement."

"Why?"

Emma turned away from him then, biting her bottom lip as an old shame warmed her cheeks. "I realized I was in love with another man. Lysander was the second son of a marquess who flattered me with his attentions each time we met at a ball or while riding in the park. He would deliberately seek out my company and tease me so tenderly I soon found myself thinking of him every moment we were apart. After I went to my fiancé and broke off our engagement, I sought him out to tell him what I'd done. I thought he'd be overjoyed."

Jamie winced as if already anticipating the

inevitable outcome of her tawdry little tale.

Emma's wry smile mocked no one but herself. "He was horrified. It seemed he was on the verge of announcing his own engagement to a young American heiress — a very beautiful, very *wealthy* American heiress. He made it quite clear a passably pretty baronet's daughter from Lancashire could never be anything more to him than a flirtation — and a mild one at that." She shrugged away the remembered anguish and humiliation of having her fragile young heart ripped right out of her breast. "He was generous enough to suggest I might consider becoming his mistress after he'd been married for a respectable amount of time."

"What a perfect gentleman!" Jamie declared, his narrowed gaze more bloodthirsty than admiring.

Emma bowed her head. "When I declined, he patted me on the hand quite fondly and urged me to seek out my fiancé and beg his forgiveness before it was too late."

"But you didn't," Jamie said. It was not a question.

She shook her head ruefully. "Perhaps it's just as well because as it turned out, it was already too late. Little did I know that my fiancé's pious façade hid a vindictive nature.

He engaged a solicitor and sued my father for breach of promise. The settlement came close to casting us all into debtor's prison and the scandal destroyed any hope I had of ever making a decent match as well as casting a shadow over my sisters' prospects. No man wanted to risk being publicly humiliated as I had humiliated poor George. Unfortunately, George's tongue turned out to be nearly as virulent as his temper. He wasn't content with the monetary settlement so he spread rumors that my friendship with Lysander was more *intimate* than it had been. He didn't precisely ruin my reputation but he certainly succeeded in casting a shadow of doubt over it. The sort of shadow designed to discourage all but the most ardent of suitors. And since there were none of those . . ."

"The unfortunate bastard," Jamie muttered. "It sounds to me as if you bruised his pride instead of breaking his heart."

She shrugged. "I'm afraid the result was the same. Papa started drinking more heavily and gambling more frequently. He rarely came home before dawn, if at all." She closed her eyes briefly, remembering the muffled clatter of her father's footsteps on the stairs, the raised voices that would come from her parents' bedchamber while she and her sisters huddled beneath the blankets in mute misery, pretending to sleep. "Papa has always had a fondness for cards, but I think he deluded himself into believing he could restore the family's fortunes at the gaming tables. Of course the exact opposite was true. He ended up squandering what remained of our meager resources, leaving us at the mercy of his creditors."

Jamie's brow darkened further. "And leaving his daughter at the mercy of a randy auld goat."

Emma turned on him in frustration, surprised to find herself trembling with a passion she hadn't allowed herself to feel for a very long time. "You have no right to pass judgment on my father! Not when you've proved yourself only too willing to trade women for gold."

"All I know is that I'd never allow *my* daughter to pay off my debts in the bed of a mon like the earl!"

"Regardless of what you believe, my father is not a bad man, simply a weak one," Emma said, echoing the refrain she'd heard fall from her mother's lips a thousand times since she'd been a little girl. "He is not to blame for any of this. It was *my* indiscretion that destroyed my family's fortunes and their good name."

"Indiscretion? Is that what an English lass calls it when a man winks at her from across a crowded ballroom? Or when he dares to touch her gloved hand while helping her into a carriage? Everyone knows Englishmen have lukewarm tea running through their veins, not hot, passionate blood. Why, I'd be willing to wager this silver-tongued young suitor of yours wasn't even bold enough to lure you into some moonlit garden so he could steal a kiss!" Jamie's gaze dropped to her lips, lingering there just long enough to make them feel warm and over-ripe.

"He most certainly did steal a kiss!" Emma informed him, resisting the urge to cool her lips with the tip of her tongue. "Not in the garden but in the alcove of Lady Erickson's town house. When no one was looking, he pressed his lips against my wrist in a shockingly bold manner."

"Forever ruining you for any other mon, no doubt," Jamie retorted, the mocking edge in his voice sharpening his burr.

She stiffened. "I was the one who ruined everything. I was the one who destroyed my family."

"And now you've decided to atone for the sin of refusing to marry a mon you didn't love by marrying a mon you'll soon despise. You were naught but a child!" Jamie's green eyes flashed with fresh anger. "A naïve seventeen-year-old lass who mistook a man's lust for love and paid a costly price."

Tamping down her passions as she'd done ever since that day, Emma replied coolly, "It was a mistake I have no intention of ever making again."

Almost as if she'd issued a challenge, Jamie drew closer to her — dangerously close. Although he loomed over her in the moonlight, the threat didn't come from his height or his superior strength, but from the taunting tenderness of his caress as he reached to tuck a stray curl behind her ear, allowing the pad of his thumb to linger against the silky skin of her cheek. "Once you marry the earl, you won't have to worry about it. You'll have neither love nor lust to trouble you."

There could be no denying the truth in his words. Once she became the earl's bride, she would never again feel her heart double its rhythm when a man walked into a room. Never feel a blush heat her cheeks at the mere mention of his name. Never feel a yearning ache deep inside her in anticipation of his touch.

Like the ache she was feeling at that very

moment as she gazed up into the smoldering frost of Jamie Sinclair's eyes.

Before she could heed the warning her heart was thundering in her ears, his mouth was on hers, moving over her lips with beguiling tenderness. He might look and behave like a Scots barbarian but he kissed like a prince. He gently feathered his lips back and forth over hers, knowing precisely how much pressure to apply to coax her lips apart, to entice her to relax her guard and allow his tongue to slip inside of her.

Emma had shuddered to imagine her first real kiss coming from the earl's dry, cracked lips. But it was a shudder of another kind that danced over her flesh as she allowed this stranger to lick deep into her mouth. She had never even dreamed of allowing Lysander to take such shocking liberties, not even when her every waking thought had been consumed by him and the future she had believed they would share, filled with chaste kisses and long walks through sunny meadows spent discussing the books they both loved.

There was nothing chaste about this kiss. As Jamie's tongue had its wicked way with her, her hands splayed once more against the muscled planes of his smooth, hard chest, her fingertips tingling as they grazed his pebbled nipples. It seemed she hadn't run far or fast enough after all. The shadows had finally caught up with her. As their seductive darkness enveloped her, she lost the urge to escape altogether, her body succumbing to a delicious languor that made it impossible to do anything but gently rock in the cradle of this man's arms.

She felt as if she was right back on that narrow ledge, on the verge of taking a fall that might shatter not only her bones, but her heart.

She might have been able to cling to a ragged shred of her self-respect if Jamie hadn't been the first to pull away. Or if she hadn't had to fight the shocking urge to tug him back down for another taste of his delectable mouth.

He gazed down at her, his thick, sable lashes veiling eyes nearly as wary as her own. If he had sought to give her a taste of what she'd be missing if she married the earl, then he had succeeded beyond his wildest expectations. And if kissing her was his way of chastising her for her disobedience, then she had underestimated him. He was far more diabolical and dangerous than she had feared.

A ragged sigh shuddered from her lips. She forced herself to hold his gaze, keenly aware that her hands were still lightly poised against his chest. "Was that my punishment for running away?" she whispered.

"No," he replied, the grim set of his jaw making him look even more ruthless. "That was my punishment for being fool enough to come after you."

Before she could try to make sense of his words, he seized her by the wrist and began to haul her away from the bluff.

"Did you forget your chains or your rope?" she asked, her bewilderment giving way to anger as she was forced to take two steps for each one of his long, masterful strides. "I'm sure you've pilfered your share of livestock in your day. I'm surprised you don't try to slap the Sinclair brand on me like some heifer or ewe that's strayed too far from its pasture."

"Don't tempt me," he growled.

"Have you even thought about the anguish you must be causing my family? Why, my mother and my sisters are probably sick with worry! And what about my father? What if this drives him straight back to the bottle?"

"Your devoted family didn't mind selling you to the earl. I'm sure they won't mind if I borrow you for a few days."

Emma could feel her frustration — and

her temper — mounting. "If you don't let me go, I'll just run again. I'm not going to let some silly Highland feud destroy my family!"

Jamie stopped so abruptly that she nearly crashed into his back. He swung around to face her, his expression fierce. For a breathless moment, she thought he was going to kiss her again, or do something even worse. But he simply leaned down until his nose nearly touched hers. "You know nothing of Highlanders or their feuds, lass. You may consider it your duty to your family to run, but I consider it my duty to my clan to stop you. You might want to think long and hard before you go charging off into the wilderness again." He raked his gaze down her with a bold familiarity that made her shiver anew. "Because if you do try to run again, I just might decide your virtue is of more value to me than to the earl."

Still holding her wrist fast, he resumed his unrelenting pace, leaving her with no choice but to stumble along after him or be dragged. He couldn't have made his intentions any clearer. The battle lines had been drawn. If Emma decided to cross them, she would do so only at her own peril.

Jamie marched on, fighting to ignore the

prick of his conscience. Emma had left him with little choice but to threaten her with the worst. It was a miracle he'd been able to pluck her off that ledge before it went tumbling into the gorge. If she tried to run again, he might not arrive in time to rescue her from some clumsy tumble down a ravine or hungry mountain cat. It made his blood run cold to imagine the sight that would have awaited him had he arrived at the bluff a few scant minutes later.

He gave her hand an impatient tug. If she didn't step up her pace, he'd soon be hauling her dead weight up the mountain and all of his hopes for making it back to camp and stealing a few precious hours of sleep before the sun rose would be dashed.

When she stumbled into his back, nearly knocking them both off balance, he swung around, his exasperation on the verge of exploding into anger. "Damnit, woman, if you don't pick up your —"

All it took was one look for Jamie to realize Emma hadn't deliberately been trying to slow their pace. She was swaying on her feet, her eyes half-closed. Even as Jamie watched, her knees began to buckle.

Cursing his own thick-headedness, he lunged forward, catching her before she could fall. When sweeping her up into his arms like a babe earned him nothing more than a slurred murmur of protest, he knew she was indeed spent and not simply trying to vex him by slowing their progress. Her eyes had drifted shut and her freckles were standing out in stark relief against her pallid cheeks. It was clear she couldn't continue, either on foot or in his arms. He had no choice but to make camp for the night.

He propped her limp form against a fallen log with painstaking care, then set about collecting enough wood to build a fire. Aside from the dense thickets of aspen and evergreen, there was no shelter on these lower slopes of the mountain, not even an abandoned barn or crofter's hut. He used the steel tinder he always carried with him to coax a tangle of brush into reluctant flame, then turned to find Emma still huddled there against the log with her eyes closed — plainly too cold, miserable and exhausted to do anything else. Her bonny gown was starting to look like the tatters of a cobweb; the soles of her slippers were worn bare in spots, exposing slender feet that were bloody and bruised.

This was hardly the wedding day — or the wedding night — any woman deserved. The lass had gone utterly still except for the gentle rise and fall of her chest, a fact that troubled Jamie even more than if she had still been shivering uncontrollably. A faint blue tinge shadowed her lips, those same lips that had warmed and flowered beneath his own only a short while ago, inviting him to explore the silken heat of her mouth.

As a surge of treacherous lust shot through his body, Jamie raked a hand through his hair, hating himself for feeling so damnably helpless. He was used to looking after his men, but they were a hardy lot, as rugged as a flock of mountain goats. They didn't need to be protected or coddled so much as herded.

He had gone charging after her without so much as a coat or cloak. All he had to warm her was the fire and the heat of his own body. But after being foolish enough to steal a taste of her lips, the last thing he wanted — or needed — to do was bed down with the Hepburn's bride for the night.

CHAPTER EIGHT

Emma drifted out of slumber to find herself enveloped in a delicious cocoon of warmth. She was accustomed to waking up with Ernestine's cold feet pressed to her calf or Edwina's pointy little elbow digging into her ribs. This felt more like being bundled up in her favorite quilt next to a cozy fire on a snowy winter day.

If this was a dream, she had no desire to wake. She yawned and wiggled her backside, snuggling even closer to the source of that seductive warmth.

She heard a pained grunt, dangerously close to her ear. Something hard and obstinately unyielding pressed against the softness of her rump, nudging her out of her drowsy stupor.

Her eyes flew open. Her heart stuttered into an uneven rhythm. It wasn't a pillow shielding her head from the hard ground, but a man's arm — well muscled and lightly bronzed from the kiss of the sun. Trying not to move or breathe, she slowly shifted her gaze downward. A matching arm was curled possessively around her waist.

As her dream turned into a nightmare, Emma lunged forward and gathered her breath to scream. A hand clamped over her mouth, muffling the sound before it could escape. The arm around her waist cinched tight, forcing her back against her attacker's unyielding body.

He must have been awake all along, just waiting for this moment.

A helpless shudder raked her as Jamie Sinclair's husky whisper poured into her ear like a shot of warm whisky. "Hush, lass. I'm not going to hurt you."

She remained as rigid as a board.

"Or rape you," he added, his voice deepening to an impossible octave.

Emma squeezed her eyes shut, heat rushing to her cheeks. She'd never heard such a shocking word on any man's lips. Where she came from, women weren't raped. They were compromised. Or ruined. Or were foolish enough to allow a gentleman too many liberties, or careless enough to take a wrong turn down a shadowy alley. Whatever grim fate befell them, it was always somehow implied that they'd had a hand in their own destruction.

When she remained frozen in his arms, Jamie must have realized his promise sounded less than credible with his rock-hard arousal still nudging her bottom.

His beleaguered sigh tickled the tiny hairs behind her ear. "I know you don't know much of men and their ways, but this is a state they often find themselves in when they first awaken. It has naught to do with you."

Even he didn't sound completely convinced. Oddly enough, it was the strained note in his voice that gave her the confidence to trust him. As she slowly relaxed into the warm cup of his body, he slid his hand away from her mouth.

He was right. She'd grown up with a mother, three sisters, and a father who had been absent more often than not in the past few years. She knew very little of men and their ways, and what she did know was becoming increasingly perplexing.

After an awkward moment of silence, her curiosity overcame her fear and she whispered, "Is it painful?"

He pondered her question before quietly saying, "At the moment, I believe I'd prefer a pistol ball between the eyes."

"If you'll hand me your pistol, that could

be arranged."

She would have almost sworn she heard a rueful chuckle. As she wiggled cautiously around to face him, his hand drifted down from her waist, coming to rest lightly against her hip as if it belonged there. She gazed up at him in the murky half-light of dawn. The beard-shadow on his jaw had darkened during the night, giving him the lean, hard look of a pirate.

He really was an uncommonly beautiful man. For a common ruffian. Before she could stop the wayward turn of her thoughts, she caught herself wondering what it might be like to wake up in the arms of such a man every morning.

And to sleep in his arms every night.

His next words jerked her back to the reality of the cold, damp dawn. "You were half-froze and damn near to falling down from exhaustion last night. I had no choice but to build a fire and make camp for the night."

"How very considerate of you," she said stiffly, her tone implying the opposite. "I suppose you had no choice but to cuddle me as well."

His eyes darkened. "I thought I made it clear last night that you have naught to fear from me on that account as long as you

100

don't try to run away again."

If that was true, then why did his touch leave her feeling as if she had everything to fear and everything to lose? "You promised not to hurt me as long as the earl gives you what you want. But what if he refuses?" she asked against her better judgment.

Jamie's only answer was a tightening of his rugged jaw and a flash of something in his eyes that might have been regret.

By the time they reached camp, Jamie's men were just beginning to roll out of their bedrolls and mill about. Some scratched at their bellies or their heads while others stumbled off toward the shelter of the trees to relieve themselves. Emma hung back at the edge of the trees, watching their disheveled and bumbling pantomime with a wide-eyed mixture of amusement and horror. She was torn between giggling and clapping a hand over her eyes. Even at his most dissolute, her papa had always appeared at the breakfast table with nary a hair out of place. His purse might be empty and his eyes bloodshot from the ravages of swilling too much gin the night before but his waistcoat was always pressed and his cravat neatly tied.

Given the amount of whisky she'd witnessed these men imbibing the previous night, she was amazed that any of them were stirring before noon.

A gangly lad with an untidy shock of saffron-colored hair paused in mid-yawn to send a curious glance their way. Emma clutched at Jamie's elbow, seized by a sudden wave of mortification. "What about my reputation? If your men see us returning from the woods together, won't they imagine the worst?"

"They might," Jamie admitted, a thoughtful look dawning in his eyes. "But only if we let them."

"I don't understand. How do we stop them?"

He shrugged. "What better way to protect your reputation than to give you a chance to defend it?"

"Against what?"

"This," he said, flashing his white teeth in a lazy grin that set her pulse to wildly pounding. Before she could heed its warning, Jamie wrapped one arm around her waist and bent her back over his other arm, his lips laying claim to hers with a lusty hunger that took her breath away.

Even through her haze of shock and yearning, Emma had to give him credit. It was exactly the sort of kiss a bandit might steal from the lady he had abducted. The sort of kiss a pirate might press upon a damsel's lips before forcing her to walk his plank. The sort of kiss the Lord of the Underworld might have thrust upon Persephone before carrying her off to his lair to introduce her to darker and even more irresistible delights.

By the time he allowed her a shuddering breath, she was dangerously near to forgetting all about the presence of his men. As well as her own name.

"Hit me," he muttered against her lips.

"Pardon?" she gasped.

"Hit me," he repeated. "And make it convincing."

As he leaned away from her, a smug smile curving his lips, Emma wanted nothing more than to seize him by the ears and drag his mouth back down to hers.

Instead, she drew back her fist and slugged him in the jaw hard enough to make him stagger.

She half-expected him to break his promise not to harm her by clouting her into insensibility with one of his big fists. But he simply cocked one eyebrow, his expression bemused, and rubbed a hand gingerly over his jaw.

Emma's voice rose on a shrill note deliberately calculated to reach every eardrum within hearing. "I don't know what makes you think I'd want to kiss a beast like you. Why, I'd be willing to wager you Scots treat your sheep with more respect than your women!" Turning slightly so that Jamie's powerful shoulders would block his men's view of her face, she smiled sweetly at him and added *sotto voce,* "There . . . was that convincing enough?"

The quizzical gleam in his eyes slowly deepened to an admiring one. "A ladylike slap would have been sufficient," he muttered. He leaned toward her in a menacing fashion and said in a booming voice, "I'll have you know that our sheep don't require kisses when we're courting them. A simple pat on the rump will usually suffice."

A choked hoot of laughter went up from one of Jamie's men. They had dropped all pretense of scratching and pissing and were now standing goggle-eyed and open-mouthed, shamelessly eavesdropping on their exchange.

Emma rested her hands on her hips, beginning to get into the spirit of the thing. In happier days, she and her sisters had put on pantomimes and amateur theatricals for their parents each year at Christmas. At eleven, she'd made a very convincing Kate in *The Taming of the Shrew* opposite Ernestine's lisping Petruchio. "Your sheep may find your crude attempts at wooing irresistible, sir, but I'll thank you to keep your filthy Sinclair paws off me!"

He leered down at her. "It might surprise you to learn that I don't usually get any complaints from the ladies about where I put my filthy Sinclair paws."

"Ladies? *Ha!* Barmaids and goose girls hardly qualify as ladies, especially not when you have to pay them with stolen coin to procure their good will. A true lady would never welcome the advances of a brutish, bride-snatching barbarian such as yourself!"

He reached down to smooth a tumbled curl from her cheek, his fingers grazing her skin in a mocking caress. "You can protest all you like, lass, but I was only seeking to give you a taste of what every woman wants — lady or no. Something that withered auld bridegroom of yours will *never* be able to do."

Thanks to the kernel of truth in his words, Emma had to struggle to look outraged instead of woebegone as she watched him turn and walk away from her, his lean hips rolling in a natural swagger. As his men averted their eyes and quickly set themselves to other tasks, she touched her trembling fingertips to her lips, wondering if in defending her reputation, they had put something even more vulnerable at risk.

CHAPTER NINE

To Emma's keen relief, Jamie allowed the lanky lad with the saffron-colored shock of hair to stand guard while she performed her morning ablutions on the bank of a nearby brook. After finding herself so deeply shaken by what was only intended to be a mock kiss, she doubted she could have found the courage to disrobe if Jamie were anywhere in the vicinity.

The last of the clouds had scattered during the night, leaving the sky a dazzling shade of azure. Although a chill still hung in the air, glowing shafts of sunlight pierced the boughs of the slender birches growing along the banks of the brook, their warming rays releasing the smell of the quickening earth. Emma could not resist drawing a bracing breath of the crisp air into her lungs. It was almost possible to believe spring might yet come, even to these harsh and wintry climes.

After taking care of her most pressing need, she knelt beside the brook and splashed handfuls of icy water over her face. Eager to divest herself of the tattered rag that had once been her wedding gown, she climbed to her feet and cast a furtive glance over her shoulder. After depositing a pile of garments on a nearby stump, the boy had retreated to stand at stiff attention at the edge of the pines, his back to her.

"You're not going to peek, are you?" she called out to him.

"Oh, no, m'lady," he assured her, his nervous swallow audible even over the babbling of the brook. "Jamie said if he caught me peekin', he'd tan me hide, he would."

Emma frowned. "Does your Jamie often threaten to tan your hide?"

"Not unless I deserve it," he replied as she awkwardly groped behind her for the endless row of mother-of-pearl buttons securing her bodice. It would have been much more convenient if Jamie had abducted her maid as well.

After a brief and largely futile struggle, she hooked her fingers between the buttons and yanked. The expensive silk gave way at the seams, sending buttons popping every which way. She felt a treacherous twinge of satisfaction, followed by a sharp pang of guilt. The earl had probably paid a fortune for the gown. He'd insisted on providing an entire trousseau for her designed by the most fashionable French modiste in London. Her sisters had also reaped the benefits of his generosity. A trunk overflowing with new gowns, slippers and bonnets had arrived at the manor house just in time for their journey to the Highlands. The house rang with their joyful squeals as they pirouetted in front of the dusty cheval glass in their mother's bedchamber and sent bonnets sailing back and forth through the air as each determined which style was the most flattering to her coloring.

Emma knew she ought to be doubly shamed by how seldom her thoughts had turned to her bridegroom since being snatched from his arms. She doubted his frail heart could take too many shocks before giving away entirely. Jamie Sinclair might try to turn her against the earl with his half-truths and unreasoning hatred, but she would do well to remember where her loyalties belonged.

She peeled away the bodice's built-in stays as if she were escaping from a cage, massaging the red welts the stiff whalebone had left on her tender skin.

"You seem rather young to be riding with

a band of outlaws," she observed to her companion as she moved to investigate the pile of garments on the stump. Jamie had provided her with a long-sleeved tunic and a pair of trousers that would doubtless make a fine pair of pantaloons to be worn under her skirts. If she had any skirts.

"Oh, I'm full grown, m'lady. I'll be fourteen come summer."

The same age as Edwina, who still slept with her battered and much beloved rag doll tucked beneath her chin.

Scowling, Emma slipped the tunic over her head. The beaten buckskin covered her to mid-thigh. The fabric felt as soft as velvet against her skin yet was sturdy enough to shield her from the sharp bite of the wind. "Just how did you come to ride with such a motley crew? Did Sinclair abduct you, too?"

"Aye, m'lady. He abducted me from the Hepburn's gamekeeper just before the mon's ax could come down and chop off me right hand."

Emma spun around, clutching the trousers to her chest. True to his word the boy was still standing at rigid attention and facing the opposite way, as stalwart as any soldier beneath orders from his commanding officer.

He must have heard her gasp though

because he continued, his tone matter-of-fact, even apologetic. "I'd been caught poachin' a string o' hares on the earl's lands, ye see. It had been a long winter and the scarlet fever had taken me mum and me da. Me belly was turribly empty but 'twas still me own fault. Everyone knows the punishment for thievery and I was almost nine then, auld enough to know what I was about."

Suffused with horror, Emma clapped one hand over her mouth. What sort of monster would order his servant to cut off a hungry child's hand for poaching a rabbit? Surely a civilized nobleman wouldn't sanction such an atrocity. Perhaps the earl had been wintering at his London townhouse at the time and the gamekeeper had simply taken it upon himself to mete out such harsh and terrible justice without the earl's knowledge.

"What happened to the gamekeeper?" she asked, regretting the question the moment it left her lips.

She didn't have to see the boy's face. She could hear the smile in his voice. "The earl had to hire a new one."

Emma slowly turned back around, her fingers digging into the supple fabric of the trousers. She wanted to feel nothing but disgust and contempt for Jamie Sinclair, but all she could see in her mind's eye was an upraised ax glinting in the sunlight, a little boy's thin, dirty face blanched with terror.

Shaking off the disturbing spell the lad's story had cast over her, she slipped into the trousers. Once she had rolled up the cuffs to keep them from dragging the ground, they were a near perfect fit. Jamie must have confiscated the garb from one of his smaller men. His own garments would have swallowed her whole.

Emma stole a peek over her shoulder at her own backside, marveling at the decadent way the buckskin molded itself to her curves. A grin curved her lips as she imagined her mother fainting dead away if she saw her in this getup. Back in Lancashire a mere glimpse of feminine ankle was enough to ignite a scandal that could persist for generations. Why, Dolly Strothers and Meriweather Dillingham had been forced to wed after Dolly had tripped while exciting a carriage and inadvertently exposed the garter above her knee to the blushing young curate!

Her mother had preferred to turn a blind eye to the fact that Emma had slipped out of the house on more than one cold winter's morning, garbed in her papa's hunting coat and a pair of his oversized trousers. When a freshly roasted grouse or hare would turn up on their supper table after a week with no meat, her mother would simply bow her head and thank the good Lord for His benevolent care, ignoring the fact that her eldest daughter had risen before dawn to assist Him with His handiwork.

Emma was most relieved to find a pair of sturdy leather boots to replace her flimsy kid slippers. They would have been three sizes too large were it not for the pair of thick woolen stockings that accompanied them.

She was about to tell the boy he could turn around without risking his hide when she realized one of Jamie's offerings was still draped over the stump.

It was a narrow strip of tanned leather, the perfect length to bind back her hair and keep it from blowing wild in the wind. Bemused by the small kindness, Emma attempted to rake most of the tangles from her hair with her fingers before using the length of leather to gather the heavy fall of curls at her nape. It wasn't exactly a satin ribbon plucked from the window of some Bond Street linen drapers shop, but at the moment she would be hard pressed to find a gift more practical or dear.

Without dozens of hairpins poking her tender scalp, she felt positively light-headed.

And ridiculously lighthearted — almost as young and carefree as she'd felt as a girl when she and her sisters had tumbled about in the garden of their country house from dawn to dusk like a quartet of sturdy puppies.

But when she turned around, her young guard was waiting for her, a stark reminder that she wasn't free at all but the captive of a dangerous man willing to resort to thievery, kidnapping and even murder to get what he wanted.

The Sinclairs had always been known for three things — their quick wits, their quick fists and their quick tempers. In truth, their quick tempers were attached to a slow fuse that might smolder for days — or even decades — before finally exploding in a rage that had been known to blast through castle walls and level entire forests. They might not yell at you if you crossed them but they were perfectly capable of biding their time until the opportunity came to quietly cut you up and bury you in fifteen different graves.

As Jamie paced beside the horses, waiting for Graeme to return with Emma, he could already hear the sizzling of that fuse in his ears — low-pitched but as inescapable as the sighing of the wind through the pines. Which was exactly why, after nearly half an hour had passed, his men stopped casting him nervous glances and devoted all of their attention to polishing pommels that were already shiny and checking cinches that had been tightened a half dozen times or more.

Jamie knew they were still puzzled over his and Emma's earlier display. He wasn't exactly in the habit of forcing his attentions — or his kisses — on any woman, be she Scots or English. As he stopped glowering in the direction of the brook long enough to glance in his cousin's direction, Bon wiggled his fingers at him and blew him a mocking kiss.

In lieu of throttling Bon with his bare hands, Jamie moved to check the bridle on his own horse. They'd squandered enough time in this place. They needed to reach the higher climes of the mountain just in case he had miscalculated and the Hepburn did decide to send his men to track them before the ransom demand could arrive.

He was beginning to fear Emma had bashed Graeme over the head with a rock and was even now skipping her way merrily back down the mountainside when she reappeared at the edge of the clearing with the lad following several respectful paces behind her.

The reins in Jamie's hands slipped through fingers that had gone suddenly numb. When he had first spotted the Hepburn's bride standing in front of the altar at the abbey, she had been as pale and spiritless as a lamb being led to the slaughter. He had assumed it was fear of him that had drained the color from her cheeks and made her look as if she was wearing a grave shroud instead of bridal clothes.

But if that were so, she had returned to the clearing as the boldest of women. The brisk breeze had stirred roses into her cheeks and kindled a sparkle in her dusky blue eyes. Her fair skin with its coppery dusting of freckles seemed to glow beneath the caress of the sunlight. Even with her slender feet weighed down by the clumsy leather boots, there was a determined spring to her step.

From the corner of his eye, he saw Bon's mouth fall open. His cousin had no idea that Jamie had pilfered the garments from his saddlebag while he'd been off pissing in the woods. Even Bon would have to admit that Emma looked a damn sight better in the garments than he did. They perfectly suited her lithe grace, making her look like a wood sprite that had just emerged from a hollow tree after a restful hundred-year nap.

As she neared, Jamie's gaze strayed to the petal pink softness of her lips. Lips that had twice melted beneath his with an eagerness he had not anticipated, giving him a tantalizing taste of both innocence and a hunger that was echoed in her eyes every time she looked at him. His body was still aching from the memory. It had been a very long time since he had kissed a woman without expecting — or receiving — anything more.

As she approached, he schooled his features into an indifferent mask.

"I suppose I should thank you for the ribbon, sir," she said. "The wind had whipped my hair into a dreadful tangle."

"It wasn't meant to be a gift for m'lady," he said with a deliberate edge of mockery. "I was just hopin' if someone spotted us on the road, they'd be more likely to mistake you for a lad."

If they were daft. And blind.

"What road?" she asked pointedly, squinting at the wilderness surrounding them as if he was the one who'd gone daft.

Ignoring the question, he gathered the horse's reins, mounted, and offered her a hand.

She took a wary step backward, plainly fearing he intended to toss her facedown over his lap as he had in the abbey.

"If you'll give me your hand," Jamie said, "you can pull yourself up to ride behind me."

Still looking doubtful, she crept closer. Sensing her nervousness, the horse whickered and skittered sideways a few steps, which only caused Emma to retreat again.

Jamie blew out a long-suffering sigh. He supposed he couldn't blame her for being somewhat leery of them both.

"I promise I won't let the horse trample you. Or eat you," Jamie assured her, once again offering her his hand. Still eyeing him with poorly disguised mistrust, she slipped her hand into his. It was the first time he'd paid any heed to her hands in the unforgiving light of day.

They weren't soft and lily-white as a lady's should be, but lightly chapped. They didn't look or feel like hands that spent all their time in genteel pursuits like practicing the pianoforte or painting watercolors. As he turned her hand over, running the pad of his thumb lightly over her callused palm, she tried to tug it back, but he refused to relinquish his grip.

She scowled up at him. "You needn't pity me simply because I've had to chop a little firewood or wash a few pans of dishes in my day. I'm sure that was nothing compared to the rugged hardships the Sinclair women have been forced to endure over the centuries — felling trees, tossing cabers, birthing entire flocks of sheep with their bare hands."

A reluctant laugh escaped him. "From what my auld nurse Mags has told me about my mother, she wouldn't have known one end of the sheep from the other. My grandfather doted upon her. She was more than a wee bit pampered."

Emma scowl softened. "She died young?"

"Aye," he said, his own smile fading. "Too young."

Before she could question him further, he gave her hand a tug, urging her off the ground and into the saddle behind him.

As he spurred the horse into motion, she was forced to throw her arms around his waist and hang on for dear life. With no corset to bind them, the small breasts beneath the clinging buckskin were pressed full against his back.

He gritted his teeth and shifted in the saddle as his body responded in a way that was going to make riding for more than ten paces a hellish ordeal.

Emma slowly relaxed her death grip on Jamie as they began to follow a winding path through a forest, accompanied by an airy arpeggio of birdsong. The wind's perpetual roar had been soothed to a gentle whisper that carried on its fragrant breath a teasing promise of spring. Sunlight slanted through the silvery boughs of the birches, making the motes of pollen dancing lazily through the air glow like flecks of ground gold dust.

Although she wasn't any happier about being dragged around the Scottish wilderness by a band of surly outlaws than she'd been the day before, Emma found it nearly impossible to keep her own spirits from soaring with the sun. The beauty of the day made it easier to pretend she had simply embarked upon some grand adventure — perhaps her last before settling down to be a dutiful wife to the earl and bear his children. A chill touched her spine, as if a stray cloud had passed over the sun.

As scandalous as her attire might be, she had to admit there was something oddly exhilarating about riding like a man. She'd had little experience on horseback after her papa's ill luck at the gaming tables had emptied their stables one horse at a time. During her Seasons in London when she'd stayed with her aunt, she'd been forced to go riding in Hyde Park every afternoon so she and her cousin Clara could both be paraded before their prospective suitors. It had been nearly impossible to enjoy the rides or the fine spring days while desperately clinging to the slippery pommel of a sidesaddle and praying the wind didn't catch the hem of her skirt and blow it up over her face.

Riding astride allowed her to feel every fluid shift of the horse's rolling gait between her thighs. She didn't have to fret about tumbling off in front of a gaggle of giggling debutantes or accidentally spooking the horse with the gaudy plume of ostrich feathers glued to the oversized brim of her borrowed bonnet. While perched on his broad back like some conquering queen of old, it was almost possible to pretend the magnificent stallion was under her control.

Unfortunately, the stallion was suffering no such delusion. He knew exactly who his master was. The second they reached an open stretch of moor and Jamie drove his heels into the horse's sleek flanks, the beast took off as if winged. Emma tightened her grip on Jamie's waist and buried her face against his broad back, silently praying she wouldn't go sailing off and be trampled into dust beneath the hooves of his men's horses.

At least Jamie was wearing a shirt beneath

his leather vest today. If not, she would have been forced to lace her hands over the smooth, warm contours of his naked abdomen. As it was, she could still feel the tantalizing shift of finely honed muscle beneath the worn cambric of the garment.

Only when their mount slowed to a walk did she dare to lift her head and open her eyes. She sucked in a panicked wheeze, almost wishing she'd kept them shut. The horse was picking its way along a narrow shelf of rock more suited to the nimble hooves of a goat. On their left was a sheer wall of stone stretching as high as the eye could see and on their right was . . . well . . . nothing.

Before she could slam her eyes shut again, her fear was eclipsed by wonder. Although the snow-capped crags of Ben Nevis still towered over them in majestic splendor, they had climbed to a dizzying height, which gave them a breathtaking view of the rambling foothills and rolling moors below. The highest towers of the earl's stronghold were still visible at the base of the foothills like the spires from some ancient fairy tale castle. A single kestrel wheeled against a sky so bright and blue it hurt Emma's eyes to look upon it. But it would have pained her even more to look away.

"What a glorious view!" she breathed, unable to contain her awe. "Why, it's like stealing a peek at heaven itself!"

Jamie's only response was a surly grunt.

"And just where are we headed on this fine spring day?"

"Up."

She glared daggers at his back. "You know, I've always heard the Scots were a contentious lot, eager for any excuse to start a brawl or a war."

Jamie grunted again, doing little to disabuse her of that notion.

"So just what did the Hepburns do to prompt this ridiculous feud of yours?" she asked. "Steal one of your sheep?"

"No," he replied curtly. "Our castle."

Chapter Ten

Emma's mouth fell open in astonishment. She twisted around on the horse to steal another wondering look at the soaring towers of the earl's keep only to discover they had vanished beneath a stray wisp of cloud. "Do you mean to say Hepburn Castle was once . . ."

"Aye. Sinclair Castle," Jamie finished for her.

As the narrow path widened and they left the edge of the cliff behind for a rock-strewn meadow, his words stirred her imagination in a manner she hadn't expected. Had the winds of fate blown in a different direction, it might have been Jamie bringing a bride home to the imposing stone halls of the castle. She could almost see him standing tall and proud before the altar of the abbey, a ceremonial plaid draped over one broad shoulder, his eyes glowing with pride as he watched his bride walk down that long aisle toward his waiting arms.

She could see him sweeping her up in his powerful embrace and striding through the doorway of the tower bedchamber where generations of his ancestors had come to claim their brides. See him gently laying her back on the satin coverlet and lowering his lips to hers, kissing her tenderly, yet passionately, as his hands sifted through the silky softness of the copper-tinted curls spilling over the —

"Longshanks," Jamie muttered, mercifully yanking her out of her alarming daydream. "Clan Hepburn made an alliance with Longshanks — your own Edward I — at the end of the thirteenth century when he tried to crown himself king of all Scotland. The Hepburns pledged homage to him but Clan Sinclair refused so the bastards were able to use English swords to drive us out of our own castle. If a handful of my ancestors hadn't managed to escape through a secret tunnel in the dungeons and head for the highest reaches of the mountain, the name Sinclair would have been wiped from the history of the Highlands and long forgotten by now.

"Then during the Forty-five," he said, referring to the conflict that had devastated Scotland and its Highlanders less than a century ago, "the Hepburns took the Crown's side once again while Clan Sinclair fought for Bonnie Prince Charlie." He snorted. "We Sinclairs never could resist a losing cause."

"So you've been nursing a grudge for over five centuries now? Don't you think that's a little extreme?"

The sarcastic note in his voice ripened. "We might have been a wee bit more inclined to forgive them for booting us out of our own castle if they hadn't tried to annihilate us at every turn since then. We were forced into raiding to put bread on our tables . . . and in the mouths of our babes."

It had never occurred to Emma that Jamie might have a wife and perhaps even children waiting for his return in some humble crofter's hut at the top of that mountain. The thought made her feel oddly hollow inside.

"Is that why you raid?" she asked, choosing her words with care. "To feed your family?"

"My men *are* my family. Their clans pledged their fealty to Clan Sinclair — and to its chieftain — long before they were born. They've had to spend most of their lives hiding in these hills and poaching off the earl's lands while he and his ilk try to hunt them down like dogs. They don't have wives or children to warm their hearths. For that matter, most of them don't even have hearths because the Hepburn has made damn sure they're never able to stay in one place long enough to settle down. They may lack the manners and polish of your bridegroom and the other *gentlemen* of your acquaintance but any one of them would gladly lay down his life for me should the need arise."

His words gave Emma pause. She had never known that degree of loyalty. Not even from her own family.

"What about the grandfather the earl mentioned back at the abbey? Is he the chieftain of your clan — the one who sent you to abduct me?"

Jamie's laugh had a rueful edge. "If my grandfather knew what I was doing at the moment, he'd probably try to tan my hide. He wasn't very happy when I left St. Andrews and came back to the mountain to stay four years ago. He always wanted something different for me. Something more. He knew there would never be anything more for me here than trying to elude the noose the Hepburn was determined to slip over my neck."

"Which might be easier to do if you'd stop

committing crimes . . . like, oh . . . I don't know . . . kidnapping the man's bride."

Jamie shook his head. "It wouldn't make one whit of difference. I've had a price on my head since the day I was born. My life has never been worth anything more than what the Hepburn has been willing to pay for it."

"Why does he despise you so much?"

Jamie hesitated a moment before replying. "I'm the last direct descendant of the Sinclair chieftains. If he can rid the world of me, the Hepburns will have won and he'll be able to die a happy mon."

Emma frowned, still unable to mesh his impressions of the earl with her own. "Just what did you study while you were away at university? Sheep rustling? Bride snatching?"

"I rather fancied Kitten Kicking," he drawled. "But my most satisfying class by far was Ravishing Over-inquisitive Maidens."

Emma snapped her mouth shut, but curiosity quickly overcame her caution. "After getting a glimpse of what the enlightened world has to offer, wasn't it difficult to come back to . . . this?" she asked, waving a hand at the wilderness surrounding them.

"No, lass, the hard part was staying away."

Emma studied the rugged vista, which in a single sweep of her gaze embraced rocky slopes, snow-capped peaks, open stretches of moorland and the distant pewter shimmer of a deep and ancient loch. It was a cruel and unforgiving land where a single careless mistake might kill you. But there was still no denying the echo of longing its wild and windswept beauty stirred in her own heart.

She sighed. Jamie's words had only deepened her confusion. "Just who am I supposed to believe is the villain of this piece? The self-professed outlaw who stole me from my own wedding at gunpoint? Or the dear old man who has shown me and my family nothing but generosity and kindness?"

"Believe whatever you like, lass. 'Tis of no import to me."

Somehow Jamie's indifference cut deeper than any of his jibes. "Well, if you think the earl is going to hand over the castle his family has held for over five centuries in exchange for me, I'm afraid you've greatly overestimated both my charms and his devotion to them."

Jamie was silent for so long she was afraid he was trying to figure out the kindest way to agree with her. When he finally spoke, his voice was even gruffer than before. "The castle was just the first thing the Hepburns stole from us, not the most valuable."

With that, he kicked the horse into a brisk canter, making further conversation impossible.

Ian Hepburn burst through the door of his great-uncle's study, then wheeled around to slam the door behind him. He gave the brass key in the lock a savage twist and backed away from the door, barely resisting the urge to shove a piece of furniture in front of it — a Hepplewhite chair perhaps or the massive twelve-drawer secretary his uncle had ordered from Madrid. If he had bricks, mortar and a trowel at his disposal, he would have considered sealing the door like the entrance to some ancient Egyptian tomb.

His ears were still ringing from the cacophony he had fled, but the study itself was blessedly quiet. If he was seeking a haven, he had chosen well. His uncle had spared no expense on his part and no effort on the part of others to create a chamber that could rival any Parisian salon or Mayfair mansion in its beautifully appointed elegance.

The earl might seek to impress the local

populace by wearing a traditional kilt and plaid to his wedding but all traces of their unfashionable Scots heritage had been abolished from this room. There were no crossed claymores with tarnished blades hanging on the wall, no moth-eaten tartans draping the chairs, no ancient shields embellished with the Hepburn coat of arms on proud display.

From the plush Aubusson carpet beneath Ian's feet to the cream-painted panels of the wainscoting to the modern arched windows that had replaced the mullioned ones, the room reflected the tastes of a man who valued the display of his own wealth and power above any sentimental attachment to heritage or history.

The three-tiered chandelier hanging from the center of the domed ceiling had only recently adorned the palatial ballroom of a French aristocrat who had followed his entire family to the guillotine. His uncle had chuckled when the enormous crate containing it had arrived, saying any fool not clever enough to outwit the peasants of Paris deserved to lose both his head and his chandelier.

His uncle had always treated the chamber more like a throne room than a study; a place where he could summon those beneath him — and that included just about everyone of his acquaintance, including Ian — into his exalted presence.

Since Ian hadn't been summoned, he shouldn't have been surprised his uncle chose to ignore his rather unconventional arrival. The earl was standing in front of the massive window framing the majestic crags of Ben Nevis, his hands locked at the small of his back and his feet splayed as if the study were the foredeck of some mighty ship and he its captain. He might play the role of kindly, doddering old man when it suited his purposes — such as when courting a new bride — but here in this sanctuary, he still ruled with an iron fist.

Ian had seen him in that exact posture innumerable times before: standing in front of that very window and gazing up at the mountain as if trying to understand why he could not bring it under his dominion when he had so easily conquered the rest of the world. Ian had long suspected his uncle would trade all of his influence and every priceless treasure he had accumulated over the years for one chance to rule those peaks and the men wild and arrogant enough to call them home.

One man in particular.

Ian cleared his throat. His uncle did not

budge. Ian could feel resentment rising like bile at the back of his throat, its taste both bitter and familiar. Despite the man's advanced age, Ian knew his uncle could still hear a footman drop a fork on the carpet from two rooms away.

He approached the window, barely managing to restrain his irritation at being treated like the lowliest of servants. "A word, my lord, if you please?"

"And what would that word be?" his uncle replied mildly, his gaze still fixed on the snow-capped peak of the mountain. *"Disaster? Catastrophe? Calamity?"*

"Marlowe!" Ian spat the name as if it were a mouthful of poison. "If I were you, I'd insist that Sinclair get back here immediately and take the entire family off your hands."

"Surely you're not talking about my bride's charming relations?"

"Charming? Not at the moment, I fear. Her mother and sisters have been weeping and wailing at the top of their lungs ever since Miss Marlowe was taken. Of course young Ernestine did manage to stop sniveling and sobbing just long enough to corner me in the drawing room and suggest that you might not be the only Hepburn in need of a bride." He shuddered. "In the meantime, her father has taken it upon himself to polish off nearly every decanter of brandy and port in the castle. It seems he believes it was somehow *his* fault his beloved daughter was abducted by some savage Scotsman. If he finds the casks of whisky in the dungeons," Ian warned darkly, "I fear he'll drown himself in the bottom of one."

His uncle continued to contemplate the mountain as if pondering some scheme to wrest it from the hands of the Almighty Himself. "You've always possessed the charm and cunning of a diplomat," he said without bothering to hide the note of scorn in his voice. "I'm sure I can trust you to soothe their ruffled feathers."

Ian drew close enough to study his uncle's implacable profile, his frustration growing. "I can't very well reproach them for their concern. It's not as if they've misplaced their favorite teakettle. Sinclair has had Miss Marlowe in his clutches for over twenty-four hours now and I don't have to remind you how utterly ruthless the man can be. I pray you'll forgive my impertinence, my lord, but her family doesn't understand why you haven't summoned the law. And if you must know, neither do I."

"Because I am the law!" his uncle thundered, turning on Ian with the ferocity of a

man half his age. His eyes in their drooping pockets of flesh were no longer bleary but glittering with fury. "And everyone between here and Edinburgh knows it, including that impudent bastard Sinclair. Nothing short of the murder of one of their own would entice the redcoats into getting involved in our feud. As far as they're concerned, we're all just a passel of unruly children fighting over a favorite toy. They're perfectly content to pat us on the head and send us on our way in the hope we'll eventually annihilate one another so they can step in and take *all* the toys."

"Then just what do you intend to do?"

The earl went back to gazing up at the mountain as if the outburst had never occurred. "At the moment? Nothing. I refuse to give Sinclair the satisfaction of knowing he's succeeded in his petty little plot to best me. If I hadn't already paid her father that ridiculously extravagant settlement, half of which I suspect he's already squandered at the gaming table, I'd be tempted to let Sinclair keep her. It's not as if I have any great emotional attachment to the girl. I could probably find a new bride within the fortnight. All it would take is another trip to London and another desperate, cash-strapped father."

The earl had been Ian's guardian since his parents had perished in a carriage accident when he was nine. He'd had ample time to armor himself against his great-uncle's callousness and had long ago stopped yearning for any sign of warmth or affection. But even he couldn't quite hide his flinch at the man's heartless words.

Knowing instinctively that the most effective appeal wouldn't address the girl's welfare but his uncle's pride, Ian stepped closer and lowered his voice. "It will hardly reflect well on you if your bride is raped or killed by those savages. It won't be Sinclair and his clan they blame, my lord, but you. And when the news reaches London — and mark my word, it eventually will — not even the most desperate papa will be persuaded to turn his daughter over to your care. Not when you can't promise to keep her alive until the wedding night."

After saying his piece, Ian held his breath, waiting for his uncle to once again lash out at him in rage.

But for once the old man actually seemed to be considering his counsel. He pursed his thin lips briefly before saying, "Then we wait for Sinclair's next move, just as I had planned. Since you seem to have made such a dreadful bungle of it, I shall attend to her parents myself and tell them our hands are tied until we receive a ransom demand from the wretch. Only then can we determine how to proceed."

Galvanized by a fresh sense of purpose, his uncle retrieved his walking stick from the brass can in the corner and marched from the room. Ian started to follow but before he could turn away from the window, his own gaze was caught and held by the magnificence of the view. Twilight was just beginning to descend from the heavens. The gathering shadows cast a gauzy lavender veil over the topmost peak of the mountain.

Unlike his uncle, Ian sought to avoid that view whenever possible. When he had first come to live at Hepburn Castle, he had been a pale, thin, bookish boy of ten who secretly dreamed of roaming the mountain's crags and hollows, as wild and free as one of the eagles soaring over its majestic crest. But his uncle had quickly wearied of having a child underfoot and packed him off to school. Most of Ian's holidays and summers had been spent at the earl's town house in London in the indifferent care of one butler or another.

When his uncle had summoned him back to Scotland to attend St. Andrews at the age of seventeen, his shoulders had filled out considerably, but he was no less pale and bookish, a fact that made him a tempting target for his more muscular, less cerebral classmates.

A trio of them had been taking turns shoving him around the grassy expanse of St. Salvator's Quad one chilly autumn afternoon when a voice had called out, "Leave the lad be!"

They had ceased pummeling Ian and turned as one to cast their disbelieving gazes on the young man standing in the shadow of the stone arch just below the clock tower. He was tall and broad-shouldered, but his robes were shabby and far too short for his long legs. His rich brown hair was poorly trimmed and falling half in his eyes. Light green eyes narrowed in unmistakable warning.

The leader of Ian's tormentors — a hulking boy named Bartimus with tree trunks for calves and no discernible neck — snorted, plainly delighted to have found a new target for their bullying. "Or you'll what, Highlander? Force us to eat some haggis? Blow us to death with your bagpipes?"

As Bartimus and his cronies came swaggering toward him, a lazy smile curved the stranger's lips. Oddly enough, it made him look more ferocious instead of less. "I don't think there'll be any need for the bagpipes, laddies. From what I've seen, the three o' ye are quite capable o' blowin' each other without my help."

Their disbelief turning to outrage, the boys exchanged a glance, then charged the newcomer as one. Ian started after them, not sure what he was going to do but refusing to let a stranger take a beating on his behalf. He'd taken only a handful of steps when the first crunch of fist on bone sounded, followed by a high-pitched yelp.

He stumbled to a halt, his mouth falling open.

It wasn't the stranger taking the beating, but his attackers. And it wasn't being done with the refined rules Ian had witnessed while visiting Gentleman Jackson's Boxing Saloon in London, but with a ruthless efficiency that combined joyful abandon with brute force. By the time he was through with them, they were no longer swaggering, but staggering.

Moaning and clutching their dislocated appendages and bloodied noses, they went stumbling away, no doubt seeking some secluded corner where they could nurse their injuries away from the crowd of gawking onlookers that had materialized when the first punch was thrown. Aside from scraping his knuckles on their faces, their opponent looked none the worse for wear.

His own pride beginning to ache, Ian shot his rescuer a resentful look as he stooped to gather up his fallen books. "I'm in no need of a bodyguard, you know. I'm perfectly capable of looking after myself."

The stranger swept his hair out of his eyes. "Aye, and ye were doin' a damn fine job of it, ye were. Right after the three o' them bluidied yer lip and blacked yer eye, I'm guessin' ye were goin' to give them a scoldin' they would ne'er forget."

Ian straightened, biting back a reluctant smile. "Ian Hepburn," he said, offering the stranger his hand.

The young man hesitated, the ghost of a frown passing over his face, before accepting Ian's hand and giving it a brusque shake. "Most of my friends just call me Sin." He cast the ancient stone walls brooding over the Quad a rueful look, muttering beneath his breath, "Or at least they might if I had any friends in this godforsaken prison."

Heartened to have found a kindred spirit who hated St. Andrews as much as he did, Ian stopped trying to restrain his smile. "I'm afraid you won't make many if you try to solve every problem with those ham-handed fists of yours." Ian shook his head, marveling at the prowess of those fists in spite of himself. "Just how did you learn to do that?"

"What? Fight?" Sin shrugged his broad shoulders as if dispatching three opponents without so much as breaking a sweat was an everyday occurrence for him. "Where I come from, if a mon can't fight he won't survive."

Ian frowned thoughtfully. He had always been forced to rely on his wits to survive. Perhaps it was time to consider some other options. "Can you teach me?"

"How to scrap?"

Ian nodded.

"Aye. I s'pose so." Sin studied him with a critical eye. "Ye're a wee bit scrawny for yer height, but it's nothin' a few heapin' portions o' neeps and tatties won't cure." A wicked smile slanted Sin's lips. "Until we get some meat on yer bones, I can teach ye a few dirty tricks that'll make those witless oafs think twice aboot smackin' ye around."

Eyeing the frayed hem of Sin's robe, Ian said, "I can pay you."

Sin stiffened, his smile fading. "Ye can keep yer precious coin, Ian Hepburn. I'm not a bluidy beggar and I've no need o' yer charity!" With that, he turned on his heel and went striding away.

Ian could feel his own temper rising. "If you're too damn proud to take my coin, Highlander," he called after Sin, "then maybe I could teach you something useful in return . . . like how to talk."

Sin stopped and slowly turned, his fingers once again curling into fists. Although Ian feared he was about to be on the receiving end of those formidable fists, he stood his ground.

A grin slowly spread across Sin's face. "Och, lad, an' whit makes ye think I'd want tae learn tae gab like some prissy gent who talks like he's got a walkin' stick stuck up his crease?"

Ian blinked at him. "Was that even English? Maybe I should have volunteered to translate for you instead of teaching you elocution. You're obviously quite fluent in gibberish."

Ian felt his own lips curve in a smile as Sin responded by giving him a gesture that required no translation.

That smile faded along with the memory of that fateful day, leaving Ian standing once again before the window in his uncle's study. While he had been lost in the past, the last of the daylight had surrendered to the bruised purple shadows of dusk, forcing him to face his own pensive reflection in the glass.

He was no longer pale or scrawny but a man to be reckoned with in his own right. Thanks to the boy he had called Sin, he knew how to use both his fists and his wits to survive. Yet he remained at his uncle's beck and call, no less a puppet to the man's tyrannical whims than he'd been as a lonely nine-year-old who had come to this place in the hopes of finding a home and a family.

As he stood gazing up at that mountain, remembering the boy who was born to be his enemy but who had all too briefly been his friend, he knew in his heart that there was nowhere in the world either one of them could flee to escape its mighty shadow.

CHAPTER ELEVEN

As the moon drifted higher in the night sky, Jamie eased back on the reins of his mount, his arms forming a natural cradle for the boneless bundle nestled against his chest. Emma had tolerated the infrequent stops and punishing pace he'd set for most of the day without complaining, but when he'd felt her grip on his waist give way and her body began to sway dangerously with each of the horse's strides, he'd been forced to reverse their positions so she could ride in front of him.

She'd protested the switch with little more than a disgruntled moan and a cross flutter of her eyelashes before curling herself against his chest like a drowsy little cat. No matter how rigid Jamie held himself in the saddle, the rioting curls that had escaped the leather thong still managed to tickle his nose. How she could still smell so sweet and feminine — like lilacs washed by a gentle spring rain — after a grueling day of riding was a complete mystery to him.

When she stirred and moaned again, he slowed his horse from a canter to a walk, ignoring the impatient looks from his men. Suddenly he wasn't nearly as eager to make camp for the night as they were. Emma might have survived their grueling day in the saddle, but he wasn't sure he would survive another night with her sleeping anywhere near him.

He had hoped his forbidding glower would deter conversation but it didn't stop Bon from drawing his sorrel alongside him and casting a cagey look toward the sleeping girl in his arms. "I s'pose it's good the lass is takin' her ease now, isn't it?"

"And just why would that be?"

Bon shrugged. "Well, after witnessin' that kiss ye tried to steal this morn, I have a sneakin' suspicion she'll be needin' all o' her strength for the night to come."

Not in any mood for his cousin's teasing — or the deliciously depraved images it brought to mind — Jamie continued to gaze straight ahead.

Undeterred by his stony profile, Bon cheerfully continued. "She might buck a bit at first but once ye break her to the saddle, ye'll be able to ride her long and hard. If ye find yerself growin' weak in the legs and in need o' any help, I just want ye to know I'm yer mon. Just give a whistle and I'll be more than happy to —"

Jamie's hand shot out and closed around Bon's throat, choking off his words in mid-sentence. Still balancing Emma's weight in the crook of his other arm, he leaned toward his cousin, looked him dead in the eye and said, "I appreciate the offer but I don't believe your services will be required. Tonight or any other night."

Freeing Bon to give him a look that would have shamed the devil himself, Jamie returned his grip to the reins and his attention to the road.

Continuing to eye him as if he'd kicked a crippled kitten, Bon massaged the fingerprints from his throat. "There's no need to be so techy, now is there? One would think that havin' the Hepburn's bride at his mercy would put a mon in a more generous temper."

"Aye, one would think that, wouldn't they?" With that cryptic reply, Jamie snapped the reins on his mount's back, determined to escape the shrewd glint in his cousin's eye.

It might have been more difficult for Emma

to continue to feign sleep if Jamie Sinclair's broad chest hadn't made such an enticing pillow. As long as she kept her eyes closed and her limbs limp, each of the horse's plodding steps continued to rock her gently in the cradle of Jamie's arms.

She had drifted out of her exhausted slumber just in time to hear him rejecting his man's crude offer in no uncertain terms. That primal display of brute masculine force had sent a treacherous little thrill jolting down her spine. Unfortunately, it was quickly followed by a wave of self-contempt.

No matter how tenderly he held her or how staunchly he defended her, she could not afford to forget that Jamie Sinclair was her enemy. Perhaps he simply sought to confuse her with his small kindnesses. Instead of sheltering her in his arms, another man might have bound her wrists and tethered her to the back of his horse, forcing her to stumble along behind him until she collapsed from exhaustion. At least it would have been easier to hate that man, she thought with growing desperation, to despise him for being the black-hearted villain he was.

She'd be the worst sort of ninny to mistake avarice for chivalry. Jamie had already admitted she was worth far more to him alive than dead. If he sought to shield her from the lascivious intentions of his men, it was only to protect her innocence and his investment until he could wrangle a ransom from Hepburn. She was nothing more to him than some sort of brood mare to be bargained away to the highest bidder.

That bitter reminder hardened her resolve. It simply would not do for her to spend another night in Jamie Sinclair's company, or his arms. If she hoped to escape his clutches with her pride and her heart intact, she couldn't afford to bide her time and wait for her bridegroom to either ransom or rescue her. She had no choice but to take her fate into her own hands once again the moment an opportunity presented itself.

And this time there would be no room for failure.

If you do try to run again, I just might decide your virtue is of more value to me than to the earl.

Emma shivered as Jamie's warning echoed through her mind. It was not an idle threat. He possessed the power to ruin her. Not just for her bridegroom but for any other man as well. If he made good on his promise, no decent man would want her. And no decent woman would ever welcome Emma into her home. She would live out the rest of her life like a ghost drifting in the shadows on the fringes of society — both scorned and invisible.

She tensed as the horse ceased its rocking. The cheerful jingle of bridles and harnesses was followed by the relieved sighs and jovial banter of Jamie's men as they dismounted. They must have finally decided to make camp for the night.

She yawned and stirred, pretending she had just been roused from a restful slumber. They had stopped on a barren expanse of moor bordered by towering trees on one side. A thin layer of mist floated just above the ground, shimmering beneath the gentle glow of the moon.

Emma half-expected Jamie to dump her to her feet as he had in the clearing the day before, but instead he carefully balanced her weight atop the horse as he dismounted, then drew her into his waiting arms.

As he lowered her to her feet, her body slid all the way down his, inch by provocative inch. Her eyes flew open in shock. His battle-hardened body was in the exact same state she had found it in upon awakening that morning — the state he had claimed was more painful than a pistol ball between the eyes. She tipped back her head to meet his heavy-lidded gaze, no longer able to feign either sleep or innocence.

Keenly aware that his men were milling about only a few feet away, she lowered her voice to a tense whisper. "I thought you said that only happened in the morning. And that it had naught to do with me."

He gazed down at her, his expressive mouth unsullied by even the trace of a smile. "I lied. On both counts."

His big, warm hands were still splayed against her ribcage, his thumbs lingering only inches away from the soft swell of her breasts. She gazed into the depths of his eyes, wondering how frost could burn so hot it threatened to sizzle away her every fear and misgiving. In that moment she was no more eager to escape him than he was to set her free.

Which was precisely what gave her the courage to close her trembling hands around the grip of his pistol, slide the weapon from the waistband of his breeches in one smooth motion and press its muzzle against his abdomen.

CHAPTER TWELVE

It didn't take Jamie and Emma's unnatural stillness long to attract the attention of Jamie's men. The good-natured banter abruptly ceased. Bridles slipped from frozen fingers. Smiles began to fade and jaws to harden.

As Emma slowly backed away from Jamie, keeping the mouth of his weapon carefully trained on his heart, a dozen pistols magically appeared in the hands of his men, each one trained on her with equal precision. Jamie had warned her they would be willing to die for him. She should have known they would be willing to kill for him as well.

She could see them from the corner of her eye but she refused to take her gaze off Jamie. With the horse still at his back, there was nowhere for him to flee.

"Lower your weapons," he commanded. Although his gaze was still fixed on her, they all knew his words were meant for his men.

"But Jamie," a great hulking brute with a jagged scar carved into his cheek said softly, "what do ye expect us to do? Just stand by and whistle through our arses while the lass blasts ye to kingdom come?"

"Lower your weapons!" Jamie barked. "It was not a suggestion."

Exchanging a flurry of doubtful glances, his men grudgingly obeyed the order. They lowered their pistols, but kept them at the ready by their sides.

Emma didn't stop backing away from Jamie until there was a good ten paces between them. She had hoped she might be able to think more clearly if she was out of his reach. But the invisible chain of his gaze still bound them together, making it nearly impossible for her to hear her own thoughts over the frantic tempo of her heart.

She needed a horse. She'd already proved she had little to no chance of making it back down the mountain on foot. But with a horse and a head start . . .

Before she could fully formulate her plan, Jamie opened his arms as if to make himself an even more tempting target. "So what do you intend to do now, lass?" The coaxing note in his voice only served to deepen its husky appeal. "Take me into custody and turn me over to the authorities? Shoot me?"

Emma tightened her grip on the pistol. To her dismay, instead of easing the tremor in her hands, the effort only succeeded in worsening it. "Perhaps I just wanted you to know what it feels like to have a pistol pointed at your heart."

"The Hepburn has had a pistol pointed at my heart for twenty-seven years. I know *exactly* how it feels."

From the corner of her eye, she saw one of Jamie's men slyly ease a step closer to them. She swung the mouth of the pistol toward the cluster of men, freezing them anew. "I wouldn't test me if I were you. It might surprise you to learn that I know how to use a pistol. If I can bring down a pheasant at fifty paces, I most certainly won't miss *you*." As she watched the nervous dart of their eyes, a new thought occurred to her. "Which one of you is Bon?"

The men stood paralyzed for several seconds, then lifted their free hands as one and pointed to a wiry elf of a man in their midst. He quickly lifted his arm and pointed to the fellow standing next to him.

Emma narrowed her eyes as she studied him. He looked like the runt from a litter of runts. His inky, short-cropped hair was spiked up in all directions as if he'd let some giant cat lick it in lieu of using a comb. A dark arrow of beard furred his pointed chin. As the other men began to edge away from him, leaving him all alone to face her bloodthirsty squint, he flashed her a sheepish grin, revealing a mouthful of crooked teeth.

"P-P-Pleased to make yer acquaintance, m'lady," he stammered, offering her a nervous bob that looked more like a curtsy than a bow.

"Well, I'm not in the least bit pleased to make yours," Emma informed him. "You said some horrid things about me to Mr. Sinclair. I don't care for you at all. I do believe I'm going to shoot you first."

Bon's sallow face went from yellow to white. "Now, lass, I didn't mean none o' them things I said. I was just funnin' with the lad. In all the years I've ridden with Jamie, I've never known him to lift a hand to a —"

"Bon!" Jamie snapped. "That'll do."

Bon shot him a helpless look, plainly trying to decide whether it would be more dangerous to offend him or the steely-eyed lass holding the gun. He returned his attention to Emma, lifting his hands in supplication. "Why, I got nothin' but respect for a bonny lass such as yerself. Ye can ask any o' the lads and they'll tell ye straight. If anyone 'round these parts knows how to treat a lady, it's me. Isn't that right? Malcolm? Angus?" he said plaintively, appealing to the two men closest to him, one of whom he'd just tried to get shot in his stead.

Emma did a double take. Malcolm and Angus weren't just brothers, but twins — both with long, wild hair, full lips and compelling, slightly off-kilter features that proved there was a very thin line between comely and homely.

Malcolm — or maybe it was Angus — nodded earnestly. "Bon's tellin' the God's truth, m'lady. Why, only last week he was boastin' aboot how he treated that barmaid over in Invergarry."

"That's right, miss," Angus — or maybe it was Malcolm — agreed with equally convincing sincerity. "Bon swore he treated her right, he did. And judgin' from the squeals and moans comin' from that hayloft in the stables until the wee hours o' the morn, he weren't just boastin'."

The other men snickered and nudged each other. Bon groaned and eyed the pistol still dangling uselessly from his hand as if contemplating shooting himself before she could.

Folding his arms over his chest, Jamie cleared his throat. "I couldn't really blame you if you shot Bon, lass. Hell, I'd have shot him myself a long time ago if he wasn't my cousin."

"Eh!" Bon protested, giving him an aggrieved look.

Jamie continued as if there had been no interruption. "However, I feel it's my Christian duty to warn you that my pistol only holds one shot. You can't shoot the both of us. I'm afraid you're going to have to choose, sweetheart."

More infuriated by the tender note in his voice than by any crude jibe from one of his men, Emma swung the pistol back around and leveled it at his heart. "I'm not your lass. And I'm not your sweetheart." As she faced him with her shoulders thrown back and her chin held high, she was surprised to realize her hand was no longer trembling. For the first time in a very long while she felt completely in control of her destiny. "I don't belong to any man. At least not yet."

She had naïvely believed she had disarmed him, but she had failed to take into account the most lethal weapon in his arsenal. Tipping his head to one side to study her, Jamie gave her a lazy grin that made her toes curl in her borrowed boots. "If you want to keep it that way, I'm afraid you're going to have to shoot me."

Unfolding his brawny arms, he came striding toward her. Although his men's expressions veered wildly between disbelief and alarm, Jamie only had eyes for her.

Emma's panic swelled as the distance between his imposing chest and the mouth of the weapon shrank. Recognizing in that moment that he was a gambling man just like her papa, she took two stumbling steps backward, raking back the pistol's hammer with her thumb.

Yet still he came, as resolute and fearless as some great mountain cat stalking a field mouse. Emma's field of vision narrowed until she could count each dark lash ringing those vibrant green eyes of his. Eyes that would be forever closed in death if she called his bluff.

She squeezed her own eyes shut to block out the sight of his face. But she could still see him lying in a pool of his own blood on the cold, hard ground. Could see the sunbronzed glow fade from his face, leaving it as pale and waxen as the effigy on a tomb.

Her finger tensed on the trigger but at the exact second she squeezed it, she felt her arm jerk to the side, as if of its own volition.

She opened her eyes to find Jamie still on his feet and an acrid cloud of smoke hanging in the air between them. Through ears still ringing from the blast, she heard him let out an admiring whistle as he eyed the jagged chunk of bark the pistol ball had torn from the trunk of a nearby birch. "Not bad for an amateur marksman. Or woman. At least you didn't shoot my horse."

Emma's arm fell limply to her side. Her shoulders slumped in defeat. She didn't even protest when Jamie reached down and gently removed the smoking pistol from her hand. He tossed it to one of his men, leaving him free to deal with her.

She braced herself for the blow to come, knowing her open defiance had left him with little choice but to mete out her punishment in front of his men. His temper, as well as his pride, would demand it. She would not cry, she swore silently, even as she felt a treacherous sting at the backs of her eyes. Nor would she give him the satisfaction of begging for mercy. Whatever he did to her, it would be no more than she deserved for letting her own temper get the best of her and squandering her best opportunity to escape.

Despite all of her courageous intentions, she still flinched when he lifted his hand. He froze and she glimpsed a flash of genuine anger in his eyes. But instead of backhanding her as she'd anticipated, he simply captured her wrist and tugged her into motion, forcing her to follow him.

As he hauled her through the ranks of his men, they looked as if they'd like nothing more than to erupt in a triumphant cheer, but didn't dare. Only Bon looked subdued, the mischievous spark in his black button eyes dimmed to an ember.

Given how long Jamie's strides were, it took them less than a minute to reach the edge of the wood bordering the moonlit stretch of moor. Emma faltered but Jamie just kept walking, giving her no choice but to stumble along behind him or be dragged. As the forbidding shadows engulfed them, she realized she had sorely misjudged him.

There would be no one to witness the punishment Jamie Sinclair had planned for her.

CHAPTER THIRTEEN

Emma stumbled after Jamie, forced to match his relentless pace. The thick canopy of boughs swaying over their heads diffused the moonlight, dappling their path with a sinister web of shadows that turned every rock and fallen branch into a trap to snag her clumsy feet.

She might be in danger of stumbling to her knees with every step, but Jamie navigated the treacherous terrain with rugged indifference, his stride as sure as his horse's had been on the edge of the cliff overlooking the vale.

Emma wanted to drag her feet, to postpone the inevitable moment of reckoning when Jamie would finally prove himself to be every inch the monster the earl would have her believe he was. His kindnesses had already sent a tiny web of cracks shuddering through her heart. She feared his cruelty would shatter it into a thousand pieces.

Her breath was growing shorter, her lungs starting to burn. Her ill-fitting boots chafed her toes and heels through the thick stockings, making each step a fresh misery.

"Pardon me?" she finally gasped out, her discomfort beginning to outweigh her fear.

His pace did not falter.

"Pardon me, *sir?*" she repeated, louder and more forcefully this time.

Jamie just kept walking, as if her words were of no more import to him than the distant call of a nightjar or the pesky chirping of a cricket.

Emboldened by a surge of anger, Emma jerked to a dead halt and wrenched her wrist out of his grip. Jamie stopped and slowly turned to face her.

The look on his face tempted her to go sprinting off in the opposite direction, but Emma forced herself to stand her ground. "We've traveled far enough, don't you think? Your men shouldn't be able to hear my screams from here."

Jamie gazed down at her, his expression inscrutable. "I'm more concerned about them hearing *my* screams. Although after that idiotic stunt you just pulled, I'm convinced no appeal to reason — however earsplitting — would penetrate that thick little skull of yours." He leaned closer, close enough to count every freckle on her nose. "If you ever pull a pistol on me again, lass, you'd best be prepared to pull the trigger."

"I did pull the trigger," she reminded him with icy calm.

"Only after you made sure your shot would go astray."

She continued to glare at him. "Perhaps the weapon simply recoiled."

He cocked a skeptical eyebrow. "*Before* you fired?"

Emma swallowed her protest. She might be able to deny that moment to him, but she couldn't very well deny it to herself. Not even if she couldn't begin to understand it.

"There's a chance my men wouldn't have taken kindly to seeing me shot down in cold blood. What if one of them had been willing to shoot you to save me?"

"Then I guess you'd be robbed of your precious ransom and the earl would be forced to woo himself a new bride."

Jamie turned and paced a few steps away from her, running a hand through his thick mane of sable hair. His big body was fraught with tension, as if there was some invisible battle being waged within.

Emma could not have said what drove her forward, what possessed her to touch the back of his arm through the faded cambric of his shirt with trembling fingertips. "Can you truly blame me for trying to escape? If you had been captured by the redcoats or were locked away in one of the earl's dungeons, wouldn't you have done the same?"

He turned to face her, his expression so stern it took every ounce of her courage not to go stumbling backward in alarm. "Aye, I would. But I would have bluidy well succeeded. I wouldn't have been fool enough to end up at the mercy of a mon like me."

"Just what sort of *mon* are you, Jamie Sinclair? Judging from what your cousin Bon blurted out back there, you're not in the habit of terrorizing defenseless women."

"That was before I met you. And one could hardly call you defenseless."

"If I hadn't learned which end of the pistol to point at a pheasant or a hare, there would have been many winter days — if not weeks — when my mother and sisters would have gone without meat."

"I wasn't talking about the way you handle a pistol. You have other weapons that are far more dangerous to a man's resolve." Her breath quickened as he lifted a hand to trace the curve of her cheek with the backs of his knuckles.

It had never occurred to her that he might

use tenderness to quell her rebellion instead of brutality. Or that it would be so devastatingly effective.

"Such as?" she whispered, knowing she was even more of a fool to ask but unable to resist.

"Your wit. Your spirit. Your willingness to sacrifice everything, including any hope of happiness, for the good of your family. Even your loyalty to your bridegroom — misguided though it may be." His voice deepened to a smoky rumble that shook her all the way to her toes. "Your fine eyes. Your wee freckled nose. The softness of your lips . . ."

Before those lips could part in a wistful sigh, Jamie was on her. He seized her face in the cup of his hands, claiming her as if she had always belonged to him, *would* always belong to him.

His mouth slanted hungrily óver hers, parting her tender lips with a mastery as undeniable as it was irresistible. His tongue plundered the slick sweetness of her mouth until the whisky-and-woodsmoke flavor of him was all she could taste, all she desired. He might be holding her face captive between his hands, but he tasted of freedom, of passion, of a danger as seductive and irresistible as it was terrifying.

It wasn't the kiss of a lover, but the kiss of a conqueror, a marauder, a man who had spent his entire life being taught that he would have to take what he wanted if he was ever to have anything at all. There was no defense against such a provocative assault on the senses, no words to deny its dark and primal power.

She felt her fingers unfurling like the petals of a flower, rising to slip beneath the hem of his shirt and dig into the smooth, muscled planes of his lower back. All she could do was hold on and try to keep from being swept away by the indomitable force of his will. Especially when all she secretly longed to do was let go and ride that surge to wherever it would take her.

One of his hands slid around her throat to tug away the leather thong at her nape, sending her curls tumbling around her shoulders in wild disarray. As he raked his fingers through them, her scalp tingled with a decadent pleasure that made her want to butt her head against his hand and purr like some sort of overgrown lap cat.

He seized a fistful of those curls and gently tugged, tipping back her head to allow him to lick even deeper into her mouth. She didn't even realize she had started to kiss him back, artlessly tangling her tongue with his, until she heard him groan deep in his throat, like a man who had tasted something he could no longer live without. Something he would be willing to die — or kill for — to possess.

That sound made a mockery of all her sacrifices, tempted her to forsake everything she held dear just to give him what he wanted. And what she wanted. But she had been bought and paid for with the earl's largesse. It was no longer hers to give.

Seized by panic, she shoved at his chest. He broke off the kiss abruptly, setting her away from him with hands as unsteady as her own.

Even though she was the one who had pushed him away, all she could do was stand there, trembling and bewildered, like a child who had been abandoned in some dark and fearsome forest with no hope of ever finding her way home.

Jamie's inky pupils had nearly swallowed the green in his heavy-lidded eyes, leaving them dusky and unreadable. As he gazed down at her, she could see herself through his eyes — the wild tumble of her curls, her dazed expression, the telltale flush where his beard-stubble had abraded the delicate skin of her jaw. She ran the tip of her tongue over lips that still felt tender and ripe from the ravenous force of his kiss.

Desperate to put some distance between them, she stooped to retrieve the leather thong from the ground. Gathering her curls at her nape, she began to twist them into a tight knot. "You've won, Mr. Sinclair," she said, fighting to keep her voice steadier than her hands. "I promise I'll be an obedient little captive until you deliver me safely into the hands of my bridegroom a few days hence. I won't try to run again so you'll be spared the onerous duty of chastising me with your kisses." She smoothed the rumpled front of her borrowed tunic as if it were the most expensive of ball gowns. "As far as your men are concerned, I shall endeavor to behave as if you simply gave me a stern scolding, forcing me to recognize the error of my ways."

With that pronouncement, she turned and marched away from him as fast as her legs would carry her, her shoulders squared and her head held high.

"Miss Marlowe?"

"Yes?" She turned to find him still standing in the exact same spot, his expression inscrutable.

For an elusive instant, he looked as if he wanted to say something else altogether, but then he pointed in the opposite direction. "Our camp is that way."

When Emma woke that night, there were no warm, masculine arms to shelter her from the cold, hard ground. Her toes were numb and a thin layer of gooseflesh pebbled her arms. She sat up, blinking away the fog of confusion that came from waking up in a strange place surrounded by strangers.

On the opposite side of the dying campfire, Jamie's men lay in blanket-draped humps. If not for the occasional drunken snort or rumbling snore, they might have been mistaken for boulders.

When Jamie had marched her back into their midst, their curious glances had been quickly quelled by Jamie's ferocious scowl. After partaking of a meal of salted venison and stale brown bread washed down by some dark, bitter ale, she had retreated to her bedroll. She didn't realize how much she would miss Jamie's presence there until she awoke all alone, disoriented and shivering from the cold.

A distant yowl came from somewhere in the crags above the moor, raising the tiny hairs at the nape of her neck. She climbed to her feet and peered nervously into the shadows, wrapping the blanket around her shoulders. The night sky arched overhead like an expanse of the deepest, blackest ice, its stars glittering shards of frost. It was as if she were the only person awake in the entire universe. The only person alive.

Until she saw him.

Jamie had dozed off only a few feet away from her with his back propped against a boulder and without so much as a cloak to cover him. She frowned at the length of rope tied around his wrist, puzzled by its presence until her gaze slowly traced the other end of it to her ankle. He had evidently looped the rope around her ankle while she slept, not tight enough to bind her, but so that any suspicious movement on her part would rouse him from his slumber.

She shook her head, a reluctant smile touching her lips. She should have known he wouldn't be the trusting sort. If she had taken one more step away from him, the rope would have jerked him awake.

Apparently, he hadn't believed her when she had vowed not to run again. She could no longer afford to risk being punished for her disobedience by his kisses and caresses. He had warned her from the beginning that she just might enjoy him putting his hands on her. Had she known then just how much she would enjoy it, she might have heeded that warning.

Now that she was aware of his snare, it would have been a simple enough matter for her to extract herself from it. But instead of moving away from him, she found herself drifting toward him.

Just how many nights had he spent sleeping on the cold, hard ground with no roof to shield him from the rain, the snow, or the tenacious chill? He might be only twenty-seven years old, but constant exposure to sun and wind had already weathered his skin to burnished gold, carved deep brackets around his mouth and etched beguiling crinkles at the outer corners of his eyes.

Even in sleep, there wasn't a hint of softness in the man, no revealing glimpse of the boy he had once been. He didn't even sleep with his mouth hanging open, but compressed to a firm line, his only concession to vulnerability the smudges of exhaustion beneath his eyes. Almost as if sensing her avid scrutiny, he stirred and turned his face toward the shadows, shielding it from her gaze.

Emma sighed. He had given her his blanket, yet she was still chilled to the bone. She couldn't help but remember how cozy it had felt to be curled up against him the previous night, how his lean, hard frame had wrapped itself around her, radiating heat like a coal stove on a snowy winter's eve.

That piercing yowl came again. She shuddered and edged even closer to Jamie. She had no way of knowing what sort of bloodthirsty creatures prowled this wilderness. Wildcats? Wolves? Bears? For all she knew, there could be a dragon stomping around in the crags above them, just looking for some tasty virgin to devour.

She stole one last longing look at Jamie before bending down and slipping the rope from her ankle.

Jamie opened his eyes, going from deep sleep to sharp alertness with the peculiar ease that came from years of vigilance.

He was assailed by two immediate impressions.

There was a blanket draped over him that hadn't been there when he went to sleep.

And there was a woman beneath that blanket who hadn't been there when he went to sleep.

He blinked warily. Emma was curled up on her side facing him. Only a scant handspan separated their bodies, almost as if she had sought to get as close to him as she dared without actually touching him. Which touched him more deeply than he cared to admit, even to himself.

He was becoming accustomed to the dull ache that had plagued his groin ever since he'd been fool enough to abduct her. But this was a sharper and even more insistent pain, perilously near to his heart.

Her russet lashes were fanned against her freckled cheeks, making her look more like the vulnerable seventeen-year-old lass who had sought love in London only to find heartbreak than the woman that lass had become. Even with her arms folded around herself for extra warmth, she looked cold. She looked miserable. She looked lonely.

By waiting to send his ransom demand until they reached the higher climes of the mountain, Jamie had hoped to torment the Hepburn with hellish visions of a Sinclair stealing what belonged to him. But now Jamie was the one burning, the one tormented by visions of another sort altogether — visions of Emma's pale, freckled softness beneath him, her lush lips eagerly parting to receive his kiss as she twined her arms around his neck, opened her shapely thighs and urged him to make her his own.

His mouth thinned to a grim line. No matter how eagerly she welcomed his kiss, she was still the Hepburn's woman. She didn't belong to him and she never would.

He had no choice but to walk away and leave her to the cold comfort of her own arms.

She stirred. A frown furrowed her delicate brow. A sleepy little whimper escaped her parted lips.

Biting off a defeated oath, Jamie reached for her, drawing her up so that her cheek could rest against his chest. She nestled into the warmth of his arms with a throaty little moan of satisfaction, foolishly trusting him not to abuse the power he held over her. Before she was fully awake, Jamie knew he could have the laces of his breeches untied, Bon's borrowed trousers around her ankles and himself buried so deep inside of her she would never again be able to call her body her own.

But if he succumbed to that dark temptation, he would be no better than the Hepburn. He would have become the very thing he despised: a man who preyed on those weaker than himself, who was willing to destroy the very thing he desired the most just to keep someone else from having it.

He would have to remain vigilant if he was to extract himself from her embrace at the first stirring of life from his men. He rested his chin on top of her head and gazed into the darkness, knowing that dawn would be a very long time coming.

CHAPTER FOURTEEN

Emma awoke the next morning feeling surprisingly well rested. It was almost as if she'd spent most of the night nestled in a warm feather bed instead of sprawled on the cold, stony ground. Although the woolen blanket was tucked beneath her chin with painstaking care, Jamie was nowhere in sight.

She climbed to her feet, yawning and stretching her stiff muscles. A balmy April breeze had buffeted most of the clouds away, revealing a dazzling stretch of azure sky. Jamie's men were milling about on the other side of the campfire, breaking their fasts and making their horses ready for the day's ride.

At first she thought Jamie had decided to take her at her word after all and had failed to post a guard. But then she saw young Graeme lounging against a nearby boulder, pretending to whittle away at a block of wood that was growing more shapeless with each flash of his blade. When she started forward, he trailed a few steps behind, trying to look nonchalant. She was tempted to bolt for the trees just to see if he actually possessed the courage to stop her.

As she wended her way through the camp, her gaze instinctively seeking but not finding Jamie's tall, imposing form, his men gave her a wide berth. Several of them even averted their eyes as she passed, devoting themselves to shoveling down mouthfuls of mealy porridge or waxing their bridles with renewed vigor.

She was only able to sneak up on Angus and Malcolm because they were too busy arguing over a hunk of scorched bannock bread to notice her approach.

"Damn it all, mon, I told ye there weren't eno' left for the both of us," one of them was saying as he plucked the bread from his twin's hand.

"There would be if one of us wasn't ye!" his twin insisted, making a vain grab for the bread.

Spotting her, they lapsed into sullen silence.

Emma eyed their tangled brown locks and full lips with poorly disguised fascination. Their off-center noses even looked as if they'd been broken in precisely the same spot. "So how do the other men tell the two of you apart?"

Pointing to each other, they said in perfect unison, "He's the ugly one."

"Oh, I see." Still puzzled, she nodded politely and backed away, leaving them to return to their squabble over the bread.

"Watch yer step, lass," someone warned as she nearly backed right into the campfire.

She turned to discover Bon sitting on a rock, hunkered over a rasher of bacon smoking in an iron skillet. Although the meat was already scorched to a blackened crisp, he didn't appear to be in any hurry to remove it from the pan.

Following the direction of her glance, Bon glared up at her. "Now that ye've stolen me britches and boots, I suppose ye'll be wantin' me bacon, too."

Emma glared right back at him with all the affronted dignity she could muster. "I didn't steal your britches and boots. Your cousin stole your britches and boots and gave them to me. And I wouldn't dream of depriving you of your breakfast, sir."

Snorting, Bon stabbed the blackened strip of meat with the point of his knife and slapped it on a battered tin plate. He held the plate out to her, his impish face scrunched into a fierce scowl. "Ye might as well go ahead and take it. I wouldn't want ye to shoot me."

Emma hesitated, suspicious of any kindness on his part.

"Go on. I didn't have time to poison it." He waggled his eyebrows at her. "Yet."

Emma accepted the plate and took a nibble of the blackened pork. She couldn't hide her grimace. It was like licking an ash can.

"Have you any more?" she asked, her stomach already rumbling a hollow protest. Ever since her papa had accepted the earl's proposal, very little had been able to tempt her appetite, but suddenly she was famished. It had to be all the riding and the fresh air.

"Greedy wench, are ye? I would expect no less from the Hepburn's woman." Still grumbling beneath his breath, he speared another rasher of bacon with his knife.

Before he could slap the meat in the pan, she stayed his hand.

"Please. Allow me."

He eyed her suspiciously, then reluctantly surrendered the knife and the bacon into her hand, muttering, "Probably end up with the blade stuck in me gullet for me trouble."

She joined him on the rock and dropped the fresh rasher of bacon into the skillet. As it began to sizzle, Emma glanced over her shoulder to find the other men still giving them a wide berth. "Why are they behaving in such a peculiar manner? It's almost as if they're afraid of me."

Bon stroked his pointed black beard. "It's not ye they fear, but Jamie. He's made it clear they're not to trouble ye or they'll have to answer to him."

"And just what would he do if they disobeyed him?"

Bon shrugged one skinny shoulder. "Probably shoot them."

A disbelieving laugh escaped her. "Jamie told me he considered his men his brothers. Do you honestly believe he would kill one of them over me?"

"I didn't say he'd kill them. I said he'd shoot them." The perpetual twinkle in Bon's eye made it impossible to tell when he was joking. "But ye needn't worry the lads'll think less o' ye because of it. He's also made it clear ye're not his woman."

Jamie's woman.

Just a day ago, those words would have both outraged and terrified her. Now they sent a dangerous little thrill shivering through her soul.

She turned all of her attention to flipping the bacon with the tip of the knife, some perverse urge driving her to ask, "Has your Jamie had a lot of women?"

"Any lad born with a face like that can have as many women as he wants."

It took her a moment to realize Bon hadn't actually answered her question. When she slanted him a probing look, he blinked at her, looking as innocent as his fox-like little face would allow.

"Have you any potatoes?" she asked.

"I've got one, miss." Emma started as the hulking man with the scar carved deep into his left cheek thrust his hand over Bon's shoulder.

She hadn't realized Jamie's men had been creeping closer, drawn by the succulent aroma of the bacon she was gently coaxing to crisp perfection. Most of them were still keeping at a respectful distance, as if working up the courage to approach.

Bon scowled at the man. "Ye know better than to sneak up on a lass like that, Lemmy. With that face o' yers, ye're liable to give her a fright she won't survive."

The towering man ducked his head shyly, his drooping mustache with its curling ends making his long face look even more melancholy. "Beg yer pardon, miss. I didna mean to startle ye."

Shooting Bon a chiding look, Emma took

the potato from Lemmy's hand. "Why, thank you, Mr. . . . Mr. . . . Lemmy. That's precisely what I needed."

His offering was slightly withered and sprouting more eyes than a gorgon, but Emma made a great show of slicing it into neat cubes and dropping them into the pan next to the bacon, where they began to soften in the hot grease.

"I've more where that one come from, miss," Lemmy announced eagerly before heading back to his saddlebags.

"If Jamie were here," Emma muttered, stirring the potatoes with the point of the knife, "I suppose he'd try to convince me the earl personally cut that scar into Lemmy's cheek with his engraved letter opener for stealing a potato."

" 'Tweren't a potato, but a bushel o' turnips. And 'tweren't the earl," Bon said matter-of-factly. "The auld buzzard don't like to get his own hands bluidy so he ordered one o' his men to hold Lemmy down while his gamekeeper did it."

Emma jerked her head up, gazing at Bon in horror. "The same gamekeeper who was going to cut off Graeme's hand?"

Bon shook his head. "The one before him. Or was it the one before that?" He ticked off a few gamekeepers on his fingers before giving up with a shrug. "The earl always did have deadly taste in gamekeepers. The more bluidthirsty, the better, as far as he's concerned."

Emma swallowed, her appetite suddenly deserting her. She was still having difficulty believing the gentle soul who had rescued her family from ruin could be the monster these men were describing. Perhaps he just had terrible judgment when it came to hiring gamekeepers.

"Your cousin told me all about the long-standing enmity between the Hepburns and the Sinclairs," she said. "But this hatred between he and the earl seems more virulent somehow . . . more *personal*. Have you any idea why Jamie despises the man so?"

"All ye need to know is that Jamie Sinclair never does anythin' without a damn fine reason."

"Even kidnap another man's bride?"

When Bon looked away, no longer able to meet her eyes, she knew she had struck a raw nerve.

"Why, you don't know what those reasons are, do you?" she said, understanding beginning to dawn. "That's why you were saying those dreadful things about me, wasn't it? To try and goad him into telling you."

A muscle in Bon's jaw twitched, but he

kept his gaze fixed on the leaping flames of the fire. "He's always had a temper and a wild streak, just like his grandfather and all the Sinclairs who came before him, but I've never known him to be reckless. I don't know what he wants from the earl but I do know it's got a powerful hold on him. He's willin' to risk everythin', includin' all our necks, to get it."

Before Emma could press him further, a young fellow with moss-green eyes and a thick ginger beard appeared at her elbow to offer her a dirty package wrapped in paper and string. "I've some more bacon, miss."

"And I've some bread," said another man, shyly handing over half a loaf of brown bread so stale it felt like a rock in her hand.

"And we've some cheese," Malcolm and Angus chimed in unison. They engaged in a brief shoving match to determine which one of them would win the privilege of dusting the furry, green crust of mold off the cheese before presenting it to her with a flourish.

As the rest of Jamie's men gathered around her, Emma studied their expectant faces. They looked less like a band of fierce outlaws in that moment than a pack of grubby little boys desperate for a warm sugar biscuit straight out of the oven.

Shaking her head ruefully, she said, "Stand

back, lads. A lady needs room to work."

When Jamie came striding back into the camp, the last sight he expected to see was his men hunched over tin plates, shoveling food into their mouths with the blades of their knives as if they hadn't eaten in a month and might never again have the chance.

He might have been more mystified by their behavior if the irresistible aroma of sizzling bacon hadn't come drifting to his own nose, luring him forward. Even though he'd eaten a chunk of stale bread paired with a thin strip of dried venison before slipping out of camp before dawn had yet to blush the sky, the succulent aroma still made his stomach clench with yearning.

That yearning sharpened to something infinitely more dangerous when he saw the woman presiding over their feast. Emma was leaning over Graeme's shoulder, scraping a fresh serving of potatoes — fried up tender on the inside and crispy on the outside just the way Jamie liked them — onto the boy's plate. Graeme gave her an adoring look before stuffing a heaping portion into his already full mouth.

Jamie glanced at the other men's plates to discover more potatoes, several rashers of bacon and thick slabs of bread toasted in bacon grease with cheese melted over the top.

He shook his head in disbelief. " 'Tis a good thing we'll have food and shelter tonight since you lads appear to be gobbling down the stores of a fortnight in one sitting."

The men still had enough of their wits about them to look abashed but they didn't stop eating.

"Could I interest you in some breakfast, Mr. Sinclair?" Emma asked, the crisp formality of her tone only serving to remind him of the helpless little sounds she had made at the back of her throat while he was kissing her last night. She plucked a rasher of bacon from her own plate and offered it to him.

He reluctantly took the bacon from her fingers, knowing exactly how Adam must have felt when Eve handed him the apple.

Still eyeing her warily, he sampled a piece of the crisp pork. If the smell was heavenly, the taste was pure rapture. Before he knew it, the entire rasher was gone and he was licking the grease from his fingertips without a hint of either manners or shame.

"The lass cooks like an angel," Bon mumbled through a mouthful of potatoes.

"If she wasn't already promised to the earl, I'd marry her meself."

"Why, thank you, Bon," Emma replied, beaming with pleasure. "Even though my mother said it was a common pastime hardly befitting a lady, I've always loved to cook. When I was a little girl, Cookie used to have to chase me out of her kitchen with a broom. Fortunately, it was a passion that served my family in good stead after Cookie . . . retired."

She lowered her eyes to avoid Jamie's sharp gaze. She had probably taken over the cooking after her papa had squandered Cookie's wages on faro and cheap gin. Jamie couldn't help but wonder if any of her sisters had ever lifted a hand to help her.

Reminded of the errand that had sent him stealing out of the camp before any of them had risen from their bedrolls, he retrieved the brace of cleaned and dressed hares slung over his shoulder and tossed them at her feet.

As her startled blue eyes met his, he said, "As long as you're riding with me, you'll never lack for fresh meat on your table."

With that, he turned on his heel and headed for his horse. "Finish stuffing your faces and pack up your gear. If we wish to reach Muira's before midnight, there's no time to dawdle."

"Who is this Muira?" Emma called after him.

"A friend," he said shortly. "And don't get too attached to the lass," he tossed over his shoulder to his men. "She's not a pet. You can't keep her."

As their crestfallen groans echoed in his ears, Jamie decided he might do well to heed his own warning.

Jamie drove them at a relentless pace through that endless day, frequently glancing back over his shoulder as if fleeing some devil only he could see.

At first Emma tried to sit stiffly in the saddle behind him, pride preventing her from clinging to him. But after the third time she was forced to make a frantic grab for the back of his vest to keep herself from sliding off the horse and over the edge of a cliff, Jamie bit off an exasperated oath, dismounted and swung himself back up behind her. Sliding one arm around her waist, he tugged her into the cradle of his thighs with a grip that warned he was in no mood to be defied.

As the hills grew steeper, the trees more scarce and the terrain ever more rugged,

Emma was almost thankful for his bullying. Without his imposing chest and muscular arms to support her, she probably would have gone tumbling into some stony ravine and broken her neck.

They all had cause to be thankful they'd started their journey with full bellies since Jamie only allowed them a handful of breaks to meet the most basic of their needs for food, water and respite. Judging by the gruff impatience with which he urged them to hurry up and remount, the breaks were more for the horses' benefit than their own.

With each league they traveled, the air grew thinner, making the wind feel like the stinging snap of a whip against Emma's tender skin. Patches of dingy snow began to appear beneath the sparse clusters of birch and cedar as they left even the most elusive hint of spring far behind them.

Emma's world soon narrowed to the well-muscled cradle of Jamie's body and the steady sway of the horse between her thighs. Her memories of England — of sunlight dancing over the tender spring grass and larks singing in the budding hedgerows — seemed nothing more than the distant echoes of a dream. Just when she thought she couldn't possibly grow any more wretched, a chill drizzle began to fall from the leaden sky.

Jamie retrieved an oilcloth from his pack and used it to fashion a makeshift tent over both their heads. His efforts were wasted when the capricious wind shifted and began to drive the icy needles of rain into their faces. It was soon dripping off Emma's eyelashes and running down her cheeks like tears. Forsaking her battered pride, she huddled against Jamie, shivering and soaked to the skin.

Before long they were forced to slow their pace so the horses could pick their way over the slippery rocks. Emma's head began to droop. She could not have said if she drifted into sleep or stupor, but when she opened her eyes, it was to a world both achingly familiar and utterly alien.

She must be dreaming, she thought, her exhaustion melting to a haze of wide-eyed wonder. How else was she to explain the enchanted tableau before her eyes? She blinked, but still the vision remained, cozy and substantial enough to put a lump of longing in her throat.

The rain had shifted to snow while she drowsed — fluffy white flakes that waltzed through the clearing before them in the arms of the wind. In the middle of the clearing sat a cottage. This was no tumbledown

189

crofter's hut but a sturdy structure fashioned from weathered gray stone and crowned by a thatched roof. The cheery glow of lamplight spilled from its deep-set windows like a beacon to welcome the weary traveler.

To Emma's eyes, the cottage looked as if it should have been spun from gingerbread and marzipan instead of stone and mortar. She half-expected to see a bony, white-haired crone beckoning from the doorway, eager to offer her sugar plums and sweetmeats before stuffing her into a waiting oven.

It was a fate she might actually welcome at the moment, she thought, wracked by a fresh round of shivers.

Since the horse had finally ceased its rocking, there was only one other constant in her life — Jamie's arms. He dismounted, pulling her off the beast with him in one fluid motion. Instead of setting her on her feet, he gathered her to his chest and went striding toward the cottage, carrying her like a child.

Emma stole a furtive glance at him. Fresh snowflakes dusted the rich sable of his hair and caught like diamond dust in his lashes.

She knew she should have protested his high-handed treatment of her. Should have insisted he put her down that very instant. But she wasn't entirely sure her trembling legs would support her. So she looped one arm around his neck, telling herself it was less humiliating than going sprawling to the ground at his feet. As she rested her weary head against his shoulder, she thought how unfair it was that someone so untrustworthy should feel so strong and warm and solid.

As they approached the cottage's stone stoop, the wooden door swung open as if by magic.

Jamie ducked beneath the low door frame. They were immediately enveloped in a cloud of warm air, faintly scented with the delicious aroma of cinnamon biscuits.

It took Emma a dazed moment to realize it was no cackling crone who had granted them entry, but a ruddy-cheeked woman who was nearly as broad as she was tall. It wasn't a very difficult feat to achieve since the top of her head barely came to Jamie's elbow.

Judging by her rumpled tent of a nightdress and the long white braids draped over her shoulders, their arrival had roused their hostess from her bed. But that didn't seem to dim her delight.

She clapped her hands, a smile wreathing her rosy cheeks. "Jamie, me darlin' lad! Why, ye're a sight fer a puir auld woman's sore eyes!"

Even burdened with Emma's weight, Jamie still managed to bend down and graze the top of the woman's snowy head with a kiss. "There's no need for false modesty, Muira. You know you're still the bonniest lass north of Edinburgh. I've been half in love with you myself since I was but a wee lad."

"Only half?" she inquired coyly, giggling like a schoolgirl. "I'm still waitin' fer ye to come to yer senses and ask me to be yer wife."

"And you know I would if I thought your husband wouldn't mind." Jamie straightened, glancing around the cozy but spacious chamber that appeared to serve as both parlor and dining room for the cottage. "Where is he?"

"He's off huntin' with the lads again." The old woman's eyes twinkled with mischief. " 'Twould serve him right if he returned to find a randy young lover in me bed."

"Bite your tongue, woman. You know he'd shoot any mon foolish enough to trifle with his blushing young bride. He almost shot my grandfather once and all he did was wink at you."

She swatted Jamie on the shoulder. "After

thirty-five years o' bein' wed to Drummond MacAlister, 'twill take more than a spoonful o' flattery from a honey-tongued lad such as yerself to make this bride blush. So how is that grandfather o' yers? I was hopin' the stubborn auld rascal would come doon from the mountain and pay us a visit before the winter snows set in, but we've seen neither hide nor hair o' him all these long months."

From Emma's angle, it was impossible to miss the sudden tension in Jamie's jaw or the faint quickening of the pulse in his throat. "He's staying closer to home these days. I haven't seen him myself for nigh on two months."

Muira snorted. "Ye canna expect me to believe the auld divil's retired to his rockin' chair. If 'twas up to him, he'd still be leadin' the lads and ye'd still be in St. Andrews or Edinburgh playin' the gent."

A mock shudder raked Jamie. "I would have never survived. The whisky was weak and the lasses weren't nearly as bonny as you."

Worry dimmed the twinkle in Muira's eye as she peered past them into the shadows of the yard. "Shall I fetch the pistols and bolt the door? Are ye bein' followed?"

"Not at the moment. Except by a band of wet, hungry, weary men who would gladly trade their mortal souls for a bowl of hot neeps and tatties and an invitation to bed down in your stable for the night."

Muira rubbed her plump hands together, as if being stirred from her sleep in the dead of night to feed a dozen ravenous men was her idea of paradise. "I'll put a pot on the kitchen hearth right away. And tell young Nab to lock up the sheep," she added with a ribald wink. She turned her attention to Emma, her toffee-colored eyes as bright and inquisitive as a robin's. "And what have ye here? Did ye find some half-drowned muskrat doon on the moors?"

Any other time Emma might have balked at being likened to a rodent. But at the moment she was helpless to squeeze so much as a squeak of protest past her chattering teeth.

She felt Jamie's arms tighten around her. "I was hoping you'd look after her while I tend to the men and the horses."

"That I will, lad." Clucking like an aggrieved mother hen, Muira gave him a chiding look. "And from the looks o' the puir child, I'll do a damn sight finer job of it than ye."

Plucking a glowing oil lamp from its hook, their hostess ushered them across the room. After sleeping on the cold ground for two nights, the cozy cottage with its low plastered ceilings and neatly swept flagstone floor looked like a king's palace to Emma. A narrow wooden staircase was tucked into an alcove in the corner. Apparently, the cottage had a full second story instead of just a sleeping loft.

Fragrant bunches of dried rosemary and thyme had been hung from iron hooks set in the exposed oak rafters along with an impressive array of iron pots and copper kettles. Jamie had to duck to avoid banging his head on the largest of them.

Emma forgot about all of the room's other charms when she saw the fire crackling merrily on the stone hearth. An ancient hound with a grizzled muzzle was dozing on a rag rug in front of the fire. It was all she could do not to shoo him away so she could curl up in his place.

Jamie gently deposited her on the bench closest to the hearth, then straightened just enough to whisper something in Muira's ear.

"Aye, I'll see to that as well, lad." The woman bobbed her head, the sly twinkle returning to her eye. " 'Twill be ready when ye return."

As if eager to make good on her mysterious promise, she turned toward the back of the cottage and clapped briskly. Emma craned her neck, waiting to see if a trio of elves or perhaps a unicorn would appear to do her bidding.

But it was simply two servant girls who emerged from what must have been the kitchen, rubbing their bleary eyes. The one with the ruddy complexion and pug nose was nearly as short and stout as her mistress but the other was a tall, comely young creature with dark, glossy gypsy ringlets and plump breasts on the verge of tumbling out of her low-cut bodice.

Her eyes lit up when she saw Jamie, making Muira's welcome seem positively chilly in comparison. "Why, Jamie Sinclair, as I live and breathe," she purred, resting a hand on one shapely hip. " 'Tis been far too long since ye've paid me . . . I mean, us . . . a visit."

CHAPTER FIFTEEN

Steadfastly avoiding Emma's eyes, Jamie bobbed his head briefly. "You're looking well, Brigid. As always."

Emma could only stare, fascinated by the hint of color gracing his high cheekbones. She wouldn't have thought him a man capable of blushing.

"Not nearly as well as ye," Brigid replied, looking him up and down as if she'd like nothing better than to lure him off to the nearest hayloft for a lusty tumble. And not for the first time, if the way she was licking her ripe lips was any indication.

Emma glared at the impertinent chit through the sodden ropes of her hair, then quickly lowered her eyes when she realized what she was doing. Fortunately, Jamie had already turned and was striding back toward the door, no doubt relieved to be free of the burden she had become.

Muira shooed both the servants back

toward the kitchen. "Go on with ye now! There's no time for gawkin' and dallyin'! We've much to do and little time to do it."

Brigid spared Emma a disdainful glance before flouncing back into the kitchen with Muira and the other maidservant following at her heels.

Emma tugged off her boots and huddled in front of the fire, perfectly happy to bask in its warmth and keep company with the grizzled old hound. The moments were punctuated by the muffled clang of pots, the occasional Gaelic curse, and the sound of footsteps trudging up and down the stairs behind her. Her garments were just starting to go from soaking wet to unpleasantly damp when Muira reappeared to hand her a wooden bowl. Emma quickly spooned down its contents, caring only that they were warm and bore a vague resemblance to vegetables she recognized. She was equally grateful for the cup of hot tea Muira pressed into her still trembling hands.

She spent a blissful moment breathing in the steam wafting up from the cup before lifting it to her lips.

The liquid slid down her raw throat, burning every inch of the way. She choked, shooting Muira a betrayed look.

"Drink up, lass," the old woman urged,

settling her considerable bulk on the edge of the hearth. "The whisky'll warm ye far faster than the tea will."

Blinking the stinging tears from her eyes, Emma tentatively took a second sip of the whisky-laced tea. Muira had spoken the truth. The burn soon subsided to a pleasant glow that warmed her belly and made her numb fingers and toes begin to tingle.

Emma couldn't have said if it was the whisky or the compassionate sparkle in the woman's eyes that thawed her frozen tongue but she suddenly found herself blurting out, "How long have you known Jamie?"

"Since he was naught but a wee lad ridin' on his grandfather's shoulder." The woman's plump cheek dimpled in a smile. "Ramsey couldn't take a step in those days without Jamie tuggin' on his coattails. Oh, he would fuss and bluster, but ye could tell the lad could do no wrong in his eyes. It nearly broke his heart to send Jamie away to that fancy school when the lad turned seventeen."

"It's a shame they weren't able to teach him any manners there," Emma muttered, still feeling oddly out of sorts after witnessing Brigid's overly familiar greeting.

Muira gave her a reproving look. "Mind yer tongue now, lass. A mon doesn't need manners when he has a stout heart. There's been many a bitterly cold winter when me and mine wouldna have survived if Jamie — or his grandfather before him — hadn't brought us milk and meat in the shape of a stolen heifer or two. If not for the Sinclairs, we'd have all been driven off this mountain and into the lowlands long ago by the Hepburn and his lapdogs. The Sinclairs are the ones who put meat on our tables and coins in our purses when times are lean. Why, three o' me own lads even rode with Jamie for a season before settling down with their wives to raise bairns of their own."

"Would you be so quick to defend him if I told you he had abducted me?"

Considering the fawning welcome Muira had given Jamie, Emma hardly expected their hostess to gasp in horror and go running for the authorities. But she was still a little nonplussed when the woman leaned over and gave her a motherly pat on the knee. "I suspected as much, dearie. Me own Drummond stole me right out from under me dear father's nose."

Emma eyed the woman in disbelief. "Do you mean to say your husband abducted you as well?"

"Aye, that he did." Muira sighed, her eyes growing a bit misty at the memory. "Tossed me o'er the back o' his horse and made off with me in front o' half the village. I had six younger sisters and they were all pea green with envy."

Perhaps the woman was mad, Emma thought as she blinked at Muira's beaming countenance. Perhaps all Scots were mad.

"But this isn't the Dark Ages." She took another sip of the tea and whisky concoction, feeling her indignation begin to mount along with her body temperature. "Where I come from, a man courts the woman he fancies. He woos her. He writes poetry to praise the fairness of her face, the grace of her steps, the gentleness of her temperament. He doesn't toss her over his shoulder and carry her off to his cave. Or his cottage," she added, stealing a glance at their homey surroundings. The cottage with its worn rag rugs and scarred but sturdy furniture looked like a place where life was not only lived, but celebrated. "Where I come from, men behave in a civilized manner. Like gentlemen," she finished stiffly, "not like savages or barbarians."

"Och, but there's nothin' gentle or civilized aboot what happens between a man and a woman in the bedchamber." Muira gave her a broad wink. "At least not if a lass is lucky, that is."

"And Muira has always been among the luckiest of lasses." Emma jumped as Jamie's voice came from just behind her, warning her he'd probably heard every word of her ridiculously passionate speech. "She has seven strapping sons and twenty-seven grandchildren to prove it."

Muira rose from the hearth to smack him on the arm, her laugh a bawdy bray. "Go on with ye, lad! 'Twould be eight-and-twenty grandchildren now. Callum's wife had her seventh bairn while ye were off tweakin' the Hepburn's forked tail."

Reminded anew that her fiancé didn't have many admirers on this mountain, Emma drained the dregs of her tea in a single bitter swallow and waited for Jamie to inform Muira that he hadn't stolen her so he could make her his wife, but to sell her back to his enemy for a profit. But he simply plucked the empty tea cup from her hand and handed it to Muira before scooping Emma back into his arms.

She stiffened, no longer willing to submit to being treated like some slow-witted child. "You may put me down now, sir. I'll have you know I'm perfectly capable —"

"— of holding your tongue for another five minutes," he finished smoothly, striding toward the stairs.

Emma snapped her mouth shut, reluctant to make a scene in front of Muira or her servants. The girls had reappeared and were watching Jamie carry her off. The stout lass was gaping with open-mouthed fascination while Brigid watched through eyes narrowed to feline slits.

Muira's younger sisters must have looked equally envious when Drummond MacAlister had gone riding out of that village with his squealing bride-to-be on the back of his horse. Emma knew she should be more concerned about how Jamie's manhandling could damage her reputation, but she could barely resist a childish urge to poke her tongue out at Brigid as they passed.

Jamie turned left at the top of the stairs, carrying her to a chamber at the far end of the narrow corridor that was little more than a dormer tucked beneath the eaves. The only furniture in the room was a ladder-backed chair, a small table with a lamp on it and a round wooden tub banded in iron.

A round wooden tub with curlicues of steam rising from the heated water within.

"I'm afraid it was the best I could do since I didn't have time to compose an ode to the fairness of your face and the grace of your step. Or the gentleness of your temperament," Jamie added wryly.

Emma slid to her feet and drifted forward, forgetting all about her annoyance with him. In that moment, she would have forgiven him anything, even murder. She'd heard the maidservants trudging up and down the stairs while she languished in front of the fire but her mind had been too numbed by cold and exhaustion to realize they'd been hauling buckets of heated water. Now she knew exactly what Jamie had whispered to Muira before ducking back out into the snow to tend to his horses and his men.

"Oh, Jamie," she breathed, trailing her fingertips through the warm, silky water. "It's beautiful!"

She lifted her head to find him surveying her with an odd light in his eyes. Her smile faded. "What is it? Why are you staring at me?"

"That's the first time I've heard my Christian name on your lips." His gaze dropped to those lips, its smoldering caress warming her in places even the whisky had not been able to reach. "I rather fancy the sound of it."

Before she could fully absorb the impact of his words, he was gone, leaving her all alone to run a trembling finger over her parted lips.

■ ■ ■ ■

Oh, Jamie . . .

Jamie went striding from the cottage, trying not to think about just how badly he
longed to hear those words on Emma's lips
again, this time ending on a breathless sigh
of pleasure or perhaps even a deep-throated
moan of surrender as he knelt between her
fair, freckled thighs and . . .

He bit back a groan of his own. His restless strides carried him to the very edge of
the rocky slope behind Muira's cottage. The
snow was still tumbling from the sky but
the brittle flecks of ice did little to cool his
fevered flesh. Despite the frigid bite of the
wind, all he could see was Emma peeling
off her damp garments and sinking into the
warm water just as he longed to sink into
her.

It was far too late to entertain such a foolish notion. He'd already waited a lifetime to
wrest what he wanted from the Hepburn
and now his time was running out.

If the Hepburn gave him what he wanted,
he would have no choice but to honor his
word and send Emma back to the front of
that abbey, where she would take the earl to
be her husband, her lord and master, and

the father of her babes.

His hands clenched into fists. He'd managed to convince himself long ago that there was only one thing the Hepburn possessed that he could not live without. He'd scorned the man's greed, his arrogance, his insatiable lust for power.

After all, why should he — Jamie Sinclair — envy an ancient pile of stones when he possessed something far more precious — his freedom? He wasn't caged by four walls, but slept beneath the star-spangled expanse of the sky, the entire mountain his kingdom. Why would he require a bevy of servants to be at his beck and call when he had loyal men willing to ride by his side for little more than the promise of companionship and adventure?

And yet here he stood coveting the Hepburn's proud and prickly tempered bride. Why couldn't she have been some spoiled, grasping creature willing to sell her succulent young body to the earl for a pair of diamond earbobs or a cloak trimmed in ermine? If she had been, he might not want her so badly for himself. He wouldn't be standing out there in the cold, every inch of his body burning so hot he could almost feel the snow melting beneath his boots. He might still be content with the sort of woman who would welcome him into her bed without requiring so much as a kiss, much less a lifelong pledge of devotion.

Almost as if his thoughts had conjured them from the swirling snow, a pair of warm female arms materialized to slip around his waist.

Jamie closed his eyes, allowing himself to imagine for the space of one heavy, thudding heartbeat he felt all the way to his groin that they were Emma's arms. That it was Emma who had braved the snow to seek out his company, fresh from her bath, her skin still damp and rosy, the irresistible softness of her breasts pressed against his back.

But it wasn't the intoxicating scent of rain-washed lilacs that tickled his nose. It was a hint of woodsmoke from the kitchen fire underlaid with the unmistakable musk of female desire.

He turned, his sigh visible in the frigid air. "You should get back in the cottage, Brigid, before you freeze your silly self to death."

The buxom servant girl twined her arms around his neck, laughing up at him. "Ah, but there's no danger o' that as long as ye're around, is there? As I recall, ye've yer own special way o' warmin' a lass."

Jamie groaned as one of her greedy little

hands ventured between them, rubbing the rigid length of his staff through the soft buckskin of his breeches.

"Oh my," she breathed, shooting him a coy look. "I told Gilda ye'd be eager to see me tonight. But I had no idea just *how* eager."

Jamie didn't have the heart to tell her he'd been *eager* ever since he'd tossed a certain willowy young English miss over the front of his saddle two days ago.

It seemed she wasn't in the mood for conversation anyway. She was too busy nuzzling his throat with her moist, hot lips and rubbing her plump breasts against his chest.

Jamie knew he'd be a bluidy fool not to hike up her skirts right there where they stood and take her up on her offer. Perhaps if he could relieve the unrelenting ache in his groin, he would be able to shunt some blood back to his brain. He'd be able to quell his growing obsession with another man's bride.

Biting off a savage oath, he wrapped his arms around Brigid and gave himself over fully to the ripe, open-mouthed carnality of her kiss.

Emma rested the back of her head against the rim of the tub and closed her eyes, letting the water melt the last of the chill from her bones. A delicious drowsiness stole over her as the lingering burn of the whisky in her belly mingled with the seductive warmth of the water lapping at her breasts.

The serving girls had left a clean rag, a ball of soap and a linen towel perched on the rim of the tub. Although the crude soap was no doubt made by Muira's own hands, Emma would have found it no more divine had it been French-milled in Paris and reeking of lavender. She had worked up a generous lather with it and taken her time scrubbing the grime of their journey from her skin and hair.

She sank even deeper into the water and listened to the wind whistling around the eaves, biting back a moan of pure pleasure. She knew she would have to emerge from the tub eventually. If she dallied too long, she was afraid Jamie might just come strolling back in and decide to join her.

Against her will, her wayward imagination conjured up an image of him sinking into the water as naked as on the day he was born, reaching to tug her into his arms with a wicked come-hither smile, his well-muscled body as wet and sleek as a seal's. A heat of another kind swept over her, tightening the rosy peaks of her breasts and making the fire in her belly snake lower until it settled into a dull ache between her thighs.

She sat straight up in the tub, her eyes flying open. Despite the brisk air caressing her cheeks, she suddenly felt feverish and cross. She pressed the back of her hand to her brow. Perhaps the exposure to the elements had been too much for her. Perhaps she was taking a fatal ague. She'd spent countless hours mooning over Lysander in the privacy of her bath — the only place she could escape her sisters' inquisitive eyes — but she'd never before been troubled by such disturbing visions. Even in her boldest fancies, Lysander had been garbed in the full regalia of a gentleman, his fashionable Hessians perfectly polished, his cravat flawlessly knotted. She'd never dared to imagine him doing anything more audacious than stealing an innocent kiss from her puckered lips.

She frowned. Now that she thought about it, she could hardly recall his face. Features that had once been incredibly dear to her eyes were nothing more than a vague blur. His curling hair no longer gleamed like gold in her memory, but seemed as pale and lifeless as corn husks. His perfectly modulated voice with its precise diction and crisp consonants sounded as tepid as a day-old cup of tea. There had been no hint of smoke in that voice, no echo of simmering passion to make a woman dream about more than just kisses when she was alone in her bath.

As that unsettling fever swept through her once again, Emma quickly clambered out of the tub, toweling herself dry with the rough linen. She was already dreading the prospect of trying to wriggle her way back into her clammy garments when she spotted the nightdress hanging on a nearby peg.

She drew the crisp, freshly laundered folds over her head. A stray gust of wind struck the window beneath the dormer, sending it banging open. Cold air flooded the room, pebbling Emma's damp skin with gooseflesh.

She rushed over to close the window but her fingers froze on the latch when she spotted the two figures locked in a torrid embrace at the edge of the slope below.

CHAPTER SIXTEEN

The snow seemed to cast a supernatural glow over the stony terrain behind the cottage, making it that much easier to spot Jamie in the arms of another woman.

The sight made Emma feel strangely hot, then cold — as if the icy flakes were no longer swirling outside the window but inside her heart.

As she watched, longing to avert her eyes but unable to look away, Brigid twined her arms even more tightly around Jamie's neck and tipped her head back to laugh up at him, her teeth a flash of white against her swarthy skin. Emma couldn't hear what the woman was saying, but when her hand glided downward and disappeared between the two of them, Jamie threw back his head and gritted his teeth, his expression only too easy to interpret.

It was the expression of a man in the throes of some sort of terrible, yet exquisite, pain. A man willing to do whatever it took to turn that pain into pleasure.

Pressing her advantage, Brigid nuzzled his throat and rubbed her breasts against the broad chest where Emma had so recently rested her head. Then Brigid's head fell back in wordless invitation, baring the graceful line of her throat. Emma squinted through the falling snow, almost willing to swear she saw Jamie hesitate. But it must have been nothing more than a trick of the spinning flakes and the ghostly light because the next thing she knew Jamie had wrapped his powerful arms around the woman and was devouring her lush mouth with a hunger that refused to be denied.

Resisting the urge to slam it with enough force to shatter the glass, Emma gently eased the window shut without a sound.

Brigid moaned against Jamie's lips, her voice deepening to a throaty purr, "Oh, Jamie . . ."

Jamie's eyes flew open. Even with Brigid's voluptuous curves in his arms, it was Emma's voice he heard sighing his name, Emma's eyes he saw shining up at him, Emma's lips he felt moving beneath his — parted and wet and hungry for his kiss. And for all the pleasures she would never know at the earl's hands.

Closing his hands around Brigid's upper arms, he set her gently — but firmly — away from him. "You'd best get back to the kitchen before your mistress finds you gone. It's been a very long journey and I'm wearier than I realized."

Brigid rested her hands on her hips, her eyes slowly narrowing. "Not too weary to cart that scrawny bag 'o bones up the stairs. Since the rain didn't do the job, I was rather hopin' ye were goin' to finish drownin' her in the tub."

If Brigid in the throes of lust was an impressive sight, Brigid in the throes of jealousy was even more magnificent. Jamie half-expected the buxom, raven-haired beauty to start hissing and spitting at him like some furious cat.

"Why don't you let me walk you back to the cottage?" he offered, hoping to distract her from clawing his eyes out.

"Don't trouble yerself overmuch on my behalf, sir," she snarled with mock sweetness. "I'm sure Angus or Malcolm won't be too weary to warm a bonny lass on such a cold night." She gave her curls a defiant toss. "Or Angus *and* Malcolm."

Eyeing the saucy twitch of her rump as she whirled around and went storming off toward the stables, Jamie shook his head and muttered, "God help the lads."

Unfortunately, he might be in even greater need of the Almighty's assistance. His brief encounter with Brigid had only succeeded in rendering him more *eager* than ever, sharpening the dull ache in his groin to an incessant throb that was as painful as it was impossible to ignore.

Still shaking his head, he started back toward the cottage, already cursing himself for being a bluidy fool.

When Jamie's knock failed to garner an answer, he gingerly pushed open the door of the bathing chamber to find Emma sitting in the ladder-backed chair, her hands folded primly in her lap.

Muira's billowing nightdress enveloped her slender curves. Her freckled face was still pink from the bath. A halo of damp ginger curls framed her face.

"Well, *that* certainly didn't take very long," she said, shooting him a vaguely contemptuous glance from beneath her lashes.

Studying the sulky bow of her mouth, Jamie frowned. When he'd left her, she'd appeared to be on the verge of throwing her arms around his neck and smothering his face with grateful kisses. Now she looked more inclined to hold his head under the cooling water in the tub until the bubbles stopped rising.

It seemed to be his night for infuriating women. At least he knew what he'd done to send Brigid stomping off in such a snit. Emma's sudden bout of ill temper was a complete mystery to him.

"I was hoping to leave you enough time to finish your bath," he said cautiously.

"How very generous of you to consider my needs before your own," she replied with a scornful sniff. "From what I understand, most men are only concerned with satisfying themselves. By any means necessary . . . especially the most convenient" — her delicate upper lip curled in a disdainful sneer — "or the most common."

Almost as if responding to her mood, the wind whining around the eaves surged to a howl. The window in the corner rattled in warning, then flew open with a bang, sending a dervish of icy wind and snow whirling through the room.

Jamie strode over to secure it, but paused with his hand on the faulty latch when his gaze fell on the stretch of ground below. The thin blanket of snow reflected every available scrap of light, including the gentle glow of the lamplight streaming through the kitchen windows, making the night seem as bright as dawn.

He glanced over his shoulder at Emma. She was still staring straight ahead, her delicate jaw squared. Her shoulders were rigid, her spine so stiff it wasn't even touching the back of the chair. A knowing smile began to steal over his face.

He eased the window shut, then sauntered back into her line of view, hiding his budding grin behind an exaggerated yawn. "I'm so spent I can barely keep my eyes open. I wager I'll sleep like a babe tonight."

"I dare say you will." She slanted him a look that made him glad he'd left his pistol belowstairs in his pack. "Sudden and violent exertion frequently has that effect."

He extended his arms in a mighty stretch, deliberately giving her a languid look from beneath his shuttered lids. "I don't think I can remember the last time I felt so turribly . . . drained."

The temperature in the room dropped another ten degrees, prompting him to steal a glance at the window to make sure the latch had not failed again.

"I'm surprised you still have the strength to speak. Much less stand."

As if in total agreement with her, he leaned against the tub, bracing his weight on its edge, and heaved a lusty sigh of contentment. "Aye, my legs are as weak as a newborn lamb's. I'd like nothing more than to just collapse."

"Well, by all means, don't let me stop you!" Springing to her feet, Emma gave his chest a surprisingly hearty shove, sending him teetering backward into the tub. He landed with an impressive splash, the water closing over his head.

When he surfaced, still sputtering with surprise, Emma was stalking toward the door as if she had every intention of marching all the way back down the mountain in her nightdress and bare feet.

Jamie struggled to his feet, his garments plastered to his body, and tossed his dripping hair out of his eyes. "And just where do you think you're going, lass?"

"To sleep with the hound on the hearth rug. I'm sure you won't have any trouble finding someone to share *your* bedroll. My companion will probably have better manners than yours, though. And fewer fleas."

Bracing one hand on its edge, Jamie vaulted out of the tub and caught up with her in two long strides. Without slowing his pace, he swept her into his arms and tossed her belly-down over his sodden shoulder.

"Put me down this instant, you overgrown

oaf!" she snapped, beating on his back with her small fists. "I'm tired of being hauled all over this godforsaken country like a sack of potatoes!"

Ignoring the furious scissoring of her feet, he carried her out the door, his water-logged boots squelching with each step. "I really wish I could be there when the earl discovers he's wed a wee wildcat instead of some mewling English kitten. In case no one has ever told you, lass, you're quite fetching when you're jealous."

She sucked in a scandalized gasp. "Jealous! Don't be ridiculous. Why would I be jealous just because I saw you pawing some slattern in the kitchen yard? Why, I'm not the least bit jealous! I'm relieved! Now that you have your very own trollop to satisfy your baser needs, you can stop finding ridiculous excuses to kiss me and put your hands all over me. And you can stop looking at me in that intolerably impertinent manner!"

Jamie addressed the shapely rump draped over his shoulder. "And just what manner would that be?"

"As if I were a fresh strawberries and cream trifle and you'd had nothing but bread and water for all your miserable life."

Jamie stopped in his tracks, his stillness so

complete Emma stopped kicking and pounding and simply hung limp over his shoulder like a side of mutton.

When he started forward again, his strides were even more determined. Muira's maidservant Gilda had just emerged from a chamber at the end of the corridor, her stout arms piled high with rumpled linens. As Jamie came barreling toward her, she let out a startled shriek and plastered herself to the wall.

Both of her chins quivering, she jerked her head toward the door. "The mistress had me lay a fire on the hearth. She says the puir wee lass can have her bed fer the night."

"Tell your mistress the puir wee lass and I are much obliged," Jamie replied, striding right past her and using his heel to kick the door shut in her astonished face.

He marched over to the bed and tossed Emma none too gently on her back in the middle of the heather-stuffed mattress. The dampness from his shirt had transferred itself to her nightdress, rendering the linen translucent. The fabric clung to the soft globes of her breasts, outlining the tantalizing thrust of her pert nipples with a diligence that made him want to lower his head and taste them with the tip of his tongue.

She blinked up at him like an upended turtle as he prowled over her on hands and knees until they were nose to nose, their lips only a breath away from meeting. "I can assure you, lass, that Brigid was more than willing to satisfy my 'baser needs.' But I didn't take her up on her offer. If I had, I'd be down there right now doing all the things to her that I so desperately want to do to you."

CHAPTER SEVENTEEN

Jamie's smoky growl made Emma shiver deep inside, in some dark secret place no man had ever touched.

She struggled to catch her breath, imprisoned by the seductive softness of the mattress beneath her and the muscular heat of the man above her.

He wanted her. Now that she'd driven him into confessing it, there was nowhere for either of them to hide from the truth. Not behind fruitless denials and petty bickering. Not behind his contempt for the earl and her loyalty to him. And certainly not within the cozy confines of Muira's bed.

Sharing the cold, hard ground with Jamie Sinclair was one thing. Sharing a bed with him was another matter entirely. With his weight poised so precariously above her, it was only too easy to understand just how seven strapping sons could have been sired in that bed, or how a man and a woman might best spend the bitterly cold Highland nights when the hours between sunset and dawn seemed as dark and endless as the winter.

Emma licked lips that had gone suddenly dry. "You're dripping on me."

Jamie waited until another drop of bath water splashed like a tear against her cheek, then leaned back on his heels. With his knees still straddling her hips, he peeled his soaked shirt off over his head and tossed it aside, revealing an alarming expanse of bare skin. The sculpted muscles of his chest glowed like bronze satin in the firelight. He used both hands to slick his wet hair back from his face. His unshaven jawline only served to emphasize the striking symmetry of his features.

He was a beautiful man. And a dangerous one.

His sodden breeches were clinging to his lean hips and powerful thighs like a second skin, giving Emma even less reason to doubt his words. She jerked her wide-eyed gaze back to his face, half afraid he was about to divest himself of the breeches as well.

"I'm doing it again, aren't I, lass? Looking at you as if you were a trifle made from fresh strawberries . . ." His hungry gaze caressed the vulnerable pout of her trembling lips, then rode slowly downward, taking in the pulse beating madly at the side of her throat, the uneven rise and fall of her breasts, the provocative way the damp fabric of the nightdress was clinging to the mound between her thighs. His burr deepened on a hoarse note. "And cream." His gaze drifted back up to her lips. "I suppose next I'll be trying to find another ridiculous excuse to kiss you."

"Such as?" she whispered, knowing even as she did so that her foolish challenge would not go unanswered.

He leaned down and touched his mouth lightly to her ear, his whisper a low-pitched vibration that made her shudder with desire. "Because I'm bluidy tired of bread and water."

Before her chest could hitch with another uneven breath, Jamie's mouth was on hers, devouring her lips with such delectable tenderness it was impossible to resist inviting him to partake even more deeply. Her arms went around his neck as his tongue parted the ripe softness of her lips, urging her to join the feast. Her tongue danced over the smoky velvet of his with a wanton hunger that shocked even her. This wasn't just a tantalizing taste of pleasure. It was a banquet for her starving senses.

His kiss made her crave delights she could not name. She yearned for something sweeter than honey and infinitely more filling than ambrosia. As she stroked her fingers through his damp hair, sweeping it into a veil of silk around their faces, he groaned deep in his throat.

If his mouth on hers had been pure bliss, there were no words to describe the moist heat of it gliding over the sensitive satin of her throat, nibbling at the tender swath of skin behind her ear, giving her earlobe a sharp nip, then turning her startled squeak into a gasp of raw pleasure by gently suckling the place he had nipped.

His mouth captured that gasp with another ravenous kiss, warning her that his appetites could never be satisfied by pressing his lips to a lady's wrist or stealing a chaste peck in some ballroom alcove.

Jamie Sinclair was no gentleman. He was a man.

Despite the ferocity of his kiss, his hand was irresistibly gentle as it closed over her breast through the damp fabric of the nightdress. He fit her softness to his broad palm as if she had been fashioned by God just for him. Any fears that he might find her lacking in comparison to the buxom Brigid were laid to rest by the reverent sigh he breathed into her mouth.

Emma had never dreamed such strong hands could be so gentle — or so nimble. Jamie tenderly brushed the callused pad of his thumb over the rigid bud of her nipple again and again, creating a friction so exquisite it was almost painful. She moaned and clenched her thighs together against a delicious little throb, his deft caress making her feel as if he was stroking her everywhere at once.

Taking her moan as one of invitation, Jamie lowered his weight, covering her fully. Although the snow continued to cascade past the bedchamber's darkened windowpane, it was impossible to believe she had ever been cold or that she ever would be again. Not with Jamie's arms to warm her, his tongue to kindle a scorching spark of desire in the depths of her mouth and his clever hands to stroke that spark into a living flame. That flame soared to dangerous heights when he used one knee to nudge her thighs apart and settled his hips between them.

He groaned into her mouth, warning her that if it wasn't for the rumpled folds of the nightdress and the wet buckskin of his breeches, he wouldn't just be on top of her; he would be inside her.

Lacing his fingers through hers, he gently imprisoned her hands on either side of her head. Bracing the weight of his upper body against their intertwined hands, he rocked between her legs in a rhythm new to her but as ancient as the mountains surrounding them. Waves of pleasure began to fan out from the tender cleft where his body sought to join with hers. She arched her hips, straining toward him instead of away.

As Emma trembled on the very precipice of something both terrifying and wondrous, she realized she was doing it again — bringing herself and her family to the brink of destruction just to satisfy her own selfish desires. Perhaps she really was one of those women her mother had spoken of with such contempt: a woman willing to sacrifice everything that was noble and proper and court ruin for nothing more than a few stolen moments of pleasure beneath a man's hand . . . a man's body. Yet even in that moment, she couldn't bring herself to feel ashamed. She was too breathless with longing to feel anything but exultation. Oddly enough it was that lack of shame, that overwhelming sense of *rightness* she felt in Jamie's arms, that shocked her into turning her face away from his kiss.

He immediately stilled, lifting his head to

gaze down at her.

Although all she wanted to do was weep with frustration, she forced herself to meet his wary gaze. "Please. This isn't what I want."

Even as she whispered the words, she knew he possessed the power to prove her a liar with nothing more than a nudge from his lean hips.

The grim set of his jaw couldn't hide the unspoken entreaty in his eyes. "There are things I could do to you, lass. Things I could do *for* you. Pleasures I could give you without compromising your innocence. He would never know. No one would ever know."

Despite that innocence, Emma understood what he was offering. But she also understood just how much it would cost them both.

"He might not know," she said softly, unable to keep the note of despair from creeping into her voice. "But I would."

Jamie continued to gaze down at her as if weighing her words. With his fingers laced through hers and her thighs splayed open in wanton abandon, she was his prisoner in every sense of the word. She could still feel every inch of his manhood — hot, hard and heavy — pressed against her throbbing flesh. Mercy was his to grant . . . or deny.

He rolled off her and to his feet in one abrupt motion, as if to linger would make such a feat impossible.

Emma had been wrong. She could be cold again. It was almost as if the snow drifting past the window was falling inside the room, casting a chill no fire could dispel.

Without looking at her, Jamie retrieved his wet shirt and shrugged it on over his broad shoulders. The cut of his breeches made it impossible for him to hide his unabated arousal.

As he strode to the door and swung it open, Emma scrambled to her knees in the middle of the bed. "Are you going to her?"

He stopped dead in the doorway but did not turn around. "No, Miss Marlowe," he finally said. "I'm going to finish my bath."

Although Emma sensed he would have liked nothing more than to slam the door hard enough to rattle the rafters, he pulled it shut behind him with painstaking care.

As his clipped footsteps faded, she flopped to her back among the rumpled bedclothes and gazed up at the ceiling, knowing she'd had no right to ask that question.

And even less right to be relieved by his answer.

■ ■ ■ ■

Emma emerged from the cottage the next morning to discover the spell that had so enchanted her upon their arrival had been broken. Sometime during the night, the rain had returned, washing away any lingering trace of snow or magic. It was no longer raining but clouds still hung low over the glen, casting a brooding shadow over the clearing.

She had expected to spend half the night tossing and turning after sending Jamie away, but she'd been seduced into sleep by exhaustion, the lingering effects of the whisky and the irresistible warmth of the patchwork quilts heaped high upon the bed. She had awakened to find a plain but serviceable merino gown and a pair of thick plaid stockings draped over the foot of the bed. Hoping rather spitefully that they didn't belong to Brigid, she had donned the garments and tugged on Bon's boots before making her way downstairs. When she found no one to greet her but the grizzled old hound, she had sliced a warm slab of bread from the freshly baked loaf sitting on the table, slathered it with creamy yellow butter and wandered outside, nibbling on her pilfered prize.

Although several of Jamie's men were already leading their mounts into the muddy yard, readying them for departure, their leader was nowhere in sight. She could not help but wonder if Jamie had come to regret his rash pledge to her. If he was even now still dozing in some cozy hayloft with a naked Brigid curled up in his arms.

Or not dozing, she thought, her appetite suddenly deserting her.

At that moment Angus — or it might have been Malcolm — came staggering into the yard with Malcolm — unless it was Angus — nearly trodding on his heels. Neither one of the twins looked as if they'd slept a wink. Angus was yawning and Malcolm's heavy-lidded eyes were at half-mast. Emma winced as Malcolm stumbled right into the back of another man's horse, earning himself a sound cursing from the man and narrowly avoiding a nervous kick from the horse.

The mystery of their lingering exhaustion was solved when Brigid came sashaying into the yard a few seconds later, a feline smile curving her lips and pieces of hay poking out of her tangled nest of curls. Her ample breasts were in even *more* danger of tumbling out of her half-unlaced bodice than they'd been the night before. Emma wolfed down the rest of the bread, her appetite miraculously restored.

The other men looked on in open amusement as Brigid wiggled her fingers at the twins. "Farewell, me sweet lads," she sang out. "I do hope ye can come again."

One of the men let out a bawdy hoot while the others burst into laughter. As she preened before her appreciative audience, Brigid's gloating gaze combed the yard. When she failed to find what — or whom — she was searching for, her gloating smile turned into a pout.

She sauntered over to where Bon was slipping a bridle over the head of his sorrel. "Ye can give yer cousin a message for me," she said, her voice loud enough to carry all the way down the mountain. "Tell him Angus and Malcolm are twice the mon he'll ever be."

Giving her curls a saucy toss, she continued on to the cottage, plainly aware that every man's gaze in that clearing was glued to the exaggerated roll of her shapely hips.

"Or one might argue it took two men to replace Jamie in the lass' . . . er . . . *affections*," Bon pointed out when she was gone, earning a fresh round of laughter from his companions.

Emma gingerly picked her way through

the mud to Bon's side. Giving his sorrel's sleek russet throat a shy stroke, she asked, "Have you seen Mr. Sinclair this morning?"

Returning his attention to his task, Bon jerked his head toward the mouth of a narrow path that wound away from the clearing and deeper into the forest. Emma frowned. Bon wasn't like the other men. It wasn't like him to avoid her eyes.

She was turning to follow the path when he muttered, "Mind yer step, lass. It can be treacherous out there."

Unsettled by his warning, she followed the winding path through the forest. The rain had banished the snow and now the wind was rapidly whisking away all traces of the rain. She had never known a place with such mercurial weather, but she supposed it suited the rugged character of the men who called this mountain their mistress.

After traveling a short distance, she swept aside the gnarled branch of a rowan and emerged from the thinning trees to find herself standing on a broad bluff. The windswept glen below might have looked barren and ugly were it not for the gauzy mist of purple just beginning to creep across its rock-strewn face. The breathtaking sight gave Emma a sharp pang in her heart, almost making her regret she wouldn't be around to see the heather in full bloom from that particular vantage point.

Jamie was perched on the edge of a large rock that bore a fanciful resemblance to the head of a sleeping lion, his sable hair blowing in the wind. His jaw was clean-shaven, making him look both younger and somehow less approachable.

He glanced up as she neared, the pen in his hand poised above the scrap of foolscap resting on a smaller rock he appeared to be using as a makeshift desk.

Emma's steps faltered. After watching Brigid return from her torrid tryst in the hayloft, she was only too keenly aware that if she hadn't banished Jamie from her bed last night, it could have been *her* curls in such wild disarray, *her* lips flushed and swollen from his kisses, *her* eyes misty with memories of the forbidden delights they had shared.

Given how they had parted, she wasn't expecting the warmest of welcomes, but Jamie's expression was even more guarded than Bon's had been. "Who told you where to find me?"

"Your cousin."

"I should have known," he muttered, dipping the nib of his pen into the bottle of ink resting beside his knee. "He's been meddling in my affairs since he was auld enough to crawl. He used to drop bugs into my cradle just to hear me yell."

"Did you decide it wasn't too late to write an ode to the gentleness of my temperament?" she ventured, nodding toward the paper.

He scrawled another line on the cheap paper. "You're probably surprised an uncivilized Scot can write at all. Or read."

"I assumed you wouldn't have been accepted at St. Andrews without passing some sort of proficiency exam."

"My grandfather taught me how to read and write English and Gaelic." He slanted her a mocking glance. "I taught myself Latin and French." He dipped his pen in the ink again, using it to make a bold stroke across the foolscap.

"And just where did you get all the books?"

"Oh, we didn't just steal gold, silver and cows. Whenever my grandfather got word that the Hepburn was expecting a new shipment of books for his library . . ." He trailed off, his devilish smile making it only too easy for her to imagine the rest.

"Well, at least you're putting the skills your grandfather taught you to good use."

His smile faded. "He wouldn't be very

happy with me at the moment if he knew I was using them to pen a ransom demand."

Emma suddenly felt as if he'd plunged the sharpened nib of the quill into her heart.

But she had no right to feel betrayed. It wasn't as if she hadn't known this moment would come. If anything, she should feel relieved. He was just fulfilling his vow to her, was he not? Once the earl delivered his ransom, Jamie would set her free. She would be free to return to the loving bosom of her family, free to resume her role as dutiful daughter and be the bride of a man she neither loved nor desired.

She could hardly reproach Jamie for looking *at* her when she talked instead of looking *through* her as her family tended to do. She couldn't scold him for making it clear he'd like to choke both her former fiancé and Lysander instead of blaming her for their shortcomings. She couldn't chide him for making her feel safe in his arms when he was the greatest threat her heart had ever known.

And she certainly couldn't hate him for making her believe — if only for one giddy, glorious moment while she had shared both his bed and his kiss — that she might be worth more to a man than silver or gold.

"So just how much am I worth to you?"

Jamie's pen stilled over the foolscap. A single drop of ink welled up from the nib of the pen, falling to spatter like a drop of fresh blood against the face of the paper.

Emma struggled to inject a note of false cheer into her voice. "Five hundred pounds? A thousand? My own father sold me for five thousand pounds so I'd urge you not to settle for anything less. I'm sure the earl would be willing to pay a very dear price indeed for the womb destined to bear his future sons."

Jamie's grip on the pen was so tight she was surprised it didn't snap in two. If not for the solitary muscle twitching steadily in his cheek, his profile could have been carved from the stony crags of the mountain towering above them.

When he finally turned to look at her, his piercing gaze cut straight to the quick of her heart. "You set far too low a price on yourself, Emmaline Marlowe."

Emma didn't realize she had ceased to breathe until he returned his gaze to the paper and she drew in a shuddering breath. He'd withdrawn his eyes from her a heartbeat too late to hide the flicker of emotion in their depths. Was it guilt? Regret? Longing? Whatever it was, it didn't stop him from scrawling his name across the bottom of the foolscap with a decisive flourish, sealing both of their fates.

He blew briefly on the page to dry the ink, then rolled the paper into a tube and secured a leather band around its length, his motions brisk and impersonal.

Graeme emerged from the trees, the boy's pace slowing when he saw Emma. He ducked his head, his gaze traveling shyly between the two of them. "Bon told me ye were lookin' fer me, sir."

Jamie rose and held out the scroll. "See that this is delivered into the earl's hands at the earliest opportunity. Wait for his answer and bring it to me without delay. We'll be waiting at the abbey ruins on the north face of the mountain."

Graeme accepted the missive from Jamie's hand. Tugging his spiky blond forelock, he offered Jamie a bashful bob. "Aye, sir. I'll do just what ye say. I'm yer mon, I am."

He bobbed twice more before rushing back toward the cottage clearing at a near sprint, plainly eager to prove he was worthy of Jamie's trust.

"So what do we do now?" Emma asked stiffly when the boy was gone.

"It won't take him long to get back down the mountain on his own. So we ride," Jamie replied, seizing her by the upper arm and hauling her toward the clearing as if to remind them both she would never be anything more to him than his prisoner.

When they returned to the clearing, Muira was waiting to whisk a sturdy cloak around Emma's shoulders.

The woman fastened the cloak's leather frog beneath Emma's chin, her plump fingers surprisingly efficient. "So glad to see the dress fits ye, lass. After shovin' out her fourth babe, me daughter-in-law never could quite wiggle back into it. Squealed like a sow the whole time the bairn was being born and has been eatin' like one ever since."

Emma tried not to shudder, thankful her mother hadn't made it to the rudiments of childbirth when instructing her in the duties of a wife.

After bidding Jamie a tearful farewell, Muira threw her arms around Emma, hugging her as if she was a long-lost daughter. Somewhat taken aback by the show of affection, Emma gently patted the old woman's back.

Only then did Muira whisper, "Never forget, lass, that a mon doesn't always need poetry to court a woman."

Emma glanced around to see if Jamie had

heard her but he had already mounted his horse and was holding out his hand in invitation. He wasted no time in tugging her up into the saddle behind him. As he urged the beast into motion, Emma twisted around in the saddle, surprised to find a lump in her throat as she watched Muira and her cozy cottage melt back into the woods.

Jamie ruthlessly drove them up the mountain until they could no longer outrun the gathering shadows of dusk. When a dark wood loomed up before them, those shadows threatened to engulf them completely.

The rest of the horses balked at the edge of the wood, leaving Jamie with no choice but to tug his mount to a prancing halt.

The horses milled about, tossing their heads and whickering nervously. The men sawed at the reins and fought to keep them from bolting, showing a bit too much white in their own eyes for Emma's comfort. The towering pines swayed and creaked in the wind, guarding the invisible entrance to the forest like enchanted sentinels planted there by some ancient king long forgotten by both time and history.

"Where are we?" Emma asked softly, tightening her grip on Jamie's waist as she abandoned all pretense of pride. It was almost as if they were about to cross some invisible boundary into a territory from which there might be no return.

"Nowhere of any consequence." His tones were terse but he briefly rested his big hand over both of hers as if seeking to soothe her fears.

Bon edged his sorrel toward them, still struggling to control the beast. The fitful shadows had robbed his face of color, leaving it pale and gaunt. "The lads don't want to go on, Jamie. They want to know if we can go 'round?"

"Not unless we want to add another two days to our journey. When Graeme returns with the earl's response, we have to be where he can find us but the Hepburn's men can't."

Bon stole a look over his shoulder at his companions, his Adam's apple bobbing in his skinny throat. "Ye can't blame them fer bein' sore affrighted. They've never forgotten what happened to Laren or Feandan."

Emma would have never taken Angus and Malcolm to be pious sorts, but at the mere mention of those names, both brothers signed a hasty cross on their breasts.

"No one ever found Feandan's body, only his horse," Jamie pointed out with a sigh.

"For all we know, he's in Edinburgh right now with his face buried in some barmaid's bosom. And Laren was a fanciful young fool who got spooked by his own shadow on a misty night and rode straight off a cliff."

The men exchanged uneasy glances, no more comforted by their leader's words than their horses were.

The commanding timbre in Jamie's voice deepened. "I'll be damned if I'm going to let some silly legend stand between us and what's on the other side of these woods. If you're not men enough to ride through them with me, then feel free to stay behind like a gaggle of superstitious auld women and wait for the Hepburn's men to come pick you off one by one."

He urged his horse through their ranks, forcing them to give way or be trampled. After a tense moment of hesitation, they began to wrestle their own mounts into submission and reluctantly fell in behind him.

They entered the forest in a single line, leaving behind the light of the rising moon for a dappled web of shadows. Emma shivered as a gust of wind danced past them, making the silvery leaves of the birches rattle like dry bones. It occurred to her that if these rugged men were afraid of whatever dwelled in these woods, then she might be wise to be afraid as well.

"What sort of legend were you talking about back there?" she asked, wishing she could see Jamie's face. "Just what exactly has your men so spooked?"

"The silly fools believe these woods are haunted."

Emma stole a glance at the ghostly white trunks of the surrounding trees, feeling a fresh tremor dance down her spine. "By whom?"

"My parents," he replied grimly.

Without another word, he gave the reins a sharp snap, urging their mount into a canter and driving them all deep into the very heart of the forest.

CHAPTER EIGHTEEN

"He's always refused to talk aboot it but I heard they was both found with their heads cleaved clean off."

"Well, I heard the blade of a single claymore was rammed right through both their hearts."

"What a lot o' piddle and nonsense! If that was true, then why would they still be wanderin' these woods with their bluidy heads tucked under their arms?"

Finishing off a tart chunk of cheese Muira had packed for their journey, Emma sidled closer to the circle of men seated around the fire, both appalled and transfixed by their gory gossip. A low-hanging mist was wending its way through the pale trunks of the birches that ringed the clearing. That same mist had forced Jamie to call a halt to their harrowing rush through the wood and order his men to make camp for the night. Despite their visible unease, they had complied with a minimum of grousing and grumbling. They might fear whatever haunted this wood but they also knew that to continue racing blindly through it would mean certain destruction for both their horses' legs and their own necks.

Their voices were hushed, with none of the jovial banter or ribald taunts that usually marked their conversation. Instead of competing to see which one of them would be the first to drink too much whisky and pass out, they took furtive sips from the earthenware jug being passed from hand to hand, as if they didn't wish to dull their wits on such a night.

Or in such a place.

As Malcolm — yes, Emma was quite sure it was Malcolm — cast a furtive glance over his shoulder, she could almost feel the damp, spectral fingers of the mist brushing the back of her own neck. She edged a few steps closer to the comforting glow of the campfire, inadvertently catching Bon's eye.

Giving her a snaggle-toothed grin, he patted the stretch of fallen log next to him. "Come join us, lass, before the bogles creep in and carry ye off."

"I'm afraid you're too late, sir. They already did," she retorted, drawing a chuckle from the other men.

When the fellow next to him failed to scoot over quickly enough to suit Bon, he earned a painful jab from Bon's bony elbow. Emma settled herself gingerly between the two men on the log, an effort that would have been impossible in a corset and heavy petticoats.

Bon pried the jug of whisky from Malcolm's hand and handed it to her. "Drink up, lass. 'Tis a good night fer a wee bit o' liquid courage."

Remembering her experience with Muira's whisky-laced tea, Emma took a tentative sip of the stuff. It seared a fiery path from her throat to her gullet. She sucked in a desperate breath, tears scorching her eyes.

Bon gave her a hearty clap on the back, dislodging the cough trapped in her throat. "No need to be ashamed, lass. Scots whisky is fine eno' to make even a grown mon weep with joy."

Emma had no choice but to nod, since she was still incapable of speech.

"Our mum told us Jamie's da was the jealous sort," Angus said, taking up their conversation right where they'd left off. "That he took the notion Jamie's ma was dallyin' with another mon and strangled her with his bare hands, then shot himself with his pistol."

Emma winced. When Jamie had strode off into the woods without a word of explanation shortly after they'd made camp, she had felt a ridiculous flare of alarm. Now she was almost relieved he wasn't here to listen to such terrible speculation about his own parents.

Angus leaned closer to the fire, sweeping his gaze around the circle of bug-eyed men. "They say some nights when the mist comes stealin' in from the moors, ye can still hear her beggin' him for mercy."

"Balderdash."

The voice came from just behind Emma, its crisp cadences cracking like a whip. She jumped, barely managing to bite back a startled shriek. Lemmy wasn't so lucky, which earned him a flurry of snickers from his companions. He ducked his big head, hiding his sheepish grin behind his untidy fall of hair.

Jamie slanted her a mocking glance as he came sauntering around the fire, making Emma wonder if he had been eavesdropping even longer than she had. The shadows from the firelight flickered over his features, making it impossible to tell if he was annoyed or amused to discover that she had once again been invited to join his men's ranks.

"I'm sure our guest appreciates a good yarn as much as the next lass," he told them, "but you should remember that Miss Marlowe's notions of entertainment are far more sophisticated than ours. She wasn't raised on gruesome tales of kelpies, goblins, baby-stealing bogles . . . or ghosts. You should take better care not to offend her delicate sensibilities."

As he moved to claim a low, flat rock on the opposite side of the fire, Emma said, "I can assure you I'm not so quick to take offense as you would have your men believe, Mr. Sinclair. Even Lancashire has its share of headless horsemen and white ladies."

Stretching his long, lean legs out before him, Jamie tilted his head to the side to survey her. "So you do believe in ghosts?"

"I most certainly do not. We *are* living in the Age of Reason after all. Science has judged most apparitions to be nothing more than the inevitable result of superstition and ignorance."

Of course she hadn't believed men like Jamie Sinclair still existed either until he had come riding into that abbey. It was almost as if he'd materialized from another age, an age where might was prized over manners and passion over propriety.

"Is the lass callin' us ig'nrant?" one of the

men demanded, looking more wounded than outraged.

Bon snorted. "If ye weren't so bluidy ig'nrant, ye'd know, wouldn't ye?"

"Perhaps a more apt word might be *unedu-cated,*" Emma said gently, extending the jug of whisky to the man as a peace offering. Before he could take it, an eerie cry splintered the night.

No amount of fine Scots whisky could have burned away the chill that shot down Emma's spine in that moment. For a tense eternity, there was no other sound except the fitful crackle of the fire and the echo of that unearthly cry. They all held their breath, scanning the shadows that surrounded them. Emma had to fight a treacherous urge to leap over the fire and into Jamie's arms.

"There's no need to wet your breeches, lads," he drawled, leaning back on one elbow. " 'Twas naught but a bird, or perhaps a wildcat. Now pass that jug over here before our wee Miss Marlowe drains it dry."

His men hastened to obey, more than one hand betraying a lingering tremor as the jug traveled their circle. When it arrived at Jamie's hand, he tipped it back and took a long, deep swig. His gaze met Emma's over the leaping flames of the fire, as if to deliberately remind her that his mouth was where hers had just been. And to remind her just how tender and persuasive that mouth could be.

He lowered the jug. "You might as well continue with your tales. You heard Miss Marlowe. She's not some nervous Nell afraid of her own shadow. I'm sure she's as eager to hear more of your gruesome gossip as I am."

Jamie's men took a sudden and keen interest in the cleanliness of their boots, looking as if they wished themselves anywhere else in the world — including the Hepburn's deepest dungeon.

Emma cleared her throat, the whisky giving her even more courage than she had anticipated. "It's been my experience that the only weapon strong enough to still the wagging tongues of gossips is the truth."

Jamie's eyes narrowed to frosty slits. She had allowed herself to forget — if only for a moment — that he just might be more dangerous than whatever was lurking in those woods. At least to her. "This isn't some Lancashire sewing circle or London drawing room, Miss Marlowe. Out here the truth can be a dangerous thing. It can even get you killed."

"Is that what happened to your mother?

Did the truth get her killed?"

The hush that had fallen after that eerie cry seemed like a cheerful hubbub compared to the silence that descended over them now. It was as if the night was holding its breath along with Jamie's men. Emma refused to relinquish Jamie's gaze.

When he finally spoke, his voice was soft but edged with reluctant admiration. "Apparently ghosts aren't the only things that don't frighten you. If my men were half so bold, we'd have routed the Hepburn long ago."

Emma swallowed, thankful he couldn't hear her heart hammering in her throat.

"If 'tis the truth you want, lass, then 'tis the truth you'll have." While his men exchanged shocked glances, he took another swig of the whisky, then wiped his mouth on the back of his hand. "When my mother, Lianna, was little more than a girl, she was out collecting mushrooms in a wood very much like this one when she met a bonny young stranger who had lost his way. Their flirtation was probably harmless enough until they both made the greatest mistake of their lives."

"What did they do?" Emma asked.

Jamie was gazing at her as if she was his only audience and his men were as insubstantial as the ribbons of mist curling around them. "They fell in love."

It was impossible to mistake the note of warning in his voice.

Emma shook her head. "I don't understand. Why was that such a terrible mistake?"

"Because they were born to be enemies, not lovers. She was the daughter of the last surviving Sinclair chieftain . . . and he was Gordon Hepburn, the only son and heir of the Hepburn."

A wave of shock rippled through Emma but it was clear from the bleak expressions on the faces of Jamie's men that they were already all too familiar with this chapter of the story.

Jamie went on in his hypnotic burr. "Every time she could escape her father's watchful eye, she would steal away to meet him. This went on until the inevitable happened . . . she realized she was with child."

"But . . . but . . ." Emma stammered, "wouldn't that make you —"

"A bastard." Jamie's glower warned her to tread with care. "And a Sinclair. Just like my mother."

Emma snapped her mouth shut, reeling with astonishment. She searched Jamie's face — his regal cheekbones, his strong blade of a nose with its lightly flared nostrils, the rugged planes of his jaw — but could find no trace of the wizened old man to whom she was promised. A man she now knew to be Jamie's paternal grandfather. For the first time she understood why their enmity was so personal . . . and so bitter.

"They both knew their fathers would be outraged if they discovered the truth," Jamie continued. "So they ran away together and set up house in a crofter's hut deep in the forest with only her loyal auld nurse to tend to them. They were determined to keep her safe and hidden from both their families until after the babe was born."

It was all too easy for Emma to imagine the two young lovers playing at domestic bliss in some cozy cottage, desperately trying to ignore the storm clouds gathering over all of their hopes.

"After the babe was born, they left him with the nurse, then set off down the mountain in the dark of night. Their plan was to elope, then come back, retrieve the babe and break the news to both their families after it was too late for them to be stopped. They truly believed their union would put an end to the feud between the Hepburns and the Sinclairs once and for all. That their love was strong enough to defeat the hatred between their clans."

Resting her chin on her hand, Emma sighed wistfully. "Such a romantic dream."

"Aye, it was." Jamie agreed, his voice so dispassionate he might have been talking about a pair of strangers. "But also a hopelessly naïve one. They died in a misty glen not far from here that very same night. They were found lying on the ground with their hands outstretched toward each other, yet still a fingersbreadth apart. She had taken a pistol ball to the heart. He was shot through the head."

Emma might have felt self-conscious about the tear she was forced to dash from her cheek if Malcolm hadn't tugged a grimy kerchief from his pocket and honked loudly into it before passing it to his brother.

"Who would do such a thing?" she whispered when she could speak again.

Jamie shrugged. "The Hepburns blamed the Sinclairs. The Sinclairs blamed the Hepburns. Accusations flew and the feud continued, more bitterly and violently than before."

"What happened to the poor ba—" She hesitated, knowing he was more likely to scorn her pity than appreciate it. "To *you?*"

"The Hepburn despised the very fact of my existence so my mother's father took me in and raised me as his own." Jamie's gaze traveled the circle of his men's rapt faces before returning to Emma. "So now you all know why there are some who say my parents' shades still drift through these woods, calling out to each other on misty nights. 'Tis still whispered they're doomed to wander this place where they died — together yet ever apart — until their murderer is revealed."

His words sent a fresh shiver dancing down Emma's spine. "Is that what you believe?"

"Of course not. As you pointed out so eloquently, Miss Marlowe," he said, lifting the jug of whisky to her in a mocking toast, "we live in the Age of Reason. And the Hepburn has certainly proved there are more turrible monsters to fear than ghosts."

It was far too easy for Emma to believe in ghosts — and even more sinister agents of darkness — while lying on her side in the middle of a strange wood and watching the mist come creeping out of the trees toward her. The spectral tendrils seemed to ripple and curl, weaving themselves into forms that were alien and yet all too recognizable — a hollow-eyed skull, a snarling wolf, a beckoning finger, inviting her to rise from her bedroll and come meet her doom.

She flung herself to her other side, starting to feel like some overly fanciful heroine from one of the Gothic novels Ernestine would sneak between the pages of her Bible when their mother wasn't looking.

She'd been kidnapped by a gang of Highland ruffians. She had far more substantial threats to fear than a pair of restless ghosts.

Like the man who still sat gazing into the dying flames of the fire, the empty jug of whisky dangling from his strong, tanned fingers.

Jamie's men had been snoring in their bedrolls for quite some time now, leaving him to face the night all alone. The flickering shadows played over his strong jaw and the stark planes beneath his cheekbones. Emma could not help but wonder what images he might be seeing in those waning flames.

Did he see the face of an innocent young girl foolish enough to trust her heart to a man born to be her enemy? Or did he see the wizened visage of the Hepburn — a vindictive old man who would deny his grandson's very existence before admitting his son had fallen in love with a Sinclair?

Was it truly a ransom Jamie was demanding from the Hepburn in exchange for her return? Or simply the inheritance that right-fully belonged to him?

And if the Hepburn refused him, would she be the one to pay the price? Would it be her body found in some deserted wood? Her ghost doomed to wander the misty night without even a lover to drift by its side?

Or would Jamie's revenge be even more diabolical?

This time, her shiver had nothing to do with ghosts and everything to do with the dangerous power a mortal man might wield over a woman. The breathless moments they had shared in Muira's bed had only given her a taste of that power. If he unleashed its full might against her, she wasn't sure her body — or her heart — would survive.

Yet here in this dark and forbidding wood, she was oddly comforted by the sight of him, by the knowledge that he was watching over them all. Her eyes began to drift shut as her weary body succumbed to exhaustion.

A shrill cry shattered the peaceful hush.

Unsure how long she had been dozing, Emma sat bolt upright, her every nerve jangling with alarm.

It was the same cry they had heard earlier, but closer this time. And there was no denying its chilling resemblance to a woman's scream. It sounded like the cry of a woman who was about to lose everything she held dear and could do nothing to stop it.

Emma pressed a hand to her thundering heart. She could still hear Jamie's men snoring, their sleep undisturbed. Wondering if the cry had simply been the echo from a nightmare she couldn't remember, Emma glanced over to see if Jamie had heard it.

The fire was deserted. Jamie was gone.

"Mr. Sinclair?" Emma whispered as she picked her way through the dense undergrowth surrounding their campsite. "Mr. Sinclair, are you out there?"

A silence as thick and cloying as the mist greeted her words. At least she hadn't been answered by that dreadful cry. If she had, she feared she would have leapt clear out of Bon's boots.

She brushed aside a curtain of tangled vines, venturing a few steps deeper into the forest. The mist drifted past her in a billowing veil of white, obscuring all but the most determined beams of moonlight. She couldn't have said what had possessed her to go after Jamie. She only knew she couldn't bear the thought of him wandering these woods where his parents had been murdered all alone.

She had no intention of straying very far from their camp. Glancing over her shoulder, she caught a comforting glimpse of the waning campfire through the trees.

A loud crack, like that of a boot snapping a branch, whipped her head back around. "Mr. Sinclair?" she called out softly, drifting forward with the mist. "Jamie?" she added in a hopeful whisper, the name as unbearably intimate as a caress on her lips.

The forest seemed to hold its breath, silent except for the quaking of the aspen leaves in the wind.

Wasn't she the one who had insisted to Jamie's men that they were living in the Age of Reason? She wasn't superstitious. Or ignorant. But even so, it was growing difficult to ignore the atmosphere of brooding menace that seemed to be deepening with each step she took.

What if these woods *were* cursed? What if that piteous cry had been nothing but a trap to lure some foolish wanderer to their doom? Hadn't Jamie and his men already lost two of their own comrades-in-arms beneath these very boughs?

From what his men had said, one had disappeared without a trace while the other had ridden his mount straight off a cliff.

Emma wondered just how many other unfortunate souls had vanished or perished in this place since that terrible night when Jamie's parents had been murdered.

She wondered if she would be next.

She did an abrupt about-face, deciding it would be wiser to return to the camp without Jamie than to risk letting her own fancies drive her over the edge of some cliff.

The campfire had vanished, its flickering light extinguished by a dense shroud of white. It was almost as if the mist had deliberately closed in behind her, making it impossible for her to retrace her steps.

Her heart skittered into an uneven rhythm. She briefly considered screaming but was half afraid of just exactly who — or what — might answer her cry for help.

She wove her way among the ghostly white trunks of a stand of birches, keenly aware of the irony of her situation. If Jamie returned to the camp to find her missing, he would assume she'd used the mist to stage another escape attempt. He would never believe she had been running *to* him instead of *away* from him. She could hardly believe it herself.

There was no need to panic, she told herself sternly. She couldn't have wandered very far in such a short time. She would simply start off in the most promising direction and soon arrive safely back at her bedroll.

Her plan seemed a sound one but after trudging past a towering clump of pines utterly indistinguishable from the clump of pines she had passed nearly a quarter of an hour ago, Emma finally had to admit she was hopelessly, irretrievably lost. The mist made it impossible to tell if she was wandering in circles only a stone's throw away from their camp or if each step was carrying her farther away from where she wanted to be.

Another twig cracked. She froze, holding her breath. Was it just her overwrought imagination or did she hear stealthy footfalls behind her, muted by the mist?

She had thought it a fearful thing to be alone in this forest. It was even more terrifying to realize she might not be alone after all.

Had the mist been this treacherous on the night Jamie's parents had died? Had someone come upon them without warning, catching them unawares? Or had they been stalked through the shadows, hunted like animals, their breath coming so fast it made their chests ache? Their panic would have grown with each frantic step until they finally turned to see that deadly pistol gripped in the hand of a ruthless stranger. Or even worse, in the hand of someone they trusted, someone they might even have loved. Someone determined to punish them for daring to believe their love could conquer centuries of hatred.

Almost as if conjured up by her bleak thoughts, a hazy shape seemed to separate itself from the pallid trunks of the birches just ahead of her. Was it another tendril of mist or a woman garbed in a flowing white gown? Emma blinked to clear her vision but the spectral figure continued to drift toward her, its mouth gaping open as if frozen forever in a mournful cry.

A piercing yowl that was all too real sounded practically in her ear. She whirled around to find a pair of malevolent yellow eyes glowing down at her out of the darkness.

A scream tore from her throat. Spinning sideways, she took off at a dead run, plunging blindly through the mist.

Jamie despised this place.

He would have gladly risked his neck and those of his men driving their horses through the wood at a dead gallop just so they wouldn't have to pass the night there.

But he wasn't willing to risk Emma's slender neck.

It was far too valuable to him.

He swept a drooping pine bough out of his way, knowing exactly where his determined steps were leading him. Neither the brooding shadows nor the creeping veil of mist slowed his pace. He could have found his destination on a moonless night while blindfolded. He had been halfway there earlier in the evening before forcing himself to turn around and return to camp.

Earlier he hadn't had half a jug of whisky burning a hole in his belly and Emma's bold questions echoing through his mind. It wasn't as if sleep would be possible anyway. Not here in this place and most certainly not with Emma sleeping only a few feet away from him in her bedroll, as sleepy and warm and ripe for the taking as she had been in Muira's bed.

His long strides didn't slow until he reached the bottom of a steep slope and emerged from the shelter of the trees. Here the mist hung low to the ground. The moonlight played gently over it, bathing the entire glen in an unearthly glow. It was the perfect place for two lovers to meet.

Or to die.

Jamie drifted forward. His grandfather had

brought him to this place for the first time when he was just a boy. He had knelt down and touched his fingers to the grass, his craggy face lined with pain as he described the night the bodies of Jamie's parents had been found in such detail Jamie had almost felt as if he had been there. He could almost see them splayed out on their backs in the grass, their eyes open wide yet unseeing, their bloodstained fingers ever reaching but never finding.

Jamie squatted down and touched his own fingers to the grass. One would think the ravages of twenty-seven years of sun and wind, rain and snow, would wash away every trace of tragedy. That there would be no lingering miasma of loss or grief poisoning the air.

Emma had been courageous enough to face him and demand the truth, yet he had offered her only lies. He did believe in ghosts. How could he not when they'd been haunting him for most of his life?

Despite that admission he felt no fear, only grim determination. Because he knew these woods weren't cursed. He was. It wasn't his parents who were doomed to wander this mountain until their murderer confessed his guilt.

It was him.

He had no fear of the mist drifting through the glen or of the shadows lurking beneath the trees or of the mysterious cries that pierced the night. His only fear was that he might fail them.

A bloodcurdling shriek echoed through the glen.

Jamie froze, the hair on the back of his neck standing straight up. That hadn't been the cry of a night bird or some woodland creature stalking its prey. It had been a woman's scream, hoarse and ripe with terror.

It took Jamie a numb moment to realize the scream hadn't come from the ground beneath his hand — ground that had once been soaked with his mother's blood — but from the line of trees behind him.

He rose and turned just in time to see a slender figure come flying out of the forest, heading straight for his arms.

CHAPTER NINETEEN

Emma came hurtling out of the woods, desperate to escape whatever was crashing through the underbrush behind her. Her relief at leaving the trees behind rapidly evaporated when she realized it would only be that much easier for her pursuer to run her to ground.

Gasping for breath, she threw a wild-eyed glance over her shoulder. Her foot snagged on a hillock, nearly sending her sprawling. She managed to recover her balance just in time to see a dark shape come looming out of the mist in front of her. Between one frantic footfall and the next she realized it wasn't some terrible specter with an hourglass in one bony claw and a scythe in the other, but Jamie himself.

Without an ounce of conscious thought, she threw herself at him. His arms closed around her, holding her fast. Unable to help herself, Emma buried her face in his chest and clung to him, quaking with a mixture of terror and relief. He smelled like woodsmoke and leather and everything that was warm and safe in a cold, scary world.

Rubbing her back as if his only purpose in life was to ease her violent trembling, he murmured, "There, there, lass. It's all right now. There's no need to be afraid. I've got you."

"Not for long," she mumbled through her chattering teeth. "Once the earl delivers your precious ransom, you'll have to return me."

His chest rumbled beneath her ear in a reluctant laugh. "If this was yet another escape attempt on your part, you really should give it up. You're bluidy turrible at it."

"I wasn't trying to escape this time. There was a ghost chasing me."

His big hand tenderly stroked her hair. "I thought you didn't believe in ghosts."

"So did I." She tipped back her head to meet his gaze, still fighting to steady her breathing. "But that was before one had the temerity to chase me."

Jamie gazed down at her for a long moment, his heavy-lidded gaze warning her that there were other things he'd much rather be doing with her in his arms than hunting ghosts. But he finally sighed and gently set her away from him, his watchful gaze scanning the line of trees bordering the glen.

Emma continued to clutch at his sleeve, fully prepared to leap back into his arms should it prove prudent to do so.

"There!" she cried, pointing toward the trees. "Don't you see it?" A fresh shudder raked her. "As long as I live, I shall never forget the sight of those horrible eyes glowing down at me from the shadows!"

As Jamie stared at the spot she indicated, a smile slowly began to curve his lips. "If it's a ghost, lass, then it's naught but the ghost of a wee wildcat."

Emma squinted. It took her a moment but she finally picked out the shadowy outline of a striped creature with phosphorescent eyes and pointed ears crouching at the very edge of the underbrush. Her mouth fell open. "Why, he's not much bigger than Mr. Winky!"

Jamie lifted a quizzical eyebrow.

"Mr. Winky is Elberta's tomcat," she hastened to explain. "He lost one of his eyes in a fight with one of the barn toms so he looks as if he's always flirting with you."

"You must have wandered into the wee lad's territory. They can be very dangerous but they don't usually trouble humans unless they're crossed. They're notoriously shy."

As if to prove his point, the wildcat gave them a haughty look before turning and slinking away without a sound.

Emma scowled at the place where he had been. "He certainly didn't seem very shy while he was chasing me. He seemed savage. And hungry." She shook her head, her terror melting to chagrin. "I can't believe I let him give me such a fright."

"You needn't feel like a fool. You're hardly the first person to mistake a wildcat's mating call for the wail of a banshee."

"I might not have been so quick to panic if I hadn't just seen —" She snapped her mouth shut. She wasn't about to tell him she had also seen an apparition melting out of the mist. An apparition that had borne an eerie resemblance to his murdered mother.

His smile faded. "Seen what?"

She shook her head. "Nothing of any import."

He studied her face. "If you weren't trying to escape, then just what were you doing?"

She inclined her head, hoping the milky moonlight wouldn't expose the flush she could feel creeping into her cheeks. "If you must know, I was looking for you."

"And just what did you intend to do with me once you found me?" he asked, his burr even more silky than usual.

He was so close she could feel the whisper of his breath stirring her hair. She took a few steps away from him, afraid he might be on the verge of pulling her back into his arms, and even more afraid that she would go.

She peered down the long, narrow glen, taking in their surroundings for the first time. The mist was thinner here, drifting close to the ground like ribbons of tattered lace.

"This is the place, isn't it?" she whispered, realization slowly dawning. "The place where your parents died?"

He didn't have to answer. His expression — or lack thereof — told her everything she needed to know.

While she had been out chasing imaginary ghosts, he had been here in this clearing facing real ones. One would have expected some ugly echo of rage or horror to linger at the scene of such tragic violence. But all Emma felt was an overwhelming sadness that made her heart feel heavy in her breast.

"This isn't the first time you've been here,

is it?" she asked him.

He shook his head. "My grandfather first brought me here when I was nine. Told me the whole tragic tale. He was the one who found them, you know, after Mags — my mother's auld nurse — told him they were headed down the mountain to elope on the night they disappeared. Poor Mags went half-mad with grief for a while after they were found."

Emma felt a flare of mingled pity and anger, imagining the boy Jamie had been standing in that exact same spot, his dark hair falling in his eyes as he was forced to relive the final desperate moments of his parents' lives. "What on earth was your grandfather thinking? Why would he lay such a heavy burden on such young shoulders?"

The corner of Jamie's mouth quirked in a smile that was both fond and rueful. "My grandfather is a harsh mon, but a fair one. He never believed in shying away from the truth, no matter how unpleasant. He knew the truth could kill you, you see, but he also knew it just might keep you alive. If I was going to have to dodge the Hepburn's arrows for the rest of my life, he wanted me to know why."

"Is there any chance they might have

271

simply stumbled upon some heartless band of robbers? Was anything of value missing when they were found?"

Jamie's eyes darkened. "Only one thing — the necklace my mother always wore. Her own mother had given it to her before she died and she was never seen without it. But it wasn't silver or gold. It was naught more than a worthless trinket smuggled out of the dungeons by one of our ancestors on the night the Hepburns captured the castle. It wouldn't have been of value to anyone but a Sinclair."

Emma paced away from him, so caught up in her pondering that she forgot she might be trampling the very spot where his parents had breathed their last. "Did anyone else know their secret besides the auld nurse? Could someone else have betrayed them? Someone who wanted the feud to go on?"

She turned to face Jamie. With the moonlight playing over its stoic planes, his face looked as if Michelangelo himself might have hewn it from a block of the finest Italian marble. She had never seen him look so beautiful . . . or so ruthless.

"Your grandfather believed the earl had something to do with their deaths, didn't he?" Her voice faded to a stunned whisper.

"And so do you."

"I know he would have rather seen his son dead than wed to a Sinclair."

"Do you honestly believe the earl could have murdered your mother — and his only son — in cold blood?"

"Had them murdered, more likely. The Hepburn always keeps someone around to do his dirty work for him." A bitter smile played around Jamie's lips. "He's been trying to rid himself of me since the day I was born. Trying to wipe out all evidence that his precious son was ever fool enough to love a filthy, no-good Sinclair."

If there had been a stump or even a particularly inviting stretch of grass available, Emma would have sank down on it just to give her unsteady knees some relief.

Jamie's vendetta against the Hepburn wasn't just about greed or even claiming an inheritance he believed he'd been denied. It never had been.

It was about justice. Retribution. Avenging the blood crying out from the very soil beneath their feet.

"If it was revenge you wanted, then why didn't you just shoot me in the abbey that day and be done with it?" she demanded, her heart already beginning to ache as if he had.

"He took something that belonged to me. So I took something that belonged to him."

It took Emma a dazed moment to realize he wasn't just talking about the earl taking his mother's life. "The necklace," she breathed. "You're not just after the man's gold, are you? You want the necklace. You want him to admit he was the one who had your parents murdered."

Jamie's silence was all the answer she needed. He had claimed the necklace was nothing but a trinket, worthless to anyone but a Sinclair. Which, she supposed, was not an exaggeration since he was willing to sacrifice everything — including her — to recover it.

"You must have waited your whole life for this chance. Why now?" She shook her head helplessly, the words spilling directly from her battered heart. "Why *me?*"

"If it had been up to my grandfather, I never would have come back to the Highlands. But when I did, I discovered that he was no longer strong enough to lead his own men. He's dying, you see. His time is running out. He's lived for twenty-seven years with half the people on this mountain still believing it was a Sinclair hand that committed those murders. I won't let him die with the shadow of that suspicion still hanging over him. I owe him that much, especially after all he's done for me."

"And if the earl agrees to give you this necklace in exchange for me, if he all but confesses to the murder of your parents, just what are you planning to do then?"

Jamie shrugged. "The authorities will never believe a Sinclair or arrest a Hepburn so I guess I'll take the necklace to my grandfather, then sit back and wait for the devil to come collect the Hepburn's rotten soul."

"Without any help from you?" Emma had never known it could hurt so much to laugh. "Do you honestly believe that?"

"I don't know." He scowled, still possessing enough grace to look sheepish.

She wrapped her arms around herself, her laughter dying on a broken note. She might have had a hope of competing with silver and gold, but she couldn't compete with this. No matter how desperately Jamie wanted her, he would always want the truth more. She would never be anything more to him than a pawn to be moved about the board at his discretion until he could capture the king.

For the first time, Jamie's stoic countenance showed signs of cracking. "The earl won't live forever, either, you know, and I refuse to let that bastard take his secrets to his grave. This may be my last chance to find out what happened in this place on that turrible night. Can't you understand that, lass?"

He reached for her but Emma backed away from him, no longer able to trick herself into believing there was any shelter or solace to be found in his arms. He was a far greater danger to her now than he had been when he stood in that abbey with a gun in his hand.

She should have heeded the warning he had tried to give her back at the campfire.

The truth really could kill you. Or at least break your heart.

"You were right all along, sir," she said coolly, squaring her chin to hide its trembling. "Your parents did make the greatest mistake of their lives when they fell in love."

Gathering her skirts, she turned and started back across the glen, deciding she would rather brave the ghosts drifting through those woods than the ones still lurking in Jamie's heart.

CHAPTER TWENTY

A furious howl echoed through the high-ceilinged corridors of Hepburn Castle. Doors came flying open with maids and footmen popping out of them like startled jack-in-the-boxes to see who — or what — was making such a tremendous racket.

As the dreadful din swelled, shattering the tense hush that had hung over the castle since the earl's fiancée had been abducted, the three Marlowe sisters came running in from the garden, their freckled faces flushed and their bonnets all askew. Their mother trailed after them, her pale face drawn with a heartbreaking mixture of terror and hope, while their father emerged from the conservatory, his cravat untied and a glass of half-finished port dangling from his unsteady hand.

Ian had spent most of the morning closeted in the library, reviewing the estate's account ledgers and avoiding the stricken eyes of Emma's family. When he heard the racket he came rushing into the corridor without bothering to snatch up his coat, even though he knew his uncle would most likely chide him for appearing in public in his shirtsleeves. Even if the castle was under attack or on fire.

Especially if the castle was under attack or on fire.

It turned out the only one under attack was the lanky lad being dragged through the cavernous entrance hall by a thick shock of his bright yellow hair. Silas Dockett, his uncle's gamekeeper, was the one doing the dragging. The boy had clamped his thin hands around the man's meaty wrist to lessen the pressure on his scalp. His booted heels tattooed out a desperate rhythm on the slick marble floor, fighting for purchase. A steady howl poured from his throat, punctuated by a blistering stream of curses questioning both the temperament and virtue of Dockett's mother.

Appalled by the casual violence of the scene, Ian fell into step behind the man. "Have you lost your wits, man? What in the devil do you think you're doing?"

Without missing a beat of his stride, Dockett drawled, "Package for the master."

By the time the gamekeeper reached the

earl's study, his curious followers had swelled to a virtual parade with Ian in the lead, several of the bolder servants and Emma's mother and sisters padding the middle and Emma's father bringing up the rear, staggering slightly.

Dockett didn't wait for the flustered footman standing at attention outside the door to announce him. He simply flung open the door with his free hand, dragged the boy across the study and dumped him in the middle of the priceless Aubusson carpet.

The boy scrambled to his knees, shooting Dockett a look of raw hatred and cursing him in a burr so thick most of the oaths were mercifully indecipherable.

Before he could climb the rest of the way to his feet, the gamekeeper gave the boy's ear a brutal cuff. The boy collapsed back to his knees, a fresh trickle of blood coursing down his rapidly swelling jaw.

"Mind that cheeky tongue o' yours, mate, or I'll cut it out for you, I will."

"That will be quite enough," Ian snapped, striding forward to place himself between the gamekeeper and his quarry.

Ian had never cared for the man. After the untimely death of his uncle's previous gamekeeper, the earl had returned from a trip to London with Dockett in tow. Ian suspected his uncle had plucked the hulking East Ender from the bowels of the London slums for the very qualities Ian most despised in him — brute strength, unquestioning devotion to whoever paid his salary and a sadistic penchant for cruelty. A sinister scar ran from just beneath his left eye to the top of his upper lip, drawing his mouth into a perpetual snarl.

Dockett gave Ian a look that left little doubt he would be just as pleased to cuff him bloody if the earl would allow it. But Ian coolly stood his ground and the man was forced to back away.

The earl rose from his chair, peering over the desk at the boy as if he were a piece of sheep's dung someone had scraped off the bottom of their shoe. "And just who is this upstanding young fellow?"

"I found 'im lurkin' outside the dovecote, m'lord," Dockett said. "Claims 'e 'as a message from Sinclair."

"Oh, my baby!" Mrs. Marlowe cried, clapping a hand to her ruffled bosom. "He's brought word of my lamb!"

She began to sway on her feet, going as white as a sheet. Two of the footmen lurking by the door rushed forward to shove a delicate Hepplewhite chair beneath her. As she collapsed into the chair, Ernestine began to fan her with the Gothic novel she had been reading in the garden while Emma's father drained what remained of his port in a single gulp.

"Well, don't just sit there bleeding all over my carpet, lad," the earl said. "If you've a message to deliver, then spit it out."

Ian stepped back as the boy staggered to his feet, plainly the worse for wear after Dockett's manhandling. Still glaring daggers at the gamekeeper, the lad swiped a smear of blood from the corner of his mouth with the back of his hand before tugging a rolled up and slightly battered piece of foolscap from the inside of his jacket.

The earl reached across the desk and plucked the missive from the boy's hand with two fingers, his upper lip curling with distaste. While he took his own sweet time retrieving a pair of steel-rimmed spectacles from his blotter and perching them on the tip of his nose, Mr. Marlowe rested a trembling hand on his wife's shoulder. Ian couldn't tell if he was doing it to comfort her or steady himself.

The earl used one yellowing fingernail to slide the leather band from the tube of paper. "Let's see just how much of my hard-earned gold the insolent lad plans to steal from me this time," he said, snapping the paper open with more than just a hint of unseemly glee.

Even from where he stood, Ian recognized the untidy scrawl. He'd seen it often enough on school assignments and on notes addressed to him, many of them containing private jokes and clever little sketches of their classmates designed to make him laugh.

As his uncle scanned the missive, an expectant hush fell over the room. The servants kept their eyes glued to the floor, thankful no one had remembered to order them to return to their duties. Mrs. Marlowe revived from her near swoon and rose to her feet, pressing a lace-trimmed handkerchief to her trembling lips. The Marlowe sisters huddled together in a nervous knot, their freckles standing out in stark relief against their fair skin.

Finally Ian could no longer bear the suspense. "What is it, my lord? How much is he demanding for her return?"

His uncle slowly lifted his head. A rusty sound rattled up from his throat. For one chilling moment, Ian thought it was a sob. Then it came again and Ian's blood ran even colder.

His uncle was laughing.

They all gaped in astonishment as the earl

collapsed into his chair, his papery cheeks growing even more sunken as he gasped for air.

Ian took an involuntary step toward the desk. "What is the meaning of this? Are his demands so outrageous?"

"I should say not," the earl replied. "They're perfectly reasonable . . . for a *mad-man!*" He pounded on the desk, crumpling the ransom demand in his fist and wheezing himself right into a fresh gale of laughter. "So the lad thinks he's canny enough to outwit me, does he? Well, we'll just see about that!"

Despite his uncle's unfettered amusement, there was a sparkle strangely akin to admiration in his eyes. Ian had never once seen that look in his uncle's eyes when his uncle looked at him. The man might deny his bastard grandson with his dying breath, but he also considered him that rarest of creatures in his Machiavellian mind — a worthy adversary.

"But my daughter, my lord?" Mr. Marlowe stepped forward, the beads of sweat on his brow betraying the effort it was taking to remain on his feet. "What's to become of her?"

The earl rose and came around the desk, still looking alarmingly amiable. "Have no fear, Marlowe. Young Emmaline is my concern now and I give you my word that I'll look after her. I don't want your wife or your other daughters to worry their pretty little heads about any of this." He beamed at the girls, who could not help brightening just a bit beneath the unexpected flattery. "Just continue to be patient and I'll make sure Sinclair gets what's coming to him. *Everything* that's coming to him."

Still murmuring a stream of soothing re-assurances, he somehow managed to use the sheer force of his will to steer the entire Marlowe family past the gawking servants and right out the door.

"Wot should I do with 'im?" Dockett gave the young messenger a wolfish look as if he could think of any number of possibilities, none of them pleasant or possibly even legal.

The earl waved an impatient hand. "Take him down to the old dungeon and lock him up. Both he and his master can cool their rash young heels for a day or two."

Before Ian could protest, Dockett started toward the boy, baring his teeth in a feral grin.

"Wait. Not you," the earl snapped. "I wish to have a word with you." He crooked one bony finger at the two footmen who had provided Mrs. Marlowe with her chair. "The two of you can take him."

The footmen exchanged another doubtful look. They were accustomed to being ordered to polish the silver or light the carriage lamps, not cart snarling lads off to a dungeon that hadn't been used in a hundred years.

At least not to their knowledge.

But obedience was as ingrained in them as deference to their betters so they finally shrugged and moved to seize the lad by his elbows. He put up a savage struggle, getting in a lick that would probably end up blacking one of the footman's eyes and bloodying the other's lip before they were able to muscle him out the door.

When the sounds of their struggle had faded, the earl swept his withering gaze over the remaining servants. "I'm not paying you to stand around and eavesdrop on matters that are none of your concern. Get back to your posts immediately before I dismiss the lot of you."

As they hastened to obey, bobbing a flurry of awkward curtsies and bows as they departed, the earl turned and gave Ian an expectant look.

Ian frowned, growing ever more bewildered by his uncle's peculiar behavior. He had made it clear from the first moment

Ian had set foot in Hepburn Castle that Ian would never be anything more to him than a burden and a disappointment. But that had never before stopped him from confiding in Ian or using Ian as an audience while he gloated over his latest triumph or plotted to avenge some petty slight, either real or imagined.

"You heard me," his uncle said coldly. "I have business with Mr. Dockett."

"But, my lord, I think we should discuss Miss Marlowe's situation and —"

"*Private* business."

Ian stood there for a moment, feeling as if the gilt hands of the ormolu clock on the mantel had somehow gone sweeping backward. He was once again a lonely ten-year-old boy, mourning his parents and desperate for a scrap of his uncle's affection, no matter how bitter or stale.

The clock chimed the half hour, breaking the spell and reminding him that he was no longer that boy. He was a man now. The man his uncle's indifference had made of him. It was his uncle who had taught him how to hate, but he was only now beginning to realize just how well he had learned that lesson.

His pride still stinging, he offered his uncle a curt bow and went stalking from the study. Before the footman could sweep the door shut, blocking the room from his view, Ian glanced over his shoulder and caught one last glimpse of Dockett standing in front of the desk, his beefy arms folded over his chest and a smug smile twisting his lips.

CHAPTER TWENTY-ONE

Jamie could hear the fuse attached to the legendary Sinclair temper smoldering in his head. It grew louder each day as they waited at the auld abbey ruins carved out of the stony hillside for Graeme to return with word from the Hepburn.

Jamie had spent a lifetime striving to master that temper, but he feared it was only a matter of time before that slow, steady hiss drowned out all patience and reason, resulting in an explosion that could destroy them all.

The last time he'd lost it, a man had ended up dead. Some might argue the man had needed killing, but no amount of justification could wash the stain of his blood from Jamie's hands. That stain had cost him his dearest friend and it would be there until the day he died.

He had spent the long hours waiting for the Hepburn's response prowling the crumbling ruins, his burning gaze searching the vale far below for any sign of an approaching rider. The morning of the fourth day found him simply sitting at the foot of a flight of stone stairs leading to nowhere, his stillness more ominous than the brooding underbellies of the clouds hovering over the mountain.

His men sought to relieve their tension by stuffing one of Angus' auld shirts with dead leaves, hanging it from a tree and using it as a target to practice their archery. Which wouldn't have been so distracting if they hadn't invited Emma to join them.

Jamie's eyes narrowed as her merry laughter rang out like one of the bells that had once graced this abbey. She'd barely spoken two words to him since following him to the glen where his parents had died but now she was grinning at Bon as if they'd been lifelong mates. It was impossible to tell if she was oblivious to the brewing storm or just didn't give a flying fig. Jamie suspected the latter.

She'd somehow managed to twist her rebellious copper curls into an untidy knot, exposing the graceful curve of her throat and the downy dip of her nape where Jamie longed to touch his lips. His eyes narrowed further as Bon put his wiry arms around her slender shoulders to help her nock the arrow and draw back the string. The arrow left the bow with a sprightly *zing,* sailing across the clearing to pierce the crooked heart Malcolm had traced on the chest of the target with berry juice.

The men set up a hearty cheer but it died in their throats when one of them glanced over his shoulder and saw Jamie watching them. Emma marched blithely over and wrenched the arrow from the target, a triumphant smile curving her lips.

She was probably wishing it were one of his shirts, Jamie thought grimly. And that he was wearing it.

He ran a weary hand over his jaw. It was no wonder his nerves were shot. It wasn't as if he'd been sleeping very well.

Or at all.

How was he supposed to sleep when Emma's bedroll was only a few feet from his own? He was too busy glowering at the back of her tousled head to sleep. Too busy remembering what it had felt like to pass that first night on the road with her nestled trustingly in his arms. Too busy reliving those magical moments in the cottage when she had twined her fingers through his hair and kissed him as if she was on the verge of letting him do all of the tender, wicked things he had been aching to do since the first moment he had laid eyes on her.

He hadn't even wasted his time trying to sleep last night. He had simply climbed to the top of a crumbling stone arch and spent the endless hours until dawn listening for the distant echo of hoofbeats.

Just like the ones that were now drowning out the steady hiss of the fuse in his head.

He surged to his feet, wondering if he'd dozed off into a dream. But the faint vibration of the rubble beneath his feet left little doubt that someone was coming. Emma glanced over at him, her smile fading.

He'd been waiting for this moment ever since his grandfather had taken him to that glen when he was nine years auld and shown him where his parents had been shot down in cold blood. So how was he to explain the sudden dread blunting the edges of his anticipation; the sinking sensation that finally getting what he had been waiting for just might cost him everything he had ever wanted?

A lone rider topped the edge of the bluff. Jamie's dread and anticipation had both been for naught. It wasn't Graeme returning with word from the Hepburn but simply the lookout Jamie had dispatched the previous night to scout the floor of the vale below.

Carson slid off his mount, his downcast eyes and the brief shake of his head telling Jamie everything he needed to know.

For a moment that seemed to hang suspended out of time, there was nothing but a white hot silence as the smoldering fuse finally reached the powder keg in Jamie's brain.

He exploded off the steps, pacing the length of the clearing in long, furious strides.

"Take cover, lads," he heard Bon murmur through the roaring in his ears. "Here we go."

"What in the bluidy hell does that miserable whoreson of a Hepburn think he's doing?" Raking a hand through his hair, Jamie wheeled around only a step before he would have crashed into a tree at full tilt. "Has the mon gone completely daft? Why would he be fool enough to leave his helpless bride in the hands of a band of desperate men, knowing full well that every second he delays they could be doing any number of *turrible* things to her?"

He went charging back across the clearing. His men had heeded Bon's warning and all retreated a step or two. Only Emma was bold enough to remain in his path, forcing him to either stop or trample right over her.

He jerked himself to a halt and stabbed a finger toward her chest, thankful to have found a target for his ire. "Why, look at you! You don't belong here! You're just a wee Sassenach lass without the good sense God gave a mushroom."

She blinked up at him, her dusky blue eyes strangely serene, the loose tendrils that had escaped her untidy knot of hair blowing gently in the breeze.

"You should never have been let out of your bedchamber without a nursemaid and a fully armed guard, much less out of England! Isn't your doting bridegroom the least bit worried about what might be happening to you right now? Why, if you were *my* woman . . ."

His words echoed through the ruins like a crack of spring thunder, followed by a silence so complete you could have heard a caterpillar inching its way across a leaf. A ridiculous wave of heat began to creep up Jamie's throat as he realized that not only Emma but everyone on that hillside was holding their collective breath, waiting for him to finish.

"What, Jamie?" Emma finally asked softly, her use of his Christian name stinging more than a slap. "If I were *your* woman, just what would you do?"

Unable to answer the bold challenge in her eyes, Jamie turned his back on her, turned his back on them all. He paced a few steps away to the edge of the bluff and stood with hands on hips, gazing off into the misty gray haze that hovered over the distant moors. That was when he heard a most unexpected sound behind him.

Emma was laughing.

He slowly pivoted to find his men retreating yet another step, as if they feared a fresh explosion of his temper, this one even more damaging than the last.

"Haven't you figured it out yet?" Emma asked, her eyes sparkling with tears. His men might mistake them for tears of mirth but he knew better. "The joke is on you. The earl wouldn't waste so much as a handful of shillings to save me. I have no value in his eyes. I was never anything more to him than an empty womb where he could plant his seed. And God only knows there are plenty of those for sale between here and London."

She shook her head, her husky ripple of laughter mocking them both. "You've tortured my poor family and dragged me halfway to hell and back for naught. He's *never* going to give you what you want. He doesn't care what you do to me. So there's no longer any need for you to play the gentleman." This time it was her turn to close the distance between them. Stopping so close he could see the agitated pulse fluttering in the creamy column of her throat, the enticing quiver of her bottom lip, she tipped back her head to look him in the eye. "So go ahead, Jamie Sinclair. *Do your worst.*"

For one dark moment, Jamie was tempted to do just that. Tempted to seize her by the hand and haul her deep into those ruins where he could show her just exactly what he would do if she were his woman.

Everything he would do if she were his woman.

"Jamie?" Bon's voice was barely a whisper.

Jamie continued to gaze down into Emma's eyes, transfixed by the unforeseen power of her passion.

"Jamie?" Bon repeated, more urgently this time.

"What in the bluidy hell do you —" Jamie swung around just in time to see Graeme come staggering out of the trees on foot.

CHAPTER TWENTY-TWO

Graeme was clasping his ribs in a white-knuckled grip. One of the boy's eyes was swollen shut and an ugly bruise, already beginning to yellow around the edges, stained his clenched jaw.

Several of the men rushed to aid him but it was Jamie who reached him first. He slipped an arm around Graeme's shoulders just as the boy's legs began to crumple beneath him.

"Would've been here sooner . . ." he rasped out, leaning heavily against Jamie's chest. "Damn horse threw a shoe a few leagues back."

As his men gathered around them, Jamie eased Graeme to a reclining position on the ground, stricken by guilt. He should have known Hepburn wouldn't have any qualms about shooting the messenger. He should have sent Bon — someone who was as crafty as the Hepburn, someone who wouldn't have underestimated the auld buzzard's potential for treachery.

"What did those bastards do to you?" Jamie demanded, wincing along with Graeme as he ran a careful hand over the boy's battered ribcage.

"Nothin' I won't survive." Graeme grinned up at him, his split lip giving his smile a rakish tilt. "Got in a few good licks meself, I did. Made those fancy footmen o' the earl's think twice aboot knockin' heads with Graeme MacGregor." Reaching inside his jacket, Graeme tugged out a leather pouch, his hand trembling ever so slightly. "I did just what ye said, Jamie. I gave the Hepburn yer letter and he said to give this to ye."

Jamie accepted the offering, managing a pained smile of his own. "You did us all proud, lad. Especially me."

As Jamie rose, Lemmy dropped down to take his place, tugging Graeme's head into his lap with a gentleness that should have been impossible for his enormous hands.

Jamie gazed down at the Hepburn's missive. No cheap foolscap this but a thick sheet of creamy vellum, folded into perfect thirds and sealed with a daub of crimson wax bearing the Hepburn's crest.

He broke the seal and carefully unfolded

the paper beneath the watchful eyes of his men.

Even though he'd never learned to read, Bon bounced up and down on his tiptoes in a desperate attempt to see over his shoulder. "Don't leave us danglin', lad. What does it say?"

It didn't take Jamie long to scan the handful of curt words scrawled on the paper. He refolded it with painstaking care. He had imagined this moment for so long, had anticipated the dizzying rush of triumph he would feel.

But as he lifted his eyes to meet Emma's questioning gaze, he felt nothing but a piercing stab of regret. "He's agreed to our demands. The ransom is to be delivered on the morrow."

He only managed to hold Emma's gaze for an elusive moment before she turned and disappeared into the ruins without a word.

Emma sat at the edge of the round stone platform that had once housed the old bell tower of the abbey, hugging one knee to her chest. The roof and most of the walls of the structure had collapsed long ago, leaving the platform open to the sky and reachable only by a flight of narrow stone stairs worn nearly smooth by rain and time.

The wind that usually raged so passionately over this mountain had subsided to a mild breeze that sighed against her cheek and toyed with the loose tendrils of hair at her nape. The moon hung over the uppermost peak of the mountain like a glowing pearl, twice the size it had been in Lancashire yet still far beyond her reach.

A loose pebble went skittering off the far edge of the platform.

She turned, unable to stop a treacherous surge of hope from leaping in her heart. But it was only Bon who emerged from the shadows at the top of the stairs. He hovered at the fringes of the moonlight, plainly uncertain of his welcome.

"Don't worry, Bon. It's safe," she assured him. "I'm not armed."

He moved to stand beside her, his snaggletoothed grin no longer menacing to her eyes but winsome. "The way ye were handlin' that bow today, I'd wager a man's heart will never be entirely safe as long as ye're around."

"Perhaps that's why your cousin is so eager to be rid of me," Emma replied lightly, hoping to hide the bitter edge in her voice. "Why aren't you down there celebrating with him? He must be beside himself with joy. After all, the earl is about to give him his heart's desire."

"He still won't tell me or any o' the lads what that is. And it's not like Jamie to keep secrets from me."

"This may be the first time he's ever had one worth keeping."

"We wouldn't begrudge him nothin' he wanted," Bon admitted. "He's sacrificed too much for us. He's allus been a canny lad, ye know, haulin' around books he was barely big enough to carry. He could have stayed down there in the Lowlands and made his own fortune like a proper gent. But when he heard his grandfather was ailin', he came back here. To take care o' us. To take care o' everyone on this mountain who've always depended upon the Sinclairs for their survival." Bon hesitated as if he longed to say something else. Something more. But he finally just ducked his head, gazing down at his feet. "I just come to tell ye I'm sorry we ruined yer wedding. And I hope ye and the earl will be" — he cleared his throat, plainly struggling to choke out the words — "verra happy together."

"Thank you," Emma whispered, the sudden tightness of her own throat making it impossible for her to offer him any other absolution.

After he had made his way back down the stairs, leaving her alone, she turned her face back to the moon only to find it shimmering behind a watery veil. The girl who had gazed upon that same moon from her bedchamber window as it drifted over her father's orchard seemed like a stranger to her now — a naïve child who had believed a man's quality could be measured by the eloquence of his speech or the fine cut of his coat.

How was she to accompany the earl's men back down that mountain on the morrow and pretend she was still that girl, who had never tasted Jamie's kiss, never felt her body begin to melt beneath the smoldering heat of his desire for her? How could she be content with jewels and furs and gold or even a nursery full of children conceived not out of love or passion but desperation and duty?

After feeling her body and her heart come alive beneath Jamie's touch, how would it be possible to lie night after night in long-suffering silence with the earl grunting and heaving on top of her, her teeth clenched to keep from screaming? Especially now that she knew he might not be a kindly old man after all but a murderer, ruthless enough to cut down his own son for daring to love the wrong woman.

She blinked back her tears, bringing the moon into crisp focus. She *wasn't* the same girl she had been and she would never be that girl again. No matter the cost, she was no longer willing to deny her own passions, her own desires, simply to preserve the peace of those around her. Her mother had spent Emma's entire life living just such a lie, sacrificing her own happiness so she could go on making excuses for Emma's papa.

But she was not her mother. And she was no longer the girl who had stood before that altar in the abbey of Hepburn Castle, prepared to pledge her heart to a man she would never love.

All she needed was someone to help her prove it.

Jamie braced both his hands against the rough stone of the abbey's altar. That single stone had somehow survived the devastation of battle and years of neglect, proving there were some things even time could not destroy.

He wondered how many christenings it had seen, how many weddings, how many burials. How many lives had begun there? How many had ended?

The small church had been a ruin for as long as he could remember, no doubt destroyed in one of the many wars and skirmishes that had left their scars on this rugged and beautiful land. Even though it had been reduced to little more than roofless walls and moss-covered rubble, an air of dignity still hung over the place, as if neither God nor time had forgotten this had once been holy ground.

He ran his hands over the pocked stone, wishing he had the words to express the tumult he was feeling. Although he'd always been a believing man, he'd never been a praying one. He'd assumed it would be best if he and the Almighty didn't discuss their differences of opinion.

For how could God claim vengeance was His when Jamie could feel the weight of it resting so heavily on his own shoulders? They'd always been strong enough to bear that burden in the past but now he felt as if it was dangerously close to crushing his heart. Tomorrow he would send Emma down the mountain. He would never again sleep with her warm body tucked into the shelter of his own. Never again hear his name on her lips. In a few days she would be standing before an altar just like this one, preparing once again to become the Hepburn's bride.

He dug his fingertips into the stone, wishing he could smash the altar to rubble with his bare hands.

"Jamie?"

At first he thought he had imagined that melodic whisper of sound, that it was nothing more than a product of his own feverish longings.

Relinquishing his grip on the altar, he slowly turned.

Emma stood there at the edge of the moonlight like the ghost of all the brides who had come to this place to pledge their hearts to the men they loved.

"What do you want?" he asked hoarsely, no longer able to pretend her answer didn't matter to him.

She lifted her chin, her gaze as cool and steady as it had been on the night she had pointed his own pistol at his heart. "I want you to ruin me."

CHAPTER TWENTY-THREE

Swallowing her trepidation, Emma drifted toward Jamie, exposing herself fully to the moonlight and his burning gaze. In that moment he looked like every virgin's worst nightmare — desperate and dangerous and only to be approached with tremendous caution, if at all.

"I've always been a very good girl," she said, each measured step carrying her closer to him, "and a dutiful daughter — the one who was always called upon to set the example for my younger sisters. It was always 'Yes, sir' and 'No, ma'am' and 'As you wish.' I wore what my mother selected for me. I ate everything that was put in front of me, whether I liked it or not. I went everywhere I was told to go and did everything they asked of me." She stopped just out of Jamie's reach. "But I will not marry the earl. And you and I both know there's only one sure way to convince him I'm no longer fit to be his bride."

Jamie didn't say a word. He just continued to gaze at her, his expression as unreadable as the petrified pages of the Holy Bible moldering in the corner.

She managed an awkward laugh. "Bon was right all along, wasn't he? I know you've convinced yourself you'd have to be content with proving the Hepburn murdered your parents. But wouldn't your vengeance be even more satisfying if you returned his bride to him having been ravished by a Sinclair? Especially a Sinclair who just happens to be his bastard grandson."

"More satisfying for me, certainly." Jamie folded his arms over his chest, the smoky heat of his gaze making her shiver somewhere deep inside. "What about that ramshackle manor house in Lancashire you love so well? If the earl demands his settlement back, how will your father keep his creditors from seizing the house and tossing the lot of you in the poorhouse?"

"I'm confident the earl will graciously insist he keep the settlement. Especially if he doesn't want everyone in London to learn that he's suspected of having his own son — and the mother of his grandson — murdered in cold blood."

Jamie cocked his head, eyeing her with

reluctant admiration. "I never would have guessed such a bonny face could hide such a ruthless streak."

She flashed him a bitter smile. "Since coming to the Highlands I've had the opportunity to learn from the best."

"Your home may be spared and your father may avoid debtor's prison but have you thought about the consequences you'll suffer once you return to England with your family?" Jamie moved forward to circle her while he spoke, his husky burr weaving a web she no longer had any desire to escape. "The earl has a tongue like a viper. Rather than let anyone believe he was fool enough to let his young bride be stolen out from under his nose, he'll start spreading rumors that you went into my arms — and my bed — willingly. And even if he doesn't, it won't matter to society if you were seduced or raped. The shadow your first fiancé cast over your reputation will be nothing compared to this. Decent folk will turn their heads when you walk by in the street. No one will receive you. You'll be a social pariah and you'll be giving up all hope of ever finding a husband or having a family of your own."

"Then I'll be free to return to Lancashire and live out my life in peace." She faced him, giving her curls a bold toss. "If I get bored, I can always take a strapping young lover. Or two."

He saw right through her bravado, just as he had the first time she had said those words. He reached up to trace the delicate curve of her jaw with the backs of his knuckles, his voice even more gentle than his touch. "There are other considerations, lass. What if I should put my babe inside you?"

Emma didn't bother ducking her head to hide the blush she could feel creeping over her cheekbones. She knew it was no use. "You may find me distressingly naïve but thanks to my mother's tutelage I'm not completely ignorant of the ways of the world. Or of men. If there weren't ways to prevent such things, then there would be more by-blows than legitimate heirs walking the streets of London."

He nodded, conceding her point. "So you truly believe this is the only way to keep the Hepburn's lecherous hands off you? To make sure you're free to live out your life as the mistress of your own fate?"

She nodded, her voice finally deserting her now that her courage was spent. There were a thousand other reasons for going to his bed that she might have confessed to him in that moment had pride not stilled her tongue. She could have told him she wanted to feel alive at least one more time before burying herself beneath the crushing censure of society. That she didn't think she would survive spending the rest of her life alone without first spending one night in his arms.

"Then what choice do I have?" He leaned down, his lips grazing hers like the brush of angel wings.

Emma's breath caught in her throat. How was it that she could feel more like a bride standing here in this crumbling ruin of a church than she had ever felt in the Hepburn's majestic abbey?

"Wait here," he whispered, drawing away from her with palpable reluctance.

She waited in an agony of suspense until he returned with the blankets from her bedroll draped over one arm. This time when he took her hand, she went with him willingly. As he led her out of the moonlight and into the shadows, she laced her fingers tightly through his, not wanting him to know she was quaking all the way down to her toes.

He led her to the corner of a small chamber where two walls still stood, defying the ravages of time. They had set up camp in the trees bordering the bluff so Emma knew

Jamie had deliberately chosen this spot to protect her from his men's prying eyes.

But before he could spread out the blankets, she grabbed his arm. "Wait!"

He eyed her warily, plainly fearing she had changed her mind.

She inclined her head toward the crooked stone arch that had once housed a door, indicating that it was his turn to follow her. Judging by the look in his eye, he would have followed her to the very ends of the earth.

They climbed those worn stone steps to the old bell tower, emerging in a misty pool of moonlight. She took the blankets from Jamie and spread them out in the center of the tower, leaving only the sky and the moon to witness what was about to happen.

When she was done she faced him, feeling impossibly shy. "So what's it to be, Mr. Sinclair? Do you plan to seduce me or ravish me?"

His lazy grin made her heart double its rhythm. "Both."

He drew her against him, surprising her anew with his size, his strength, his irresistible heat. For a long moment, he simply held her, letting her grow accustomed to the feel of his arms around her, the whisper of his breath in her hair. She rested her cheek against his chest, feeling each shuddering beat of his heart as if it were her own. After a moment, she grew bolder, slipping her hands around his waist and beneath his shirt, marveling at the smoothness of his skin, the supple flex of the muscles beneath her palms as he lifted one hand to stroke her hair.

"Oh, dear," she mumbled, suddenly overwhelmed by the magnitude of what she was about to do with this man.

"What is it?"

She kept her face buried in his chest. "My mother's instructions seem to have deserted me. I'm not entirely sure how we should proceed from here."

"Why don't you leave that to me?" he murmured, tipping her chin up with one finger and lowering his mouth to hers.

He gently feathered his lips over hers, his undeniable expertise leaving little doubt that he knew *exactly* how to proceed. He didn't kiss like a man who considered it simply a means to an end — some sort of quaint ritual required by females to coax them into taking off their clothes. He kissed her slowly and with exquisite deliberation, as if he would be content to spend all night just making love to her mouth.

She had always scorned women who

swooned at the slightest provocation, but the tender flick of his tongue over hers left her so breathless and dizzy that she felt her knees go weak and her ears begin to ring as if there were still bells in the tower. She might have succumbed to the temptation but she didn't want to miss a moment in Jamie's arms. So she simply closed her eyes and hung on, tasting his tongue with her own until she heard a groan rumble up from deep in his throat.

When her eyes finally fluttered open, she was surprised to find them both on their knees in the middle of the blankets. Perhaps Jamie's legs had failed him as well.

"That went very well indeed," she murmured, sighing against his lips. "What would you suggest we do next?"

He leaned back to survey her face, his expression disarmingly earnest. "I thought we'd both take off all our clothes."

Apparently she had been wrong about the kiss. "But . . . but . . . then we'd both be . . . unclothed."

He pondered her words for a moment. "Well, if you'd like, you could just take off *your* clothes. I could keep mine on . . . for now."

Emma eyed him, growing increasingly suspicious. "My mother never said a word

312

about disrobing. I think I would have remembered that."

It was Jamie's turn to sigh. "Just what did she tell you?"

"She said I was to lie back and close my eyes and the earl" — Emma could not quite suppress her shudder — "my *husband* would simply fold the hem of my nightdress up a few inches — after the lamps were extinguished, of course — and perform his husbandly duty."

"While the idea has its charms, it simply won't do." The callused pads of Jamie's fingertips played lightly over her sensitive nape. He lowered his voice to a husky growl, his breath moist and hot in her ear. "Because I'm going to go mad, lass, if I can't see you naked."

This time Emma's shudder was one of desire. "Perhaps you could coax me into taking my gown off. If you put forth your best effort."

His throaty chuckle warned her that was just the challenge for which he had been waiting. Lifting the weight of her hair with one hand, he ever so gently laid his seeking lips against the wildly beating pulse at the side of her throat. Emma gasped. Judging by the scorching sweetness of his lips against her flesh, it must be his intention to *melt* the gown from her body.

Her head fell back of its own volition, giving his mouth full dominion over the graceful column of her throat. After a few breathless moments of that delicious torment, she was forced to dig her fingernails into his sleeve just to remain upright. "For a brutish Highlander, you've a rather persuasive touch, sir."

"Those fancy English gents are the ones who start all those nasty rumors about us and our sheep. They just don't want their lasses to know what they're missing."

As his tongue swirled around the delicate shell of her ear, making her toes curl with pleasure, she bit back a moan. "Maybe they don't want their sheep to know what *they're* missing."

Jamie's laugh was a deep-throated rumble that warmed her from the inside out. While his mouth was having its way with her ear, his hands were gently easing her gown down to bare one creamy shoulder. Emma was ever so grateful to Muira for gifting her with such a simple gown, not one adorned with slippery pearl buttons or rows of sharp, steely hooks. Or painful stays to contain flesh already aching for Jamie's touch.

All it took was a deliberate tug and one of her breasts was freed from the confines of the bodice. Jamie gazed down at her in the moonlight, his expression so dark with hunger it made both her pulse and her stomach flutter. She could feel her nipples begin to swell and throb in anticipation of the pleasure she sensed was coming.

That pleasure arrived with a jolt of pure sensation when Jamie leaned down and touched the very tip of his tongue to her. As he laved that pebbled peak with maddening tenderness, then drew it into his mouth, suckling deep and hard, Emma could no longer bite back a moan of raw delight.

She moaned again when he dipped his hand into the other side of her bodice and claimed that breast for his own as well, molding it to his palm and gently squeezing.

How was it possible a man could be possessed of so many hands? One of them had taken advantage of her breathless distraction to work its way beneath her skirt. Even now it was sliding between her knees and up, up, up until it brushed the silky curls between her thighs.

As Jamie closed his hand over her as if she no longer belonged to herself, but to him, Emma shook her head, nearly mute with shock. "But my mother never —"

Jamie withdrew his other hand from her

bodice to lay it over her mouth, his eyes sparkling with amusement. "Would it be possible for you not to mention your mother again, sweeting? During lovemaking most men find that something of a . . . distraction."

As he removed his hand, Emma laughed. "You'd have found her instructions for discouraging a woman's husband from seeking her company in the bedchamber even more . . . distracting."

Jamie surprised her by leaning down and kissing the very tip of her nose before lowering his mouth to hers once again. His lips slanted over hers, encouraging her to open wider for him, to welcome him deeper as his tongue began to take her mouth in a rhythm that was both carnal and irresistible. Before long they were breathing as one, her every sigh becoming one with his own.

Only then did his seeking fingers breach those curls between her thighs, finding a silk that was even hotter and slicker beneath them. He trapped her helpless whimper between his lips, his deft fingertips coaxing the tender petals of her body open like some exotic flower ripe with the sweetest and thickest of nectars.

Emma had never known such pleasure was possible. She was torn between clenching her thighs tightly together to ease the growing ache between them and letting them fall apart so Jamie could do it. But his touch only deepened the ache and before long her breath was coming in fierce little pants.

Ignoring the fact that she was already grinding herself against his palm in a frenzy of need, he stroked and petted and fondled her slick, swollen flesh as if there was nothing else in the world he would rather do and he had all night to do it. Just when she thought his exquisite torture couldn't possibly get any more diabolical, he began to brush the pad of his thumb over the hooded little nub at the crux of her curls in maddening circles. Even as he did so, his longest finger slid lower, dipping gently once, twice, a third time before delving deep inside of her.

His name broke from her lips on a sob as Emma's body erupted in one long, glorious, blinding shudder of rapture.

The second she could see and breathe and move again, she dropped to a sitting position and tugged off her boots.

"What are you doing?" he asked, clearly alarmed.

"Rewarding your efforts," she replied, peeling off her stockings.

"Oh, I was just getting started," he warned as she returned to her knees and drew her gown over her head.

Tossing it aside, she boldly faced him, knowing she must look like the most shameless of hoydens kneeling before him with her hair tumbling every which way and her cheeks and breasts still flushed from the pleasure he had given her. But any fear that Jamie might find her lacking was dispelled by the mingled lust and adoration in his eyes as he gazed upon her naked body for the first time.

"You're so fine," he whispered hoarsely, his eyes slowly devouring every inch of her. "You don't deserve this. You deserve a grand bed carved o' the finest mahogany. And mountains o' feather pillows. And candlelight. And silk sheets. And —"

It was her turn to lay her fingers across his lips. "I may deserve every one of those things. But all I want is you."

He reached for her then, crushing her naked softness against him as if he could somehow make them one with the sheer passion of his embrace. He was hard where she was soft, unyielding and angled where she was gently curved. Emma twined her fingers through his hair and buried her face against his throat, surprised to feel the sting of tears in her eyes. He smelled like wood-smoke and spring rain and the wind blowing through the pines on a cold winter's night. He smelled like a freedom she had never known before this night.

"So what must I do to coax you into taking off your clothes?" she murmured, dusting the broad column of his throat with her kisses.

He gently set her away from him, a rakish grin curving his lips. "You, my lady, have only to ask."

Before Emma had time to catch her breath, he had divested himself of shirt, stockings and boots. She might have perished from mortification as he reached for the leather laces of his breeches if she hadn't noticed that his hands were less than steady.

As he peeled off his breeches and rose back to his knees, Emma's curiosity quickly overcame her maidenly shyness. His was a beautiful body — sleek and taut and masculine, even more thickly muscled than she had imagined.

Unable to resist the temptation, she reached out and trailed a hand over his chest, marveling at the havoc her touch was wreaking on him. Despite the chill in the air he was sweating, his brawny body coated with a glistening sheen of perspiration.

Encouraged by the glazed look in his eye, the uneven hitch in his breath, her hand wandered lower — skating over the incredibly well-defined muscles of his abdomen — then lower still, closing gently over the part of him that was jutting forward as if begging for her touch.

He threw back his head with a guttural groan.

Emma's surge of desire was matched by a surge of delight. He no longer held all the power. She had power over him now, the power to bend him to her will, both literally and figuratively; to mold him with her palm and watch him lengthen and swell even further, although she would have sworn that wasn't even possible. As she drew her hand along his rigid shaft, a single drop of seed — like the most rare and precious of pearls — welled up from its velvety crown to dampen her fingertips.

"You once told me it hurt," she reminded him solemnly, her gaze flicking to his face.

"Aye, lass," he replied, panting out the words between clenched teeth. " 'Tis the sweetest pain I've ever known."

They both knew there was only one way to alleviate his suffering. As he eased her down on the blanket and covered her, shielding her from the moonlight, she realized she had brought him to this place because his was the only shadow she was seeking, the only darkness to which she was willing to surrender herself.

She clung to him, trembling with both anticipation and terror. She was going to do it. She was going to let him inside of her — where no man had ever been before.

He rubbed the heavy ridge of his arousal between her legs, laving himself in the rich cream his caresses had coaxed from her body. As she felt those delicious little tremors begin to dance over her flesh once more, she feared he was seeking to prolong her torment. But when she felt his thickness probing the entrance to her body, she understood it wasn't his intention to leave her wanting at all but to give her everything she was aching for. And more.

So very much more.

She dug her fingernails into his back as her untried body fought to accept him. She tensed and bit her lip to keep from crying out when she felt a painful tearing sensation. But he did not relent until his throbbing length was sheathed deep within her.

"I'm sorry, angel," he whispered, touching his lips to her sweat-dampened brow. "Hesitating would have only prolonged the pain."

"Mine or yours?" she quipped, letting him

know she was going to survive.

His big body shuddered with something that might have been laughter in a less urgent moment. "Both."

As he began to move within her, sipping tenderly from her lips all the while, the pain faded to a dull throb that only sharpened her awareness of the incredible intimacy of what they were doing. She was truly his captive now. There was no escaping him. He surrounded her. He enfolded her. He made her every breath she drew his own, her every wish one only he could fulfill. It was almost as if there was no part of her he was not touching — including her soul.

When he abruptly stopped, she wanted to weep with disappointment.

She opened her eyes to find him peering down at her, his expression quizzical. "Emma? Sweeting? Is there something wrong? Why are you being so still? Is the pain too great for you to bear?"

"My moth—" She clamped her mouth shut and began again. "I was *informed* that if I wriggled a bit beneath the earl, his exertions would be over that much more quickly. So I thought if I stayed completely still . . ."

She trailed off, allowing him to draw the obvious conclusion.

When he did, a strangled laugh escaped

him. "You may wriggle all you like, lass. I'm still going to make this last for as long as I can. Of course, given how incredibly tight and hot and wet you are" — he gritted his teeth against a fresh groan as she gave her hips an experimental shimmy — "that may not be nearly as long as either one of us would like."

With that warning, Jamie began to rock against her, setting an irresistible rhythm she had no choice but to follow. Soon she was arching her back, lifting her hips to draw him even deeper inside of her. He rewarded her boldness by angling his own hips so that each downward stroke brought him into direct contact with that exquisitely sensitive little bud nestled in her damp nether curls. With each tantalizing stroke, he made good on his promise to both seduce and ravish her.

He must have felt her begin to shiver and clench around him.

"Come with me, Emmaline," he growled. "Come for me."

And then she was — in shudder after shudder of raw bliss that sent her soaring over that precipice of ecstasy once again. But this time she would not fall alone. Jamie surrendered to his own plunge over that precipice with a muffled roar, withdrawing from her just in time to spill his hot seed over her belly.

Jamie awoke before sunrise with Emma cradled in his arms, much as he had on the morning after he had abducted her. But this time there was one major difference — neither one of them was wearing any clothes.

And a delightful difference it was, Jamie thought, burying his nose in her sweet-smelling curls. Although his arousal was already nudging the softness of her rump in a shameless bid for attention, he was loathe to wake her and put an end to this moment.

He traced the graceful slope of her hip with his palm. After living so long in this rugged land, it was still difficult to believe anything could be so soft, so impossibly silky to the touch. How was he supposed to send her back to the Hepburn in a few hours when all he wanted to do was spend the rest of the day kissing each of the freckles scattered like nutmeg over the glowing alabaster of her skin?

He ought to be celebrating. He had triumphed over his enemy once again. Emma would never belong to the Hepburn. But the satisfaction he had anticipated was blunted by a jagged edge of desperation.

Because she would never belong to him either. These few stolen hours between midnight and dawn were all he would ever have of her.

When she had come to him last night he would have agreed to almost anything just for the chance to hold her in his arms this way. But he'd been a fool to believe he could love her for one night, then let her go without her taking a sliver of his splintered heart with her.

He had already spent much of the night teetering on the edge of disaster. Each time he had made love to her, it had been nearly impossible to force himself to withdraw from her tight, silky sheath when he really wanted to spill his seed deep within her, to mark her as his own in a way that neither the Hepburn nor the rest of the world would ever be able to deny. But he'd been driven to honor their bargain. It was bad enough to send her back to England in disgrace without risking sending her back with his bastard in her belly.

If Gordon Hepburn hadn't been so careless in such matters, Lianna Sinclair might be alive today. Jamie wasn't about to make the same mistakes his father had made. As far as he was concerned, the man had been every inch a Hepburn, seeing what he

325

wanted and then taking it with no thought whatsoever to the cost or the consequences. Jamie had spent his entire life seeking to prove it was Sinclair blood that ran through his veins. He would never be a Hepburn. He would never be his father. He wasn't greedy or selfish enough to ask Emma to risk her own life just so she could share his.

She didn't belong with the likes of him. She belonged in some cozy rose arbor in Lancashire taking tea with her sisters with a cat curled up in her lap and a book in her hand. The Hepburn had taken her away from all that but it was within his power to send her back where she belonged. She could live out the rest of her life in comfort and safety, far away from ancient feuds and their terrible casualties.

She stirred, pressing her rounded little bottom against him. The musky scent of their lovemaking lingered on her skin, making him feel positively savage with the desire to possess her again.

"Don't fret, lass," he whispered in her ear. " 'Tis a state men often find themselves in when they awaken."

"Mmmm . . . I'm so glad to know it has absolutely nothing to do with me. Do you realize this is exactly how we woke up the first time I slept in your arms?"

"The thought had occurred to me. But there is one wee difference."

Tightening his grip, he slid up and into her from behind, sheathing himself all the way to the hilt in one smooth motion.

She shuddered and arched against him. "Forgive me for quibbling, sir," she gasped out, "but I don't believe anyone could call that 'wee.' "

He captured her pert nipples between his thumbs and forefingers and gently tugged. "Does that mean I'm strapping enough for you, lass, as lovers go?"

She nodded her breathless assent. "I do believe Brigid was wrong. You must be twice the man Angus and Malcolm could ever hope to be."

Closing his eyes and burying his face in her hair, Jamie began to move deep within her, determined to stave off the dawn for as long as he could. "And I have you to thank for letting me prove it."

CHAPTER TWENTY-FOUR

Jamie was already mounted astride his horse when Emma emerged from the ruins of the abbey. With perverse timing, the sun had chosen to make its first appearance in days, burning off the last of the mist and coaxing a hopeful serenade of birdsong from the budding branches of the surrounding birches and aspens.

But the slanting rays of the morning sun failed to warm him. Despite the crisp white clouds drifting across the dazzling blue of the sky, a chill had settled deep in his bones, making him feel as if winter lurked just over the southern horizon instead of spring.

He sat motionless in the saddle, watching Emma cross the clearing. Muira's cloak was draped over her shoulders. She had used the leather thong he had given her to neatly bind her unruly curls at the nape just as she'd used the water he had warmed over the fire for her to wash his scent from her skin.

Unlike the abbey lying in rubble behind her, she did not look ruined to him. Her freckled cheeks were flushed, her lips still slightly swollen from his loving, her eyes slumberous. She looked gloriously . . . *un-ruined.* Jamie felt a smoldering fury that society would now deem her less worthy of their regard. They would consider her sullied by his touch, when she was glowing from within like something so fine and precious it hurt his eyes just to look at her.

He had taunted her once by telling her the Hepburn would probably insist that she be examined by a physician to determine if she was still worthy to be his bride. Now the thought of some stranger putting his hands on her, even for such a dispassionate purpose, made Jamie want to smash something with his fists.

As she approached the horse, she glanced around the deserted clearing, her expression troubled. "Where are Bon and the rest of the men?"

"They've been waiting at the meeting place since before dawn. You won't see them. And with any luck, neither will the Hepburn's men."

He offered her a hand, both of them

knowing it was the last time he would ever do so.

As she settled herself in the saddle behind him, slipping her slender arms around his waist, Jamie had never been so keenly aware of the cold, heavy weight of his pistol against his belly. Or of the centuries of hatred and violence that had brought them to this place.

For one wild, desperate moment, all he wanted to do was kick the horse into a gallop and ride as fast and far as he was able, to whisk her away to some distant haven where the Hepburn could never find them. But he wasn't as naïve or foolhardy as his parents had been.

He knew there was no outrunning fate and nowhere he could flee to escape his own destiny.

As Jamie and Emma rode into the mouth of the long, narrow glen from the north, the cheerful chirping of the birds in the surrounding trees seemed to mock them. Jamie had chosen the place for the exchange with deliberate care. Birds weren't the only creatures sheltered by the lush green boughs of the cedars flanking the glen on both east and west. His own men were tucked away there as well, their pistols and bows cocked and held at the ready. If they spotted any sign of treachery, they would be able to fire before the Hepburn's men could even draw their weapons, then flee back into the hills without leaving a trace.

Jamie was not surprised to see half a dozen of the Hepburn's burliest henchmen sitting on horses strung out across the gentle rise in the land at the south end of the glen. They were simply obeying his own instructions to the Hepburn not to allow them to come any closer.

But he was surprised to find Ian Hepburn himself sitting straight and tall on the back of a chestnut gelding at the very heart of the glen, his dark hair blowing in the wind. With his snowy white cravat and handsome mulberry-colored frock coat, he might have been on his way to take tea with a duchess instead of delivering a ransom.

Jamie had expected the Hepburn to send his latest gamekeeper, not his nephew. This was a development he hadn't anticipated, one that upped the stakes in an already dangerous game.

He and Ian had spent too much time fighting on the same side, even if it was only against the bullies at St. Andrews. Despite the casual disdain of his bearing, Ian had to know Jamie would never march into battle without his men. He would have already guessed there were unseen pistols trained on his heart and that if anything went wrong, he would be the first to die.

Jamie flicked a tense glance toward the trees, silently praying his men would use every ounce of the restraint he had tried to teach them.

He drew his own horse to a halt a healthy distance from where Ian sat waiting for him. He dismounted, then reached back up to lift Emma from the saddle.

"Wait here," he commanded her, his hands lingering against the gentle curve of her waist. "If anything goes wrong, run for that line of trees as fast and as hard as you can. Find Bon. He'll look after you."

She nodded. Judging by the solemn expression in her dusky blue eyes, she understood exactly what he was telling her.

And what he was not telling her.

He gazed down into those eyes, keenly aware that their every move was being scrutinized by both allies and enemies. Swallowing back all of the things he wanted to say, he gave her one last nod, then turned and began to walk toward Ian's horse.

He bridged over half the distance but when Ian showed no sign of dismounting, he stopped in his tracks.

"What ails ye, laddie?" he called out,

knowing his familiar smirk would gall Ian far more than his exaggerated burr. "Gettin' too much enjoyment from sneerin' down yer nose at a lowly Sinclair?"

Ian glared at him for a minute longer before sliding off the horse to face him. From this distance, he could have been that same proud, aloof boy who had been stoically taking a beating the first time Jamie had laid eyes on him. But as Jamie neared, the contempt written in every line of Ian's bearing reminded Jamie that he hadn't been that boy for a very long time.

Jamie didn't stop until they stood eye to eye for the first time in four years. "Usually your uncle sends one of his attack dogs to do his dirty work for him. To what do I owe the dubious pleasure of your company?"

"Perhaps he thought you'd be less likely to gun me down where I stand. Not out of misplaced sentiment or common decency, of course, but to preserve your own loathsome hide."

Despite his best intentions, Jamie felt his temper begin to rise. "Funny how you didn't hate me until your uncle told you it was expected of you."

"I'm sure I would have if you hadn't deliberately misled me. If you had told me who you were from the beginning. *Exactly* who you were."

Jamie shook his head sadly. "You still don't know who I am."

Ian's dark eyes glittered with barely suppressed fury. "I know you're a no-good thief and a murderer. When I hunted you down that day on the mountain after my uncle told me how you had tricked me — how you had played me for a fool all those years at school and made me a laughingstock in his eyes — you didn't even have the decency to deny shooting down his gamekeeper in cold blood."

"You just proved my point," Jamie said softly. "If I had to deny it, you never knew me at all." He could almost feel Emma's gaze on his back, knew she was watching every nuance of their exchange even if she could not hear their words. "I didn't come here today to argue with you. I came to keep my end of our bargain. As you can see," he said, jerking his head toward where she stood patiently waiting beside his horse, "Miss Marlowe is unharmed and ready to come with you."

Unharmed but not unfooked.

Jamie had to close his eyes briefly as Bon's impish voice danced through his head, accompanied by a vision of Emma lying naked beneath him on the blankets, her lips parted in a wordless sigh of pleasure as he drove himself deep inside her.

He opened his eyes to banish the vision. "Did your uncle send what I asked for?"

Ian nodded curtly, then turned and signaled toward the far end of the glen.

The six henchmen guarding the south entrance to the glen nudged their horses apart, making room for a flatbed wagon manned by a beefy driver to pass between them. As they closed ranks once again, the wagon came trundling across the grass toward Jamie and Ian. The vehicle made a half-circle, finally rolling to a halt facing the opposite direction a few feet behind Ian.

Jamie scowled at the wooden chests weighting down its bed. "What in the bluidy hell is this?" he demanded, returning his gaze to Ian's face to search for any sign of treachery. "Some sort of trick?"

"Of course it's not a trick," Ian snapped. "It's exactly what you asked for."

As Jamie moved forward, Ian's hands curled into fists. But Jamie stalked right past him, heading for the wagon. The driver eyed him nervously over his shoulder as he snatched up a fallen branch from the ground, but relaxed when Jamie moved to use the branch to pry open the lid of the chest closest to the back of the wagon bed.

The lid fell away with a clatter. The morning sunlight glinted off its contents, nearly blinding him.

Shaking his head in mute disbelief, Jamie moved to pry open the lid of the next chest only to find exactly the same thing awaiting him.

Gold. A king's ransom in gold.

He spun around, turning his disbelieving gaze on Ian. "What is this? This isn't what I asked for! This isn't what your uncle promised me!"

"Of course it is!" Ian insisted, a shadow of bewilderment softening the contempt in his eyes. "It's exactly what you demanded in your note. Enough gold for you and your men to live on for the rest of your wretched lives."

He reached inside his frock coat, forcing Jamie to move his own hand a few inches closer to the butt of his pistol. But it wasn't a weapon that appeared in Ian's hand. It was a folded piece of vellum.

He thrust the paper toward Jamie. "My uncle also said to give you this."

Jamie strode forward and snatched the missive from Ian's hand. He tore it open, this time not pausing to admire the fine quality of the paper or the elaborate Hepburn crest stamped into the sealing wax.

There were eight words scrawled across the paper in a feeble, spidery hand: *What you seek is not mine to give.*

While Ian stood there staring at him as if he were a madman, Jamie crumpled the note in his fist, fury rising like bile in his throat. The crafty auld bastard had done it again. He'd betrayed Jamie and left him standing there empty-handed and half blind with rage.

He lifted his burning gaze to the bed of the wagon. Ian was right. There was enough gold in those chests to last a lifetime. It could keep Muira and her family and all those like them on this mountain in milk and meat for many winters to come. His own men could finally stop running, stop hiding, settle down and have cottages and wives and children of their own if they so desired.

He glanced over his shoulder at Emma. Tension was written in every line of her bearing, as if she sensed something had gone badly amiss.

She had been right as well, Jamie thought bitterly. She was nothing to the earl. Just to have the last laugh in their lifelong battle of wits, the bastard had been willing to gamble that Jamie would set her free in exchange for the gold instead of marching right back to her, shoving the mouth of his pistol against her temple and pulling the trigger.

Jamie closed his eyes briefly just to block out the sight of her. Despite what his parents had been foolish enough to believe, this feud would never end. But he couldn't keep dragging Emma all over the Highlands indefinitely. She might not survive the next drenching rain, the next surprise snowstorm, the next harrowing ride up the mountain while trying to elude the Hepburn's men.

She might not survive him.

"Wait here," he snarled at Ian.

Rubbing a hand over his rigid jaw, he went striding back across the glen to Emma.

"Did you get what you wanted?" she asked as he approached, the proud tilt of her chin reminding him that he had made her believe there would always be something in this world he wanted more than her.

He couldn't very well tell her he wasn't even sure what he wanted anymore. That everything he had dreamed of, everything he had fought for up until the day he first laid eyes on her, now seemed less than worthless to him.

So he simply said, "You're free."

She nodded, then turned and went walking toward Ian. At first Jamie thought she meant to leave him without so much as a backward glance, which would be no less than what he deserved. But she had only traveled a few feet before she turned and came running back to him.

Clutching his arm and standing on tiptoe, she touched her lips to his ear and whispered, "There won't be any strapping young lovers. There will only be you."

He reached for her but she was already gone. All he could do was stand there and watch her walk away from him, his empty hands slowly curling into fists. Her back was straight, her shoulders unbowed despite everything she had endured since arriving in Scotland.

What a bluidy fool he had been! He had tried to steal something so precious he should have been willing to sacrifice a king's ransom to possess it.

She was nearly halfway to Ian now. Jamie willed her to turn and look back at him one last time, to see in his eyes all of the things he had been too cowardly to confess. But she just kept walking.

He had to stop her, to tell her that he was even more of a fool than his parents had been. At least they had died with something to show for their folly, even if it was only a few stolen months of happiness. If he let

Emma go riding out of that glen with Ian, he would have nothing except the memory of the one night she had spent in his bed and a lifetime of regrets.

He was already taking a step when a beam of sunlight glinted off something high up in one of the cedars to the east of the wagon, distracting him. He squinted toward the tree, just barely able to make out the gleaming black barrel of a pistol protruding from the dense sweep of boughs.

Jamie frowned. His men knew better than to scale a cedar that high. If something went wrong, it would make it too easy for Hepburn's henchmen to cut off their escape route.

That was when he realized it was the wrong tree.

The wrong man.

Like a sleeper wading through the cloying fog of a dream, he followed the line of fire from the pistol to its target — not his breast but Emma's. Not his heart but hers. Oblivious to the threat, she continued across the glen, utterly alone, utterly exposed.

Jamie yanked his pistol from the waistband of his breeches and lunged into motion, knowing even as he did so that there was no way he could shoot down the assassin from this distance, no way he could reach her before it was too late.

Time seemed to unfold as if the seconds were being measured by a laboring clock someone had forgotten to wind. He was charging forward but the distance between him and Emma seemed to be growing — each step he took carrying her farther and farther out of his reach.

"Emma!" he bellowed.

She stopped and turned toward him, a desperate hope shining in her eyes.

A blast rang out.

He saw her body jerk. Saw a look of blank shock descend over her face like a mask. Saw the crimson stain begin to blossom across the shoulder of her gown.

Jamie had seen the exact same scene a thousand times in his imagination. He'd heard the pistol blast thundering in his ears. He'd seen the crimson stain blossom and spread until it seemed to obliterate all of the other colors in the world. He'd witnessed the look of betrayal on a woman's face as she fell.

A roar of pure anguish exploded from his chest. Time resumed at twice its normal pace as he raced toward Emma, firing wildly toward the cedar where the gunman had vanished.

The glen exploded in a storm of gunfire.

Through the crimson veil that had descended over his vision, Jamie saw Ian standing frozen beside the wagon, a stricken look on his face as he gazed at Emma's crumpled form. He saw his own men come spilling out of the trees, yodeling fearsome battle cries and firing at anything foolish enough to move. He saw the driver bring his whip down on the backs of his team with a savage crack, sending the wagon careening wildly out of the glen. He saw the Hepburn's men spur their horses into motion, driving them down the rise and into the thick of the fray to join the ambush.

Ian reached into his coat. This time his hand emerged not with a note, but with a pistol. Gritting his teeth, Jamie swung the mouth of his own weapon around, pointing it at Ian's chest. No power on earth was going to stop him from getting to Emma, not even a gun in the hand of the man who had once been his dearest friend.

Their eyes met for the briefest of seconds, but before Jamie could fire, Ian shouted, "Get her, damn it!"

Ian turned and went sprinting toward the cedar where the assassin had disappeared, running low and hard to try to avoid the pistol balls whizzing around him.

From that moment on, Jamie only had

eyes for Emma.

If she was still alive, he knew he had only one hope of keeping her that way. He broke his stride just long enough to scoop her up in his arms like a child and went racing for the nearest boulder.

Collapsing to his knees behind the boulder, Jamie gently cradled Emma across his lap. She gazed up at him, her beautiful eyes glazed with pain and shock.

"It's all right, lass," he said hoarsely, desperately trying to staunch the flow of blood spilling from her shoulder with his free hand. Her freckles were standing out against her pallid cheeks in stark relief. He rested his forehead against her cold, clammy brow, willing her to focus her eyes and look at him. To really *see* him. "I've got you now. I'll not let you go."

"It's too late," she whispered, a lifetime of tenderness and regret shining in her eyes as she struggled to lift her hand to his face. "You already did." Then her eyes fluttered shut and her fingers fell open, going as limp as the petals of a dying flower against his cheek.

CHAPTER TWENTY-FIVE

Throughout the rest of that endless day Jamie rode as he had never ridden before — through the waning sunlight, through the rising mist of twilight, through a cold, driving rain that only deepened his desperation, and finally through a night as deep and dark as any he had ever known.

Once the Hepburn's men had realized they were both outgunned and outmanned, they had wheeled their horses around and beat a hasty retreat. Jamie had been left with no choice but to trust Bon to tie up any loose ends. He'd never abandoned his men before, but he couldn't afford to wait for them. Not when every minute lost might be another minute of Emma's life ticking away.

He couldn't even afford to linger in the glen long enough to deal with Ian. He'd only had time to bark out quick instructions that he was not to be harmed if captured, but brought directly to his grandfather's stronghold for questioning.

By the time Jamie finally reached that stronghold himself, it was well after midnight and Emma's makeshift bandage was soaked through with a mixture of blood and rain. As he dismounted, drawing her into his arms and tugging the hood of the cloak over her head to shield her face from the worst of the downpour, she was as still and limp as a corpse in his arms. Her breath against his throat felt more insubstantial than a will-o'-the-wisp drifting across the moors on a moonless night.

As he staggered through the mud, churning gusts of wind drove the rain into his face, blinding him. He stumbled and nearly fell before finally reaching the ancient keep perched at the crest of the steep hill.

The earth and timber structure had served as both home and fortress to the Sinclairs ever since they had been driven out of their own castle over five centuries before. The gatehouse and most of the outbuildings had burned long ago, leaving only the central tower standing to battle the elements. Even that was beginning to crumble in spots, making it impossible to predict just how many more seasons it would survive.

Cradling the lifeless bundle Emma had become against his chest, Jamie pounded on the rough-hewn door with his fist. *"Open the bluidy door!"*

There was no response to his pounding or his desperate roar. He and his grandfather hadn't exactly parted on the best of terms the last time they'd spoken, but he'd never known his grandfather to turn his back on him in a moment of need. He continued to slam his fist against the door and shout until both his knuckles and his voice were raw.

His desperation gave way to rage. He wasn't about to just stand there in the pouring rain while Emma died in his arms. He was backing up and preparing to give the door a mighty kick when it began to swing inward with a rusty creak. The darkened crack between frame and door slowly widened to reveal a face as familiar as his own.

Jamie glared at his grandfather, his expression both fierce and pleading. "Stand aside, auld mon. Your grandson has come home."

The last thing Emma remembered after the glen had exploded in a fiery cloud of pain was falling. Falling so hard and so fast that not even Jamie's arms could catch her.

Then everything had gone as dark as the blackest night. But even in the murky hours and days that followed, Jamie had been there — his big, callused hands easing her to a sitting position with a tenderness that should have been impossible for them; his gruff burr coaxing her to open her mouth wider so he could spoon a bitter-tasting broth between her lips; his cool lips brushing her brow when it was ablaze with fever; his warm arms enfolding her when she was wracked with chills; his head bowed as he clutched her limp hand and pleaded with God to let her live.

So it was no surprise it was his presence she sensed when the first glimmers of light began to pierce the receding shadows. She slowly pried open her eyes, waiting for her head to stop spinning and the wavering world to come back into focus. When it finally did, she found herself gazing into the gentle eyes of an enormous brindled beast sitting in front of a crackling fire on a crude stone hearth.

"Why is there a pony in here?" she asked, surprised by how rusty her voice sounded to her own ears.

" 'Tis not a pony, lass. 'Tis a dog."

She frowned at the towering creature. "That, sir, is no dog."

"Aye, it is. 'Tis a deerhound."

As the creature folded its long limbs and sank into a reclining position, her frown deepened. "Are you sure it's not a deer?"

347

She gingerly turned her head, wincing at a lingering twinge of stiffness, only to find herself gazing up into a pair of arctic green eyes fringed with thick silver lashes. A wave of shock rippled through her. The man she had been arguing with wasn't Jamie at all, but Jamie as he would look forty years from now.

His thick hair might be the snowy white of hoarfrost and his face as craggy as the side of a mountain, but time hadn't robbed this man of his vigor as it had the Hepburn. He still possessed the impressive shoulders and rugged vitality of a much younger man. He wore a green-and-black tartan kilt and a ruffled shirt with falls of lace at the throat and cuffs that made him look as if he belonged in some Gainsborough or Reynolds portrait from the previous century.

Realizing she couldn't have possibly been asleep for *that* long, she whispered, "You must be Jamie's grandfather." She blinked up at him, unable to drag her gaze away from those oh-so-familiar eyes. Everything about the man was larger than life, including the wooden chair he had drawn next to her bed. Still too muzzy-headed to censor her words, she blurted out, "I thought you were dying."

Ramsey Sinclair leaned forward, his eyes

twinkling as if he was about to confide a delicious secret. "Well, for the past few days, I thought ye were dying, too."

"Mind yer tongue," a voice croaked. "I've worked too hard to keep the lass alive to let ye scare her to death."

Emma could not stop herself from recoiling on the pillow as a woman who looked ancient enough to be the Hepburn's grandmother came shuffling toward the opposite side of the bed, the rounded hump in her back forcing her to stoop almost double. Stringy strands of hair the color of tarnished silver hung around cheeks so sunken as to be nearly hollow. As she drew closer to the bed, Emma realized what she had mistaken for a toothless grimace was meant to be a smile.

"There, there, dearie," the woman crooned, patting Emma's hand. "Don't let the auld rogue affright ye. The worst is o'er. Ye're goin' to be just fine now."

"Mags is right about that," Jamie's grandfather said dryly. "If ye have a strong enough constitution to survive the foul stench o' her poultices, then gettin' shot certainly isn't goin' to kill you."

This must be the Mags Jamie had mentioned, Emma realized with a start of shock. The woman who had once been his mother's nursemaid.

The old dame wagged a bony finger at the Sinclair. "If it weren't for me foul-smellin' poultices, Ramsey Sinclair, ye'd have been molderin' in yer own grave a long time ago." She gave Emma a gloating look. "For years, he could barely leave the fortress without gettin' his fool self shot or takin' a tumble off o' his horse. Lucky for him, that stubborn neck o' his was too hard to break."

The Sinclair made a sound that sounded suspiciously like a harrumph. "It was ne'er as hard as yer head, woman."

As they continued to trade barbed insults, Emma's fascinated gaze bounced between the two of them. They weren't behaving like master and servant but bickering like an old married couple.

"Bluidy hell, auld mon!" Jamie exclaimed from the doorway. "Why didn't you tell me she was awake?"

As Jamie strode toward the bed, Emma ignored Mags' fretful clucking and struggled to push herself up on the pillow. The sight of him gave her a fresh shock. His handsome face was haggard, his jaw unshaven, his eyes bloodshot with dark smudges beneath them.

His grandfather settled back in his chair, waving away Jamie's concern. "Pshaw! I wasn't about to wake ye from the first nap ye've had in four days. Don't ye think ye can trust me to play nursemaid for a few hours? God knows I did it often enough for ye when ye were squallin' from the colic or had stuffed yer wee face with too many green apples."

Mags retreated from the bed, making way for Jamie to kneel beside it. He laced his fingers through Emma's, his fierce gaze searching her face as if to assure himself that she was truly awake, truly alive.

"What happened?" she asked him.

"It was an ambush," he said, gently squeezing her hand.

"What about your men?" she asked. "Were any of them hurt?"

He shook his head grimly. "As soon as the Hepburn's men realized they were outnumbered, they scattered like the rats they were. You were the only one who was wounded."

"Me?"

"Aye. The Hepburn sent an assassin. The wretch must have been hiding in the tree before my men even arrived." When she reached up to touch the edge of the clean bandage peeping out from the neckline of her nightdress, he managed a strained smile. "Thank God it was a clean shot. The pistol ball went right through your shoulder. It cost you a lot of blood and there was some infection but Mags was able to fight it off with her poultices. A wee bit more rest and you'll be as good as new."

Emma touched two fingers to her brow, struggling to recall the moments before the world had gone dark.

She remembered walking away from Jamie across a sunlit meadow, knowing she would never see him again. She remembered the birds singing while her heart was breaking.

"I heard you call my name," she whispered. "If I hadn't turned . . ."

She lifted her gaze to his grim face, reading the truth in his eyes. If she hadn't turned toward him at the precise moment the assassin had fired, the pistol ball would have gone straight through her heart.

"Don't know what you thought ye were doing draggin' such a scrawny lass up here anyway," the elder Sinclair said cheerfully. "She doesn't look hearty enough to survive a Highland spring, much less a winter." His disparaging gaze dropped to Emma's hips beneath the fur coverlet. "Won't be much of a breeder either, I'll wager, unless ye plump her up with some bluid puddin' and haggis first."

Emma gasped, outraged at being judged and found wanting like some sort of prize sow at the village fair.

"Now do you understand why I haven't spoken to him in two months?" Jamie drawled. "Given his irresistible charm, it may surprise you to learn we had a wee bit of a falling out."

The Sinclair glowered at his grandson. "Pay no heed to him, lass. That's just his way o' sayin' I was right and he was wrong. He should have never returned to this mountain in the first place. He could have escaped its shadow forever."

"Like you did?" Jamie ventured, the mocking note in his voice unmistakable. Freeing Emma's hand, he rose to his feet. "This mountain is my home, just as it's been home to every Sinclair who came before me. I'll not abandon it. Nor will I be driven off of it by the likes of the Hepburn. Or by you."

His grandfather's voice was rising, his face growing more flushed by the minute. "If ye'd have listened to me and let the Hepburn be, the lass wouldn't be lying there in that bed right now with her bonny shoulder all shot up."

Genuine anger flashed in Jamie's eyes, but there was no arguing with the ring of truth in the old man's words. "If you had wanted me to let the Hepburn be, you should have never told me he was the one who slaughtered my parents."

"Well, I'm older now. And wiser. I've learned there's nothin' to be gained from stirrin' up ghosts. Leave them to their rest, I say, or they'll ne'er leave ye to yours." His grandfather struggled to rise, but only made it halfway to his feet before being forced to sink back down in the chair. Laboring for breath, he gripped the broad wooden armrests, his visage robbed of both its vigor and its color.

"That'll be quite enough o' that!" Mags scolded, shuffling to the man's side with more haste than should have been possible. "If ye won't think o' yer own health, ye auld fool, then think o' the wee lassie's. The last thing she needs right now is to listen to the two o' ye tearin' at each other's throats like a pair o' ornery hounds."

"It's all right, Mags," Emma said. "I'm guessing their barks are worse than their bites. Or at least I hope so."

Shaking the old woman's hand from his arm, Ramsey Sinclair made a second attempt to reclaim his dignity by getting to his feet. This time he succeeded.

He faced his grandson across Emma's bed, the proud set of his shoulders painfully familiar to her. "Ye're as rebellious and hard-headed as yer mother. I'm just tryin' to stop ye from meeting the same fate."

With that last salvo in what appeared to be a longstanding battle of wills, he turned and went lumbering from the room with Mags shuffling at his heels. After a moment, the enormous hound rose without a sound and padded after them.

Jamie stood gazing at the empty doorway for a long moment, his eyes still stormy. "He's never stopped fancying himself the laird of a powerful clan and ruler of a mighty kingdom. He forgets his only subjects are a balmy auld woman and a devoted deerhound."

"It's his heart, isn't it?" Emma asked quietly, having once had an aunt who suffered from a similar ailment. It had eventually killed her.

"Aye. He hides it well but the weak spells are growing more severe and more frequent. I might not have known just how frequent if Mags hadn't pulled me aside and told me the last time I was home."

"And that's when you realized your time to prove the Hepburn had murdered your parents was running out. You decided the quickest way to accomplish that would be to steal his bride."

Jamie gazed down at her, a wealth of

regret in his eyes. "My grandfather was right about one thing. I meant to steal her . . . not to get her shot."

Emma reached for his hand but he was already moving away from her toward the only window in the chamber — an expansive square of glass that occupied much of one wall.

While he gazed out over the brooding sky, she carefully eased herself to a sitting position, finally alert enough to really take in her surroundings.

It was as if she'd stumbled upon the only dwelling in Scotland constructed from timber instead of stone. With the window drawing the eye from every angle, the large octagonal room wasn't so much a bedchamber as an eagle's eyrie. Everything in the chamber — from the massive hand-carved bed with its plush nest of fur coverlets to the yawning hearth with its rough-cut stones to the oak rafters over Emma's head — was oversized, as if fashioned for a race of Gaelic giants.

Despite its potential for grandeur, an air of neglect hung over the tower. Cobwebs drifted from the rafters in ghostly veils and the dog had been allowed to leave an array of half-gnawed bones around the ash-strewn hearth. There wasn't so much as a hint of feminine comfort visible. No pillows aside from the one beneath her head, no graceful wax tapers in silver candlesticks, no dressing table littered with brushes and bottles of scent, no floral watercolors or family portraits to adorn the rough-hewn walls. It was easy to understand how such an environment might have bred a man as virile and rugged as Jamie.

"Have you told your grandfather you have proof the Hepburn murdered your parents?" she asked him.

He spoke without turning around. "There's nothing to tell. The Hepburn didn't send the ransom. It was all for naught."

Emma shook her head, wondering if blood loss had dulled her wits. "I don't understand. I saw you talking to Ian. I saw him hand something to you."

"Oh, the Hepburn delivered a ransom, but he didn't send the necklace. He refused me the one thing I asked for — the truth." Returning to the bed, he drew a folded piece of vellum out of his shirt and handed it to her. "He sent this instead."

Emma unfolded the paper. It looked as if it had been crumpled and smoothed more than once. "What you seek is not mine to give," she read aloud, puzzling over the words.

"I should have known the bastard was too canny to hand over the evidence that could have convicted him of murdering his own son."

"Maybe he didn't want to spend the rest of his life — however short that might be — looking over his shoulder, waiting for you to come for him."

"He's going to have to do that now anyway," Jamie said grimly, a bloodthirsty glint dawning in his eye.

She shook her head. "None of this makes any sense. Why would the earl refuse you the necklace, yet send all of that gold?"

"The gold was never meant to be anything but a distraction. He had no intention of parting with it. The wagon driver took off the minute you were shot."

His words deepened both her bewilderment and the dull throb in her shoulder. "I can understand why the earl might want to kill you, especially now that he knows you believe he murdered your parents. But what on earth would he stand to gain by killing me?"

He leaned over to brush his lips over her brow, the ruthless set of his jaw sending a shiver of foreboding down her spine. "Now that we know for sure the bastard didn't succeed, that's exactly what I intend to find out."

Unlike Hepburn Castle, the Sinclair stronghold had no elaborate labyrinth of dungeons buried beneath impenetrable layers of stone, no rusty chains dangling from dank stone walls, no secret passages winding their way through the earth. But it did boast a small chamber — really more of a cave — that had originally been dug out of the side of the mountain below the tower to serve as a root cellar. It was plain and practical . . . and utterly impossible to escape.

Small rocks skittered beneath Jamie's boot heels as he made his way down the steep slope. He paid no heed to the warmth of the spring sun on his shoulders or the fat woolly clouds frisking across the crisp blue of the sky.

Bon was waiting for him outside the wooden door that had been set directly into the rock face of the mountain. The impish twinkle in his cousin's eyes had been extinguished, leaving them as cold and black as the deepest loch in winter.

"Miss Marlowe?" he asked, plainly fearing the worst.

"She's awake," Jamie replied, telling him

everything he needed to know.

Bon sighed with relief, then nodded and unlocked the door, swinging it open without a word. Jamie ducked beneath its rough-hewn frame. The shadowy cave was lit by a single torch. After Bon closed the door behind him, blocking out the sunlight, it took a minute for his eyes to adjust.

A man sat with his back to the opposite wall and one long leg drawn up to his chest. His fine mulberry frock coat was missing, his silk waistcoat rumpled and his expensive linen shirt ripped at the shoulder. His left arm was in a filthy makeshift sling and an ugly bruise darkened one of his aristocratic cheekbones. His dark hair hung around his face in lank, dirty strands.

Although he was plainly the worse for wear, Ian still managed to struggle to his feet to face Jamie. "I was wondering when you were going to make an appearance. Have you come to finish the job your men started?"

"Perhaps. But not until I have some answers."

"I'd like some answers of my own, if you please. I'm afraid your men haven't been particularly forthcoming. Did Miss Marlowe survive?"

"If she hadn't, we wouldn't be having this

conversation." Jamie drew nearer to his old friend, struggling to keep the ragged edges of his temper from unraveling. "Now it's my turn. Why her? Why would your uncle try to kill an innocent woman?"

"After being in your hands this long, I doubt she's still an innocent."

Ian's mocking snort was cut off along with his breath as Jamie closed the distance between them in two strides, seized him by the throat and slammed him against the wall. Ian clawed at his arm with the hand not trapped by the sling. Jamie had taught Ian how to fight well and how to fight dirty, but when it came to brute strength, Jamie would always have the advantage.

"Now let's try this again, shall we?" Jamie said, his teeth clenched in a feral smile. He relaxed his grip just enough to allow Ian to speak. "Why did that wretched uncle of yours try to murder Miss Marlowe?"

Ian glared at him, his dark eyes smoldering with contempt. "Your merry band of cutthroats seized me before I could find the man who fired on her. How do you know for sure that it was one of my uncle's men? Perhaps one of your own men misfired and accidentally shot her."

Jamie tightened his grip again. "Wrong answer. I saw the barrel of the pistol at the top of one of the cedars before she was shot. Someone knew where we were going to meet. Someone who arrived the night before and took cover before anyone could spot him."

Ian frowned, his mask of defiance slipping for a minute to reveal his bewilderment. "Dockett," he finally breathed, all of the fight going out of him.

Jamie released him and he sagged against the wall. "Who in the hell is Dockett?"

"Silas Dockett. My uncle's gamekeeper."

Jamie folded his arms over his chest, unable to resist a mocking smirk. The one thing he hadn't been able to forgive his friend was that Ian had been so willing to believe his uncle's lies. To condemn Jamie for cutting down a man in cold blood without giving him a chance to explain the circumstances. "One I haven't had the pleasure of murdering yet, I gather."

"More the pity that," Ian admitted, straightening and jerking the wrinkles from his waistcoat. "Dockett is even more ruthless than the last one. It had to have been him. My uncle insisted on speaking to the man alone after that lad delivered your demand. That's when he must have given the brute his orders." For an elusive instant, Ian looked more like the friend Jamie had once known than the embittered stranger he had become — the friend who had spent hours teaching him how to speak properly so he could disarm the bullies at St. Andrews with his words instead of his fists. "My uncle had to send me to the rendezvous, you see, so you'd believe he was sincere. But he didn't dare tell me his scheme because he knew I'd never go along with such a thing."

Jamie shook his head in fresh amazement at the earl's audacity. "So he betrayed us both. He had to know there was a chance you'd be captured or even killed once Emmaline was shot. But none of this explains why he wanted her dead."

His old friend disappeared into the past as an all too familiar sneer curled Ian's lips. "Oh, he could care less about Miss Marlowe. The chit means nothing to him."

Time flashed backward and Jamie was standing in that sunny meadow once again, watching Emma turn toward him after he'd called her name — her hair blowing in the breeze, her blue eyes shining with a hope that was about to be vanquished forever. This time when he closed his hand around Ian's throat, it was in earnest.

Through the roaring in his ears, he heard

Emma's voice coming to him like an echo from a distant place. *"Jamie, no!"*

CHAPTER TWENTY-SIX

Jamie threw a stunned glance over his shoulder to find Emma standing in the doorway of the makeshift cell, a wide-eyed Bon beside her. The sunlight haloed her tousled curls and filtered through the folds of her white nightdress, making her look like an angel.

Or a ghost.

She swayed on her feet, forcing him to release Ian so he could rush over to catch her before she could fall.

"What are you doing out of bed, you wee fool? Trying to spare the Hepburn the trouble of killing you himself?"

He tried to sweep her up into his arms, but she resisted, clinging to his forearm but staying on her feet. Her face was nearly as bleached of color as her nightdress, but there was no denying the determined set of her delicate jaw. "I didn't care for the look in your eye so I followed you. I didn't want you to murder someone on my account."

Jamie shifted his glare to Bon. "And just how did she force you to open the door? Steal your pistol and hold it on you?"

Bon offered him a sheepish shrug. "She asked."

Ian coughed pointedly, reminding them all of his presence. He was still slumped against the wall, massaging his throat. "Good day, Miss Marlowe," he said with excoriating courtesy. "There's no need to trouble your pretty head over me. I can assure you that I much prefer these accommodations to being trapped in a castle with my uncle and your charming family."

Emma clutched at Jamie's forearm, her face brightening. "How is my family? Have my mother and sisters worried themselves sick over me? Is my papa . . ." — she hesitated for a telling moment — ". . . quite well?"

Jamie narrowed his eyes at Ian, warning him it might not be in his best interests to add to her concerns.

"Your mother and sisters are bearing up with admirable fortitude and I can assure you that your father is in . . . robust health." When Emma looked less than convinced by his words, he quickly added, "Before your hot-headed young champion here tried to choke the life out of me with his bare hands for the second time in this interminable day, I was getting ready to explain to him that it's not you my uncle wants dead. It's him."

"Then why didn't he order his gamekeeper to shoot *me?*" Jamie demanded.

Ian's laugh had a bitter edge. "Because my uncle is first and foremost a gentleman. He would never dream of sullying his own lily-white hands with Sinclair blood. Especially the blood of his own bastard grandson."

Jamie scowled, his precarious patience still running dangerously thin.

Ian straightened, as if he wanted to be on his feet for this particular fight. "When you first abducted Miss Marlowe, my uncle told me the redcoats would never get involved in some silly Highland bride-snatching. That they'd just as soon we all feud to the death and leave them to pick our bones clean after we're gone. But if one of their own were killed . . ."

Jamie's breath froze in his throat. "So he has Emma shot . . ."

". . . and claims you were the one who did it in an attempt to double-cross him after he delivered the ransom. The redcoats might be loathe to get involved in our affairs but even they couldn't very well ignore the ruthless murder of an innocent young Englishwoman."

"So they would be forced to come for me and my men."

"And hang you all," Emma finished for the both of them. "Leaving the Hepburn looking as blameless as a newborn babe."

This time when her knees betrayed her, she allowed Jamie to whisk her off her feet and into his arms. She looped her arms around his neck and rested her head against his chest as if Ian's revelation had drained what remained of her scant strength.

"Do you swear to me that you knew nothing of your uncle's plan?" The look Jamie gave Ian over the top of Emma's head left little doubt that Ian's very life might depend on whether or not Jamie found his reply convincing.

"If I had, do you think I would have been standing out there in the open when the firing started?" This time Ian's smile held no rancor, only a bittersweet echo of days gone by. "You taught me better than that, didn't you?"

Jamie pondered his words for a moment, then nodded and turned to go, determined to get Emma tucked safely back in her bed before she collapsed altogether.

"So what happens to me now?" Ian called

after them. "Are you just going to leave me here to rot or are you going to give me a chance to help you bring down that miserable whoreson who calls himself my uncle?"

As Jamie carried Emma from the chamber without a word, Bon drew the door shut behind them, leaving Ian alone in the shadows.

Emma drifted out of sleep that night to the delicious sensation of someone gently stroking her hair.

"Oh, Jamie," she murmured, snuggling deeper into the feather pillow.

If this was a dream, she had no desire for it to end. She wanted to cling to it long enough for Jamie to tenderly brush his lips over hers, to coax them apart so he could give her a tantalizing taste of all the pleasures they were about to share.

"Sweet dreams, me bonny lass," someone croaked in her ear.

Emma's eyes flew open. It wasn't Jamie's handsome face hovering over hers but a dried brown apple with a shriveled slash of a mouth frozen in a toothless grimace.

Emma let out a startled shriek, realizing too late that it was only Mags. The nurse went scrambling backward to cower in the corner. She lifted her wizened hands to shield her face, keening a low-pitched lament.

Emma sat up in the bed, favoring her injured shoulder. The chair beside the bed was empty. After Emma had promised Jamie she would obey his stern order to remain abed, he had retreated to his own bed to get a full night of sleep, his first since she had been shot.

Before he had left her, he had secured the heavy shutters over the window to hold the chill night air at bay. The fire on the hearth was dying but silvery ribbons of moonlight leaked through the wooden slats of the shutters. Emma could just make out Mags rocking back and forth in the corner like a frightened child. Her fear that the Hepburn had sent another assassin to finish her off quickly melted to chagrin.

"I'm so sorry, Mags. I didn't mean to startle you," she said softly, as if waking to the sight of the woman hanging over her bed like a vulture hadn't taken half a year off her own life.

At the sound of Emma's voice, the woman abruptly stopped keening and lifted her head. She hesitated for a moment, then scrambled to her feet and came creeping back toward the bed. She bore little resemblance to the sharp-tongued old biddy who had sparred with the Sinclair over Emma's bed earlier that day.

The woman perched on the edge of the bed and lifted a gnarled hand to stroke Emma's disheveled curls. "So pretty," the woman crooned. "Me bonny wee lass. Me sweet Lianna."

A chill danced down Emma's spine. Jamie's words echoed through her memory — *Mags went half-mad with grief for a while after they were found.*

Perhaps the woman was still half-mad with grief. Or perhaps Emma's arrival had simply stirred up old memories, some of which were better left buried. For all she knew, this might be the very chamber where Mags' young charge had once slept.

"It's Emma, Mags," she said gently, taking care not to make any sudden moves. "Not Lianna. Lianna doesn't live here anymore."

The woman continued to chant in her eerie singsong as if she hadn't spoken. "Ye were always such a good girl. Such a fine daughter. Ye hadn't a rebellious bone in yer body. Ye always had such pretty manners and did what yer papa told ye to do."

Emma's chill deepened as she realized the old woman *could* have been talking about her. She didn't know if it would be kinder to try to correct her again or to allow her the brief comfort of believing Jamie's mother had finally returned. "You loved your Lianna very much, didn't you?"

"Aye. I loved ye like a mother would. That's why I knew ye'd come back to us someday. I told him he just had to be patient and never give up hope." The nurse leaned closer, lowering her voice to the same hoarse croak that had awakened Emma. "I told ye I'd look after it fer ye and I did. I've kept it safe all these years. He tried to bury it so deep no one would ever find it but auld Mags knew just where to look."

Emma watched with reluctant fascination as the woman drew something wrapped in a scrap of fabric from the pocket of her homespun skirt. She placed her offering on Emma's lap, then nodded toward it, beaming with pride.

Hoping she wasn't about to find the rotting corpse of some bird or mouse, Emma gingerly unfolded the cloth to reveal a simple cherrywood box with a hinged lid. The box smelled damp and moldy, like something that had been in the ground for a very long time.

Emma gently brushed away the bits of dirt clinging to the lid to reveal an oval miniature of a young girl set into the wood.

"Her father gave it to her when she turned seventeen," Mags said, warning Emma that she was once again drifting between past and present. "Had the likeness painted from a sketch done by a traveling artist, he did. She was so proud of it! I still remember how she threw her arms 'round his neck and smothered his face with kisses."

Emma turned the box toward the window, studying the miniature by the gentle glow of the moonlight. Although she would have sworn Jamie was the very image of his grandfather, he carried something of his mother in him as well. It was there in the regal angle of his cheekbones, the beguiling way his eyes crinkled at the corners when he smiled.

Emma squinted at the likeness, struggling to make out the shape of the necklace adorning the graceful column of Lianna's throat. It appeared to be some sort of Gaelic cross.

"Go ahead," Mags urged. "Open it."

Emma reached for the lid, her hand trembling ever so slightly.

"Mags! What do ye think you're doin'?"

Both Emma and Mags jumped guiltily, jerking their heads toward the doorway.

Jamie's grandfather was standing there. He looked even taller and more imposing with his broad shoulders draped in a cloak of shadows. "Ye mustn't trouble our guest, Mags. The lass needs her rest."

"Aye, m'lord. I was just checkin' to see if she wanted another quilt."

Emma moved to throw a fold of her coverlet over the box only to discover it had already vanished back into Mags' pocket. Before the old nurse turned away from the bed, she startled Emma anew by giving her a mischievous wink.

Jamie's grandfather stood aside to let her shuffle past him. "Don't mind auld Mags, lass," he told Emma. "Sometimes late at night when she can't sleep, she wanders — both in mind and body."

For an elusive moment, he looked nearly as wistful as Mags had when she'd come creeping toward the bed to stroke Emma's hair. Emma wondered if he, too, still spent sleepless nights wandering the fortress, haunted by memories of his poor doomed daughter.

"Sleep well, child," he said gruffly before melting back into the shadows, his shoulders more stooped than when he'd appeared.

Emma collapsed against the pillows with a sigh, still troubled by her brief glimpse of Jamie's mother and wondering why her lonely bed had to be visited by everyone

except the one person she most desired to
see.

CHAPTER TWENTY-SEVEN

When Emma awoke the next morning the chair beside the bed was still empty, making her feel oddly bereft. A mournful sigh drifted across the chamber, warning her she was not alone.

She sat up to discover the deerhound stretched out in front of the hearth, his shaggy head cradled on his massive front paws.

"Nice pony," she murmured, eyeing him nervously and wondering if he'd broken his fast yet. He looked large and fierce enough to leave *her* bones scattered around the hearth.

In response to her greeting, he simply sighed once more and closed his soulful brown eyes, looking more inclined to nap the rest of the day away than to gobble her down in a single bite. Perhaps he only ate deer.

Someone had already slipped into the

room while she slept and wrestled open the wooden shutters, inviting the sunlight to come streaming into the chamber. She gave her wounded shoulder an experimental shrug. It was far less stiff and achy than it had been the previous day.

"M'lady?"

Mags appeared in the doorway, struggling to balance a fat bundle of cloth and a ceramic washbasin filled with steaming water.

"Good morning, Mags," she said tentatively, wondering if the old woman still believed Emma was Jamie's mother or if she even remembered their moonlit encounter.

Mags shuffled over to deposit her burdens on the rough-hewn table to the right of the hearth, her eyes bright and clear. There was no sign of the adoring creature that had crept into Emma's room to stroke her hair while she was sleeping. "And a bonny mornin' it is, lass! I've brought ye a fresh gown and stockin's and everythin' ye'll need fer yer bath."

Puzzled by the change in the woman's demeanor, but eager to test her growing strength, Emma climbed out of the bed and padded over to the table. "Your master didn't punish you for disturbing me last night, did he?"

"Ha!" Mags leaned closer, the mischievous twinkle Emma had so briefly glimpsed the previous night returning to her eye. "I stopped takin' orders from the master a long time ago. Now I'm the one tellin' him what to do." She reached over to pat Emma's hand. "Don't ye fret, lass. I've brought ye *everythin'* ye'll need," she repeated, as if the words should have some special significance.

As the old nurse went shuffling from the room, the deerhound unfolded his lanky form to follow. Emma moved to close the door behind them both, wondering if Mags was simply a bit balmy or if she might actually be dangerous.

The basin of steaming water quickly distracted her from her worries. She tugged the nightdress over her head, taking care not to dislodge the bandage on her shoulder. As she dipped a rag into the heated water, she couldn't help but remember sinking into the bath Jamie had arranged for her at Muira's cottage. Had she known then what she knew now, she might have invited him to join her.

With her eyes closed and the warm water dribbling between her breasts, making her sigh with pleasure, it was only too easy to imagine herself and Jamie entwined in that tub, their bodies sleek and wet and straining toward that perfect bliss that could only come when they were joined.

Her eyes flew open. It would hardly do for Jamie to come striding through that door only to find her melted into a puddle of longing. For all she knew, he was perfectly content with the one night they had shared. He might even have spent those long hours at her bedside nursing her back to life out of guilt, not devotion.

Growing increasingly out of sorts, she finished bathing and dried herself off. The gown Mags had found for her was more of a kirtle. It was cut from midnight blue wool and had a graceful bell of a skirt with a hem that swept the floor. As she donned it, struggling with the front laces of the old-fashioned bodice, she wondered if it, too, had once belonged to Jamie's mother.

It wasn't until she lifted the stockings that she realized Mags had left her more than just the garments.

Lianna Sinclair's box sat on the table, just as it might have thirty years before. Emma's heart took an unexpected plunge toward her toes. She stole a look at the door, knowing exactly how poor Pandora must have felt. She should probably just wait for Jamie or his grandfather to appear so she could return the box to its rightful owner.

There was probably nothing of any import inside anyway. Mags had most likely just been hoarding some cherished trinkets from her young mistress's childhood — a watercolor landscape the girl had painted or perhaps some flowers she had collected and pressed.

Emma ran a finger over the miniature portrait set in its lid, surprised to discover how unsteady her hand was. She wondered if Jamie's mother had already met her young lover when the miniature was painted. Lianna might have the demure smile of a girl, but she had the knowing eyes of a woman — a woman with a dangerous but delightful secret to keep.

He tried to bury it so deep no one would ever find it . . .

The echo of Mags' words both frightened and tantalized her. For it wasn't Lianna's secrets Emma longed to discover. It was her son's.

The next thing Emma knew, she was lifting the lid. A handful of off-key notes drifted through the room, as haunting as they were beautiful. It wasn't just a box. It was a music box. A yellowed piece of paper was nestled within its oilcloth-lined interior.

Emma pulled the paper out and gingerly unfolded it, taking care not to tear the brittle edges. Squinting at the faded ink, she carried it over to the window.

Sunlight streamed over the paper for the first time in years, illuminating the words scrawled across its face. Emma studied it for several minutes before lifting her disbelieving gaze to the snow-capped crags beyond the window. Apparently, Mags wasn't the only one who had lost her wits. Because she couldn't possibly be seeing what she thought she was seeing.

"I'm obviously not making enough of an effort to keep you in bed, am I?"

Emma whirled around to find Jamie standing in the doorway, looking every inch the Scottish laird in a maroon and black tartan kilt and a cream-colored linen shirt with full sleeves and a fall of lace at the cuffs. She had been so preoccupied with her find that she hadn't even heard him open the door.

Still speechless with shock, she tucked the hand clutching the paper behind her back. She could only pray he wouldn't notice the open box sitting on the table.

He cocked his head to the side, looking increasingly suspicious. "Just what have you been up to?"

"Nothing," she said hastily. "Nothing at all."

"Then why do you look so deliciously guilty?" He sauntered toward her, favoring her with an indulgent smile. "What is it, sweeting? Have you managed to get your hands on one of my grandfather's pistols? Now that you're on the mend, are you planning on shooting your way out of here?"

As he advanced on her, Emma shot a panicked glance over her shoulder. Unless she planned to back right out the window, there was no escaping him. But she could evade him, at least until she figured out a way to tell him that everything he had ever believed about himself was a lie.

She planted her fists on her hips, still keeping the paper carefully concealed, and glared at him. "And why would I have to shoot my way out of here? You proved in that glen that you were only too eager to be rid of me."

He stopped in his tracks, eyeing her warily. "Perhaps I should go tell my grandfather to lock up the pistols."

"Don't bother denying it! The earl didn't even give you what you asked for, yet you couldn't wait to let me go." As Emma felt her temper begin to rise in earnest, she was surprised to discover that she meant every word she was saying. "All he had to do was wave a little gold under your nose and you practically shoved me into his arms. I'm surprised you didn't offer to trade me for a horse. Or maybe even a . . . a . . . sheep!"

Jamie's lips twitched, as if he desperately wanted to smile but knew he didn't dare. "After spending the night in your arms, I have to confess that even the most devoted sheep has lost its appeal."

"Why, Jamie?" she asked, refusing to let him charm his way out of answering her question. "Why did you let me go?"

"Because I didn't believe you were mine to keep."

She turned back to the majestic view beyond the window, not wanting him to see she was on the verge of bursting into tears. She'd tried to be strong for so long but the events of the past few days seemed to be catching up with her all at once, compounded by the shock of what she had just discovered.

When Jamie's voice came again, it was a husky whisper in her ear. "But I was wrong." She could feel his strength, his heat, warming her deeper than any beam of sunlight ever could. "Even before you were shot, I knew what a bluidy fool I'd been. I was already coming after you. That's why I was able to react so quickly when I saw the gunman. Because I realized that I —"

Emma turned to gaze up at him, so mesmerized by his words that she forgot all about her shoulder . . . and all about the piece of paper in her hand. Until it slipped from her limp fingers and went fluttering to the floor at their feet.

She scrambled to retrieve it, but unhampered by a wounded shoulder, Jamie was able to reach it first.

"And what's this, lass?" he asked, shooting her a bemused glance as he straightened. "Were you penning a ransom note of your own? Because at the moment I don't think my grandfather would give you two shillings for me."

He studied the piece of paper briefly before giving her a curious look. "It looks like a page torn from some auld church register. Where on earth did you get it?"

"Mags gave it to me," she reluctantly confessed.

"Ah!" He returned his gaze to the paper, shaking his head fondly. "Mags has always been like an auld crow, collecting odd treasures to feather her nest — pretty rocks, auld coins, shiny . . ." His voice trailed off, fading along with the color in his face. When he lifted his eyes to her again, they had gone dark with shock. "I don't understand," he whispered. "What is the meaning of this?"

She attempted a weak smile. "Apparently you're not as much of a bastard as I thought you were the first time we met."

He glanced back down at the paper, his lips moving as he read the last two signatures on the page once again.

Lianna Elizabeth Sinclair.

Gordon Charles Hepburn.

"I know this must come as something of a shock," Emma said gently. "But your father didn't just seduce your mother. He married her. According to this, your parents must have secretly eloped months before you were born. You're not a Sinclair after all. You never were. You're a Hepburn and you always have been."

Jamie glanced up at her again, his look of abject horror almost comical.

She shook her head, marveling anew at their discovery. "You're not only the Hepburn's grandson but his legitimate heir. The heir to an earldom."

Jamie spun on his heel and stalked across the room, crumpling the fragile proof of his lineage in his fist as if it was so much garbage.

He drove his other hand through his hair, ruffling it beyond repair before wheeling around to face her. His expression was as savage as she had ever seen it. "So they weren't eloping the night they headed down the mountain?"

Emma shook her head. "Apparently not. Perhaps they were going to tell the Hepburn that they'd been wed all along, that he would have no choice but to acknowledge their love . . . and their son." She took a few steps toward him, longing to smooth the tousled sable strands from his brow, to lay her lips against the troubled furrow between his eyes. "This doesn't change who you are, Jamie. You're still the same man. What are you so afraid of? That if you lay claim to your inheritance, you'll have to give up your wild ways? Your freedom?"

"I'm reasonably certain the Hepburn only requires your soul to enter his service." He shook the fist holding the paper at her. "You know damn well the auld goat will never acknowledge this. Where did it come from anyway?"

She lowered her eyes. "I told you. Mags gave it to me."

"And where did she get it?"

Not sure just how many more shocks his battered heart could take, Emma reluctantly nodded toward the table where the old nurse's offering still sat. Jamie crossed to the table and picked up the empty box, jarring a few more off-key notes from its rusted works.

The look on his face as he lowered the lid, coming face to face with his mother's miniature, made Emma's own heart clutch in her breast. "I've never seen her before," he whispered. "She's even more beautiful than I imagined. But where did Mags find it?"

"She left me with the impression that your mother had trusted it into her keeping but that someone else had taken it from her after your mother's death and buried it to keep it from being discovered."

Their eyes met, both of them realizing in the same breath exactly who that someone must be.

"Why?" Jamie asked hoarsely. "Why would my grandfather do such a thing? Why would he pretend to love me, yet lie to me with his every breath?"

Emma shook her head helplessly. "I have no idea. Perhaps he was afraid of losing you to the Hepburn. If the earl had known from the beginning that you were his legitimate heir, he might have tried to claim you for his own. Perhaps your grandfather felt he had no choice but to bury it — along with the truth."

"Then I wish to hell it had stayed buried!"

Before Emma could stop him, Jamie hurled the box to the floor.

The rotting wood gave way, splintering wide open to reveal a false bottom and sending a necklace spilling out at Jamie's feet.

CHAPTER TWENTY-EIGHT

The necklace was a tarnished Gaelic cross on a chain of braided pewter. Even before Jamie knelt to gather it into his hand, Emma recognized it from the miniature on the lid of the box.

It was his mother's necklace.

The necklace she had been wearing when the artist sketched her likeness. The necklace that had vanished on the night she died, ripped from her throat by the hand of her murderer.

But both the chain and the clasp of this necklace were intact, as if someone hadn't torn it away from its wearer but tenderly removed it from her lifeless body.

Emma heard Jamie's words echo through the room as clearly as if he had just uttered them: *It was naught more than a worthless trinket. . . . It wouldn't have been of value to anyone but a Sinclair.*

Jamie slowly lifted his eyes to hers. It

wasn't the emotion in the arctic wasteland of those eyes that froze her soul, but the damning lack of it. Without a word, he straightened and went stalking from the chamber, the chain of the necklace dangling from his clenched fist.

Emma stood staring at the empty doorway in dumb shock for several precious seconds, then went racing after him, fearing this was one murder she might not be able to prevent.

Emma's throbbing shoulder forced her to slow down on the narrow spiral stairs that wound down into the heart of the tower. When she reached the long, high-ceilinged room that must have once served as the great hall of the keep, it was to discover that the large oak door at the far end of the room was standing wide open.

She hurried across the hall, afraid she might already be too late. If Jamie reached his grandfather before she reached him, she feared he would be lost forever, not just to her but to himself.

She emerged from the gloom, blinking in the bright sunshine. As her eyes adjusted, she saw Jamie just topping a small rise to the east of the keep. She called his name but he kept walking as if he hadn't heard her, his stride as ruthless as his countenance.

She lifted the hem of her gown and hastened after him. When she reached the top of the rise, she saw Ramsey Sinclair tilling the stony ground of the slope below with a heavy iron hoe, his snowy white mane of hair blowing in the wind.

Fearing the hoe could end up being used as a weapon, she quickened her steps.

"So are you burying more secrets, auld mon? Or perhaps some actual bodies this time?" Stopping right in front of his grandfather, Jamie lifted his fist to dangle the tarnished necklace in the man's face.

Ramsey Sinclair didn't even look surprised, only resigned. It was as if he had been waiting twenty-seven years for this moment to arrive and now that it finally had, it was almost a relief.

"Jamie, please," Emma said softly, stopping a few feet from the two men.

He took his eyes off his grandfather just long enough to point a finger at her. "This is none of your concern, lass. And don't you dare swoon! Because if you do, I'm bluidy well not going to catch you."

Emma held her tongue. Despite Jamie's warning, she knew that if she keeled over at that very moment his arms would be around her before she could hit the ground.

To her keen relief his grandfather moved to sink down on a rounded boulder at the edge of the garden, laying the heavy hoe aside. With his shoulders stooped beneath the weight of Jamie's contempt, he looked every minute of his age.

"I adored yer mother, ye know," he said, squinting up at Jamie in the sunlight. "She was all I had left after the fever killed your grandmother. It broke my heart nigh asunder when she ran away with that rogue." He shook his head, his craggy face lined with sorrow. "I searched for months to no avail. I might have never found them until they wanted to be found if Mags hadn't managed to get word to me that Lianna's babe had been born. But by the time I reached the crofter's hut, it was too late. They had already gone."

"So you hunted them down." Jamie's flat words were not a question.

Anger flared in the elder Sinclair's eyes, making them look eerily similar to his grandson's. "How can I expect ye to understand when ye've ne'er had a daughter o' yer own? My Lianna was always a good girl. And he was just another miserable greedy Hepburn used to takin' whate'er he wanted, no matter the cost. It wasn't the first time a

Hepburn had preyed upon an innocent young lass he happened upon in the woods. Why, yer own grandmother ➤ my sweet Alyssa —" He broke off, his voice strangled by rage and remembered anguish.

Emma closed her eyes briefly, understanding all too clearly how this legacy of hatred had been passed from generation to generation.

"I knew the young rogue had seduced my Lianna. Maybe even raped her. Made her his whore."

"She wasn't his whore!" Jamie thundered. *"She was his wife!"*

His grandfather lifted the back of one trembling hand to his mouth. "I didn't know that then. I didn't find the page from the weddin' register in the pocket of his coat until after they were dead. By then, it was too late." His voice faded to a choked whisper. "Too late for all of us."

Emma wondered how he had borne it all these years — knowing he had murdered his daughter and her husband for a crime neither one of them had committed. No wonder his heart was finally failing beneath the crushing burden of his guilt.

The Sinclair turned his beseeching eyes back to his grandson. "I never meant to hurt her, lad. I swear it! I just wanted to bring her home. When I caught up to them in the glen, I drew my pistol, thinkin' it might frighten that young whelp into givin' her up without a fight. But he shouted that she was too good, too fine to spend the rest o' her life with the likes o' the Sinclairs. That she belonged to him now. That he would *never* let her go. Then everythin' went red and all I could hear was the roarin' in my ears as I lifted the pistol and pointed it at his heart. At the very instant I squeezed the trigger, she threw herself in front o' him."

Jamie pressed the fist holding the necklace to his lips as his grandfather continued. "I'll ne'er forget the look in her eyes. The shock, the betrayal and worst of all, in those last precious seconds of her life — the pity."

The elder Sinclair bowed his head, as if already knowing he had forever relinquished any right to his grandson's pity. "Hepburn caught her as she fell, just sat there rockin' back and forth with her in his arms, weepin' like a babe. I couldn't believe what I'd done. But all I could think was if not for him, if not for all the Hepburns who had pissed all over the Sinclairs through the centuries, my precious baby girl would still be alive. So I walked over to him and put the mouth of my pistol right between his eyes. He didn't even fight. He just gazed up at me as if daring me — no, begging me — to pull the trigger."

"So you did," Jamie said bleakly.

"Aye. And there they lay. Dead in each other's arms." His grandfather's jaw hardened. "I couldn't bear the thought o' him still touchin' her, tryin' to lay claim to her even in death. So I pulled them apart. Made sure he would ne'er touch her again. I was about to turn the pistol on myself when I heard it."

"What?" Emma asked softly, well aware that both men had probably forgotten her presence. "What did you hear?"

He cocked his head as if haunted by the echo of a moment long past. "A gentle cooin' like that of a dove. I walked over to the bushes and there ye were. They must have tucked ye away when they heard my horse approachin'."

The look on Jamie's face broke Emma's heart anew. "I was there in that glen on the night they died? But you told me they'd left me with Mags."

His grandfather shrugged. "What's one more lie added to a thousand?" A shadow crossed his face. "For one dark moment, I was tempted to kill ye, too — to destroy the last remainin' evidence of their love. But when I reached down to do it, ye just looked up at me without cryin'. Without blinkin'. Then ye grabbed my finger in yer tiny little fist and held on for dear life." The old man turned his face to Jamie, tears of remembered wonder glazing his eyes. "In that moment, I knew ye weren't theirs after all. Ye were mine."

When Jamie continued to gaze down at him, his face as beautiful and merciless as an avenging angel's, the Sinclair swiped away the tears, his hand growing ever more steady. "I didn't want to live with what I'd done. But I knew I had no choice if I was to look after ye. So I took ye back to Mags at the crofter's hut and swore her to silence, then returned to the glen late that night with my men so there would be witnesses when yer par—" He swallowed. "— when the bodies were found."

Jamie's voice was dangerously dispassionate. "And I suppose it was easy enough to blame their murders on the Hepburn. After all, he and his kin had been responsible for most of the ills around these parts for centuries."

"Aye. That was the only part of my divilment I couldn't bring myself to regret. At least not until now."

Emma's heart nearly stopped when he reached into a hidden fold of his kilt and withdrew an ancient-looking pistol with a flared muzzle. But he simply offered it to Jamie, butt forward.

"Go on, lad. Take it and do what I should have had the courage to do all those years ago."

Jamie gazed down at the weapon in his grandfather's hand, his eyes as cold as Emma had ever seen them. "You always told me the truth could kill you. Or it could keep you alive. I believe I'll let you just keep on living with what you've done."

His grandfather struggled to his feet, leaning heavily on the handle of the hoe. "I don't want yer mercy, lad! I have no need of it!"

A scornful smile curved Jamie's lips. "Oh, I haven't any mercy where you're concerned. There's just no need for me to hasten your journey to hell. You'll get there soon enough on your own."

With his mother's necklace still dangling from his fingers, Jamie turned his back on his grandfather. As he walked past her, Emma reached for him. But he continued on as if she wasn't even there.

She hesitated for a moment, then turned to follow. She half expected to hear the thundering report of a pistol behind her. But when she paused at the top of the rise to glance over her shoulder, it was to discover that Jamie's grandfather had already taken up his hoe and gone back to tilling the rocky soil.

She would have hated him as much as Jamie did in that moment but she knew he was simply doing what the Sinclairs had always done.

Surviving.

When Emma reached the balcony crowning the very top of the keep, Jamie was already there, standing with his back to her and his hands gripping the wooden balustrade.

As she emerged into the sunlight, an involuntary gasp escaped her. The Highlands were sprawled below them in all of their rustic splendor. A misty veil of green draped the lower passes and glens while dazzling patches of white still crowned the highest crags. Winding streams poured down the mountainside, fattened by the melting snows and glistening silver beneath the kiss of the sun.

As an ethereal wisp of cloud drifted right past the balcony, she understood how Jamie's grandfather might have come to fancy himself the ruler of some mighty kingdom. Why live among the mere mortals down in the foothills when one could reside among the clouds? While overlooking this breathtaking view from such a dizzying height, a man might very well fancy himself the ruler of heaven itself.

At the moment, Jamie looked more like the dark prince of some Stygian underworld where doomed souls were sent to await their punishment.

"You shouldn't be here," he said without turning around. "You belong in bed."

"Whose bed?" she asked softly, joining him at the balustrade. "Yours? The earl's?"

He turned to face her, his expression so distant it sent a dark shiver of dread down her spine. "Your own bed. The one in your bedchamber in Lancashire. The one with the robin's nest right outside your window and the family of mice living in the dining room baseboards. You belong a thousand leagues away from here — away from all the deceit and treachery . . . and death."

"Away from you?"

His hesitation was so brief she might have imagined it. "Aye." He returned his gaze to that grand sweep of moor and mountain, his profile as stern and intractable as a stranger's. "As far away from me as the road can take you."

"And what if I don't choose to go?"

"You don't have a choice. Didn't you hear

my grandfather? I come from a long line of men with a history of destroying the very thing they love the most."

Hope surged within her, pushing the dread aside. "What are you trying to say, Jamie? That you love me? Is that what you were about to tell me before you discovered the page from the marriage register?"

She touched his sleeve but he pulled away from her. He hadn't been able to keep his hands off her before, but now it was as if he couldn't bear to look at her, much less touch her.

"What are you trying to do?" she cried, her frustration growing. "Pretend that night in the bell tower never happened?" Could he pretend she had never lain beneath him, shuddering in helpless wonder as his nimble fingers and powerful body gave her the sweetest and most devastating pleasure a man could give a woman? "Can you truly tell me that night meant nothing to you?"

He turned to look directly at her then, the indifference in his eyes even more chilling than the contempt he had shown his grandfather. "I kept my end of our bargain. You asked me to ruin you, not pledge my eternal love. If you're well enough to travel on the morrow, I'm taking you down the mountain. Your family may very well believe you're dead. I need to get you back to them before they leave Scotland for good."

Emma shook her head, reeling from his curt dismissal of all they had shared. "What about the Hepburn? He might not have murdered your mother but he did try to murder me. And I'm sure he'll be only too delighted to learn that there's no need for him to find himself a new bride since he already has an heir."

A grim smile canted Jamie's lips. "Oh, you can leave the Hepburn to me. He's no longer your concern. I'll deal with him."

He turned on his heel to go, then paused, frowning down at his hand as if he was surprised to find his mother's necklace still looped through his fingers.

Emma felt her heart stutter with hope as he took her hand in his and dropped the necklace into her palm.

He lifted his gaze to hers, the regret shadowing his eyes extinguishing her fragile hope. "I tried to warn you, lass, that it was naught but a worthless trinket." He gently folded her fingers around the necklace, then turned away.

After he had disappeared into the shadows of the stairs, Emma opened her hand to gaze down at the simple Gaelic cross.

It was a symbol of faith. A symbol of hope.

The Sinclair who had smuggled it out of the castle as he and his kinsmen were being driven from their home must have known it would inspire the dreams of the generations to come. The woman who had worn it last had refused to relinquish her own dreams. She had been willing to risk everything — her home, her father's love . . . even her life — to make them come true.

Emma closed her fist around the necklace, lifting her eyes to gaze out over the rugged land she was coming to love. Jamie Sinclair was about to discover that this tarnished trinket was not so worthless after all and that he just might have found himself an adversary more ruthless and determined than the Hepburn.

CHAPTER TWENTY-NINE

As Jamie descended into the hall of the keep the next morning, the last thing he expected to hear was Emma's merry ripple of laughter. He scowled, wondering if he was still dreaming.

But how could he be dreaming when he hadn't even slept? When he'd spent the entire night pacing the floor and fighting the temptation to slip back into Emma's bedchamber . . . and her bed? How could he be dreaming when all of his dreams had died only a few hours ago, crushed beneath the iron fist of his grandfather's treachery?

He reached the foot of the stairs, his mouth falling open when he saw the unexpected scene of domestic bliss.

The long table in the middle of the hall had been draped with a clean cloth. Emma was bustling around it, a tray of steaming scones balanced in her hands.

If not for the bandage peeking out from

the bodice of her harebell-blue gown, one would never know she'd been shot and nearly died only a few days before. Her hair was loose around her shoulders, but drawn back from her face by two ivory combs Mags must have found somewhere. Jamie was even more riveted by the sight of his mother's necklace fastened around the slender column of her throat.

She leaned over the table, offering fresh scones and an enchanting view of the gentle swell of her bosom to the two men seated on one of the long benches that flanked it. One of the men was Bon.

The other was Ian Hepburn.

Although his left arm was still confined by the sling, his bruised face was scrubbed clean and his sleek, dark hair was neatly secured at his nape in a leather queue, exposing the dramatic swoop of his widow's peak. If Jamie wasn't mistaken, he was wearing one of Jamie's own shirts.

Spotting Jamie, he cocked a mocking eyebrow in his direction. "Good morning, Sin. Or would you prefer 'my lord'?"

Jamie turned his disbelieving gaze on Emma. "You told him about the marriage register?"

She shrugged. "And why not? The whole world will find out you're the earl's heir soon enough."

"Not if I have anything to say about it," Jamie retorted.

Bon tucked another plump bite of scone between his lips, rolling his eyes in pure pleasure. "Ye're a damn sight finer cook than Mags, lass. If I can ever catch ye between fiancés, I just might swear off me bachelor ways and court ye meself."

"Why, thank you, Bon," Emma replied, visibly preening. "It's always gratifying for a woman to find a man who appreciates her skills." She turned her innocent smile on Jamie. "*All* of her skills."

Jamie was forced to squeeze out his words from between clenched teeth. "Funny, Bon, but I don't recall giving you orders to release our prisoner."

"He didn't require orders." Emma gave one of Bon's pointy ears a fond tweak. "He only required the promise of a piping hot scone fresh from the oven."

Shooting Jamie a droll look, Ian helped himself to another scone. "You needn't worry I'm going to stab you in the back just so I can steal your inheritance. As you can imagine, I was rather nonplussed when Miss Marlowe first told me the news. But upon reflection, I've decided I'm rather pleased by this fascinating development, if only to

imagine the vexation it will cause my uncle."
He lifted one shoulder in an elegant shrug.
"Better to lose my inheritance to you than
some mewling infant I'd be tempted to
smother in his crib. Perhaps now I can
finally be free of that godforsaken castle and
the petty tyrant who rules it."

Jamie folded his arms over his chest. "I
wouldn't have thought you'd have been so
eager to allow a cold-blooded murderer to
take your place."

"Interesting that you would bring that up.
While I was enjoying your . . . *hospitality,* I
struck up a conversation with a young man
named Graeme who was sent to guard me.
Of course, I had made his acquaintance
once before when he came to the castle to
deliver your ransom demand, but we had
limited opportunities for discourse since it
wasn't exactly a social call." Ian used the
blade of his knife to slather some fresh
cream on his scone. "He was kind enough
to help me pass the long hours of my captiv-
ity by telling me a most intriguing tale about
a vicious gamekeeper and a noble savior
who came riding out of the mist to stage a
most daring rescue. A rescue that resulted
in the lad being fortunate enough to keep
both of his hands."

"What a thrilling story!" Emma exclaimed, ignoring Jamie's glare as she slid onto the bench opposite Ian.

"Indeed." Ian cast Jamie a narrow look. "A pity my dear cousin here didn't share it himself instead of letting me believe the worst of him for four years."

"Something you were only too eager to do. Even if I'd have told you the truth that day you rode up on the mountain to confront me, I doubt you would have believed me."

Ian snorted. "And why should I have believed you when my uncle had just informed me that nearly every word you'd ever uttered to me was a lie?"

The flush creeping up Jamie's throat only made him feel sulkier. "I didn't lie when we were at St. Andrews. I just neglected to tell you that our families had been enemies for over five centuries and you were supposed to hate me and wish me dead with your every breath."

"I wanted to do more than wish you dead that day," Ian muttered, shifting his gaze to Emma. "When my uncle found out exactly who I'd been keeping company with at St. Andrews, he laughed so hard I thought he was going to give himself an apoplexy. He told me Jamie had doubtlessly been laughing behind my back the entire time, mocking me to our classmates and to the rough-and-tumble lads he rode with whenever he returned to the mountain. He told me that no matter how well I learned to use my fists, I could never hope to be half the man that Jamie Sinclair was."

"That bastard," Jamie breathed, despising the Hepburn anew for driving such an indestructible wedge between two devoted friends. "No wonder you tried to kill me that day on the mountain."

"I thought it was time to put some of the skills you'd taught me to good use. You have to admit that I did manage to get in a few decent licks."

Jamie glowered at him. "You broke two of my ribs and my nose."

"But I was still no match for him," Ian told Emma. "He could have easily killed me but he chose not to. I hated him even more for that. We never saw each other again after that day . . . not until he came riding into your wedding."

"You poor dear! What a terrible ordeal it must have been for you!" Emma reached across the table to pat Ian's hand with a tenderness that made Jamie stiffen.

"Aye," Bon agreed, gesturing with his own knife. "The puir lad is lucky to be alive."

"He broke two of my ribs and my nose,"

Jamie repeated. But no one seemed to be paying him any heed. They were too busy clucking in sympathy over poor Ian's terrible plight. "Now that we've all suffered through that touching little tale, perhaps one of you would like to tell me what in the bluidy hell is going on here."

Bon and Ian took a renewed interest in their scones but Emma rose, coming around the table to face him. "We're plotting my revenge against the Hepburn."

"*Your* revenge?"

"Yes, my revenge." She lifted her chin, looking every bit as defiant and magnificent as she had the first time she'd stood up to him. "Do you think the Sinclairs have some sort of monopoly on revenge? It was me he tried to kill this time, not you. What right do you have to deny me the satisfaction of watching that shriveled little toad of a man crawl at my feet?"

"I told you I'd take care of the Hepburn."

"I don't need you to take care of the Hepburn. Or me, for that matter." She drew even closer to him, so close he could smell the tantalizing fragrance of her skin. He could remember every nuance of what it felt like to trail his fingertips over that skin. "I've never fought for anything in my life. Don't you think it's time I started?"

Something in her expression warned him that she was talking about more than just defeating the Hepburn. And that she just might be a far more formidable opponent than he'd anticipated.

He shifted his gaze to Ian. "And I'm just supposed to believe you're willing to throw in your lot with us? With your family's sworn enemies?"

Ian rose to his feet, a mocking smile curving his lips. "And why not? There's obviously no love lost between me and my uncle. He didn't even care whether or not I survived the ambush. And besides, lest you've forgotten, you *are* my family."

"And if he's *yer* family," Bon said, rising to clap Ian on the back, "then he's my family, too!"

Jamie studied Emma through narrowed eyes, allowing his curiosity to overrule his caution. "So tell me, lass, just how do you intend to bring the earl to his knees? To make him rue the day he crossed Miss Emmaline Marlowe?"

She exchanged a glance with the other two men before giving him a bright smile. "How else? I'm going to marry him."

CHAPTER THIRTY

Silas Dockett didn't even flinch when his master's bony hand went whipping across his face, leaving a vivid print against his pock-marked cheek. He was too well compensated to complain about a little abuse. Being an earl's lackey was much better than fishing bloated corpses out of the foul-smelling muck of the Thames for hours on end, all in the unlikely hope of finding a gold tooth or a crested signet ring.

"You *fool!*" the earl spat. "How dare you come crawling back here just to tell me you haven't succeeded in finding my bride! She can't have just vanished into thin air!"

"Your men and I 'ave spent the last week combin' every inch o' mountain around that glen, m'lord. There's no sign o' your bride. Or your nephew."

The earl waved away his words. "I'm not worried about that fool nephew of mine. I should have known the hapless idiot

411

wouldn't even have the good sense to take cover once the firing started. If Sinclair's men captured him or put a pistol ball in his worthless hide, it was no more than he deserved. It's the girl I need. *The girl I must have!*"

Dockett shook his shaggy head, wadding up his hat in his hands. "I'm tellin' you, sir. I saw 'er go down. I'm a crack shot. There's no way I could 'ave missed from that distance and there's no way she could 'ave survived."

"Then you mustn't give up until you find her. I want you to take the men back out there without delay and keep searching." The earl grabbed the much larger man by the lapels of his cheap woolen coat and shook him, spittle flying from his lips. "If I'm going to bring the redcoats down on Jamie Sinclair's head and rid myself of him and his kind forever, I need a body!"

"M'laird! Is that you over by the fountain?"

The earl shuddered as Mrs. Marlowe's voice came drifting to his ears. Mrs. Marlowe and her remaining daughters had spent most of the past week weeping and honking into their handkerchiefs so violently one would have sworn a flock of consumptive geese had invaded the castle.

He had deliberately chosen this secluded corner of the garden for his meeting with Dockett, hoping to elude the ever-present Marlowe family. But it seemed there was no longer any corner of the castle free from their wretched interference. He couldn't wait for the day when they could take their daughter's body and go, never to darken his doorstep again.

Ever since they had received word that Sinclair had double-crossed them all — shooting Emma, capturing Ian and making off with the ransom — they'd been fluttering about the castle like a flock of vultures. They had no way of knowing that it was his own gamekeeper who had shot Emma and that both the wagon and the gold were hidden beneath a bale of hay in his stables.

As the days passed without any trace of Emma's body being found, he had gently encouraged them to return to England, promising to send word as soon as there was news. But they'd refused to go, insisting that they could not possibly abandon their daughter as long as there was any hope she might still be alive.

When the earl turned to find the entire family descending upon him en masse, it was all he could do not to duck behind Dockett's beefy shoulders and order the man to shoot them all.

Mr. Marlowe led their bedraggled little parade with his wife clinging to his elbow. The daughters followed, carrying parasols to protect their already freckled complexions from the threat of the afternoon sunlight. They certainly weren't any more attractive with their noses and eyes reddened from their incessant weeping.

The earl moved to intercept them on the flagstone path, plastering what he hoped was a sympathetic smile on his lips. "I do hope you'll forgive me for being such a wretched host. I often enjoy a walk in the garden as the day begins to wane. I find the *solitude* to be a balm to my aching heart."

They all blinked dully at him, showing no sign of taking or even understanding his hint.

Mr. Marlowe cleared his throat awkwardly. The earl peered at him, wondering if the cloudiness that had plagued his own eyesight for the past few months was worsening. As unthinkable as it was, he would almost swear the man was . . . sober.

"My wife and I have been discussing the current situation. We would never presume to question your experience or gainsay your judgement in these matters but we think it might be time to call in the proper authorities to assist in the search for Emmaline."

The earl felt his smile begin to thin. When an Englishman used the word *proper,* he could only mean one thing — another Englishman.

"I can assure you that I have every intention of contacting the *proper* authorities, but I fear it might be a bit premature to seek their intervention. They're usually reluctant to get involved until the time comes to bring the suspected culprit to justice."

"But perhaps they would have the resources to enable us to find our dear Emma," the chit's mother offered timidly. "Aside from the testimony of your men, we have no proof that her wound was mortal. She might still be alive out there somewhere, just waiting for us to come for her."

The earl gently gathered the woman's gloved hands into his own, giving them a fatherly pat. "My dear Mrs. Marlowe, I wish I could share your hope, but I feel it would be cruel to allow you to entertain such an unlikely scenario. My own Mr. Dockett here saw your daughter fall after that miserable wretch Sinclair opened fire on her. If not for the resulting confusion, he would have been able to retrieve her body before it was snatched by those ruffians. I can assure you my own men will continue to search until it — until *she* — is found."

Exchanging a glance with his wife, Marlowe deliberately squared his sagging shoulders. "While we appreciate the efforts of your men, my lord, I'm afraid they are no longer enough to satisfy us. I simply must insist that the authorities be notified."

"Fortunately, that won't be necessary."

As that mellifluous voice rang out, they turned as one to find Ian standing beneath the elaborately scrolled arch of the iron trellis that separated the garden from the churchyard. Despite the yellowing bruise on one of his cheekbones and the sling binding his left arm, he seemed to be standing even taller and straighter than when he'd left.

A strangled gasp escaped the earl as Emmaline Marlowe appeared at his nephew's side.

A dazzling smile lit her face as she came flying toward him. She threw her arms around him, nearly knocking him off his feet. "Darling! I've come home to you at last!"

CHAPTER THIRTY-ONE

Emma felt the earl's slight form stagger beneath her overly enthusiastic embrace. "Oh, my dearest," she crooned, suppressing a shudder as she leaned down to press her cheek to his dry, papery one. "What a joy it is to be back in your arms! You can only imagine my distress when I thought I'd never see you again!"

He stood frozen in her embrace like a mummified corpse for several awkward moments before finally lifting one bony hand to give her back a feeble pat. "There, there, dear. I was just explaining to your family that it was far too soon to give up hope for your return."

"My baby!" her mother sobbed, running forward to wrest Emma from the earl's arms.

Even though her healing shoulder throbbed a sharp protest, Emma was only too happy to trade the earl's embrace for her mother's. As she was enveloped in the familiar scent of rice powder and lavender water, genuine tears stung her eyes. It made her feel as if she was a little girl again. Her mother had no way of knowing she was a woman now. Jamie Sinclair had seen to that.

Her mother held her at arm's length to study her, her eyes still brimming with tears. "Why, just look at your poor hair! I do believe it's more impossible than ever. Have you been carrying a parasol to protect your complexion from the elements? No? Well, I didn't think so. You're more freckled than a brown egg fresh from the henhouse. We'll have to send one of the earl's servants to the village immediately for a new jar of Gowland's Lotion. And I do believe you're even scrawnier than before. No man is going to want you if we don't put some meat back on those bones."

Emma had to bite back a secret smile as she remembered Jamie cupping the softness of her breasts as if they were the most exquisite treasures he had ever been allowed to touch.

As her mother's gaze returned to her face, her plump bottom lip began to quiver anew. "Oh, my precious girl!" she cried out, fresh tears spilling from her eyes. "You're the most beautiful sight I've ever seen!"

As she snatched Emma back into her embrace, Emma became aware that someone else was gently stroking her hair. She opened her eyes to find her papa standing beside them. Although his face bore all too clearly the ravages of recent drink, his eyes were clear and his hand steady.

"Hello, pet," he said, offering her a shy smile. "We're glad to have you back."

Then all was chaos for several minutes as Emma's sisters descended upon them, chattering like a flock of magpies.

"So what was it like to be the captive of such a dastardly villain?" Edwina asked.

"Did he tie you up and insist upon having his way with you?" Elberta inquired, ignoring their mother's scandalized gasp.

"Repeatedly?" Ernestine added hopefully.

"In truth, this Sinclair fellow hardly paid me any heed at all," Emma lied, beset by memories: Jamie kissing her for the first time on that moonlit bluff; Jamie carrying her through the snow at Muira's cottage, the glittering flakes catching like diamond dust in his lashes; Jamie kneeling naked before her, no longer able to hide his desperate hunger for her. "Whenever he looked at me, I'm sure all he saw was the fat purse of gold he hoped to win by selling me back to the earl."

All three of the girls looked woefully crestfallen.

"Did he at least *threaten* to ravish you if
you dared to defy him?" Elberta ventured.

Emma sighed. "I'm afraid not. I spent
most of my confinement tied to a tree,
watching Sinclair and those savages who
ride with him swill whisky and make ribald
jests at my poor bridegroom's expense."

The earl ground his porcelain teeth.

"We've been positively ill with worry,
child," her father confessed. "Only last week
the earl's men returned with word that
you'd been shot when they were delivering
the ransom. He's had men out combing the
mountainside ever since. Just how were you
able to make your escape?"

The earl swallowed, looking as if he was
on the verge of being ill. "Yes, I'm sure we'd
all love to hear how you managed to slip
through the clutches of those scoundrels."

"Oh, I owe it all to your courageous
nephew here!" Emma reached back to twine
an arm through Ian's, drawing him into
their joyful little circle. "It was his astonishing reflexes and quick thinking that saved
me."

Ernestine claimed Ian's other arm, blinking up at him like an adoring rabbit. "That
doesn't surprise me in the least. From the

first moment we met, I could tell that Mr. Hepburn here had a heroic nature."

"You are too kind, miss," Ian gritted out. He tried to retrieve his arm but Ernestine dug her nails into it, refusing to release him.

"It didn't hurt that Sinclair has wretched aim," Emma said. "Fortunately, his shot only grazed my shoulder."

The earl cast a murderous glance at the beefy man standing behind him with hat in hands, making a noise in the back of his throat that sounded suspiciously like a growl.

"After he saw me fall, Ian here managed to whisk me away to safety when the other men opened fire and keep me in hiding until he thought it would be safe for us to make our way down the mountain." Emma gave Ian's arm a fond squeeze. "Who would have thought a gentleman like Mr. Hepburn here would have such a gift for surviving in the wilderness?"

"I've often said my nephew is a man of many talents," the earl murmured, refusing to meet Ian's eyes.

Abandoning Ian to Ernestine's clutches, Emma returned to the earl's side. She beamed down her nose at him, deliberately emphasizing the discrepancy in their heights. "The whole time I was having my little adventure, all I could think about was getting back to you so I could take my rightful place as your bride."

"Perhaps we should delay our nuptials until you're fully recovered, my dear. I'm thinking a thorough examination by a physician might be in order to ascertain the *full* extent of your injuries."

Despite the warmth of her bridegroom's smile, the cold light in his eyes betrayed the fact that he was talking about far more than just her shoulder.

"Oh, that won't be necessary," she replied cheerfully. "It was naught more than a scratch. Tomorrow morning there will be nothing — and no one — to stop us from standing before that altar and making our pledges to each other."

The earl took one of Emma's hands in his, lifting it to his ice-cold lips. "Welcome home, my dear," he said stiffly, offering her a formal bow. "I shall be looking forward to our wedding with great anticipation."

"As will I, my lord," Emma replied, spreading her skirts to sink into a deep curtsy. "As will I."

Ian was lounging on a leather settee before the fire in the drawing room that night, enjoying a much needed cigar and a goblet of brandy, when a footman appeared in the doorway.

"The earl wishes to see you, sir."

Ian sighed, almost wishing himself back in Jamie's humble cell. At least there he hadn't had to pretend to be free while bound by invisible chains. He stubbed out the cigar but drained the goblet in one swallow before following the liveried footman to his uncle's study.

For once his uncle wasn't standing in front of the massive window on the north wall, gazing out over the mountain. Instead, he was sitting hunched over his desk, looking like a spindly old spider in the flickering firelight. Now that he was no longer in any danger of being caught in the old man's web, Ian felt an odd calm steal over him.

As the footman closed the door behind him, leaving the two of them alone, his uncle nodded toward the chair on the far side of the desk. "Sit, sit," he barked impatiently. "I haven't all night."

Tempted to agree that his uncle's time was growing ever shorter, Ian crossed the plush Aubusson carpet and settled himself into the chair, propping one shiny black Hessian on the opposite knee.

As was customary, the earl didn't squander any time or breath on pleasantries. "I have a favor to ask of you."

Ian cocked an eyebrow in surprise. In all the years since the man had been his guardian, he couldn't remember his uncle ever asking anything of him — short of keeping himself out from under his feet so he could forget about Ian's existence for extended periods of time.

"Just what can I do for you, my lord?"

"I would have approached you sooner but I had hoped the *situation* might resolve itself. Especially after a new opportunity came to light. But alas, due to the flagrant incompetence of nearly everyone around me, that stroke of good fortune has been squandered."

Only his uncle could manage to sound utterly convincing when referring to the attempted murder of his own bride as a "stroke of good fortune."

The earl picked up an ivory-handled letter opener from the leather blotter on the desk and turned it over in his hands, gazing down at the silver blade. He actually seemed to be struggling for words. "It pains me to confess that along with age can come certain . . . infirmities. One is not entirely the man one used to be."

Ian leaned forward in the chair, fascinated against his will. He'd never known his uncle to admit to any deficiency in either health or character. And he certainly hadn't noticed his uncle being any less of a petty tyrant than he'd always been.

"As you may have observed, there is a slight age difference between my bride and I."

"It hadn't entirely escaped my notice," Ian said dryly.

"While she is young and fertile, I fear that age has robbed me of my ability to produce an heir, if not the desire. That's where you come in." He cleared his throat, his hesitation betraying just how much it was costing him to take Ian into his confidence on such a sensitive matter. "I was hoping I could impose upon you to pay a visit to my bride's bedchamber on our wedding night. And every night thereafter until I can be assured that Hepburn blood will run through the veins of my heir."

Ian felt his own blood chill to ice. "Let me make sure I understand you. After you make Miss Marlowe your wife on the morrow, you want me to visit her bed nightly until I can be entirely certain that I've succeeded in impregnating her?"

His uncle's nostrils flared in disapproval. "There's no need to be so crude. We are all gentlemen here. But yes, that's exactly what

I am asking of you. Miss Marlowe seems to have developed a certain inexplicable *fondness* for you. I'm sure she won't object too strenuously." His uncle shrugged. "But if she does, there are ways to ensure her co-operation. I can instruct one of the more discreet footmen to assist you. Or there's always laudanum to dull the senses and cause confusion."

"Yes, with enough laudanum, I'm sure she could easily mistake me for you."

Deaf to his sarcasm, the earl chuckled. "She's a comely girl if not a beautiful one. I'm sure you won't find your duties overly taxing. Of course once I've achieved my goal of installing a new Hepburn brat in the nursery, I might be forced to call upon your services once more. At my age, it would behoove me to have both an 'heir and a spare' as it were."

Ian settled back in the chair, stunned into silence by the depths of his uncle's depravity. The man wasn't a spider. He was a monster, willing to allow his nephew to systematically rape his bride just to make sure no one would question his own virility or the lineage of his heir.

"You won't inherit, of course, but I'll reward you richly for both your service and your discretion. I'm thinking that property right outside of Edinburgh might be to your liking. If I throw in a healthy annual income, you'll be able to settle down, find a suitable wife, and father a few whelps of your own perhaps."

Ian had no doubt that once Emma had provided his uncle with his heir and a spare, she would be equally expendable. But she wouldn't be offered a healthy annual income and a property outside of Edinburgh. She was more likely to be offered an overdose of laudanum and a cold, stony bed in the churchyard of the abbey next to the earl's previous wives.

If Jamie had been present to hear the shocking proposal, the earl would be sitting behind his desk right now with the blade of the letter opener jammed right through his scrawny throat.

His uncle scowled at him. "What are you smiling about, lad?"

"I was just thinking that this might be one of the more pleasant obligations I've been asked to fulfill."

His uncle nodded in approval. "I knew I could count on you. Despite our differences, I've often suspected that you were cut from the same cloth as your dear old uncle."

Ian rose, sketching the man an elegant

bow. "I am, as always, my lord, at your humble service."

As he strolled from the study, heading back to the drawing room to finish his cigar and pour himself another goblet of brandy, Ian was still smiling.

Emma stood at the window of the luxurious bedchamber the earl had provided for her, gazing toward the north. The mountain was a mighty shadow against the night sky, crowned by a shimmering slice of moon and a sprinkling of stars. She could feel its irresistible tug on her heart as surely as she could feel Jamie's presence.

Even though he and his men had been forced to part company with her and Ian before reaching the border of the earl's lands, she knew he was out there somewhere. Watching her. Watching over her.

If he had his way, she would be returning to Lancashire with her family as soon as they brought down the Hepburn. He was determined not to make the same mistake his parents had made. To him, the rewards of love would never be worth its risks. Not when risking everything might mean ending up with nothing.

When their party had ridden away from his grandfather's keep, the old man had stood on the balcony to watch them go, his broad shoulders unyielding and his loyal deerhound standing by his side. Ramsey Sinclair must have known it would be the last time he would ever see his grandson. And even though Jamie had to have known his grandfather was there, he hadn't glanced back, not even once. Emma wondered if he would be able to cut her out of his heart with such devastating precision.

She touched her fingertips briefly to the cool glass of the windowpane as if to a lover's cheek. Left with no recourse but to seek the lonely comfort of her bed, she started to turn away from the window only to gasp with shock when the reflection of the man standing behind her came clearly into focus.

CHAPTER THIRTY-TWO

Emma spun around, clapping a hand over her mouth.

Jamie stood in front of the marble hearth, dressed all in black and framed by the firelight.

"What are you doing here?" she whispered, her heart leaping with joy. "How did you get in?"

"If a Sinclair knows how to sneak out of a castle," he said solemnly, "he also knows how to sneak in."

"The tunnel in the dungeons," she breathed.

"Aye." He touched a finger to his lips. " 'Tis a secret passed down through generations of Sinclairs just in case one of us might want to sneak into the castle in the dead of night to steal a rare volume of Descartes, slit some throats . . . or ravish some bonny Hepburn lass."

His words sent a delightful little shiver of

anticipation coursing through her. She lifted her chin, giving him an imperious look. "You almost tarried too long. I'm to be wed on the morrow, you know."

"So I've heard. To a shriveled-up auld goat." He crossed to her side, reaching out to twine one of her unbound curls around his finger as if he could no longer resist the temptation to touch her. "All the more reason you might want one night with a real mon in your bed."

"Are you volunteering your services?"

"I am. But I'm afraid I'm just a penniless Highland lad. I can't give you gems or furs or gold."

"Then what can you give me?"

"This," he whispered, lowering his lips to hers for a long, lingering kiss. "And this." He wrapped his arms around her and tugged her close, letting her feel every extraordinary inch of his hunger for her against the softness of her belly.

Emma twined her arms around his neck, melting into his kiss, melting into his arms.

He might claim he wasn't willing to follow the same path his parents had trod, yet he was risking everything, including his very life, by coming to her. And even though it could spoil all their schemes and cost them both dearly, she didn't have the heart — or the will — to send him away.

Without breaking the tender bond their mouths had forged, Jamie swept her up in his arms and carried her to the bed, still taking care to guard her shoulder. As he laid her beneath him, her curls spilled over the satin coverlet in a river of copper.

She had never felt more beautiful or more like a bride as she did in that moment. She understood how Jamie's mother must have felt when she had first encountered his father in that secluded wood; understood what had driven them to run away, leaving behind everything they held dear so they could embrace a love so strong and enduring it had created the man who was gazing down at her in the firelight, his eyes shadowed by a desire so desperate he was willing to risk his life — if not his heart — to slake it.

She sifted her fingers through the thick sable of his hair and tugged his delectable mouth back down to hers, inviting him to satisfy that desire, inviting him to satisfy her.

He wasted no time in accepting her invitation. Her nightdress seemed to dissolve beneath the clever machinations of his fingers, shimmering away into thin air and leaving her naked beneath him. He took pity on her own clumsy efforts to make his garments go away and deftly disrobed between tantalizing caresses and deep, drugging kisses. Soon their bodies were straining as eagerly as their mouths toward the moment when they could be united as one.

But just when Emma thought that moment had come, he went sliding down, down, down in the firelight. His big hands gently parted her thighs, exposing the very heart of her to his hungry gaze. Overcome by a sudden wave of shyness, she tried to wiggle out of his grasp. But he refused to allow it, using his superior strength to gently but firmly hold her fast.

Then he bowed his head and touched the very tip of his tongue to her just as he had touched it to her nipple that night in the ruins of the abbey.

If that had been bliss, then this was indescribable, a pleasure beyond any she had ever dreamed or imagined. Her hands fisted in the bedclothes, desperately seeking any purchase in a world tilting madly on its axis. Soon she was writhing beneath the tender lash of his tongue, his name an endless litany on her lips.

He knew she was going to come before she did. He reached up and gently covered her mouth with his hand, muffling her cry of ecstasy before it could wake the entire castle. Then his mouth was on hers again, forcing an intoxicating taste of her own pleasure on her as he drove himself up and into her with a tender savagery that left her gasping for breath.

He seemed determined to prove that no other strapping younger lover could vie for her heart with the same expertise or stamina. It was as if he intended to offer her a lifetime of lovemaking in one night, as if his body had been created for one purpose and one purpose only — to pleasure her.

He covered her, he stole behind her like a thief in the night and after a very long time he lay beneath her while she straddled him, his powerful hips rocking in a rhythm more irresistible and hypnotic than the tide rolling into the shore. Just when that tide was on the verge of pulling her under, into a sea of unspeakable bliss, he rolled again, taking her with him.

Emma could only cling helplessly to his shoulders as he took her with long, deep strokes, making her his again and again until she knew that no matter how far or how long she traveled in this world, she would always belong to him. By that time she was so sensitive to his touch that all it took was the merest brush of his fingertips to jolt her into another spasm of ecstasy.

His powerful body began to shudder. Emma expected him to withdraw, leaving her bereft, but he only surged deeper, clenching his teeth against a ragged groan. As he spilled his seed at the very mouth of her womb, she arched off the bed in a paroxysm of rapture, her secret muscles clenching and unclenching as if determined to milk every last drop of pleasure from Jamie's magnificent body.

As those last lingering tremors of bliss ravished her sated flesh, she collapsed into the feather mattress, beset by a languor so dark and deep she didn't know if she would ever find the strength to stir again.

"Oh, Jamie," she whispered without opening his eyes. "I knew you'd come back to me."

"Shhh," he murmured, brushing his lips over hers with a possessive tenderness that made her want to weep. "Sleep, angel. Dream."

When she opened her eyes again, he was gone.

Realizing that she must have dozed off, she struggled to her elbows, shaking her hair out of her eyes. There was no sign that Jamie had even been there. If not for the musky scent that clung to the bedclothes and the pleasurable tenderness between her thighs, she might have wondered if she *had* dreamed the whole thing.

Flopping back to the mattress, she blew an errant curl out of her eyes and glared up at the medallioned ceiling. Apparently, Jamie Sinclair hadn't yet realized his days as a thief and a raider were done. He could no longer slip into a woman's bedchamber to ravish her body — and steal her heart — without paying a very dear price indeed.

She turned her face to the window and the night beyond, gazing northward until the moon sank behind the mountain and her wedding eve turned into her wedding day.

Emma was sitting at the dressing table in her bedchamber the next morning, studying the serene reflection of the woman in the oval mirror, when a knock sounded on the door. She had already dismissed a bevy of chattering maidservants from the room, needing a few minutes to compose herself before the wedding.

"Come in," she called out, assuming it was a footman sent to tell her that her father was downstairs in the drawing room waiting to escort her to the abbey.

But when the door eased open, it was her

mother who appeared in the mirror's reflection. With her pale apricot hair, fair, freckled cheeks, and gentle blue eyes, Mariah Marlowe had once been as pretty as a pastel watercolor. But time and strain had faded her to a mere sketch of herself. In the past three years, as Emma's father had turned increasingly to the bottle for comfort and less often to her, it seemed that even those lines were beginning to blur.

Her smile, however, had lost none of its charm. "You make a lovely bride," she said, gliding over to kiss Emma on the cheek before settling herself on the end of the bed.

"Thank you, Mama." Emma pivoted around on the brocaded stool to face her. "And how is Papa this morning?"

Despite the casually phrased question, they both knew what she was asking.

"Your father is fine. I'm sure it won't surprise you to learn that he had a rather difficult time after you were abducted. But he hasn't touched a single drop of liquor since word came that we might have lost you forever."

"Why? Did the earl run out of spirits?"

Emma half-expected her mother to leap to her father's defense, but she simply occupied her hands with smoothing her skirts. "I didn't come here this morning to discuss your father, Emmaline. I came to discuss you."

Emma sighed and rested her chin on her hand, bracing herself for the usual lecture about the responsibilities of being the eldest and the importance of devotion to duty, followed by the familiar assurance that they all appreciated the sacrifice she was making on their behalf.

"It occurred to me while you were gone that you may have wondered why I was so eager for you to accept the earl's proposal in the first place."

"Not really. I always knew why." Emma struggled to keep the note of bitterness from her voice. "So Papa wouldn't end up in the workhouse and the other girls might have a chance to find decent husbands of their own."

"That's what I might have led you to believe but in truth, I never wanted you to marry the earl for our benefit, but for your own."

Emma straightened on the stool, frowning in confusion. "Just how could marrying a man old enough to be my great-grandfather work to my benefit?"

"I convinced myself that his wealth and power would somehow shield you from the slings and arrows of life." Her mother shrugged. "Besides, I knew the man was ancient. How long could he possibly live?"

A startled laugh escaped Emma. She would have never expected her mother to echo the exact words that had gone through her own racing mind as she had stood before the altar with the earl the first time.

"Of course you would have to endure the unpleasant duty of presenting the man with an heir," her mother admitted with a grimace, "but once the earl was gone, you wouldn't have to answer to anyone. You could be mistress of your own fate."

"Did it never occur to you that I might want to wed for other reasons?" Emma closed her eyes briefly, unable to look at the bed where her mother was sitting without remembering the shattering pleasure she and Jamie had shared there only a few hours before. "For love perhaps?"

Her mother looked her in the eye, her gaze as uncompromising as Emma had ever seen it. "I didn't want you to make the same mistake I did. I married for love, you see, but ended up with neither money nor love, only regrets." She rose from the bed and wandered restlessly to the window, where she stood with her back to Emma, gazing out over the mighty shadow of the mountain. "Your father and I have spent the past week not knowing if we would be attending your wedding or your burial. It gave us ample time for discussion. We're both in agreement that we won't force you to marry the earl against your wishes. Your father is downstairs at this very moment, fully prepared to go to the earl and tell him that we're calling off the engagement."

"But what about the settlement?" Emma whispered, stunned nearly speechless by her mother's words. "We both know Papa has already spent a large chunk of it to settle his gambling debts."

Her mother turned to face her, her hands clasped in front of her. "We're prepared to return the unused portion to the earl immediately and find a way to pay back every penny of the rest. Even if it means selling the property that has been in my family for two hundred years. If necessary, your sisters have even volunteered to go into some sort of service with one of the more wealthy families in the parish — as paid companions, perhaps, or even governesses."

Emma knew it wouldn't do to show up at her own wedding with a reddened nose, but she couldn't stop the tears from welling up in her eyes. "They would do that? For me?"

Her mother nodded, then came rushing back to kneel by her side. She smoothed

Emma's hair with a trembling hand, her eyes beseeching. "It's not too late, sweetheart. You don't have to go through with this."

Emma threw her arms around her mother and buried her face in the sweet-smelling crook of her neck. "Yes, Mama," she whispered, smiling through her tears. "I do."

Golden rays of sunlight streamed through the tall, arched windows of the abbey, bringing with them the hope of better days to come. The uncomfortable wooden pews were packed near to bursting with the earl's neighbors and villagers from the nearest hamlet, all hastily gathered together to celebrate the safe return of their laird's bride and his impending nuptials.

Many of them were curiosity seekers, eager to see how his young bride had fared after surviving such a dreadful ordeal. There had been much speculation — some of it quite lurid — about the various indignities she might have suffered at the hands of such a ruthless band of rogues. Some even whispered that the earl must be even more noble and selfless than they'd suspected if he was still willing to wed the lass after she'd spent even a night in the company of a strapping young brigand like Jamie Sinclair.

As his bride took her place before the altar, the whispers swelled to a steady murmur. Those in the back of the abbey craned their necks to get a better look at her.

She bore little resemblance to the terrified creature who had been carried away from that altar on the back of Jamie Sinclair's horse. She held her shoulders straight and her head high, betraying no hint of embarrassment or shame at what she might have endured at the hands of Sinclair and his men. Her skin was no longer as pale as alabaster but flushed with a healthy glow. A few shimmering copper tendrils had been allowed to escape from her elegant chignon to frame her freckled cheeks and gently brush her graceful nape. There was a ripe fullness to her lips and an alluring gleam in her eye that made more than one wife in the abbey pinch her husband to stop him from gawking.

Keenly aware of all the eyes upon her, including those of her family in the front pew, Emma held her bouquet of dried heather in front of her, her hands no longer trembling but as steady as they'd once been on the grip of Jamie's pistol.

Since her own wedding gown had been destroyed during her abduction, the earl had generously offered to let her borrow one of the moldering and woefully out-moded gowns worn by his second or third wives during their weddings to him, but she had opted instead to don one of her own gowns — a simple walking dress of snowy white India muslin with a high waist and lace cuffs.

Her bridegroom appeared at the back of the church, garbed once more in the cer-emonial kilt and plaid of the Hepburn laird. Emma's eyes narrowed. If the earl's plot had succeeded, she wouldn't be wearing a wedding gown on this fine spring morn, but a shroud.

There was such a bounce in his step as he marched up the aisle she was surprised his bony knees didn't clatter together. He even deigned to wink at his nephew as he passed the family pew. Ian Hepburn stretched one arm out along the back of the pew and returned his uncle's greeting with an enig-matic smile.

As her bridegroom joined her, the minister opened the Book of Common Order and pushed his steel-rimmed spectacles up on his nose with a trembling finger, plainly remembering the last time the three of them had stood before that altar.

Just as he opened his mouth to begin the

ceremony, the double wooden doors at the back of the abbey came flying open with a mighty crash. Emma's heart soared as a man appeared in the doorway, silhouetted against the sunlight like a champion from another age.

CHAPTER THIRTY-THREE

"Oh, hell," the minister muttered, the color draining from his face. "Not again."

This time he didn't even wait for Jamie to draw his pistol. He simply tossed the Book of Common Order straight up in the air and went diving behind the altar.

The Hepburn's guests huddled in their pews, wide-eyed with both apprehension and anticipation. Emma's father rose half out of his seat as Jamie came striding up the aisle, but her mother placed a steadying hand on his arm, shaking her head. Emma's sisters couldn't stop themselves from preening a bit as he passed.

"What are you doing here, you insolent whelp?" the Hepburn demanded, shaking a bony fist in the air. He began to inch away from Emma, his hopeful expression belying his outrage. "Have you come to finish what you started?"

"Indeed I have, auld mon," Jamie replied.

"I suppose there's nothing I can do to stop you." The earl huffed out a long-suffering sigh. "You won't be satisfied until you've murdered my bride in cold blood right before my eyes."

Those eyes brightened even more as a dozen redcoats came streaming into the abbey behind Jamie.

"And what's this? More uninvited guests?" He shot Jamie a triumphant smile. "These fine officers of the Crown must have followed you. I should have known they wouldn't let a rogue like you elude their clutches forever." As the British soldiers came marching down the aisle, he addressed the officer in their lead. "I suppose you've come to nab the culprit who shot my bride, Colonel Rogen? Excellent work, men. Take him into custody."

"We already have," the officer replied, his lean face grim.

The earl gasped as their ranks parted to reveal a snarling Silas Dockett. One sleeve of the gamekeeper's coat was torn clear off his shoulder and his brawny arms were secured in a pair of irons in front of him. A nasty bruise shadowed his jaw and his lower lip was swollen to nearly twice its normal size.

"I don't understand," the earl croaked.

"What is the meaning of this?"

Colonel Rogen said, "We have several witnesses who claim that *this* is the man who shot your bride."

"That would be me," Bon said as he came swaggering up the aisle. He gave Ernestine a ribald wink as he passed the Marlowe pew, eliciting a titter from Ernestine and scandalized gasps from her sisters.

"And me," Graeme added, a particularly pleased smirk on his lips as he limped after Bon.

"And us," Angus and Malcolm called out in unison, shoving their way through the ranks of the soldiers.

"Witnesses?" the earl spat, eyeing them as if they were beetles that had just crawled out of a pile of sheep dung. "I am a peer of the realm and the laird of these lands. Surely you don't expect me to believe you would take the word of this . . . this . . . Highland riffraff over mine? Why, they're naught but a bunch of filthy, no-good *Sinclairs!*"

"Colonel Rogen might not take their word, Uncle, but I can promise you that he was more than eager to take mine." A collective gasp went up from the crowd as Ian Hepburn rose from his pew and sauntered forward, offering Emma a courtly bow and his uncle a lazy smile. "I, too, was in the glen on the day Miss Marlowe was shot and I have already presented Colonel Rogen here with a letter confirming with absolute certainty that Mr. Dockett here was the culprit who shot her."

"You swivin' bastard!" Dockett shouted, straining against his chains. "I'll 'ave your balls for breakfast, I will!"

Graeme limped right up to the man who had beaten him with such brutal enthusiasm. Thrusting his face into Dockett's, he said, "I'd mind that cheeky tongue o' yers, mate, or someone just might cut it out for ye. *Before* ye're hanged."

Ignoring Dockett's feral growl, Ian continued. "My letter also confirms that Mr. Dockett has been in my uncle's employ for a number of years and that he was acting solely on my uncle's orders on the day Miss Marlowe nearly lost her life."

"Seize him," the colonel ordered, nodding toward the earl.

The crowd watched, paralyzed with shock as two of the young soldiers hastened to obey their colonel's command. Ignoring the Hepburn's incoherent sputtering, they tugged his bony wrists in front of him and clapped them in irons.

His sputtering rose to an enraged howl.

Emma watched without an ounce of pity in her heart as they began to haul him away from the altar. But they had failed to take into account just how skeletal his limbs were. As they dragged him past Jamie, he slipped one wrist out of its iron cuff and snatched the pistol from the waistband of Jamie's breeches.

As he whirled around and pointed the weapon at the snowy white bodice of Emma's gown, a muffled hush descended over the abbey. The redcoats fell back, plainly afraid of spooking him into firing.

"You cunning little *bitch,*" he spat, the pistol wavering wildly in his palsied grip. "You knew about this ambush all along, didn't you?"

Despite having a pistol pointed at her heart for the second time in that abbey, Emma felt strangely calm. "Of course I did. I'm the one who planned it. With a little help from your nephew. And your *grand-son.*"

The Hepburn's face went from beet red to eggplant purple. "Just because his whore of a mother lured my son into her bed, that doesn't make that miserable bastard my grandson! I should have known you were no better than her. You just couldn't wait to spread your legs for the first randy young

449

buck that came along, could you?"

Emma's father surged to his feet. "I say now, sir, that's quite enough of that talk!"

"Indeed it is," Jamie said softly, reaching around to give the earl's wrist a vicious twist.

Several screams echoed from the rafters as the pistol discharged, splintering one of the windows. As a shower of glass came raining down, Emma ducked, covering her head with her hands.

When she straightened, Jamie was standing in the middle of the aisle with the pistol in his hand and murder in his eyes. The earl slowly backed away from him, clutching his injured wrist.

"What are you doing?" Emma cried.

Jamie lifted the weapon, closing one eye to sight the earl's bony chest down its long, black barrel. "What someone should have done a long time ago."

"I thought you said your pistol only held one shot?"

"I lied," Jamie said, drawing back the hammer of the pistol with his thumb.

Before his finger could squeeze the trigger, she shouted, "Wait!" and darted around him, placing herself between the two men.

Jamie immediately lowered the pistol. "Stand aside, Emma."

Ignoring him, she smiled sweetly at the earl. "There's one thing I neglected to tell you, my lord."

"Emmaline," Jamie growled.

"As it turns out," she said brightly, continuing to advance on the earl, "you never had any need of a bride after all."

"What in the bloody hell are you talking about?" the Hepburn ground out.

She drew closer to him, hypnotized by the sight of the ripe purple vein pulsing in his temple. "It seems that you had an heir all along. Prior to Jamie's birth, your son Gordon married Lianna Sinclair before a rightful minister of the kirk. I have the page from the marriage register to prove it. She was never his whore, you black-hearted old goat." He stood frozen in place as Emma leaned close to his ear, her hissed whisper audible to every ear in that abbey. *"She. Was. His. Wife."*

"His *wife?*" the Hepburn choked out, his breath beginning to rattle in his throat.

"Out of my way, sweeting," Jamie commanded.

Emma held up one finger in a plea for more time. The Hepburn clawed at his throat, his rheumy eyes bugging out as he struggled for air. A thin line of spittle trickled from the corner of his mouth. Then

451

his eyes rolled back in his head and he dropped like a stone to the floor of the abbey.

While Emma dusted off her hands, a satisfied smile curving her lips, the rest of them crept closer, gathering around to gaze down at the earl's motionless form.

But only Bon dared to nudge him with the toe of his boot. "What do ye know aboot that, Jamie? I do believe the lass just spared ye the trouble o' shooting him. I always said he wasn't worth the powder it would take to blow him up."

"Or the rope it would take to hang him," the colonel added dryly, signaling his men to drag both Dockett and the earl's body from the abbey.

"Hold on just as minute," Ian said as they lifted the earl. He yanked the Hepburn plaid unceremoniously from his uncle's shoulders. "I don't believe he'll have need of this where he's going. I've heard it's quite warm there."

When the redcoats and his uncle's body were gone, Ian draped the plaid over Jamie's shoulders as if it was the mantle of a conquering king. "Congratulations, Sin! It only took the Sinclairs five centuries to win back their castle. I hope you realize that since you're now legally my cousin and the new earl of Hepburn, I have every intention of sponging mercilessly off your extensive fortune. As a matter of fact, there's this little property just outside Edinburgh that's recently come to my attention . . ." He trailed off, peering into Jamie's face. "What's wrong? Are you already sulking because I forgot to address you as 'my lord'?"

Jamie was fingering the rich red and black wool of the Hepburn plaid as if he'd never seen it before. He slowly lifted his head, his gaze sweeping the pews. Every eye in that abbey was fixed on him as the wedding guests struggled to absorb the astonishing news that their new laird was not only a Hepburn but a Sinclair.

He wheeled on Emma, panic dawning in his eyes. "Bluidy hell, lass, what have you done? I told you this wasn't what I wanted!"

Emma stood her ground, facing him just as boldly as she had faced the Hepburn. "Just what do you want? To spend the rest of your life hiding on that mountain? To shield your heart from every risk, every ache, until you end up old and all alone just like your grandfather?" She shook her head. "Don't you see? This isn't about what you want. It's about who you are. Your parents dreamed of ending the feud between the Hepburns and the Sinclairs and they succeeded beyond their wildest imaginings. They created a link between the two clans that could never be broken. And that link is you."

He touched a hand to her cheek in a lingering caress, his eyes shadowed by a fierce sorrow. "I'm sorry, lass, but draping me in plaid and calling me a Hepburn doesn't make it so. I'll always be a Sinclair at heart. I can't be caged by castle walls."

Tugging the garment from his shoulders, he tossed it back to Ian. Emma could only watch in stunned disbelief as he turned his back on her and went striding toward the door, rejecting not only his destiny but her love. She drew his mother's necklace from the bodice of her gown, taking comfort in the weight of that ancient cross in her hand.

"I know what you believe," she called out, both her heart and her eyes spilling over with love for him. "But your parents' love didn't destroy them. It saved them. Because it was their love that created you and as long as you live on in this world, there's a part of them that will always survive."

Jamie just kept walking.

As he approached the pool of sunlight spilling through the abbey doors, Emma discovered that the Sinclairs didn't have a monopoly on either revenge or tempers.

"Go ahead and run, Jamie Sinclair! Run away from the only woman you'll ever truly love. Why, the Hepburn was right about you all along! You're nothing but a miserable coward! But don't worry. I'm sure you'll be very happy with nothing but your memories and your pride to warm your bed during those long, cold Highland winters. And your *sheep!*"

Jamie froze in his tracks.

"Aw, hell, lass," Bon breathed into the stunned silence that had fallen over the church. "Why'd ye have to go and say that?"

Jamie's men began to back away from her as Jamie slowly turned, gazing at her with such scorching intensity she wondered how she could have ever thought his eyes were cold. Everyone else seemed to disappear. It was as if they were the only two souls in that abbey, the only two souls in the world.

Shaking his head, he came striding back toward her, his eyes narrowed and his jaw as hard as granite. She had seen that look on his face before, the very first time he had driven his horse down that aisle to steal her away from another man.

"What are you doing?" she whispered as he drew nearer, torn between hope and alarm.

"Making the biggest mistake of my life,"

he said grimly, before dragging her into his arms and claiming her lips in a wild and desperate kiss that stole both her breath and her heart away.

It was the kiss of a lover, the kiss of a conqueror, the kiss of a man who was not only willing to seize his destiny but to fight for it — and for her — with every breath in his body until the day he died.

By the time he finally surrendered her lips, she was light-headed with desire and giddy with joy.

He cupped her cheek in his big, warm hand with devastating tenderness, no longer trying to hide the desperate desire — or the love — shining in his own eyes. "I wasted so many years searching for the truth when I should have been searching for you. I didn't ruin you, lass. You ruined me. Ruined me for any woman that isn't you."

She gazed up at him through a shimmering mist of tears. "Then I suppose I have no choice but to marry you, do I? Because no one else will have you."

His brow furrowed in a mock scowl. "How do I know you're not just a greedy English lass marrying me for my title and fortune?"

"Oh, but I am! I want it all! Jewels, furs, land, gold . . . and a strapping young lover to warm my bed."

"Only one?"

She nodded solemnly. "The only one I'll ever need."

As their lips met for another wild and tender kiss, Bon leaned over to peer behind the altar.

The minister was still cowering there, his eyes squeezed shut and his hands clasped in fervent prayer.

"Now that yer prayers have been answered, sir, I do believe the new earl and his bride are goin' to have need o' yer services."

"Ah, just look at the dear lass! She's all a'tremble with joy."

"And who could blame her? She's probably been dreamin' o' this day her entire life."

" 'Tis every lass' dream, is it not? To wed a handsome young laird who can afford to grant her every wish?"

"And the lad should consider himself blessed to have snared such a Great Beauty. Her freckles are so becomin' I'm thinkin' o' tossin' me own jar o' Gowland's Lotion right in the trash."

Emmaline Marlowe smiled at the women's whispers. She *had* been dreaming of this day her entire life.

She'd dreamed of standing before an altar and pledging her heart and her lifelong fidelity to the man she adored. She'd never caught a clear glimpse of his face in those misty dreams but now she knew he had

458

broad, powerful shoulders, thick sable hair and frosty green eyes that flared with desire every time he looked at her.

A wistful sigh drifted to her ears. "And just look at him! He cuts a magnificent figure in red and black, doesn't he? I've never seen anyone wear the Hepburn plaid with such . . . *vigor.*"

"Indeed! It does one's heart proud. And you can tell he positively dotes upon the lass."

Agreeing with them wholeheartedly, Emma lifted her eyes to meet the adoring gaze of her bridegroom.

There could be no denying the passion smoldering in Jamie Sinclair's eyes as he vowed to love, honor and cherish her for the rest of their days. Once the minister pronounced God's blessing on their union, he would be free to sweep her up in his powerful embrace and carry her to the tower bedchamber where generations of his Hepburn ancestors had come to claim their brides.

He would lay her back on the satin coverlet and lower his lips to hers. He would kiss her tenderly, yet passionately, as his hands sifted through the silky softness of the copper-tinted curls spilling over the —

The minister cleared his throat, jerking

Emma out of her dreamy reverie and giving her a disapproving look over the top of his spectacles.

She dutifully repeated her vows, only too eager for him to pronounce them man and wife.

But instead of doing that, he began to read another endless passage from the Book of Common Order.

Jamie scowled. That scowl continued to deepen until he finally reached down and seized the book by its spine, snapping it closed. "Excuse me, sir, but are we done here?"

The minister blinked up at Jamie, plainly fearing he might be on the verge of drawing a pistol from his plaid or perhaps sending one of his men for a horse to trample them all. "I . . . I suppose so."

"So Miss Marlowe here is my wife?"

"Y-y-yes, my lord."

"And I'm her husband."

The minister bobbed his head, terror having finally succeeded in robbing him of all power of speech.

Jamie grinned. "That's all I needed to know."

As the last hope of the Sinclairs and the future hope of the Hepburns swept his bride up in his arms and went striding down the aisle of the abbey with her, his men set up a rousing cheer, her sisters squealed their delight and the poor beleaguered minister collapsed on the steps of the altar in a dead faint.

ABOUT THE AUTHOR

Teresa Medeiros is one of the most beloved and versatile voices in romantic fiction. She has appeared on every national bestseller list, including the *New York Times, USA Today,* and *Publishers Weekly,* and has more than seven million books in print in over seventeen languages. Her new contemporary novel, *Goodnight Tweetheart,* is coming soon from Gallery Books. She lives in Kentucky with her husband.

Visit Teresa's website at www.teresa medeiros.com.

We hope you have enjoyed this Large Print book. Other Thorndike, Wheeler, Kennebec, and Chivers Press Large Print books are available at your library or directly from the publishers.

For information about current and upcoming titles, please call or write, without obligation, to:

Publisher
Thorndike Press
295 Kennedy Memorial Drive
Waterville, ME 04901
Tel. (800) 223-1244

or visit our Web site at:

http://gale.cengage.com/thorndike

OR

Chivers Large Print
published by AudioGO Ltd
St James House, The Square
Lower Bristol Road
Bath BA2 3SB
England
Tel. +44(0) 800 136919
www.audiogo.co.uk

All our Large Print titles are designed for easy reading, and all our books are made to last.

LARGE TYPE
Medeiros, Teresa, 1962-
The devil wears plaid